Graphic: Adobe Stock

Graphic Designer: Dallas Ann Designs
NYX Art Work By: Lunamist
Cailian Art Work By: Penn Cassidy
Rarity Art Work By : Chelsea Chira

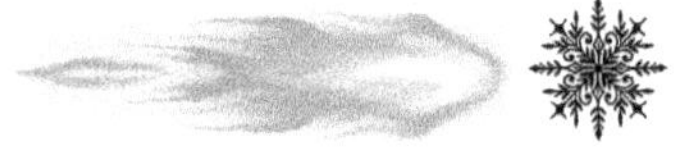

ALSO BY
January Rayne

<u>Shallow Cove™ Dimensions</u>

The Eternally Series:

Book 1: Eternally Hers

Book 2: Eternally Damned

Book 3: Carnival of Creeps

Book 4: Eternally Cursed

<u>Shallow Cove™ Dark Dimensions</u>

The Monster Stalker Series:

Book 1: Honeysuckles

DEDICATION

To those who have gotten double stuffed.
And no, I do not mean the Oreo cookies.
I have questions.

AUTHOR'S NOTE

This is a figment of my imagination. This book isn't realistic, please know that going in. Also, the beginning focuses on the M/M relationship. So if you're reading and you think "Oh, when does Rarity come in." She does, but the M/M aspect needs attention first.

TW: Blood play, mention of suicide but no details just a brief mention, spanking, knotting, spitting, anal bleeding, rough sex, double penetration, female and male pregnancy (at the end), docking, drinking, and death.

Prologue

CAILIAN

Eight hundred years ago

My best friend is a dragon, and he wants me to kill him.

I stare at him in confusion, astonishment, anger, and one hundred other different emotions while they pass over my face just as I experience them.

"You must," Dreven insists, sitting with me on the boundary while we enjoy our daily breakfast together.

He remains in flames while I am in my element of ice. Our table, plates, everything is catered to our needs to withstand our power. I look forward to breakfast every day. Dreven and I have known one another for years. We took over as the Princes of Elementalu when our fathers died and decided to rule as allies, as friends. Our land is united. Our people are united. The balance is unlike anything I've ever seen. No other planet, no other dimension I have seen has come close to what we have built here.

We are the future of what so many other dimensions should be, and he wants me to destroy it.

I drop my ice cup holding my tea. The liquid freezes across my side of the table but stays in liquid form as it travels to his. Small pieces of ice scatter onto the ground, some making their way across the boundary, and I hear a few sizzles from hot meeting cold.

Studying his face, I wait for him to tell me it is a joke, but his face is still, even a little ashen. His gorgeous obsidian color is ill. There's the typical dark undertone and usually, when the light hits it, various amounts of colors dance upon his skin. It is said that his species of dragon are born in a volcano, the magma drenching the eggs and making them glass.

They are the Volcanic Dragons, needing heat and flame to survive.

Dreven's colors are pale. The gorgeous aura of colors seems distant. Even the scales on his shoulders are dry and do not hold the beautiful shine they typically hold.

"Why?" I whisper, keeping my voice low yet filled with rage. Ice begins to grow on my shoulders, dangerous spikes forming as my emotions get the best of me.

"You have to calm down. You'll bring attention. It isn't like you to lose your cool."

I narrow my eyes at his bad joke. "My cool is not lost. Your mind is. You have to be insane to think I would ever do such a thing. You are my friend. I cannot, I will not do that to you."

He sighs, a large cloud of smoke billowing in front of him. "I beg of you," he whispers, lifting his large green eyes that have flashes of yellow and brown, reminding me of marbles fairies make from dreams.

Just as he begs me, a scale drifts from his shoulder to the ground.

I gasp, reaching for his hand. When our palms meet, the temperatures of our bodies clash causing steam to rise.

"What is happening to you, Dreven? You have to tell me. I cannot kill you if you do not give me a damn good reason."

"I've met my firebond," he says, a half-smile forming on his lips before it turns to sorrow. "I was flying a few weeks ago... Alone. She was beautiful."

"I do not understand. Is it not a dream to meet your firebond? Why didn't you tell me sooner?"

He nods. "It is. You know I have children already. I needed an heir. I've never met my firebond, but I knew when I saw her, she was meant to be mine. I experienced her touch just as a troll took her from me. She was a dragon as well, visiting from another dimension. She wanted to see Elementalu."

"Took her? I'll gather my soldiers. We will go get her. This is not the end." I will not ask why he kept his mate from me for weeks. It is not important to the circumstance. I refuse to be selfish in his agony.

But as flames take over his eyes and drip down his face while he cries, it hits me that she was not simply taken.

Her life was.

"Oh, Dreven," the words are a gust of broken wind leaving my lungs. "What happened?"

"They came at night while we were asleep. They were shockingly quiet. I didn't hear them, Cailian. I didn't. I wish I would have. I wish—"

"—I know. I know." I keep a hold of his hand and he tightens his grip.

"They ripped her heart out. Trolls love dragon hearts. It's their favorite thing to eat."

I gasp, hating he had to see his firebond die. To meet her and feel bliss only to watch her die, is nothing but torture.

"We did not mate which means my fire is killing me. I'm burning from the inside out. It hurts, Cailian. I feel my bones becoming weaker

as they lose their strength. My scales itch as they dry, and my chest constantly burns."

Tiny ice droplets hit my cheeks as I cry. I try not to, truly, but my friend is dying, and there is no way to save him. It's been weeks since he has met her, and it seems his fire is doing what it is meant to do— burn— and it's scorching him from the inside.

"I do not know if I can be the strength you rely on, Dreven. You are my best friend, a rareness only found in special lifetimes. Please, do not ask this of me."

"My children are gone for the day," he continues. "They will not see what happens to me. Freeze me, shatter me, and let the wind carry me to my firebond."

My eyes widen in horror when his words set in. "You... you want me to do this today?" I stand from the table, sweeping my hand across the surface. Dishes fly to the left, smashing somewhere in the distance. "You have known for weeks," I sneer, trying to swallow my heartache. "You have planned this. You did not want to give me time to think or mourn you."

He tilts his head, his kind eyes squinting as he forces a painful, but genuine smile. "No, I didn't. I know you, Cailian. You are my best friend. You would have tried to find a way to save me, spending your time going insane looking for a cure for my fire. The elves have amazing capabilities, but you and I know, there is no such thing as beating Fate. This is her plan for me."

"How are you okay with this?" I shout at him, stepping forward, uncaring about the fire licking my skin. "How do you expect me to live with the guilt of ending your life?"

He stands next, calmly tucking the seat under the table I've ruined with my temper. I wish I could be as calm and collected as Dreven. He's always been even-tempered, even in the most weathered times.

"I'm okay because I know I can count on you. I'm okay because I know my friend won't let me burn until I am nothing but a pile of ash on my bedroom floor. I don't want to die like that. I don't want to die alone, and I don't want my children to see. They have never seen a dragon die like this. Not yet. I'm okay because I know your face will be the last I see and I'll die with your friendship by my side. Do not live with guilt, Cailian. Live knowing you gave your friend his dying wish. I only ask that you promise me one thing."

"Anything," I tell him.

"Don't tell anyone the truth about what happened. I can't have my reputation tainted because I gave in to the pain and didn't die like a noble dragon."

"You are noble. Do not die thinking otherwise." I glance around, taking in the last of the peace between neighbors. "The dragons will hate us," I state, staring at nothing while I gather my thoughts. "They will think we betrayed them, that we are murderers, that I killed you for..." I wave my hand in the air. "Something. Name anything. Stories will be weaved and told. Lies will be spread about me, about my people, my land. If I do this—" I stare at him once more. "Everything will change."

"And I know you. You will conquer change. Everything will work as it should. Nyx, my oldest, will take my place."

I give a slight nod, not wanting to meet his son.

"And when do you want this to happen?" I ask him.

He growls, smoke billowing from his mouth as flames lick his dried skin. "Now." He shoves me in the chest.

I trip and fall, my body landing on the soft, snow-blanketed ground. I stare up at him, shocked he would show such violence toward me, but I know he's trying to make this easier.

"I can't," I sob, "Please, my friend, please, do not make me."

He picks me up by my long white hair, my scalp burning from his claws digging into my skin. His mouth gets closer to my ear and he whispers, "Please, free me from this agony my soul is in."

"In front of witnesses?" I ask, yanking myself from his grip. I stop my soldiers from coming closer by raising my hand, letting them know it's okay. "Leave us," I tell them, and the tall sentinels give one another unsure expressions.

"That's even better," Dreven states, releasing fire at me, and I cross my arms in front of me, releasing an ice shield that protects me from the flames.

"Dreven, enough!" I yell, not wanting to use my power on him. "Not like this."

He wraps a hand around my throat but doesn't squeeze. He is acting. I see the desperation in his eyes. The more he uses his flame, the more exhausted he is. More of his scales fall from him, drifting through the air like pieces of dust.

I press my palm against his chest, not once taking my eyes away from his. "You are loved. You will forever be my friend. I hope you find peace. I hope you see your firebond. I'm honored you trusted me with this." I take a deep breath and force the power in my body, through my palm, and into his chest, letting the cold seep into his heart. With every pump, it travels through his veins. "You will be missed, my friend."

I cry silently, doing my best to stay strong so I do not give away the truth of this circumstance. Ice spreads across his decaying skin, freezing the scales in place. I watch the frost glisten on his frame before I lift my eyes to his.

He smiles in relief, one last tear dripping from his eye. "Thank you, my friend. Thank you," he rasps one last time, the words a frozen cloud as the last bit of air escapes his lungs. His eyes close, a small smile remains, and he seems peaceful.

His hand is still around my throat, but I do not have it in me to pull away just yet.

The tear that fell before he froze is hanging on his jawline, a small icicle reminding me that it isn't a tear of sadness, but of relief.

"Be at peace, Dreven," I whisper, forcing a cold gust through him.

His body shatters, freeing my throat from his grip, and the wind wolves howl just in time, creating a massive windstorm that steals him from me. Dreven drifts away, frozen bits of him twinkling in the reflection of the light. I watch until he is no longer in sight.

Only a memory.

Only a moment.

And only ten minutes ago did my life change forever.

"The Prince of Dragons is dead!"

"Dreven is dead! The elf killed him!" another dragon shouts. "Murderer. Betrayer!"

My sentinels take my side as dragons fill the sky. "We are going to need more soldiers. Call everyone. We are at war."

"Yes, Prince," he says, lifting a long, thin ice whistle that lets out a high-pitched frequency only elves can hear.

I drive an ice spear through a dragon, killing yet another I called a friend.

But I made a promise, and if that promise kills me, then I will die an honorable elf.

Chapter One

RARITY

There isn't enough time in the day to try and explain the ache of the heart when it bleeds from unseen wounds. Any attempt is a waste of time because the explanation is simple: There are no words for a heart in agony. It's almost as if silence is weighing down on your chest, forcing you to drown in the absence of what used to be.

Or perhaps the absence of what never will be.

"Rarity?"

I shut my eyes when I hear my name, annoyed with the therapist my brother, Alexander, is making me see.

I look out the window of the Veiled Library, watching different species walk to and from the main entrance on the long bridge. It's a beautiful thing to see, but for some reason, the only person I want to see is a tall, elegant, ice elf.

And I won't.

It's only been two days, six hours, twenty minutes, and sixteen— seventeen— eighteen— seconds since he left to go home.

I didn't go with him.

"Rarity, I can't help you if you don't talk to me," he says gently, his voice soothing and calm. The soft baritone makes me relax. My shoulders sag as stress escapes me.

I lift my head, causing tears to break free from my eyes. Vampire tears are sacred. They are life-changing. They can heal and even give longer life spans to humans. There are creatures out there that would kill and torture us for a simple vial, so it's important we never let our tears fall.

I wipe them away quickly, not knowing this man well enough to trust he won't kill me for them.

He lifts his hand in reassurance, leaning against his desk. "I have no use for your precious tears, Rarity."

"Why not?" I ask him, pulling my shoulders back to stand up straight. "They give life."

He narrows his eyes at me and smirks. "I am life." He spreads his arms and gorgeous red and gold feathers take their place. Flames engulf his body, and his eyes hold the heat of fire. Ashes fall from his body and onto the floor. "I can be born a million times, Rarity. Your tears are just as valuable as my ashes."

"You're a phoenix," I gasp, taking a step forward. "I've never met one of your kind before."

"We keep to ourselves," he lifts a brow. "You understand why. The Veiled Library is the safest for my kind."

"Of course, I do. Your secret is safe with me." It dawns on me, why I felt at ease suddenly, then narrow my eyes. "You used your powers on me."

"I simply eased your emotions. I can't help it sometimes. When I sense someone who needs help, my heart must answer the call. We are spiritual in that sense. Not religious, but in tune with a body's

spirit." He tucks his hands in his pockets just as the ashes on the floor disappear. "Apologies, Rarity."

I lace my fingers together as I feel my anxiety begins to rise. "It's alright, Dr. Almenara. I do feel better, so thank you."

I glance to the window again, the unease of being in the veil has my heart racing. It's always me easing everyone's pain or freezing their painful memories, but when it comes to myself, I can't do anything.

"You don't like it here," he states. He doesn't ask. "Your brother told me that you and a few members of your family were stuck in the veil. Not here at the library, but in the veil, between worlds."

Anger ignites in my chest, and I let out a cool breath, the air freezing with my exhale. A reminder of how I'm so different from the rest of my family. I have more in common with my beloved than I do with my brothers, my father, and even my mother. There's so much I'm bitter about while being so sad over it as well.

"We were," I tell him. "But—" I rub the back of my neck, shutting my eyes as I try to figure out why we aren't talking about the real issue. "Aren't I here because I rejected my beloved? Isn't that what you want to talk about?"

"I do, but we will get to that. I need to understand you more, Rarity."

I snort, watching the tips of my fingers glisten with ice. "What's there to know, Dr. Almenara?" Tears fall down my cheek in cold rivers. "I spent so many years in the veil, remembering how hard it was to survive, begging for the portal to open, begging for someone to hear us as we pounded on the veil walls to be set free. I remember," I whisper to him, still watching the light reflect off the frozen pattern on my finger. "I remember my mother dying. It's my first memory. I remember looking up as we fell into the portal and locking eyes with her." My breath becomes more ragged as I speak. "It was only for a

moment, but it was long enough to watch her get torn apart." I lift my eyes to look at him, but he is reaching across the desk to grab a tissue. I chuckle. "Thank you."

"Take your time."

I lift my shoulders and shrug. "That's it. And then me, my father, and my uncles landed in a place that made no sense."

He sits down beside me, notepad and pen in hand as he writes. "Tell me about that place. Do you remember a lot of it? Where was it? What was it like? Was it a bad experience?"

I turn to him, meeting his inquisitive eyes. "You genuinely sound curious. You sound like you actually care. It makes it easy to talk to you."

"One of the perks of being a phoenix therapist, Rarity. I actually *do* care."

I nod, standing, feeling restless, and stroll to the window again, looking out to watch the creatures come and go. From how high I am in this castle, they are as small as ants, hurrying as if the portal might close again.

"I remember enough to wish I didn't remember at all." I tap the window, watching the ice vein across the glass, and then I pull away. The cold receding as if it was never there. "Time was odd there. I felt like we were stuck in a bubble, watching the world pass us by. There would be times when we would find a weak spot in the veil and we'd just sit there for hours, watching the outside world exist. People walking, talking, and laughing."

"It sounds lonely."

"I guess it was. I don't know. I had my family and we met others stuck there as well, but my dad was the worst, I think. He had to raise me and mourn his wife and my two brothers. He didn't know my brothers were alive. He had the hardest time, but we survived."

"How? If you weren't near the library, how did you survive?"

"I have no idea where we were. It was like an abandoned town. It was thick with fog every day. We ate..." I curl my lip in disgust. "Any animal we could find. It was as if we were on an island. Every day was the same. Wake up, eat, explore, try to find a way out, eat, sleep, and the cycle started over again. I matured so time still went on, but compared to the outside world, it's as if time didn't exist. No one aged. No one died. No one could die."

"What do you mean?"

"My Uncle Greyson. He tried to kill himself. A tree branch to the heart. He died but only for a few seconds before gasping for breath and yanking the branch from his chest. Time knew no end. It went on and on. And then Alexander met his beloved and it changed everything. We could communicate with her. We had hope and she set us free."

"She set us all free. Remember, while you were stuck, others were too."

"And now we are finally back," I whisper. "I have my family again." I grab the windowsill and press my weight against it. "I finally have my family back. We have all been through too much to not be together." I raise my voice, the memories of isolation switching to anger. "We are a coven again, even if my father seems to want to waste away. My brother is still in a coma. My friend's brother's spirit is locked in purgatory. I'm an aunt now. My best friend is having triplets soon. I have a family!" I shout. My chest rises and falls as freezing temperatures sweep across my chest. "I have everything I didn't have for years, and he just expects me to pick up and leave? I can't just... I can't just go, Dr. Almenara." I exhale and the glass behind me shatters. I step away, my eyes darting up and down the walls to see I froze the glass. "I'm sorry."

"Don't be. It's just glass. The gargoyles will fix it later. Go on." He crosses his legs, his focus on me.

"I want my beloved more than anything. I miss him. I'm... hungry for him," I admit with embarrassment.

"So soon? You are no longer able to stomach another's blood?"

"Just the thought makes my stomach roll," I answer.

"So I'm assuming you have no experience considering you were in the veil for the majority of your life. Is that another reason why you are avoiding your beloved?"

"No, that's ridiculous." There is a small part of me that's worried. I'm still learning so many things about the world. What do I know about pleasing a prince?

"Is it? It's okay to be scared of what you don't know and it's okay to be afraid of losing your family again."

He says the words and I have to cover my face with my hands to hide how hard I cry. The doctor's influence begins to infiltrate the air and seeps into my sadness. I still weep but his solace is like a warm balm soothing the inside of my chest.

"Isn't that what this is all about? Your fear of loss. It's understandable. You've lived a life that has been difficult and you're in a good place. You're building what you lost so many years ago, but Rarity, it is different now. You won't lose your family. You're only a sunset magnolia powder toss away. You can see them whenever you like, but if you aren't careful, you will lose the greatest thing your heart will ever feel, and it will kill you, Rarity. It won't be like the veil. You won't get another opportunity to live." He stands in front of me, the shimmer of his phoenix is a ghost around his form.

"Are you willing to risk the best part of your life because of fear? Are you willing to risk your life? Because now, there are no second chances, Rarity. And it isn't just your life at stake. You aren't losing anything. You're gaining."

"I'm going to miss so much. What if my friend has his triplets? What if my brother wakes up and I'm not there? What if…" My breath hitches.

"I have a feeling none of that will happen because you won't stop seeing them and you'll communicate. Do you really think your beloved will allow you to miss out on your family? You'll only lose what you don't try to have. Just… try. See what happens."

"I'm not typically like this. So out of touch with myself. I'm usually the one people come to. I'm used to being the strong one, the one that's put together, the one—"

"Who is allowed to be strong, put together, but just a little out of order."

I give him a sad smile.

"I forgot to ask," he says, picking up his notepad. "Does it bother you that you're so different than your siblings?"

I nod. "I almost feel like I'm not their sister at all. I know I am, but there's this huge piece of me that feels like I don't belong in their world. I don't know why I am the way I am. No one knows, but my beloved—" I blush remembering him. "He said I have ice elven in my blood, I just— I don't know how."

"Maybe you don't belong in their world because you belong in his," Dr. Almenara states simply. "Have you ever thought of that?"

I haven't, but I am now.

Maybe that one piece of my life's puzzle I've been searching for to feel complete isn't with my family. Maybe Elementalu is my home and Cailian is the missing piece.

Chapter Two

DOVENYX

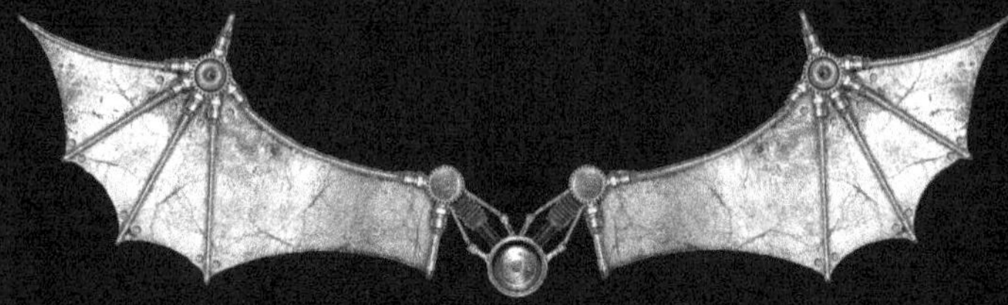

I growl under my breath, fire brewing in my chest, threatening to unleash and burn my surroundings. My heart yearns for the elf in the ice castle, my dragon roaring in my blood to claim what is rightfully ours, yet my mind is furious.

Fate is cruel.

What did I do to deserve for my firebond to be the one who killed my father? The Ice Prince is a murderer, a betrayer, and he can't be trusted. He befriended my father for years, only to kill him with his ice. He couldn't even give us the honor of burning him ourselves, to have a traditional dragon funeral.

Prince Cailian disgraced us and while the wars between us have eased in the last five hundred years, it is only because there has been a silent agreement.

We leave each other alone.

He was tired of losing elves and I didn't want to lose any more dragons. Our numbers have decreased, and it is more important to

me to save my kind than to keep losing them in an
eight-hundred-year-old war.

Shockingly, in all these long years, I've only recently seen him for
the first time. We do what we can to stay away from each other, but
again, as Fate would have it, when I was in flight back to the castle, I
saw him.

I took my chance and nearly had him in my grasp. I was so fucking
close to killing Cailian. So close, I could almost taste the fucking ice
that makes his silver skin. I had my claws in his skin only for my dragon
to pull away because the Ice Elven Prince is my firebond.

It's funny how the world works. To hate him for centuries, only to
be forced to yearn for him with my entire being, is a burn not even my
dragon can heal from.

"Nyx?" Raiden, my second in command calls for me from the
doorway of my chambers.

I've also told no one, not even my best friend that I have found
my firebond. I can't speak of it. The castle would fall, dragons would
demand answers, and I have none. Our world as we know it would be
over. Chaos would ignite and that would be catastrophic.

"What? I told you not to bother me," I shout before blowing fire
onto my bathwater until it boils. I've been in the bath long enough,
but I can't seem to get out when my eyes keep straying to the ice castle
across the boundary.

His witch has put up guards to protect the elven territory from us,
so I can't cross the magic she has used. I haven't used my wizard to
create guards. Every Prince has a witch or wizard to aid in their power.
I haven't because I want to show the elf, I'm not afraid of him. I don't
consider him a threat.

Smoke escapes my nostrils, my dragon becoming more impatient
with every second I decide to stay away from Cailian.

For every second we are not mated, we creep closer to death.

Perhaps that should be my vengeance letter.

"You're testier than usual," he remarks, letting himself into my bathroom.

He perches himself on the stone windowsill, peeking out the window. "What ya lookin' at?"

I grunt, slipping down in the tub. "You're aggravating."

"You're a dick, but we both already knew that."

My eyes turn to slits as he crosses his arms and smirks at me. His wings spread from behind his back before tucking into place.

But I must be begging for his questions, because like a damn fool, my eyes slide from the bubbling bathwater to the ice castle again. And I hate myself for wondering what he is doing, if he is okay, if he is as angry as I am about this pairing, if he longs for me as much as I despise him.

So many conflicting emotions, but one will always win over the other.

Rage.

A shadow falls over my shoulder and Raiden's chin grazes my cheek.

I growl again. "What the fuck, Raiden? Why are you so close?"

"I just want to see what you're looking at. You're just such an open book, you don't leave much for us to guess what's going on." The sarcasm drips from his tongue.

"You're overly cheery attitude is ticking me off more than usual. Is there something you need? Why are you interrupting my morning bath?" He knows it's essential to how I start my day.

My left wing is slowly deteriorating. Years ago, I protected the fireside of Elementalu and it nearly cost me my life when I came across a forest basilisk. The damned beast spit its venom before my dragonfire

finally killed it and while I dove out of the way, it was too late. My left wing had begun to burn immediately. It was like acid eating away at my flesh. The pain was unlike anything I had ever felt before.

The leather-like flesh has holes in it now, the bones peeking through the worn, tired, and injured tissue. It only hurts after the day is over, after flying and exerting myself, but one day, soaring the skies will be a memory.

I'll be a lesser dragon, and another will take my place.

Just like I took my father's.

"I know. Apologies, Prince," he bows his head, and I can't help but roll my eyes.

"You know you don't have to call me that. Out with it. Tell me what's going on so you can leave me in peace." And so I can stare out the window, daydreaming about what it would be like to have the elf under me, taking my dragon cock.

In another world, in another time, when he wasn't a killer.

Lust, need, and desire pool south, my dick stirring for my firebond. I might detest this pairing, but he is still meant to be mine, and fighting this mating is the most difficult thing I have ever done.

Gods, I'll never forget when I first saw him. He was just about to jump through the portal when my eyes locked on his long, sleek, snow-white hair. His beauty was so off-putting, so mind-melting, I forgot my goal was to kill him. Instead, my dragon scratched him, marked him, and I know he must be walking around with a scar.

I'm both proud and annoyed by that.

"Nyx?" Raiden snaps his fingers in front of my face. "Have you heard anything I've said?"

"Hmm?" I blink. "What? No, sorry. I was preoccupied."

He narrows his yellow eyes at me, the blue scales on his shoulders reflecting the light. "You've been saying that a lot lately. What's going on?"

"Nothing," I lie.

"Nyx." He pinches the bridge of his nose. "You need to tell me. I can't help you if you don't, especially with the rogue trolls heading in this direction."

"Trolls? How many?" Battling trolls is so dangerous for dragons. They love dragon hearts and fighting while trying to protect ourselves is exhausting. Our attention is split, leaving us vulnerable. We do our best to stay away from the violent creatures as we always end up losing a dragon in the process.

I'm not sure if I'm up for a battle that will force me to fly.

"Around ten according to our enforcers."

"Ten? So many. That's unheard of."

"Well, the portals are open now. Who knows where they are all coming from? I'm sure this is just the beginning of what we will see."

I nod in agreement, my damn gaze finding the ice castle again.

"How far are they? How long do we have to prepare?"

"A few days, maybe," he states, standing from his causal sitting position on the windowsill. His wide frame blocks the light pouring in the window, his shadow casting onto the brown stone of the room.

"We'll be ready."

"Will you?"

I cut my gaze at him, then stand. The water rushes down my body and splashes into the tub. I spread my onyx wings, my dragon preparing to tear Raiden to pieces for challenging me like that.

"How dare you question me," I hiss, stepping out of the tub.

Dragons don't care about nudity since we are always shifting in front of one another.

"I have proven myself time and time again."

"I'm asking as your friend, Nyx, not as your second in command. Everyone here would die for you. They aren't questioning if you'll be ready."

I dry off by allowing my inner flame to dance over my skin, the water evaporating quickly.

"Then why are you?" I get dressed, tugging on a pair of pants, I forgo the shirt the clothsmith weaved with his magic, a special piece of clothing that doesn't trap our wings, but the fabric makes my skin itch.

He steps closer to me, his eyes searching mine for truth, and I'm so close to telling him. What would he think? What would he do? Would he fight for me? Would he go against the will of Fate?

"What's bothering you, Nyx? Talk to me."

"Nothing. It's just my wing. It's bothering me more than usual."

He presses his lips together, not believing me but accepting my answer. "Okay, what would you like for me to do about the trolls?"

"Prepare the enforcers and the elite. We need to be ready."

"Maybe... maybe we should notify our neighbors, Nyx."

I snarl, pinning him against the wall. My claws lengthen, tearing into his blue scales. "What the hell did you just say?" Fire threatens to release from my throat, wanting to burn him where he stands.

Raiden doesn't flinch. He shows no pain as blood spills down his chest. "I said maybe we should tell the elves. Maybe it's time to find peace and let go of what happened eight hundred years ago."

"Peace? Peace to the elf who killed my father? Royalty. A prince. You want peace to come to them."

"Him," he clarifies.

"What?" I snap.

"Him. It was only he who killed your father. Not the rest."

"So you want to forget about the other dragons they have killed?"

"You're being a hypocrite. We've killed elves too in countless battles. We were all protecting ourselves. Just imagine—"

"—There will be no imagining!" I roar so loud that my room trembles as my dragon makes itself known and my fangs lengthen. I slam my fist against the wall next to his head, the stone crumbling to the ground. "Do I make myself clear?"

"Yes, Prince," he says the word with irritation. Raiden shoves my chest, the only person in any fucking dimension besides my firebond who could get away with treating me that way. He growls, but relents by showing me his throat, a form of submission and respect since I'm the prince. "I'll keep you updated about the trolls." My best friend storms out of the room, leaving me in the havoc of my own emotions.

If we lived in the world that my father lived in, where we shared technology and magics, the fight against the trolls would be easier.

But we live in a new world, a world where betrayal was born and bred from a decision my damn firebond made.

I walk over to the window that overlooks his castle, resting my arms above my head on the stone. Firegrass blazes while snow peacefully falls on the other side. My land probably looks like hell to him, but his looks like heaven. The snow is white, and it almost seems quiet, unlike the roar of fire that constantly happens here.

Down the middle of the boundary is heartsnow, a rare flower that burns down one half, but is cold on the other. The werewolf who killed two of my dragons came here on a difficult journey to get the heartsnow for a spell.

"What are you doing to me?" I whisper as I fight every instinct to call on him so we can claim each other. My claws dig into the brimstone as my eyes lock on one of his castle windows. The tall, iced

mansion glistens, not once succumbing to the raging heat emanating from my kingdom.

Needing to get away, I leap from my window, spread my wings, and call on my dragon who yearns for my enemy.

Chapter Three

CAILIAN

Eight hundred years ago, I never thought the promise I made would be the death of me. It's ironic that my best friend's son is my mate. A son who hates me.

"You have to do something," Zyrl begs of me. "Surely, Raltena can do something."

"I will not ask her to dive into magic that dark, brother. That is unfair. You know what that can do to a witch."

He charges at me while I sit on the oversized ice throne, leans down, and grabs the arms of the chair to block me in. I remain calm and collected, knowing his anger isn't at me, it's at the situation. He is sad. He is desperate. I cannot be angry at him for caring so much.

"I do not care what it does to her!" he roars, his eyes watering but immediately the liquid turns to tiny ice droplets rolling down his cheek. He glances away and shuts his eyes, seething between clenched teeth. "I. Do. Not. Care."

I place my hand on his cheek, turning his head so he can look at me. "Yes, you do. You do not mean that."

He nods eagerly, the youth embedded in his veins becoming apparent with his quick temper. "I do. I do mean it. It isn't fair, Cailian. Why aren't you angry? Why aren't you screaming? Killing? Demanding—"

I stand from my seated position which causes my baby brother to take a step back. "Demand, what, Zy? Demand that my mates love me? Where is the fairness in that?" I keep my words soft, but there is power in every sentence spoken. I am older than any elf here which means my power is stronger than any they will ever hold. "Love does not demand. They will come to me when they are ready. And if they don't, fates be it." I wave my hand in the air as if it doesn't matter.

"Fates be it?" he scoffs, staring at me as if he has no idea who I am. "You are leaving this up to Fate? Fight for them. Fight for your mates."

My head begins to pound, the ache in my bones becoming more apparent with each passing day I am not mated.

The secret I hold dear to my chest is threatening to explode from me for the millionth time. It would explain everything. My baby brother would see that it isn't as easy as he is making it seem, but so much harder than he could ever imagine.

My best friend's son will never accept me after killing his father. I can't even gain his forgiveness. How can I expect his love?

"You know I cannot be where Rarity is. My body cannot withstand the climate. She will have to come here. I know it." I hope when she does, her mate bond is enough to keep us alive. She doesn't know of Nyx yet, so her soul is spared.

For now.

"And the dragon?" he sneers, a secret no one else knows beside Anwyll, the wolf who needed my help when he fell through a portal.

And it needs to stay that way.

"Events happened before you were born. You don't know what life was like eight-hundred years ago."

"You mean before you killed the Prince of Dragons and made life difficult for all of us?"

A slice of pain cuts open the wound that cannot heal on my heart. "Yes, Zyrl. Before I brutally killed my best friend. Look at me now. Did my evil plan work?" The question drips with impatience and anger, maybe even a little regret.

There is a small part of me that wishes I didn't grant Dreven's wish, then there is the other part of me, the one that is mad at him for making a choice that would leave my life like this. Is that selfish of me to think? I hate to have such horrible thoughts about Dreven, but was it selfish of him to make me promise to live this life of lies?

It's a fight within myself I deal with every day.

"I am sorry, Cailian." He sighs, taking a step toward me. "I am so angry for you. I am worried. Especially now that your mate is that... beast."

I do not know what gets into me, but I wrap my hand around my brother's throat, calling upon my power. Wind whips around us, swaying my robes and fluttering my hair over my shoulders. My iced crown glows as ropes of ice trap my brother's body.

"Cailian," he chokes, tugging on my wrists. His wide eyes do not deter me.

"He is many things to us, but he is still my mate, and you will show me that respect."

"I will not show respect to a beast that would gladly kill us or refuse you. I will not show respect to him knowing you'll melt without him."

"It is the way of our kind, Zy. He knows of the repercussions. His own fire will eat away at him. That's his choice."

"At the expense of you?"

"It is the way of Fate!" I yell at him, losing my patience with my brother. "Accept it."

"I do not care of Fate. I do not care of the rules. I do not care of what was. I do not care that we have a silent treaty with the dragons. I only care that my brother lives. I will deal. I will learn to be happy with the new age of life, but I refuse to accept your death."

I sigh, tired of going around in circles with him. We have had the same fight ever since I came back from Salem. Only my brother knows of my situation. It was hard to hide with my blue veins turning orange, a sign of warmth, a sign I've met my mate, or in my case, mates.

My dragon has already scarred my back, three of his claws managed to dig into my skin before I jumped into the portal, and there is a small part of me hoping he marked me on purpose. It is the only hope I have to hold on to.

Having met both of my mates' warmth, it's heating me from the inside out, melting the ice that is embedded in my blood. It's killing me slowly to live without their mating bites, without balance, without acceptance.

It is a shame Fate is so cruel. We either have to love each other, or we die from the consequence of choosing not to.

I know of the history between elves and dragons. Dreven and I started it. We are the reason for the long history lessons we give our young. I know of the death and animosity, the hostility, the hate, but I have never been the one to care about history. It can change. Time can heal. Death can mean life. I believe Fate brought us together for that reason, to change this dimension and to rewrite the history I have paved.

And while I accept that, others do not, I fear. This union could mean war before we know peace if we ever walk down that road.

This journey is going to be filled with hot coals and if it means burning myself alive to get to the end, I will. I'll prove myself to my mates. I'll prove I am worthy.

"I plan to go to the dragon now. I would have told you earlier if you had not spent the last hour insisting I was dying."

"You are dying. I can already see it, Cailian, and so will the others, soon enough."

"I do not care what they see as long as they do not know. Not yet," I clarify. "You need to give me time. Rarity is afraid. The dragon, what is his full name, anyway? Do we know? It can't simply be Nyx. Dragons always have beautiful names."

He shrugs. "No. I only ever call him—"

I lift my hand to stop him. "The dragon is dealing with the same issues we are. He is a leader— ruler of the dragons— and I have no doubt many of them hold the same issues you do. Remember, I am the reason for all this strife. Your hate is misplaced. It does not need to be on them but on me."

He opens his mouth to say another word, but I stop him. "Enough, baby brother." I grab his shoulders and give him a genuine smile. "You take on worries that do not exist yet. I promise everything will be okay." I cup the back of his head, and a flash of him as a baby splits through the depths of my memories. "There used to be a time when you fit in the palm of my hand. Now, you fight with me every chance you get. I often miss the times when you couldn't speak."

He shoves me playfully, a small grin finally threatening the worried lines on his face.

I continue walking to the main doors of the castle, with no plan in mind. This issue cannot be rectified if no words are spoken. We need a plan.

"Do you want me to come with you?" Zyrl asks. "Going alone is not a good idea. It will be very hot over there and you said when you saw Rarity, it was too warm."

"There you go worrying again." I clap him on the shoulder. "That was over a course of a few days. Speaking with the dragon will not take that long." The main door begins to lower, the chains rattling together from the force, and a burst of cold air rushes over my skin.

Two guards come from either side, waiting for orders.

"At ease, you can maintain your post. What I need to do, I need to do alone."

Zyrl grabs my arm, stopping me mid-step. "They could kill you."

"Then according to your worry, that should not matter since I am dying anyway."

"Cailian—" his eyes become rounder, his brows dipping in the middle while he shakes his head.

"Worrying now will only cause doom." I kiss the top of his forehead. "I will be back. Tell the others I went for a walk, and I will not be available for the rest of the night." I give him my back before he can say another word and before I lose my courage.

I'll tell Nyx the truth of what happened to his father and maybe that will be enough for him to give us a chance.

I keep my head high, hands laced behind my back at the base of my spine, strolling with ease. My demeanor is a lie because my insides are havoc.

The snow continues to fall, gathering on my cheeks before becoming one with my skin. The burst of cold empowers me, trying to repair my heat-infested system. It's so odd how different our lands look when all that separates us is heartsnow. On my side, we have snow, ice, and beyond we have a forest and a meadow with big, beautiful flowers.

I hope there is more to this dragon's land than what I see before me. The ground flickers orange and red, firegrass, if I remember correctly. The castle is all stone, made from the volcanoes they derive from. It's dark, a bit dooming, yet eerily beautiful. Dragons fly above it, their

scales glittering, reflecting the flames reaching toward the sky from the tops of the towers.

Everything burns.

Even the sky is darkened by smoke but glows the beautiful orange from how bright the flames are as they climb the castle.

I open my palm, watching the snowflakes fall into my hand, so calm, so elegant, as if they are dancing. Then, I watch the fire, its own dance captivating, but menacing, as if its sole purpose is to grab onto what is in its way just to watch it burn.

Dragons are intimidating. Their powers are frightening, and I'd be lying if I said I wasn't afraid.

This would be easier if Rarity was at my side. My dragon doesn't even know he has another mate and maybe he'd prefer her over me. Perhaps *that* needs to be my plan.

Yet...

My heart just wants to see him even if he kills me.

Even if he spits his fire at me, I will take it if it is all I will ever get from him. If he wants to burn me at the stake, I will spread my arms and let him turn me to ash.

What is life now anyway? If I do not have the love of my mates.

Calling upon my power, the snow swirls around me, and I guide my hands in front of me, imagining an ice pathway that connects to the dragon's doorstep. I keep my palms face down, focusing so the ice stays intact.

The firegrass sizzles from the freezing temperature and steam rises from either side of the frozen walkway. The heat from underneath warms the bottoms of my feet, but it is not uncomfortable. I am wondering if maybe the power of flame is not as strong as I thought it to be.

A dragon lands just a few yards away from me in a worn part of the yard. Smoke billows from his nostrils as his red eyes follow me as I walk the path. An elf has never been so close to the main entrance of their home.

Not since the day I took Dreven's life.

I give a friendly nod, hoping he knows I mean no harm.

I step from the ice path to the steps of the castle, turning my head over my shoulder to see not just one, but three dragons watching me.

Two seem ready to kill while the other sits, tucks his wings, and tilts his head.

He seems nice.

I wave my hand to them in greeting and the two hungry-looking ones show their very sharp teeth. The other dragon lifts its paw. Is it a paw? A hand? And waves at me in return. He also shows his teeth, but I think it's a smile.

The one next to him roars in his face, but the kind dragon with blue scales does not stand down. He growls in return, one that I feel in my core, shaking the fragile marrow.

Another dragon lands in front of them, his back to me, his body towering over the others. He is huge. His tail alone is the size of an old tree trunk, whipping and slashing through the air. His wings stretch beyond his body, an abyss of a shadow falling over me. Fire leaves his mouth aimed at the three dragons creating issues. The black scales remind me of ink, dark and never-ending, an abyss of night, yet there is the same rainbow aura across this body that Dreven had. The only difference is the edges of his scales. They glow orange, similar to the grass below me that's burning, a constant rolling blaze.

The light pierces through his wings and I notice the left one, tattered and scarred. I'm curious about what could stop a dragon from

healing. If he gave me a chance, I could fix his wing. If he allowed me to get close enough.

The massive dragon turns and when I see his eyes, I know who it is.

It's *him*.

My mate.

Chapter Four

DOVENYX

The audacity of him to cross the heartsnow and come onto my land while looking more beautiful than a morning sun heating the firegrass irks me.

It only makes me hate him more. These conflicting emotions eat away at me, pulling me into a spiral of destruction. Fighting my natural instincts to claim him, to show him who he belongs to, to show him he is my property and that no other will ever get to experience his touch, is a sickness I wish on no one.

I want no other to have him. I want no other to experience the cool touch of his silver skin.

All while I don't want him at all.

Yes, you do. We must. You want him more than your next breath.

My dragon always has something to stay.

Ignoring my beast, I stare at Cailian, and I'm caught in his hypnotic blue gaze. I etch every curve of his face, the defined pout of his lips, and the exquisite curiosity of his eyes into my memory. I forget who we are for a moment. I get lost in the trance of my

firebond, the history between us is nonexistent, the murder of my father erased, and all that's left is hope for our future.

Huffing behind me from the other dragons pulls me away from my enchantment, reminding me of who I am and who *he* is.

The man who stole the time I had left with my father. Anything I had to learn from the man who ruled for a thousand years, was taken.

Now is my chance.

I breathe in and release my blaze from my mouth to burn him where he stands. He crosses his arms in front of him, a thick sheet of ice blocking my flames. The heat meets the cold, steam rising violently as our powers clash. We lock eyes, his blue sparkling like freshly fallen snow, the veins in his neck glow the same bright orange that is trying to kill him.

To my shock, the ice begins to crackle along my fire, inching up, slowly freezing it.

That's impossible.

I run out of breath and snap my jaw shut, blowing out black smoke from my nostrils.

"Now that we have that out of the way—" he leans to the side to p eek at the other dragons before his gaze falls on me again. I happen to like his attention on me rather than my guards. "—We can speak like adults. I believe we have much to discuss, Nyx, The Prince of D ragons." He bows his head slightly, showing me respect like any visitor would, but immediately my mind is imagining something else entirely.

He bows for me, bending his neck while falling to his knees to worship me. Would his mouth feel cold on my cock? Could he handle the heat of a dragon's knot? I'm not sure he could with his lean, elegant, nearly feminine body. He's so small. One wrong move and I'd ruin him.

"Nyx?" My name falls from his lips and my entire body shivers, the glowing of my scales intensifies, and a small piece of the iron walls I have around my heart when it comes to him, crumble. "I know I do not deserve your time, your patience, and I do not expect your forgiveness. In the eight hundred years we have been fighting one another, I have noticed that silence has been too loud between us. It has accomplished nothing but death and regret. Nothing can be mended without the strike of the first word."

I shift into my human form, tucking my wings behind my back, and do my best to ignore the ache in my left wing. Rolling my head over my shoulders, my neck cracks, and I can't hide my want for my firebond. My cock betrays me, as it plumps semi-hard against my thigh.

"Oh," Cailian whispers so quietly, no one else can hear him but me.

I smirk, scenting how much he enjoys the sight of me. His eyes widen before lifting to my face, a blueish hue gathering on his cheeks.

Is he blushing?

If I didn't want to despise his existence, I would admit how adorable he is.

Dragons have three testicles, a bit of an anomaly compared to other creatures because when we mate, we want to breed. The more come we have, the better the chance of our firebonds becoming pregnant, increasing the dragon population.

Male or female.

It doesn't matter.

We force their bodies to become pregnant, changing their system until they have no choice but to adapt to us. Is it wrong not to give them a choice? It is, but we can't help our instincts, and every fucking part of me is pushing me to pin my firebond against the door, lift his fancy fucking robes, and claim his ass.

But I won't.

Not in this lifetime.

I turn my head, my chin touching my shoulder. "Raiden. Get everyone out of the castle now. Leave us."

Raiden grunts in reply, leaping into the air, and lands on the edge of the upstairs tower. A loud bellow followed by two short one's echo through the air, ordering all dragons to leave the castle at once.

Cailian takes a step back, craning his head back to look toward the sky as the castle rumbles. Pieces of stone crumble at his feet, dust clouding the air before loud, ear-piercing calls ease the slight suffering in my chest.

Dragons of all shapes, sizes, and colors twist into the sky, flying from the open space in the center of the den.

"Wow."

I cast my gaze to Cailian, reeling in every urge I have to kill him to take a moment to appreciate my firebond without him noticing.

Unable to stop myself, I take a step forward, then another, watching as his eyes dance to each dragon flying through the clouds. Shadows fall over us from their bodies soaring up above and he smiles at the sight.

He fucking smiles.

And it's devastating because I want to consume that happiness until it fills my core. That hurts me more than he will ever know.

I'm close enough to see the way his silver skin glimmers and the ice patterns on his cheeks. His lashes are long, curling to his perfectly arched white eyebrows.

Those fucking lashes.

I grumble with every flutter they make shadowing his cheeks, and as I look closer, I notice small flecks of ice on the strands.

He is the most stunning man I've ever seen, and I've imagined killing him countless times.

Now, I'm not sure if I can do it.

I grab the back of his neck and the simple touch makes the tips of my fingers turn cold. His veins glow brighter, and his hair begins to stand, the tips coming toward me.

He lifts his hands and gathers his hair. "If it makes you feel better, you can keep your hold on me while we speak. I cannot use my powers with your touch. You negate them."

I try to warm his neck to prove I'm better than him, but I can't.

My magic is useless too.

Tightening my grip in my frustration, I rip the iron doors open with my free hand. I shove my firebond inside before I spin around, peek outside, and then close us inside by sliding the steel bar into place.

He looks so out of place in my den. It proves how much he doesn't belong here and how we do not belong together.

"I've dreamed of this," I say, crossing my arms and leaning against the door. "Of having you alone just so I can kill you."

He doesn't seem surprised. Cailian nods, the action causing his hair to fall down his shoulders. He's wearing a long robe that nearly touches the floor, the sleeves cupping his delicate wrists, and the fabric stretches over his back before diving down his chest, showing defined pectorals.

That robe is covering the mark I left on him, and it agitates me. Has he been hiding it the whole time? Would he be ashamed to be mated to me?

"So do it," he says, walking around the obsidian throne that was forged in the volcanoes we originated from. His finger glides over the glass. "It is beautiful. It's as if rainbows were caught in the glass." His eyes peek at me, those damn lashes making me question my every belief when it comes to him.

He seems so unbothered by my statement.

"Did you not hear me? I said I wanted to kill you."

His eyes never leave the throne. His palm strokes the glass, and a frozen sequence travels across the leg of the oversized chair that appears to be dipped in the green and blue lights that take over the sky at night.

"Am I supposed to be surprised?" He straightens, placing his hands behind his back as he faces me. "We have been at war for centuries. Why would your feelings for me change because Fate deemed so?"

I growl in annoyance. Why does this man have to be so reasonable? I expected this to be harder. I expected a fight. I wanted him to beg for his life.

I want him to beg me to mate him just so he can breathe another day. So he knows that his life solely depends on me.

"You agree? Fate made a mistake."

He purses his blue-tinted lips as he ponders my question. "I do not believe Fate makes mistakes. I believe I was put on this planet for you." He takes a step forward and I step away, forgetting I'm already leaning against the door.

I lift my hand. "Stop," I snarl, not wanting him to come closer.

He spreads his arms wide as he listens to me. "I believe I am yours to do what you want with. If it is your wish to kill me, I will not fight you, Nyx. I will not battle you any longer." His foot slides across the stone, daring the distance between us. "If it is what you want, then it is what I want."

"It is what I want." My voice is gruff with lust, betraying the words I just said. He takes a step closer, a cold breeze drifting over my skin. A welcome change from the heat.

He nods, the pain radiating from his eyes, and sparkling pools fill them. "May I have your full name before you kill me? I would like to know so in the afterlife, perhaps then, I'll be able to find you in another world where your father's death does not taint my hands."

His tears fall, but they are unlike anything I've ever seen. They are tiny beads of ice rolling down his face. I catch one in my hand, staring at it in amazement as it twinkles like a diamond before melting in my palm.

"Dovenyx," I choke on a broken, agonizing breath. "That is my full name." Because I want us to find each other in another life too.

"Mmm." He shuts his eyes, smiling, letting my name roll through his body. "I knew it was something beautiful. Nyx did not seem to fit a dragon like yourself." His lashes flutter until the cold glaciers of his irises somehow melt me further. "Okay, My Dove. I am ready."

He looks down when he sees I don't move. "Let me help you." He takes my hands and places them on his throat.

Anger of another nature makes itself known. "Why are you doing this?" I snarl. "Why are you making it so easy?"

"Because making it difficult is too much energy. I do not have it. I would rather die in peace than in battle, and this is as peaceful as I can imagine this situation. No?"

So many times, so many years where I've dreamed of having my hands around his throat, but feeling his skin against mine has me brushing my thumb along his collarbone. He's softer than I thought he'd be.

"Do it," he urges.

I try to, I do. My arms shake and my hands tighten slightly, but not enough to make him suffocate. I lean, dipping my head, my mouth inching closer to his.

"Your father would not hesitate. Is that what you need to hear? Do you need to hear that your scales are just like his? I know what they look like as the color is drained from them. You have me right where you want me. Do it."

My chest rises and falls as the air becomes thicker and harder to breathe. My vision swims and that's when I feel the hot tears on my cheeks while fighting the embedded instincts in my blood to kiss him. I haven't cried in eight hundred years.

And kissing him would be my suicide.

"Do it!" he yells. "Do it, My Dove. Fucking do it already!"

A roar breaks free from me, my dragon letting go of his pain, and it's so loud, the castle's foundation quakes. I shove him away, my body bursting into flames.

"Enough! Stop. Stop calling me that. Stop making this simple." I wipe the mourning away from my cheeks, the wetness is odd, and a surprise. Tears proving that my heart will always want to stop me from hurting what is destined to be mine.

An evil smile twists his lips. "Your father asked me to stop too."

I lift my hand in the air and call on my fire until a burning sphere floats in my palm. I sling it toward him, and he dives to the left. The wall behind him bursts into flames as the orb hits the stone.

He's quick, flinging sharp icicles in my direction, they hit my chest as I stalk forward, barely piercing my thick scales.

"I might as well have a little fun with my mate before I die."

"Do not call me that, you murderer."

Something flashes across his eyes, but it's gone. From the ground, an iced trident is born, and he flings it at me. It whooshes through the air and pins me against the nearby wall. My throat is caught between two spikes. My hands wrap around the ice and it's as if I'm trapped within a glacier. My breath puffs in frozen clouds and even my natural heat is taking its fucking time melting it.

He walks so effortlessly, that it's as if he is floating on a cloud as he stands in front of me. "Remember, as long as we do not touch, we can use our powers."

"Good," I snarl, leaning my throat against the weapon. "The thought of your hands on me makes me fucking sick. How dare Fate give me a firebond who killed my father?" I try to break free. "Why would Fate think for one moment I'd want those hands on me? I'd only think about how you froze him, you traitor."

"I am many things, but I am not a traitor." He eyes me up and down. "You are gorgeous, My Dove."

"Do not fucking call me that," I hiss.

He drags his hand down my chest, my scales coming alive at his touch. My cock responds, growing hard for him to my dismay.

"I have never seen a dragon naked," he admits, biting his bottom lip as he stares at my hard cock. "You are a sight painted beyond the beauties of the universe." He lifts his eyes from my leaking shaft, precome dribbling free, and heat pools in the wide length.

Beyond the beauties of the universe.

Why does that statement make me fall a little more out of hate with him?

"You know what is amazing about ice, Cailian?" I hiss, water splashing at our feet as the icicle melts.

He tilts his head, curious.

"It will never stand a chance against fire." I break free, pick him up by his neck, and then toss him to the side only for him to land on his feet.

I open my mouth and let my fire free.

Only this time, Cailian doesn't protect himself, and a red-hot blaze engulfs his body. Pain hammers in my heart as my firebond dying punctures the solidified anger that's in my soul.

I can't.

Burning him would be a sweet victory, almost poetic, but I can't kill him. I close my mouth and run to him, his beautiful silver skin is

marred, and his veins crackle as the ice that empowers him turns to liquid on the floor.

"Do not... stop. It... will... take... more...." he rasps, his lips the color of soot that lives in my blood.

"I can't. I fucking can't." I lift him into my arms as gently as I can. He cries out from the agony. Guilt eats away at my insides. My dragon panics.

We did this to our firebond.

"I'm so sorry, Cailian. Fuck. I'm sorry." I step into a puddle that's from his body disintegrating as I make my way to the door.

"I am not," he whispers. "I will gladly sacrifice the tundra in my heart to experience the fury in yours."

I hate how reasonable he is. I'm not sure how I'm going to be able to live with myself now that I've done this to him.

We're locked in and I can't slide the bar free without jostling Cailian.

"If only you knew," he trails off. "If only you knew what your father asked of me," he croaks before falling unconscious.

"Cailian." I gently shake him. "Cailian! What did he say? What are you talking about?"

His eyes remain closed, his body lifeless in my arms.

"Fuck!" I roar loudly, the grumble reverberating off the walls. I lean down and press my ear against his chest. His heart pounds, slowly, but at least it beats. "Thank Fate," I whisper before, squatting down, holding my firebond to my chest, and leaping into the air.

I spread my wings, holding in a painful cry as pain almost paralyzes me. My left wing struggles to flap, but I force it, flying through the sky to take Cailian back to his land.

"You'll be okay," I tell him. "I'm going to get you home and then we will figure this out." I'm not sure what I mean by that, but I want to be better than the bitterness that has made itself at home in my bones.

I don't want to be a mindless killer, but I truly don't know if I can mate with him. There's too much history.

A loud high-pitched ring fills the air and the wards surrounding his castle vibrate and wave from us slamming into it. How could I forget about the stupid wards?

Cailian falls from my arms, unaware of how much his life is in danger. I try to grab him, but I can't get my wings to cooperate because of the impact with the wards. I shift, calling upon my dragon, and burst through my human form.

I dive, my eyes locking on my firebond. His arms reach out to me, but his eyes are still shut. The heat of my land, the blaze from my fire, is still killing him.

The high points of his cheeks begin to turn onyx, then peel away into dust. He's still burning. He's still dying. I can feel his death creeping in like a dark shadow looming.

I manage to get under him, and he lands on my back before I crash against the ground. We slide a few hundred feet, firegrass and soot shoot up in chunks. A large crater is left from the destructive path.

Getting to all fours, I limp to the wards, getting as close as possible. I angle my wing down and tilt the side of my body, allowing Cailian to slide free. He crosses the heartsnow, landing in a pile of snow.

And I watch as magic repairs the damage I've caused.

His body soaks up the cold. His cheeks mend, his skin heals, and his hair lengthens to its previous state.

He gasps awake, his eyes snapping open. Cailian turns his head, his eyes brimming with questions.

"You did not kill me," he states to himself, watching the burns on his arms vanish.

I begin to back away, huffing as pain shoots up my leg and then my wing falls limp. That's embarrassing. For a dragon, not being able to get his wing up is equivalent to being emasculated.

He eyes my wounds and pushes himself from the ground into a seated position. "I can help you," he offers. "Let me before your wing is too far gone."

I want to. I do, but like most dragons, my pride is a powerful entity all on its own.

So I turn around and limp away, hoping that Fate is kind enough to put me out of my misery.

Chapter Five

RARITY

"I order you to go," Alexander says from across the counter. He splays his arms out, gripping the edge, and with every exhale, I hear the growl growing in his chest.

He's furious with me.

"You can't make me go." I cross my arms over my chest, tilting my head in defiance. I've never been the type to back down from authority. I won't let my brother try to bully me now. "I'm not ready to go."

He blurs until he is standing in front of me, his eyes glowing the color of rage, and his fangs lengthen. He has the longest cuspids I've ever seen, and I won't lie, if he could, he'd scare the immortality out of me.

"I am not speaking as your brother." He tilts his head, narrowing his gaze at me. One of his children coos from behind him and I peek around his shoulder to see Maven standing there with Esmeray in one arm and Enver in the other. "I am not speaking as your friend."

That statement has my attention back on his as he looms over me.

"I am speaking as your master. You will go to your beloved. You will at least have a conversation with him. Do I make myself clear?"

I swallow, those pesky tears burning my eyes again. "Lexy—"

"Do not call me that," he roars.

Uncle Luca is suddenly in front of me, shoving Alexander in his chest. "And I am not threatening you as a coven member, but as your uncle. You will not speak to her like that. You have no idea what we went through in the veil. You have no clue!" he screams, shoving Alexander again, and I gasp from the outburst.

If he continues, Alexander might take that as a challenge.

Esmeray and Enver begin to cry from the noise.

Alexander rushes to his family and strokes his children's cheeks. They calm at his touch, their loud wails silenced with love.

"Beloved, please go into the library while I deal with this. I do not want to upset the twins."

Maven nods, standing on her tiptoes and giving Alexander a kiss on the cheek. She whispers something in his ear before leaning away and narrowing her eyes at him. My brother casts his gaze to the floor, nodding as if he is a child being scolded.

The only person in existence who can put him in his place is our coven witch.

Uncle Luca spins around, one hand on my shoulder while the other slides under my chin, forcing me to look at him.

"Are you okay?" he asks, a worried tone replacing his usual light-hearted one.

I nod. "I'm fine. He's only worried about me. He's handling it the best he can."

"We are all worried about you." A sad smile ghosts over his face, his thumb rubbing under my eye. "You don't have much time. We've

come too far to get to where we are, we have fought to stay alive, and we have beat the fields of the veil to be in this exact moment."

There it is again, the familiar fear rooted inside me that while they finally get to live here, in peace with the family, I'll be absent again, missing out on all the moments that make this coven my home. No one understands.

Paranormals wait their entire lives for a mate, some believing that they are only alive to meet their other half. Everything in our lives seems contingent on what Fate has in store for us.

And Fate scares me because, for the first hundred-plus years of my life, she has not been kind to me.

I don't want my life to be dependent on anyone else. I want to be able to live my life how I want. I'm tired of being an inch away from death. There's a part of me that wishes I never met Cailian, that he stayed away, but then there's another part that misses him so much, my breath is stolen, and all I want to do is breathe him in.

It isn't fair. I know that might sound childish. Many would call me stupid for prolonging this pain instead of giving in to my beloved, but I don't want to mate with him because I *have* to.

I want to *want* that bond more than I want to be here at home with my family.

"I know, Uncle Luca, but I need more time. I just…" I ring my fingers together, then press the heel of my palms against my eyes to stop the tears. "I'm not ready to leave you or anyone else. Please," I choke, falling against his chest. "Not after everything. I need to be here. With you and… and Greyson." My words begin to sound desperate. "What if he isn't okay? What if he tries to…" I stop before I can say it because watching him die one time was enough.

"I'll be fine." Uncle Greyson's voice startles me, and I jump, spinning around to see him by the window, staring at the new lake in our

field for Irving and a few others. "Don't miss out on your beloved because of me or for anyone." He crosses his arms, turning his head to look at me as he leans against the wall. "We are home now, Rarity. Home will never disappear, but your beloved will. You will. My mind is free from death. I promise."

"I just worry about you," I state.

"And we worry about you." Alexander's commanding voice cuts through our conversation.

Luca and I turn to him while Greyson pushes off the wall to stand next to me. He wraps an arm around my shoulders, tugging me close.

"I'm sorry for losing my temper." He runs his hands through his hair, sighing before rubbing his eyes.

It isn't often vampires get tired but being the coven master with newborns can't be easy. He pulls me away from Greyson and wraps me in a hug. His arms are tight as he clings to me, and I remember how different they felt when he held me as a baby. He was gentle, afraid he'd break me.

Both times, are nothing but love.

He cups the back of my head when he pulls away. "I can't lose you again, Rarity. I can't bear to see you fade away like Father is. We have too many of our member's lives in question. Atreyu is still in a coma, Anwyll's brother is lost— which is horrible because all I want to do is bring him home, but I can't do anything about that. Father is on the brink of death and I'm doing what I can with that. I can't control any of those situations, but I can try with you. I can't save any of them, but perhaps I can save you. I understand you don't want to go but know, this will always be your home. Reuel can make you all the sunset magnolia powder you need. Heck, they probably have it there. His world seems very magical. You never have to be without us again." He palms my jaw. "I promise, Rarity."

"How about one of us goes with you to visit?" Uncle Greyson offers, taking a step forward so he is next to Alexander. "I'll go with you to see Cailian. We will talk to him and then come home. You'll get to see the new part of your life. Maybe then it won't be so intimidating if you don't go alone."

"Really? You'd go? You'd do that for me?"

"Of course I would. I need to make sure you're okay."

"I would also want to go," Reuel appears in the chair next to us and Uncle Luca shouts, slapping a hand to his chest.

"Jesus, Reuel. You're going to give a vampire a heart attack doing that."

He chuckles, flashing his pretty white teeth. "Apologies, Luca."

"You're not sorry," Luca grumbles. "You like doing it."

Reuel lifts a shoulder. "Perhaps. I need to get my kicks where I can."

"I'll go too." Finnick, our grouchiest coven member inserts his thoughts before slamming the fridge door shut and holding up a bag of blood. "And who the fuck keeps drinking my O negative? I have my name written on the bag." He points to his name written in marker. "Finnick. It's there. Right fucking there." Finnick pours the blood into a cup before putting it in the microwave. Watching the red liquid fill the clear glass has my mouth watering. I'm so thirsty, but the only blood I want is Cailian's.

Maybe a trip would be best. I can clear the air with Cailian and take a step forward in the direction I'm fighting too hard to steer clear from.

"I don't want you to go," Reuel says, reminding me how they are back to their old ways. "You'll ruin the trip with your..." He waves a hand around. "Bad attitude towards everything."

"I don't really care what you want, elf. My life doesn't revolve around you."

"Thank Fate for that," Reuel mumbles. "I couldn't imagine being mated to you. I'd have an endless headache."

Finnick takes his glass from the microwave and chugs half of it before slamming it down on the counter. He has a red mustache before licking it clean. "You are the headache. I feel bad for anyone who gets stuck with you."

Reuel vanishes, only to reappear at Finnick's side. "Me?" The tips of Reuel's ears wiggle the angrier he becomes. "At least I'm not a grinch. Who in their right mind would be happy with your cranky ass?" Reuel lifts his fist to hit Finnick, who has a wicked smile on his face, but Alexander steps in, picking Reuel up by his shirt.

"That's enough out of you two. No speaking for the rest of the night."

"Let me at him. I'm going to put his ass in the woods again."

"I'd like to see you try," Finnick challenges.

Alexander points a finger at the grumpy vampire. "That's enough out of you." He plops Reuel in a chair and holds him down. "And you, don't even think about poofing in and out when I'm not looking. I'll know."

"I'm going to see Irving. The company is so much better." Reuel disappears in the next blink of an eye.

"Finally. Peace," Finnick sighs, taking another long swallow of his cup of blood.

Greyson pinches the bridge of his nose. "Shut the hell up, Finnick. You're making my head hurt."

"Maybe going to see Cailian isn't such a bad idea," Alexander says. "Too bad I can't go. Finnick, you aren't going. Reuel might be from there and you won't ruin it for him. Luca, Greyson, you'll go with Rarity to Elementalu. You'll keep me updated every night you're there."

"Every night?" I balk, wondering how long he thinks I'll be staying there. I twist my hair around my finger nervously, then chew on my bottom lip. "I figured we'd just pop in, you know? Bring a bottle of wine to say thanks for having us. Isn't that what humans do? Then talk, shake hands, and you know, leave."

Luca, Greyson, and Alexander are staring at me with big, knowing smiles on their faces.

I blink, feeling a bit peeved. "So we don't do the wine?" I ask, unsure.

Greyson snorts and Luca keels over laughing, holding his stomach with every obnoxious snort that escapes him.

Alexander is the only one who keeps his cool, but he's obviously amused. "Do you really think a quick meet and greet with your beloved will be enough to solve all your problems?"

"No," I grumble. "It would be a start though."

"What are you so afraid of, Rarity?" Greyson asks. "That maybe you'll find happiness outside of the place where you thought you'd spend the rest of your eternal days?"

"Yes," I answer quickly. "And so many other things when it comes to my family."

"Aye, don't be worried about us," Drayce announces as he opens the front door, an axe thrown over his shoulder. The blade on it seems sharper as it shines against the light. "We won't be going anywhere. Considering we can't go into the sunlight, it isn't like we have many options," he jokes, but I don't miss the regretful flinch from Alexander.

"I'm sorry," my brother says. "Maven is still researching a temporary solution."

"It isn't a big deal. I happen to think the night sky is prettier than the daylight. I have no regrets."

"Says you."

The sound of my father's voice coming from the archway has us all turning our heads. I haven't seen him in a few days. He lives down in the catacombs now. He refuses to leave our brother Atreyu.

I gasp when I see him. He doesn't even look like the same man. His cheeks are losing their fullness and dark circles shadow under his eyes. He has lost so much weight; his shirt seems to hang on his frame.

"Christ, Severide, you look like shite." Drayce whistles under his breath. "You might want to drink some blood."

"I would if the sun could touch me," he sneers hatefully.

His attitude has changed since we have come back through the portal. It's been a slow transition, but a noticeable one. He is withering away, mind and body.

"Bullshit," Luca calls his brother out. "You aren't thinking clearly. I go hunting at night all the time and have no issues. You are choosing to be like this. You are choosing to starve yourself. You're blaming Atreyu because you don't have your son, but it's more than that. It's because you don't have Esmeralda."

My father blurs to Luca, wrapping his hands around my uncle's throat. His eyes burn the classic bright red of a vampire who is hungry and has lost all control.

"Don't you dare speak of her! Don't you fucking dare." Spit flies from his mouth, landing on Luca's chin.

Alexander is on our father, ripping him off our uncle by grabbing his shirt. "Do you think you're the only one who misses her? She was my mother. Our—" he points to me "—mother."

Severide smacks against the wall before flashing his fangs and launching himself through the air. Drayce is there, grabbing Father by the leg, then slinging him across the room.

Finnick has to move out of the way as Father lands on the kitchen island.

"I hated to have to do that, old friend, but you're losing yer fucking mind." Drayce stands over him and Father groans, too weak to continue. "I'll take that. Thanks, Fin."

Drayce snatches the glass of blood from Finnick.

"Hey—"

"Shut it, Finnick. Open another bag." Drayce glares daggers at the grumpy vampire.

Luca and Greyson run to help Drayce when they notice what he is trying to do. They hold him down and Drayce pries father's mouth open.

"Apologies, Severide. I am doing this because I care."

"No," Father mumbles weakly. "No. Let me die. I want to be with her again. Just let me be with her again."

Tears prickle my eyes as I hear the desperation in my father's voice. His weak hand wraps around Drayce's wrist, showing how slim father's arm is.

"I can't do that because you don't realize what you have here in this house. You're blinded by grief, and I won't let it take you from us." Drayce peers to Luca, then Greyson, then side-eyes Finnick. "Make yourself useful. Hold his mouth open."

Finnick stands still, not wanting to obey Drayce.

"Finnick! Get your head out of your arse and fucking hold his mouth open!" Drayce roars and at the same time, lightning strikes in the kitchen, Dottie appearing out of thin air.

"Do it before I slide this bolt through your neck," she threatens, a sword buzzing with electricity in her hand, the tip under Finnick's chin.

My mouth opens in shock, the creature surrounding Dottie pulsates.

Finnick rushes to obey, grabbing my father's chin and prying his mouth open.

"She's hard not to listen to," Drayce smirks.

"Focus, Drayce," Luca says.

"Right. Sorry. She's a bit distracting." He clears his throat, then places the rim of the glass against Father's lips.

"Don't," Father pleads the best he can, the word a garbled slur.

Drayce rolls his lips together, tilting the glass until the blood rushes free from the glass. Father coughs, and Finnick forces his mouth shut, then plugs his nose to force Father to swallow.

"Get me more blood. I'm afraid we will have to force-feed him, Master Monreaux." Drayce informs my brother and everyone in the room turns their attention to him. "If not he will die."

Alastair and Alaric come into the room. "Someone called for blood?" He tosses a blood bag to Drayce. "I have more too. Don't worry."

"Me too," Alaric says.

Alexander nods. "I understand. I didn't want us to be at this point, but it seems we have no choice."

"I'll hate you forever if you do this to me," Father sneers with disdain.

"I'll bear the weight of your hate if it means you stay alive," Lex says, sadness tinting his tone.

"You expect me to leave when this is happening here?" I whisper to my brother, changing my position to stand in front of him. "Lex, I can't."

"I can save our father because our mother wasn't his beloved." His eyes move from the men forcing blood down father's throat, then to

me. "But I won't be able to save you. You will die, so tomorrow night, just as the sun sinks below the earth, you'll go to your beloved. You'll see there is nothing to fear because what is happening at home will continue to happen, whether you are here or not."

"Lex—"

"—That's it, Rarity. There is nothing else to say. There is nothing you'll be able to do to convince me otherwise. That's the end of the conversation. Do you understand me?"

I grind my teeth together from being told what to do. "I understand."

He grabs my shoulders and gives me a slight shake. "I am doing this because I love you. You can even take your bottle of wine if it makes you feel better."

I can't help but smile. "It might."

"Good. Why don't you go see Maven? See if she needs help with the twins or Irving. I don't want you to see anything else that will happen here."

"He's my father too, Lex. I'm not a little girl anymore."

"Stop being stubborn and listen to me for once," he informs stern yet controlled. He's losing his patience.

I rip myself from my brother's arms, then push my way between Alaric and Alastair.

"Rarity," Alexander calls for me. "Rarity!"

I ignore him, throwing open the kitchen door, and jumping from the porch. The stars glitter in the sky by the millions, the wind breezes through my hair and dries my tears.

A deep bark from beside me has me turning my head to see Whiskey moseying over to me, taking his sweet time.

I grin at him, patting my thigh to call him over quicker, but he only plops his tongue out and keeps at the same pace. When he finally

reaches my side, I'm in a better mood just because of his fluffy cuteness.

"Hey, good boy." I scratch behind his ears. "You want to go for a walk with me?"

He woofs, deep and short.

"Sounds good." I pat his head, keeping my hand in his soft fur as we walk to the lake Maven has made for the water creatures we have welcomed into the coven.

The journey to the new lake is beautiful. Maven's magic keeps the plants alive all year. I pass large, towering sunflowers and black roses, mixed with snapdragons and lilies. Even the scent is sweet emanating from the middle of the flowers. It helps ease the tension that's been constant since I've met Cailian.

"He must hate me," I say to Whiskey, knowing he can't reply back, but I don't need anyone to.

I sit on the bench Greyson made to enjoy the new view and speak with our new coven members. Whiskey groans as he lies at my feet, huffing just as his snout plops on my foot.

"I hope you're right," I reply to his nonsense, imagining he said, "Cailian doesn't hate you."

"I wouldn't blame him, you know. I've been a difficult mate. I've been emotional, stubborn, and fighting the bond." A small manic chuckle fills the silent air. "Fighting is useless when it will end the way fate intended it to." I tilt my head back, resting it against the edge of the bench, staring up at the stars again. "It's crazy to think that one of those dots is a galaxy that holds Elementalu, where my beloved is."

"It's a beautiful thought, isn't it?"

I scream, holding a hand to my chest, whipping my head around to see who spoke.

Irving walks out from the lake. "I am sorry, Rarity. I did not mean to frighten you. May I?" He points to the spot next to me.

My heartbeat tries to return to normal. "Of course."

"Next time, I will try not to creep out of the darkness."

A laugh bubbles free. "That's a good plan. It might not be me you scare next time, and they might not be as nice."

"Like Finnick," we say in unison.

Our laughter fills the space and water drips from his body, the gills in his neck expanding with every breath. He mimics me, lying his head back to look up at the sky.

"I wonder if my mate is up there amongst the stars," he says, a stab of guilt ricocheting off my bones.

"I'm sure they are." I pat his webbed hand. "You're too kind to be alone, Irving."

"As are you, Rarity. So may I ask, why you want to be alone?" He turns his head, his large dark eyes blinking at me inquisitively.

"What? I don't want to end up alone."

"Then why put off the inevitable if loneliness is not your goal?"

I don't know what to say to that, so I stay quiet, thinking of his question. "It isn't that I want to be alone. I want to be with Cailian. I'm scared, but it's more about choosing my own way to get there. I envy humans and their ability to choose who they want to love. I feel I'm being forced into something I'm not ready for."

"How do you know you're not ready unless you try?"

I open my mouth to answer, but nothing comes out.

"Your heart will feel better once it's fully healed."

"Healed? I'm fine, Irving."

He exhales a long breath. "It aches from the past and it will never be full until you go to your beloved. You'll be surprised just how

much your life will change once you open those wounds again to allow yourself to heal. Your beloved is the cure."

"Having a beloved isn't a cure."

"I never said it was instant," he says, scratching his arm. "I envy you. I'm nervous my mate will see me and run. Who wants to be mated to a monster?"

"You aren't a monster, Irving!"

"I am anything but normal. This is my form. I have no other."

"Your mate would be stupid if they ran."

"Then you should stop being stupid and running from yours."

I click my tongue, nudging his arm. "I see what you did there."

"Good. I wanted to be obvious."

"Goal achieved." I tap my fingers against my stomach. "I'm going to see my beloved tomorrow, actually."

"You should go now. Why wait another night?"

"My uncles are coming with me."

"You are a child who needs parental guidance? Rarity," he scoffs. "I'm disappointed."

I frown at his statement, but now that he has said it, he is right. I am acting like a child. My beloved is someone I need to face on my own. Having my uncles there will show my beloved I don't trust him.

And maybe I don't, but that's between me and Cailian.

No one else.

"Thanks, Irving." I stand. "If anyone asks, tell them where I went."

He doesn't look away from the sky. "I will. I swear."

I begin to walk away, patting my leg for Whiskey to come with me but he stays plopped at Irving's feet.

The closer I get to the large, white mansion, the louder the yelling coming from inside becomes. Quietly, I inch my way up the steps, opening the lid of the sunset magnolia powder that Reuel keeps by the

door. The powder is in individual bags, so I snag three, stuffing two in my pocket.

Running down the steps, Reuel pops in front of me.

"Where do you think you're going?"

I toss the powder in the air, thinking of Cailian and Elementalu. "A place I've been putting off for far too long." A portal appears, the ring shining bright orange, and I can see the ice castle.

Fear is the last thing I feel as I step through, and peace overcomes me.

A voice in the back of my head whispers, "Home."

And as much as that scares me, I welcome it.

Chapter Six
CAILIAN

It is only been a few hours and I cannot stop thinking about him.

My mate saved me.

He had his chance to finally kill me, to finally have his revenge, but he did not take it. He couldn't.

He chose me. Even if he hates letting me live, that means something. I do not care if I have to live in the depths of his regret—what matters is that I live somewhere in his soul.

I will swim in the regret because now I know he won't let me drown.

"That dopey smile is a good change of pace," Zyrl says in the entry of my bedroom doorway.

I sit up in bed, deciding it was best to rest after getting burned by dragon fire and then slammed against the invisible walls. Even though I've healed, my body is exhausted.

I rub my shoulder where he scarred me. "It could have been worse." My dragon has a more even temper than I thought. I figured once he had me alone, he'd attack me and not think twice.

"Apologies, Prince Cailian," one of the guards interrupts us, clearing his throat and standing tall. His uniform glistening with the frozen threads weaved in the silver material. "For interrupting, but you have a guest in the lobby."

My heart hammers with hope. "Is it a dragon, by chance?"

He tilts his head in confusion, his eyebrows wrinkling in the middle as he stares at me. "No, Prince. It's a woman. She smells of us, but isn't? She says her name is—"

"—Rarity?" I rush to say, cutting him off.

"Yes, my Prince. She also brings wine from the humans. Sir, what are humans?" he asks and if it were any other guest, I would answer him, but it does not matter.

My other mate is here.

I rush out of bed, nearly tripping on the blankets before righting myself. "Such a small detail to what is truly important. I will answer you later." I push by him, uncaring that he loses his footing and smacks against the wall.

"Cailian!" my brother calls for me and hear him say to the guard. "I'm sorry. This guest is of the utmost importance. Let the entire castle know now."

I am sprinting down the wide, spiral staircase, wondering if today could bless me further than it already has. I stop at the bottom of the steps when I see Rarity, stunned to stillness by her beauty.

Immediately, I am in love with watching her. Every move she makes is graceful and curious. Her long white hair falls just above her hips. My mouth waters from her figure. She's wearing an odd outfit like the one I saw her in the last time I was in Salem. Black jeans, she calls them, with a plain long-sleeve emerald-green shirt that makes her skin appear flawless, almost like a frozen sheet of ice from a river that has been unbothered.

She reaches for the chandelier, curious as ever, and touches one of the ice crystals. It falls and breaks in half on the ground. Rarity gasps, looking left and right but has yet to sense me. I smirk, watching her panic.

Bending down, she picks up the pieces, desperately looks around, and tosses it in one of the few planters I keep by the door.

"Damn it, Rarity. You're not here five minutes and you're breaking things," she whispers to herself.

"As long as it is not my heart, I do not care what you break, My Snow," I finally greet her.

She spins around, clutching the bottle of wine to her chest.

I stroll forward steadily, not too fast to scare her away, but with enough determination to show her I am ecstatic to see her.

"How long have you been there?" she asks, the words wavering with nerves.

I stand in front of her, bending down until we are nose to nose, but my hand sinks into the planter, picking up the two broken pieces from the chandelier. Her breath catches as we touch and our hair decides to dance again, daring to twist and hold onto one another.

"Long enough to watch you do this." I pull my hair to the side, not wanting her to feel rushed and pressured, and lift the crystal into the air with a sly smirk on my face. "It is only ice, My Snow. Watch. Let me see your hand."

She holds her hand out, palm up, and I place the two pieces there, pressing each in together.

"We can fix what is frozen," I inform, holding my hand over hers and never looking away from her violet eyes. Magic pulsates between us, my palm vibrates as blue glows from our palms.

Removing my hand from hers takes all the cold I have inside me.

I lift the ice crystal in the air, the light from outside shines through the windows. An array of different colors radiates from the small insignificant object in my hand, but Rarity's eyes are wide with excitement.

She is impressed.

I cannot help but feel as if I have done something monumental as she stares at the crystal. I stretch my arm and she follows it, watching as I freeze it to its rightful place.

"Can you do it again?" she nearly squeals with giddiness.

I chuckle, lifting my hand over her head, and then snow begins to fall, completely disappearing in her hair since the color is the same. The long tendrils glitter, coming to life as they feel the power of where Rarity belongs.

Her smile does not fade, if anything, it becomes bigger. She spreads out her hands, the snow gathering in her dainty palms. The small flecks of ice land on her cheeks, absorbing into her flesh, becoming one with her body, and just like me, her own frozen pattern spreads across her cheekbones in a light lavender color.

I have never met another who holds the color violet inside them. Her eyes, the ice on her cheeks, she must be the only one of her kind.

Daringly different yet dared to be mine.

Holding out my other hand, I conjure a frozen flower in my hand, small enough to tuck over her ear. "To what do I owe the pleasure of your presence, My Snow?"

She blushes, the new pattern on her cheeks growing a shade of light purple that reminds me of the flowers that grow in the forest— the territory claimed by Woodland Elves. Her body did not react like this when I saw her in Salem, so I wonder if the ice elven in her blood is growing stronger now that she is in Elementalu.

"I— um— I brought wine." She shoves the bottle against my chest, giving me a nervous smile.

A piece of hair falls from the one braid she has in front, tickling her cheeks and she tries to blow it away. The rebellious strand gets caught on her eyelashes.

I lift my hand. "May I?" I ask softly, stepping forward to close any space between us.

An audible gulp sounds in her throat when she swallows from my nearness. Her eyes lock on my chest before gliding up ever so slowly to my face before barely nodding, giving me the permission I need to touch her.

My fingers glide across the wayward piece of soft platinum silk before I gently pull it free from her eyelashes and tuck it behind her ear. My palm cups her face, my thumb rubbing against the tops of her frozen cheeks.

"You are a glacier in a firestorm, My Snow, bringing hope to my heart when I thought all was lost."

Rarity licks her pink lips that remind me of the softest petals. I want nothing more than to experience the velvet flesh against my own. I bet those lips are softer than any cloud the Fates could ever promise me in the afterlife.

"You are very hard to resist, Prince Cailian," she whispers, those violet irises dropping to my lips, giving away what she truly desires.

"There is no need to resist me, Rarity. I am made for you. When you are ready, that is," I clarify. I never want any of my mates to agree to this mating if it is not what they truly want.

She shuffles her feet, and the scent of anxiety burns the air.

I slide my hand down her neck, appreciating the soft curve before following her shoulder, then her arm, and take her hand in mine. In unison, we release a weighted breath from how good it feels to touch.

"How about we have dinner and open this bottle of wine you have brought from…" I turn the bottle in my hand, not understanding the label on it.

"It's cheap wine. I had to use the sunset magnolia powder to travel here and once I was on your land, I realized I came empty-handed, so I turned around, and thought of any place that would have it." She nibbles her bottom lip. "It was ten bucks."

"Bucks? Like deer? How odd to pay in venison, but I suppose every dimension is different."

She laughs, a light airy sound that reminds me of a breeze that rustles leaves in the forest— a moment that brings relaxation and peace.

"No, dollars. That's how humans pay where I'm from and since we live in a world dominated by humans, we use their money."

"Ah, I see. Similar to our elements then."

"Elements?"

"It is money, but in coins. Forged in wind, fire, earth, and water."

"I love that," she says. "What do the coins look like? I have a quarter with me. We could compare."

"Only if you'll have dinner with me? You eat food, yes?"

Her smile disappears, but she plasters it back on. "I do. I'd love to have dinner with you, and we can talk? It's why I'm here."

"I knew as much." I tug her hand as I step forward. "This way. I have something to discuss with you as well. If this mating is to go forward, we have to be honest with one another."

I cannot let go of her hand, though. I finally have her here, her skin against mine, and sacrificing that is impossible.

"Your castle is beautiful," she compliments, looking around the icy space with wide, shocked eyes. "I've never seen anything like it. Is everything…"

"Ice? Yes. The cold is where we thrive."

"But you have hot water? Hot food?"

"We do," I answer all of her curious questions with a smile.

"How?"

We stop at the archway where the doors to the dining room are closed. Geometric designs are chiseled in the frozen blocks, the elven crest in the middle, and the long handles are icicles, stopping at a sharp point.

The elven crest is simple, a snowflake over the symbols for wind, earth, and fire, elements that bind us to this planet.

"Each dimension is different, I suppose. We have magic here just like you do at home with your coven."

Rarity traces the crest with her fingers, a delicate and soft touch I wish to feel on my body one day soon. "What does this mean?"

"It's the Elven crest. We are The House of Ice and Snow. Next door, is The House of Smoke and Fire. The Woodland Elves are by far the strongest out of all the elements as they bend the earth to their will—they are The House of Soil and Life. Finally, we have the Wind Wolves. They are The House of Howls and Wind." I push the doors open to the dining room, remembering the days when the wind existed. "I do miss my neighbors. I cannot remember the last time I saw a wind wolf. When the portals closed, I am afraid we lost our friends to another dimension. Now, only elves and dragons remain."

Dragons.

I need to tell her I am not her only mate.

"Oh my gosh," she gasps, tilting her head back to take in the high ceilings, ice banisters, and chandelier hanging above the table. "I've never seen anything like this before. The detail is more than I expected for a home that's frozen."

I hide most of my excitement, not wanting to seem too eager, but I have a bounce in my step as I grab the door handles. "I am glad my home does not disappoint you, My Snow, as it is your home as well."

Zyrl is standing outside the doors. "I'll make sure no one bothers you and your guest, brother," he whispers, lifting a white eyebrow.

"My mate. I told you she would come. You have little faith in Fate, Zy."

He sighs, long and tired, proving how low his energy is for not wanting to talk about this. "And perhaps you have too much. We will wait for updates, Cailian, but The House deserves to know what is happening with their leader. What will change for us? For Elementalu?"

I hold my hand up, palm facing him, and ease it in a stopping motion. "One issue at a time. First, I need to talk to my mate about the future so I can inform you what happens with ours."

Zy opens his mouth to reply but I close the door in his face, not wanting to prolong speaking with Rarity. My tomorrow is only a possibility with what Rarity will say today. She holds the power to the rest of the hours of my life.

"We will not be interrupted again," I say, keeping my back to her while I collect myself.

I stare at the veins in my hands, glowing bright orange against my silver skin. I bend my fingers, watching the fire twirl around every digit to warm the very tips.

The ache of my body for my mates pulses strongly in my bones. I squeeze my eyes shut, breathing through the pain until it eases.

Do my mates not need me the way I need them? How can they deny me for so long when I would give my life for five minutes of being mated to them?

"Let us open the human wine you brought. I bet it is delicious." I step forward, pulling out a chair for her, gesturing for her to sit. "Please make yourself at home. I will be happy to serve you in any and *every* way." I am unable to stop the desire dripping from my words.

Since Rarity has stepped foot into my castle, all I have wanted to do is bend her over my throne and place a crown on top of her head. She'd be claimed by my come, my blood, and power.

She'll be the first Princess our planet has ever seen, and I have no doubt, she'll wield more power than me and the dragon combined.

A violet hue teases the apples of her cheeks causing the new frozen pattern to deepen and glitter. My Snow peers down, tucking a piece of hair behind her ear.

"Do you like it when I compliment you, Rarity? Would you rather I stop?" I open my palm, flecks of ice swirling as I move my fingers.

A wine glass appears, the crescent etched into the ice, and the long stem is smooth to the touch.

She shakes her head.

"My Snow, please grace me with your gaze so I can get lost in it." If I have to, I will get on my knees to be the one to meet her sights.

Her shoulders rise and fall as she releases a nervous breath. Those unique purple irises finally lock onto me, making it difficult to focus on the task at hand.

"Do you want me to stop?" I ask again, pouring the wine she brought into the glasses I have created.

"No," she whispers, shaking her head while twirling a piece of her hair around her finger.

I grab the leg of her chair and pull her closer to me. She yelps, her hands gripping mine from the unexpected movement. The wooden legs hauntingly grind against the ice-tiled floor, scratching the surface.

That is an easy fix.

"You were too far away for my soul to be happy." I wrap a hand around her ankle, my eyes roaming up her long legs that I hope will be wrapped around my hips soon.

Moving her closer to me brings the havoc in my marrow solace, but I did not prepare myself for her scent to hit me like a newly blossomed meadow in spring. I growl, tugging her to me by her leg, the chair squeaking loudly from the few inches it moves.

My eyes roll to the back of my head as I inhale, dragging my nose up her leg until I stop at her knee. I peek up at her, hearing the audible broken breaths. Rarity is still gripping the arms of the chair, holding on for dear life, but I do not smell fear.

Oh no, it is quite the opposite.

Her desire is strong, mixed with nerves and uncertainty, and I am not the kind of male to push. Instead of lying her down on this table and showing her pleasure, I press my forehead against her knee, digging my fingers into her thigh to gather my control. My cock aches to feel her pussy around it, but in all my years, I have never slept with another.

While I want to bathe in her until I drown, I am afraid I will not be able to give her what she needs.

I kiss her leg before straightening, grabbing one of the glasses of wine I have poured for us, and chugging half. The dry bitter taste has me reeling back, choking mid-swallow.

"Are you okay?" Rarity's hands take mine as her gaze searches mine, then drops to my lips.

Tears well as the burn in my throat eases. "My gods, where did you get that?" I point to the glass. "It is dreadful. Humans made that? Those poor creatures. Is this what they give to people to punish them?"

Rarity giggles, flipping her long, luxurious hair over her shoulder. "It can't be that bad, Cai."

No one has ever given me a nickname. I rather find I like the shortened version of Cailian from her lips.

I roll the stem of the glass between my fingers. "Do you want to taste?" My voice deepens more than usual, wanting her to understand just how much I want her to savor me.

"I do."

I nibble my bottom lip between my teeth. "Open your mouth for me." My cock hardens beneath my robes, my words breathless as I imagine saying them to her while Nyx has her on her hands and knees. I'd guide my cock between her plump, pink lips, watch them stretch to accommodate me, witness her spit shine on my cock, and then be gifted the sight of her swallowing my come.

I want nothing more than to put my frost in her veins, in her womb.

"What?" she asks while I am daydreaming of her.

I smirk, snatching her throat with my hand before she can take her next breath. My thumb grazes her plump bottom lip, a breeze of a whimper tickling my fingertip.

"I said open your mouth," I repeat myself.

She obeys beautifully, spreading her lips wide for me.

"Good girl, Rarity." I take a swig of the harsh wine, then lean forward, keeping her throat clutched in my hand.

I spit the badly made alcohol into her mouth, the red liquid drips down her chin, and I am there, licking wine from her skin.

"Oh, My Snow, this wine tastes so much better when I am using you as the glass," I say, pushing her chin to shut her mouth. "Swallow."

Her throat bobs and a slight flinch pinches her features as the burning bite of the cheap wine makes itself known in her throat.

"I don't think it's as bad as you say." Her gaze dances from my eyes to my lips, her want becoming exceedingly clear.

I drag my finger down her angelic, delicate jaw. "Do you want to try it again?" My other finger circles the rim of the frosted glass.

She nods with an eagerness that has the primal need in me practically purring with satisfaction, but then I think of the submissive part of me, the part only our dragon can fill.

Rarity opens her mouth and I take another drink, never breaking eye contact. Our lust thickens the air, heating it to the point the chandelier above us begins to drip onto the table.

Sliding my fingers across her neck, her pulse jumps beneath my touch.

Ba-dum. Ba-dum. Ba-dum.

Her heart is steady, but fast, and I control her movements again, decorating her slender throat with my hand.

Once more, I spit into her mouth, a moan slipping free of her body, and I break. I move fast, wanting to swallow her sounds before the universe has a chance to taste them. Our lips meet in a clash, wine spilling free from my mouth.

My lips have never touched another's but the moment they touch hers, my own groan of pleasure travels through my chest. The dimensions right themselves, the planet that has felt so empty, now fills full with the hope of a future. Her kiss is eager, and the inexperience is sweeter than the aftertaste the wine left.

We are learning together.

My grip tightens on her shirt and this time when my hair drifts to her, I do not stop it. I do not have the will. Her tongue flicks out to mine, the tips teasing each other, daring the other to do more. Her hands slide up the back of my neck, her nails sinking into my scalp as she gains more confidence.

"Cai," she whimpers, dragging herself over my hard cock. Her nose buries against my neck, and she licks my vein. "You smell so good, Beloved." She sucks my flesh into her mouth, her fangs threatening to break the skin. "So pretty," she murmurs, kissing down my throat as she unties the belt to my robe. Her hand dips under the lapels, parting the material until my chest is bare. She continues to grind against me, over and over again, moaning the faster she moves.

"So thirsty." She inhales, smelling the other side of my neck. "I haven't fed since I met you. No other's blood will do."

"Are you hungry, My Snow? Do you need to feed?" I yank her head back by wrapping her hair around my wrist.

She hisses at me, flashing her sharp fangs, and glaring at me with starving red irises.

"Do not ever make yourself go hungry again when I am here for you, to sate your craving, to fill your needs. You will never go hungry again. If you need, promise you will take from me."

Using her vampire speed, she blurs us until I am on my back against the table, laid out before her like a feast with my arms spread. She bends my neck, exposing my throat further, and without warning, she snarls, cutting the sharp points into the jugular vein.

"Fuck!" I yell, arching my back from pain and pleasure. "Yes, My Snow. Drink. Take all you need." I cup the back of her head, pressing her face further into my neck.

She groans, sinking those weaponized teeth into me deeper.

"Rarity," I whisper in warning as my orgasm threatens.

She takes another long drag from me, and I toss my head back, shouting in ecstasy as I come. My undergarments become wet, yet my cock is still frozen solid, wanting more, wanting us to give into the mating bond.

To my surprise, her hand slips down my chest, and I cannot remember how to breathe.

"Ah— Oh— Rarity— I," I have no idea what I am trying to say. Speaking has never been an issue for me until this moment.

Who needs to speak when the pleasure I am feeling shouts volumes?

Her lithe fingers slip under the waistband of my undergarments. Immediately, she touches come.

"So much, Cai. Is this all for me?" She brings her fingers to her mouth, sucking the clear, glittering fluid from her flesh. "Your come is cold," she notices.

"All of me is," I slur, high from her bite still.

"Your blood isn't." She yanks my head to the other side that isn't bitten. "In fact, it warms me more than a fire, Cai. I think—" she licks the spot where she wants to feed "—I might need more."

Before I can say a word, she is biting me again, drinking more of my blood. Another orgasm rolls through me and Rarity's palm is there, cupping the crown of my cock so she can catch my release.

She straightens, teeth gleaming with red. Her eyes close and she sways as if she has had too much wine. I try to readjust my position under her, but she mistakes it for me trying to leave.

With a sneer, she pins me with her advanced strength, bites her free hand, and then shoves her palm against my mouth. Her blood touches my tongue just as she cleans her palm of my come. Her blood is power, swimming through my veins, mending the molecules inside me that have started to melt from the rejection of my mates.

Her eyes snap open when the connection between us intensifies. We are not mated yet. I know vampires have to fuck to complete the mating ritual, but sharing blood begins the bond. I can feel her every emotion, her uncertainty, her fear, her excitement, and her lust.

The red fades from her irises, violet replacing the harsh monstrous color of her vampire that I would love to see chasing me through the dark.

"Oh my gods."

I sit up, clutching the back of her neck. "Don't. Don't panic, My Snow. Everything is okay. I am okay."

"I practically attacked you. We are half-mated now. I didn't give you a choice. I— I did the one thing I didn't want to do with you."

Her words strike me, nearly hotter than Nyx's fire. "You came all this way to tell me you do not want me as your mate?"

"No!" she yells in a rush, taking my face in her hands. "No, that is not what I meant."

"Then, tell me so we no longer have to continue this dance of slow death," I beg of her.

"I lost control because I want you so badly. I came here to explain myself. You know what happened with my family, how we were in the veil until the portals were unlocked with Maven's magic."

I nod in understanding, tucking a wayward piece of her hair again.

She holds my hand to her chest. "I'm afraid I'm being taken from them. I'm afraid being here means I can't be with them anymore."

"Rarity. I would never keep you from them. I have enough sunset magnolia powder for you to travel back and forth for many eternities. Any time of day, any time of night, you are welcome there just as they are welcome here. Keeping you from them would be a horrible thing for me to do."

Everything about her demeanor changes. She brightens in an instant, then wraps herself around me, her legs wrap around my hips, her arms circle my neck tightly, and Rarity squeals.

"You promise? I can come and go?"

"A thousand times a day, My Snow, as long as you are by my side at night so I can hold onto all my dreams safely."

Her forehead presses against mine, our breaths mingling before I lean in and steal a kiss. Guilt eats away at the newly mended veins in my body, knowing the secret I am keeping could stop all progress.

But she deserves to know.

"Rarity, I need to tell you something, okay?"

"What is it?" She blinks at me, a loving aura surrounding her.

"We are mates, but we have one more."

"One more what?"

A loud roar rings through the castle, shaking the table we are lying on.

"What was that?" Rarity trembles, looking around to see where the commotion is coming from.

"Take this—" I dig into my pocket for sunset magnolia powder and fold her fingers over it. "Go home. I will come to you, but you need to know, the man you're about to see—" The door is kicked in and Nyx is standing there, fire blazing in his eyes, his scales shining bright, and his wings spread so wide, he has to tuck them in to step into the room.

"Firebond—" he growls at me, his anger sizzling the floor under his feet.

He hasn't registered that Rarity is our mate with his intent locked on me. Nyx releases fire at Rarity, but she blurs across the room to miss the flames.

"Rarity! Leave go!"

"I'm not leaving you," she argues, flashing her fangs at our dragon.

"He's mine!" Nyx growls so low, that I can barely understand the words.

"She's our mate!" I yell at him, then turn to Rarity. "He's our mate, My Snow."

"Nonsense! Three mates do not exist," Nyx argues, pointing a sharp claw at Rarity. "I will fly you to the moon just to watch you fall, vampire."

A barricade of icicles points at his throat to stop him from taking a step.

"My Dove, she is our mate. Breathe her in. You will smell it. Rarity—" I turn to tell her what to do, but she's gone.

All that's left is the swirling orange of the sunset magnolia powder becoming smaller and smaller.

"Rarity!" I shout, staring at her sweet face on the other side of the portal. I run, hoping to get to her in time. Stretching my arm out, I grab nothing but air.

I cut my eyes to the dragon, the man who seems to ruin everything he sees because anger deals with the issue quicker than communication ever would— I am assuming.

"You," I spit hatefully at him. "You couldn't help yourself, could you? You do not want me, but you do not want anyone else to have me." I fling the icicles away from him and they shatter against the wall, tiny pings and clanks randomly fill the space. "You do not get to do that to me. If my other mate wants me, she shall have me."

A murderous grumble makes my stomach flip. I know that sound.

It is a warning.

"Listen to me, My Little Elf—" black smoke sways from his nostrils. "No one else shall have you before I do."

Feeling cocky, a bit bratty, and smug, I straighten my spine and lift my chin. "Too late for that, dragon. My ice has been claimed."

His wings wrap around my body, the smooth leather gliding across my skin. They are softer than I imagined.

"Prince Cailian!" my brother yells from the other side of the locked doors. The handles shake but don't give way. "Brother! Answer me!" he shouts, but Nyx presses a finger against my lips.

"Better hush the sharpness of your tongue, My Little Elf."

"Or what?" I sass, wishing Nyx never would have walked through these doors. I was finally making progress with Rarity. How much did this incident set us back?

Weeks? Months?

"Someone open these fucking doors, now!" My brother barks his orders to my men.

Nyx drags his claw down my neck where Rarity bit me. His breathing comes out harsher, the smoke becoming blacker, his eyes burning brighter, and then he leaps into the air.

He smashes against the wall, crumbling the ice window, then spreads his wings, carrying me away from my kingdom.

"There were much easier ways to get me to talk to you," I mumble, crossing my arms as we glide through the air. "This is ridiculous."

"So is the fact that my firebond is my father's killer and that you had some other rubbing against you. I smell your come."

"And I cannot wait until she makes me come again."

The flight over the snow-capped tree-tops becomes shortened as we land in the forest a half of a day's walk from the castle.

"Bite your tongue, Cailian."

"Or what? You will burn me to death?"

I do not know why I am baiting my dragon. But it is fun.

I shall keep doing it.

Chapter Seven

DOVENYX

His words sear me to my bone, etching a permanent mark on the regret I've been battling since I released my fire on him.

"She will not touch you again," I repeat, thinking about the white-haired woman with purple eyes and fangs. She was beautiful, but to call her my firebond is a stretch. I couldn't smell her over Cailian's blood overwhelming the area. The scent of him bleeding, smelling his desire, it was too much for my dragon to handle.

"She will. She shall touch me whenever she wants. When she wants to feed, I will gladly bend my neck or spread my legs, wherever she chooses to take from me."

I spread my wings, flapping them in harsh beats until my feet are hovering above the ground. With a snarl, I launch myself toward him at full speed, catching him by his throat before slamming him against a nearby tree.

"I will rip your tongue out of your throat if you continue to speak that way to me. You are mine, Cailian, whether I like it or not. You aren't allowed to be with anyone else." My eyes drop to his

blood-stained neck and the two pinpricks on either side of his neck where that vampire fed from him.

"Go ahead and rip it out—" he inches closer, pushing his neck against my hand, my claws threatening to cut his skin from the pressure "—Then I'll shove it down your throat, dragon, and it will be the first and last time you will have me in your mouth."

I exhale a rumble, the heat of my fire brewing to catastrophic levels inside me. My claws warm from the inside out, morphing from an abyss of black to a constant color of smoldering.

My lips graze his in an almost-kiss, his frozen breath cooling my insides as I inhale, trying to be as close to him as possible without getting *too* close.

It's too late for that though, isn't it? Here I am, fighting the urge to stay away, but the more I fight, the closer to him I become.

"I don't want you," I say, the words filled with centuries of hate.

His hands wrap around my arm, trying to pry my hand away from his neck. "Then let me go."

I touch the wounds on his neck, a vibration of awareness soaking into my scales. I bend down, inhaling the vampire's scent, her saliva and blood smeared all over him. When I first smelled the aroma of them in the dining room, all of my jealous urges burst from me. Now, that I have him alone, I fucking feel it.

That vampire is my other firebond.

I have two.

I flick my tongue out, needing to have a taste.

Just a small, quick, taste. Nothing else. It won't mean anything. I'll satisfy any urges for him and her, then live the rest of the weeks I have alone.

His blood spreads over my tongue and I moan, my cock aching between my legs. "Mmmm," I moan, sucking onto his skin harder,

the reasoning for my denying him drifting further away into the back of my mind. "Fuck." My forked tongue lavishes his flesh, cleaning the dried blood from his silver body. "My firebonds." I push him against the tree, turning his head forcefully.

"My Dove." Cailian wiggles in my hold, his hips cantering.

His move to get out of my hold has his cock rub against mine, fucking with the last thread of control I have and shredding it to pieces.

"I hate it when you call me that." I drag my tongue across his throat to the other side, cleaning the remaining blood from his skin. "I am not your Dove. I will never be yours," I say with small bites along his collarbone, rutting our cocks together.

The smell of his lust permeates the air, the forest becomes quiet, and the only sound is our breaths. Every exhale fuels me. My hands become needier, my lips become desperate, my cock heats to the point of pain, and my knot is wanting to form.

Dragons can have sex with whoever they want, whenever they want, and have children, but they can only knot their firebonds.

I rip his robe from him, holding the scraps of it in my hand, needing more of my firebond all while wishing for less.

The lust calms for a moment as the scent of his clothes makes my soul lightheaded. "This is all I'll have of you then?" I roll the fabric he was wearing in my hand by balling it into a fist. My eyes burn as the tendons in my heart threaten to break. I bury my nose in the material that glimmers like the stars, scenting the winter embedded in every stitch tailored for him. "This is it? Quick nothings alone for a few moments, your smell haunting me, your beauty taking over my imagination so every time I touch myself, the only thing I think about is you. You have taken over me!" I throw the robe down in frustration.

The elf's crown is crooked, so I readjust it, unable to hide the pain I'm in because of him. "I want nothing more than to quit you. I want to tell my witch to unwind the threads of our fate so we can be free from one another, but that would probably kill one of us."

"I have also thought about consulting my witch," he admits, and hearing his soft voice spew such a statement, hurts me more than the acid that hit my wing. "But I will not ask that of her. It is dark magic. I will not put her at risk." His blue eyes swirl as he stares at me, his veins pale orange instead of bright like my fire, which tells me he is in the mating process.

But not with me.

"Quit me then," he states, tossing his long hair in a messy bun on top of his head, but leaving the braid out to frame his face.

Fuck. He looks spectacular like that. Messy, frustrated, but there is still something so fucking calm about him that no matter how hard I try to hate him more, I can't.

"You know I can't do that," I whisper.

"Then we are at an impasse." He places his hands on his hips, staring at me as if I hold all the answers on what to do next. Sighing, he bends down to pick up his robes. "I need to get back to the castle and explain Rarity to my House."

"And me?"

"I will not bring you up in the conversation. Perhaps we can live half-mated. I mate her, you mate her, but we do not mate one another."

I'm in front of him again, blowing smoke in his face. "My dragon won't allow that."

"I do not know another answer, Dove. It is the only way I can think of to not die. I know you can feel your fire inside you. I bet it is feeling bigger and hotter, and if it keeps going, it will burn you alive. I know I

can feel the freeze in my blood becoming warmer. Today, I felt better because of Rarity, but then you swept in as if you were jealous, and I am only back to feeling worse. I almost wish for death, so I do not have to go another day seeing your face!"

"You hate me that much?" I yell in return, slapping my chest as our conversation becomes a fight. My question rings through the forest, bouncing off the shadows of the trees. "You do not have the right to hate me." I somehow have him pinned against the tree again, caging his head with my hands on either side of his face.

"I do not hate you." The grace of his fingers trace my jaw and my eyes roll to the back of my head from how good that simple touch feels. "I could never hate you, but if I wished for death so I could not see your face, it would only be because the pain of not being able to look at you and call you mine, would be over. I would not have to go day to day wishing for your lips on mine. I would not be caught in the trap of dreaming about the life we could have together. I would be free to wait for you in another life, another time, and that sounds more peaceful than this." He presses his hands against my chest.

"Tell me, My Little Elf. Tell me." I know he understands what I am asking, but my words hold no meaning when I pick him up and wrap his legs around my hips.

He sobs, pressing his forehead against mine. Our eyes meet, holding for a second too long, but it's enough for me. I hold him close, squeezing his ass right as I lean in and take his lips.

The lips of a fucking murderer have never felt so good.

His kiss extinguishes the hot blaze in my body that he spoke about earlier. My body has gotten hotter, and I only give myself another week before I'm dead.

Cailian's hands rub over my wings, and I groan, the innocent strokes nearly make me come. I had no idea they were so sensitive.

My own palms have a mind of their own, grabbing every inch of his exposed body as if this will be the only time I'll get to feel him.

It might be.

We can give in now and quit each other later.

I wrap my wings around him, tugging him to me, then roll us to the ground. The long grass almost hides us from how tall it is. The tips of his ears wiggle, enticing me to bend down to take the point into my mouth.

"Dove!" he shouts so loud, that the branches of the trees sway.

"You like that?" I take one ear in my hand and begin to stroke it, rubbing the tip and then pinching it.

He arches his back, rubbing his cock against mine, and that blue hue on his cheeks returns.

"I bet I could make you come like this, couldn't I?" I grab his other ear, stroking it in unison.

He shakes his head, wetting his dry lips. "No— no, that's— I wouldn't— that's impossible," he moans loudly, snow beginning to fall upon us.

"I think you're lying." I tug on the tips, a whimper causing his mouth to turn into an 'O'.

He pinches his dark blue nipples, the erotic grunts and groans becoming more frequent.

"So sensitive." I stop stroking his ears which has his eyes snapping open.

The fucking points continue to wiggle. I've decided that is my favorite thing about him.

I take a claw and rip his undergarments from him. "If you are going to be the death of me, I deserve to fuck this pretty ass, do I not, Little Elf? And as long as we touch, we can't use our powers on one another, so what are you going to do to stop me?" I tilt my chin down, getting

the view of his lithe body, so fragile, so small, so soft under my large hands. "You are breathtaking," I admit on a low breath, barely able to get my lungs to remember to work.

Lean muscle wraps his bones and a dip at his waist reminds me of the hourglass figure a woman has. I grip his hips, my claws digging into his flesh until he hisses. A trail of white hair is groomed, the pathway to his cock laid out before me as if he's been preparing for this. I rub my fingers through the trimmed hair, the touch causing him to gasp and his stomach to tremble as he figures out a way to breathe.

Then his cock comes to view, and I have to lick my lips when I see the impressive sight. He's long, somehow elegant and slender to match him. He is uncut, the skin a darker silver than the rest of his body. The ridge of the crown is prominent and wide against the extra flesh. I wrap my hands around his shaft, igniting a wispy groan from him.

He's too pretty to deny.

I stroke him, pulling his skin down so I can expose the head. My mouth waters from what I see before me. I trace the ridges, realizing it is shaped like a snowflake.

"Do all elves have this?" I ask him, my thumb rubbing across the slit. "Or is it just you, My Little Elf."

"All elves, but we all have our patterns."

I grumble in delight, watching the pale silver tip disappear under the foreskin while I stroke him.

"Oh, gods, Dove." His arms hit the ground beside him, fisting the grass.

I hear the blades rip from the soil as pleasure coils his body.

He's very sensitive. Too sensitive.

A thought hits me and I stop stroking. "Cailian." I drop my hand to my side and grab his chin, furrowing my brows and dropping my tone. "Are you a virgin? Surely not, you're over nine hundred years old."

The blue hue on his cheeks deepens, and then he wiggles out from under me. I don't stop him this time. I'm too stunned.

With a swipe of his finger, he dresses himself in a thin white dress, it forms tightly to his body, moving with every step he takes. Snow drifts from it and I realize that is what makes his gown.

His cock is still hard against his thigh, the ridge barely covered with the layer of snow.

"It is best if we stop this now. My House will be looking for me soon and we do not want to be caught together. I am sure you would not like to answer your dragons when they ask why you were alone with the elf who killed your father."

I stand, rolling my head across my shoulders, and spread my wings, flinching to work the ache out of the left one. The heat in my cock controls my every thought. I can't focus on what is important when he is standing there in a nearly sheer snow dress that hugs his every defined line his body has. It leaves no room for imagination.

The grass crunches under me as I step forward. Cailian crosses his arms in front of him, shielding himself in a bubble of ice so I can't reach him.

"You do not want this. You do not want us, so please, leave me be. I cannot survive you if you take another step."

I stop just outside the shield of ice, his large blue eyes wide and unblinking as he waits for me to make a decision.

"I can't survive you either." I scratch the tip of my claw down the shield, a long groove left in my wake. "The destruction you will leave me in will be catastrophic. Saving me won't be possible." I tell him, tapping on the ice. I increase the pressure.

Boom.

Boom.

Boom.

I'm slamming my fist against the shield, and it cracks, but Cailian is quick. He holds out his palms, doing his best to freeze the broken surface so I can't get to him.

Opening my mouth, I release my fire, the heat melting the ice to a worthless puddle at our feet. I don't want to hurt him again, so I close my lips when he is finally in arm's reach. That fucking gown is still tight against his body, slinking down to the earth.

I never thought I'd be jealous of snow, but I am. I'm furious at the cold flakes. They get to touch his body without remorse. Inhaling a deep breath, I release the air, keeping it heated, and blow it all over his body.

The dress melts from him. His torso is exposed first, his dark grey nipples dying for attention. The dip in his waist is revealed next, then the V chiseling the pathway to his cock.

"You are more beautiful than one of your flowers that manages to bloom through ice," I explain as the rest of the gown falls to pieces on the grass before it vanishes, changing its form to water. "So tell me, Prince Cailian of The House of Ice and Snow, are you a virgin?" I step forward, having to bend down to look at him in his face. "You never answered me."

He is tall, but nowhere near as large as I am. I tower over him and seeing him tilting his head back to look at me is my new favorite view.

"I do not think that is important information. We should get Rarity here."

I barricade him against the tree with my arms. "Are you a virgin? Don't make me ask again."

"Yes," he trembles, licking his lips as he turns his head to place more distance between our lips. "Yes, I am. I wanted to wait for my mate. It did not feel right having sex when I knew my mate was out there."

"I did not wait for you," I admit to him, taking the point of his ear between my fingers again. "Dragons are not the same."

Smoke sways from my nostrils, a cloud of impatience from the dragon within me. Next, a rumble shakes my chest, and my nails drag down the bark.

"Dove?" he whispers. "Are you okay?"

"You need to run," I tell him, unable to pull myself away. "I can't hold myself back knowing you've never been with another."

He dips under my arm and isn't two steps away from me when I strike my arm out, gripping his hair by the root to stop him.

"Dove!" he cries out in pain, reaching his hands to free mine. "You are hurting me."

I yank him to my chest, his back smooth and cool against the heat of my scales. My fire is high, burning so deep, if I don't take him, I'm not sure if I'll be able to live another day.

"That's what I should be doing, isn't it? I should be skinning you alive, seeking revenge, but damn it, you're more tempting than the gift of lava, Cailian." I rub my cock against his backside.

"You cannot keep touching me. I'll— I'll go into heat, Dove. You'll make me and then what will we do?"

I nibble the tip of his ear and he cries into the forest for all to hear, stretching to stand on his tiptoes. "I guess I'll have to knot you through it, My Little Elf." I spin him around, keeping my hand cupping the back of his head so he can't run away from me.

This is bad.

This is so fucking bad.

His cold breath puffs against my mouth before stealing my lips abruptly, giving in to anger and desperation. He bites my lower lip and I growl.

The hate I've convinced myself of starts to chip away the longer he is in my arms, the longer he holds my kiss, the more he moans against me.

If I'm not careful, I'll get lost in Prince Cailian.

There's a voice inside my head whispering that I won't get lost, but I'll get found.

His fingers dig into my chest his nails dragging over my scales, and I kiss him harder.

It's punishing.

It's abusive.

His teeth clank against mine.

My fangs nip his lip until I taste blood.

And fuck me, he tastes so good.

His sly fingers travel down my chest, reaching for the button of my pants, and once they are unsnapped, I kick them off, the kiss breaking from the movement. I snarl in frustration from not having his lips on me this fucking instant and rob them again before he has a chance to breathe anything else but me.

I moan down his throat, grabbing every inch of him. His ass is round and full, bubbly for his frame, and my cock weeps with pre-come, dying to be inside him. Pressing one hand against his hip, then the other on his shoulder, I spin him around, the crease of his ass trying to hug my thick dragon cock.

My eyes fall upon his back, then his narrow shoulders and my mark is there. I trace the scars with my nails, a perfect fit.

"You hide them with your robes," my voice takes on the depth of my dragon, a baritone so low, it shakes the leaves of the trees.

"I have to hide you," he replies, gasping as I palm his ass.

I don't say anything to that because I have to hide him too.

I turn him around again, smirk into his glassy eyes, and shove him to his knees. "Suck."

Cailian stares at my cock, his eyes wide, his palms on my thighs. He reaches between his legs to touch himself and I slip a claw under his chin to tilt his head back.

"Don't touch yourself. Your cock is mine. You'll come by my hand or Rarity's, our other firebond. Do you understand? If I smell come on you at any point, ever, and I didn't make you feel that pleasure, I'll bend you over my knee, Little Elf. I'll spank that pretty silver ass until it's blue."

A burst of aroma emanates through the air, making me growl when I smell just how much he loves that idea.

"Maybe not," I say, stroking his cheek. "It seems you like that idea."

He whimpers with closed eyes. Taking my cock in my hand, I press the head against his lips which has him opening his eyes.

"That's it. Watch as I fuck this face. You aren't a prince with me, are you? You're just a dirty firebond wanting my cock, nothing more."

He hums around the crown, squeezing the base where my knot will form. I moan loudly, wrapping my wings around him so we have more privacy. Being barricaded makes the moment more intimate. Every moan and breath is louder. I become more aware of him, of our bond, of what he means to me while his mouth stretches to take more than he possibly can.

He sucks me eagerly, a bit messy, unsure, with no rhythm, but his mouth is by far the best I've ever felt. I wish I would have waited too, but unlike him, I didn't think my firebond existed. I thought my only purpose was to kill the man who is currently on his knees, trusting me not to take advantage of his vulnerability and take his life.

I could, but even the thought has tears brimming in my eyes at the mere thought of him not existing. What would life be like without being graced with him? A beauty not even the galaxy can compare to.

He takes his free hand and cups my sack, trying to fondle all three orbs. They are too big. One barely fits in his palm while the others wait for his attention. He hums happily, gagging and choking when he tries to take me deeper.

"Don't hurt yourself," I state on a groan. "Fuck, you feel good." I clench my teeth together, trying to gather my control.

My cock slips from his mouth and he whines, licking the shaft up and down eagerly. Spit sticks onto his chin, mouth, and now the tip of my cock smears across his cheeks.

"So big," he mumbles, continuing to lick down the length to the trio beneath. He sucks as much as he can into his mouth, the ball too big to fit. He releases it, kissing and nipping the second, then sucks the third, and the attention has my wings spreading free. I tilt my head back and release fire from how good he feels.

"I do not think you're going to fit inside me or Rarity."

I yank his head back and press myself into his mouth until I feel the back of his throat. "Shut up," I sneer, picking up the pace until all three of my balls slap under his chin. "I'll fit. You're my firebonds. I bet her pussy feels so good, Cailian. So tight. So wet. She'll take my cock, fucking me hard until she takes my knot. You'll be watching us, stroking yourself, begging for me to fuck you because you'll be so empty. And when I do, you'll slip into her, fucking her through my come."

His eyes roll to the back of his head as he groans. His hands lace behind his back, so submissive for me while I use his throat. With every stroke of his tongue under my crown, his own cock weeps thick pools of glimmer.

"That's it. Fuck, you were made to take my cock. Look at you." Tears drip down his face from the discomfort, the way I hit the back of his throat, and how he can't seem to catch his breath. His lips are stretched to the max, becoming swollen and irritated as I pummel and claim what is mine.

My orgasm looms, tugging my sack closer to my body, and my claws extend as I lose control. Part of my body begins to change, my dragon breaking free.

"Cailian!" I shout with fire, groaning as I empty the many streams of come into his mouth. I grunt, slowing my thrusts and burying myself as far into his throat as I can. "Fuck yes," I growl at him, pulling on his hair. "You look so pretty with my come dripping from your lips, Little Elf."

I run my claws through his hair, my dragon showing him how much I care for his attention.

"Can you take every drop? There's so much, I'm not sure you can. I have so much saved for you. Ah—" I groan as another stream fills his succulent warm mouth.

His tongue flicks out, showing me all the come drenching his tongue. The flames turn from orange to blue, dancing inside his mouth before they vanish.

"Such a good boy taking your dragon's big cock. Do you like sucking me, Little Elf?"

"Yes. You taste so good." He licks the slit before latching his mouth onto it and suckling the few drops of come I have left. "So warm."

"You swallowed my fire," I grumble in pleasure, raking my claws through his long, luxurious hair.

Already, I feel the bond between us strengthen, and the catastrophic temperature inside me eases. I'm addicted to the relief. I hadn't realized how hot my blood had gotten until this moment.

Wanting more, I pull from his greedy mouth, and pin him to the ground, tucking my good wing under his back so he can be more comfortable. I run my hands down his body, in disbelief that someone so beautiful could be mine.

The need for Cailian is an urge I can no longer deny. I take his lips in a kiss, shutting my eyes to allow my body to think for me. I taste myself on his tongue, a tease of warmth still left inside of his mouth.

I force his legs apart, settling and fitting fucking perfectly between them, which only adds fuel to pent-up aggression. I rock against him, our cocks gliding together. I break the kiss, needing to look down, needing to see us in a way I wish we could be forever.

Constant growls escape me, my primal need to consume him over-taking my dragon. My cock engulfs his. The rainbows under the ob-sidian scales shine brighter with every stroke against him. He moans, meeting me thrust for thrust, coating me in his precome. The liquid has a cooling component, draping over my cock and I shiver in delight, wondering what it might feel like inside me.

Fisting our cocks together, the skin of his pulls back, showing the impressive snowflake pattern his crown has. Every ridge against mine has me rutting faster, needing more from him, demanding he become mine.

Our shafts slip and glide across one another, wetting the space between us. I hear the filthy sounds of my sack slapping against his ass. My feet slide against the ground trying to gain leverage to move faster and harder. I circle my finger around his tight hole, my come relaxing the muscle so he can take me.

When he tweaks his nipples, I gather more come, holding it up to the sky so I can see the way it shines like ice when the sun hits against it in the mornings. I notice the small flecks of fire, reminiscent of me. The combination is thick and begins to drip down my finger. Before

it goes to waste, I slide my hand between his legs, sheathing my claws, and easing one finger inside him.

He hisses, clenching that virgin ass around me. Thunder vibrates in my throat, threatening to release a storm.

"Have you ever played with yourself, Cailian? Are you used to having your ass fucked?"

He nods, whimpering and biting his lip. "I have toys."

I insert another finger, imagining him laid out on a bed, legs spread while he fucks himself on his little toy. "You've never taken anything my size, have you? Anything you use from here on out won't be able to fill you like I can fill you. You'll feel empty and you'll beg me to fill you with my big cock, won't you?"

He flicks his tongue, swirling blue eyes cutting to mine. His fingers pinch my chin together as he leans forward. "I will never beg you to fuck me, dragon," he sneers. "I will never give in to all your demands. I am a Prince. Princes do not beg." He nips my bottom lip, but his attitude is cut short when I insert another finger. He cups my jaw, mouth parting on a silent scream.

I chuckle at his audacity to think such things. "Oh, you are no Prince when you are with me, Little Elf." I pull my fingers back and slam them inside him. "You're just a body for me to use and fuck anytime I want."

He tosses his head back, gripping my shoulders with his hands. I make him appear so small now that his hands are on me. My shoulders are giant compared to his palm and I like how large that makes me feel. He isn't delicate, but to me, against me, he is fragile, and my dragon demands we protect him.

Cailian's fingers dig into corded muscles, moaning my name so all the forest creatures can hear.

"Fuck, Dove. Oh, you feel so good. Your fingers are so thick. I've never felt anything like this before. I need to come. I want to come."

My brows raise in surprise when I hear the dirty words fly from his mouth. He slams his ass down on my fingers, adding more force with every thrust.

"Let me come," he demands through clenched teeth.

I take a glance at his cock, the crown is weeping, and the shaft is so hard it seems painful.

"Not until I'm inside you," I say, scissoring my fingers. The new angle hits that spot inside him that makes him lose his fucking mind.

His legs shake and his fingers dig deeper into my body, my scales threatening to rip from my hide if he isn't careful.

"If Rarity were here—"

"—But she isn't. You made sure of that, didn't you? You made her leave before I had the chance to tell she was my firebond." I lie him on his back, yanking his legs apart in haste, and line my cock to his hole. Come spurts free, giving me the extra lubricant I need to push inside him. "If she were here, do you know what I would do?" I inch in, holding my breath as his ass tightens around me. I can't breathe. He feels too good.

"I'd fuck her too, but I'd fuck her first. I'd fill her with all my come until her stomach is swollen with it, and then I'd fuck you, but while you take my cock, she'll silence your cries by sitting on that pretty face. You'll drink my come from her cunt."

"Dove—"

I silence him by covering his swollen lips with my hand. "—Hush. You've done enough to me, haven't you? How dare you keep her from me?" I bottom out, my cock fully sheathed by his virgin hole. "Fuckkk," I groan, dropping my head to his shoulder. My claws dig into his hips. I squeeze until my arms shake from holding onto the

small amount of control I have so I don't physically hurt him. "Do you know how good I'd make you both feel? It makes sense for Fate to give me two firebonds." I ease out, glancing down as I watch him take my scaled cock. "I have all this come to give."

His hole is stretched wide, to the point I'm worried I'm going to rip him. Cailian groans, his hands slipping down his body before wrapping around his cock. Snarling, I grab his wrists and pin him to the ground. Smoke drifts from my nose and mouth, my eyes burning bright with fire as my dragon pushes against my bones.

"What did I say about your cock, Cailian?"

He wiggles against me, arching his back until his chest is pressing against mine. I get sidetracked for a moment, locking onto his nipples, and stretch my forked tongue out. The sweet morsel tightens from my touch, reacting to me and only me.

"You are better than any dream I could ever dream," I whisper against his skin so low, that only I can hear myself.

When he begins to fuck himself on my cock, the sweet thoughts end, and I remember who I am dealing with— an elf who thinks he can take whatever he wants.

I pull out of him and flip him onto his hands and knees. Pressing my hand between his shoulder blades, I force him to stay. His ass sways in the air, his hole leaking from my precome, and fluttering from being so empty.

My knees dig into the ground and with my claws digging into his hips, I yank him back against me, my cock pressing into his ass again.

"What did I say about your cock? I said I'd make you come, did I not? That means do not fucking touch what is mine, firebond. You are to never touch yourself again unless I say so."

He stretches his arms out in front of him and hangs his head, shaking it back and forth. "You will never know if I come when you are not around, and I will not tell you."

I rear my hand back and slap his ass, a loud *smack* resounding through the swaying grass around us. Cutting his skin with my claws, I drag them up his body, then wrap my palm around his throat, yanking him onto his knees until his back is pressed against my chest. My wings spread out, flapping in annoyance that my firebond loves to be so defiant.

"Do you make a habit out of that, Little Elf? Keeping secrets that are not yours to keep?"

He lifts an arm, wrapping it around my neck. "If I must." He sinks his ass down on me, again and again, taking every long, thick inch of me until nothing but the head remains before slamming back down.

With a sneer, followed by a growl, I force him to the ground. His hands try to catch his weight, but his fingers smash into the dirt, his chest tickled by grass, and his cheek against the soil from his head being turned.

I yank his arms behind his back, clasping his wrists in my hand, and hammer into him.

My thrusts are hard.

Relentless.

Punishing.

I take my want for him, my need, and make it my fuel as I fuck him. He no longer owns me.

I own *him*.

"You fill me so much—" he groans, sucking his bottom lip into his mouth. "Oh, I never imagined it could be like this. More, more. Give me more," he cries beautifully, begging me just like he said he wouldn't.

"I thought Princes didn't beg?" I slap his ass again before grabbing it in my palm.

"I am not. I am demanding you."

With both hands, I hold him to the ground, his legs straight, his ass angled, and I pummel his hole, ruining it for anyone else but me.

"I wish Rarity were here. I bet she'd be watching, fucking herself with her fingers. She'd look so pretty under you, Cailian. I'd fuck you which would make you fuck her. Mmmm," I hum at how delicious that sounds. "All the things we could all do together…"

"Ah, Dove! Dove! Oh, fuck. You are deep. Too deep. You are— You are—"

"Right where I need to be to claim this body." I'm far enough inside where his body will change, adapting to my species' needs so he can carry my children.

The thought has my knot inflating, popping in and out of his hole as it grows.

His ass shakes with every abusive and hard thrust, but Cailian doesn't complain, he only grows louder, clawing at the grass to get away while screaming for more.

"Fuck, your cock is so good. I am addicted. I will never be able to go a day without it. So thick, take me. Fuck me, Dove. Claim me."

I tug his hair free from the bun, wanting to see it drape across his skin. I wrap it around my wrists and use it as reins, plowing into him. We slide across the ground, becoming filthy from the dirt and stained by the green grass. We become desperate as we seek our orgasms. I growl louder, a constant purr in my soul from how amazing I feel.

The only thing missing is Rarity.

My knot pushes inside him one last time and I'm unable to pull out.

"No, no! Your knot is too wide. I do not think I can, yet I want more of you." He reaches for me, grabbing my ass to press me against him more.

"You'll take it, Little Elf. Your ass was made for this." I tap my finger against his rim, the one that's stretched to the brink while my knot locks us together. I thrust against him, tugging against his hole until my wings jerk, my toes curl, and I have to tilt my head back to release my flame as I come deep inside my firebond's body. "Come for me, Cailian. Come for your firebond," I finally manage to say through the most intense orgasm of my life.

I pour my come into him just as his muscles tighten around me, milking me for every drop.

"More, more, more," he chants just before releasing a loud shout of my name. "Dovenyx!"

I would bristle at the use of my birth name if I wasn't high from the best sex I've ever had. Reaching under him, I squeeze his cock, feeling it spasm as he orgasms. My teeth begin to ache and his sweaty body lying there, trembling, pressing against my knot, breaks me.

I push his hair out of the way, then sink my teeth into the back of his neck to truly place my mark. His hair dances in the air, swirling until it can wrap around my own. It's electrifying. The official bond snaps into place and the emotions whirl, the orgasms heighten, and I come again.

And so does he.

My palm catches his come, the liquid cold, and I bring it to my mouth, licking it clean.

"You taste delicious," I say, watching as the remaining come on my palm turns to a light frost. "I could have my own popsicles of you, couldn't I?"

"Dove," he giggles, suddenly coy even though I have my knot buried in his ass.

I lick my mating mark and shiver. He manages to turn around on my knot to face me, wincing as it tugs, but he manages to wrap his legs around my hips. To my surprise, he bites my neck in the middle before blowing cold breath onto my skin.

I groan, the cool tingly sensation roams its way through my veins and more come spills into him.

"Fuck," I groan, touching the spot he bit but I don't feel anything. "No mark?" I try not to sound disappointed, but I am. There's a part of me that wants us to be firebonds and embrace. I want to be able to show everyone I'm taken.

Then the other side of me is relieved because I don't have to explain to anyone that my firebond is a betrayer.

"No bite mark, but a soft, light blue glittering tattoo. Like ice, in the shape of a snowflake. It is the Ice Elven's mating mark."

I'll have to get the shirts from the clothsmith we have. I can't have anyone seeing this.

"I cannot wait to see Rarity take this big cock, Dove. She is going to look so gorgeous on top of you." He lies his head against my shoulder, exhaling a happy sigh, and my arms wrap around him because even with all this havoc between us, I want this.

I want him.

I am not sure how a vampire, an elf, and a dragon can be together. I'm not sure how any of this can work. Dragging my claws up and down his back, he relaxes so much, he lets his guard down.

His mind becomes easy to enter with our bond in place. A curiosity takes over, one that has me push forward into his thoughts, wanting to hear what he is thinking, and wondering if I'll be able to get the truth.

"He feels so good. He is so strong. I cannot believe my best friend's son is my mate. What would he think? I'd hope he know I'd treat him well. I never imagined that day when he asked me to—"

The thoughts come to an abrupt stop and Cailian shoves my chest. "What—"

Tears brim his eyes, and he tries to get off me, but can't. He continues to try, bouncing up and down until my eyes are rolling to the back of my head because he feels so damn good. I'm nearly ready to come again when he finally pulls himself free. He sobs, lying on the ground, his hole torn and bleeding.

"Cailian!" I run to him.

"Don't touch me! Don't come near me. You are a foul, inconsiderate asshole." He throws a spear of ice at me, but I dodge it. My come mixed with his blood, flows freely onto the grass.

"Let me help you. I can take you to your witch."

"I do not need you or your help," he sneers. This is the first time I've heard true venom in his tone. Snow begins to fall around him, the cold healing the injury.

He stands, naked and beautiful while the sun peeks through the tops of the trees to radiate against his hair.

Much to my dismay, he waves his hand, hiding his body in that sexy tight snow gown again.

I groan, wanting nothing more than to mate him again when he is such a sight for villainous eyes.

"You only mated me to get the truth." He picks up his crown which must have fallen off in our mating, to place it on top of his head. The icicles remind me of deer antlers, but instead of growing to the sky, they frame his eyes and face. A blue gem sits in the middle, reflecting the dismay pinching my eyes... "You used me to know what

happened to your father. You wanted the mate bond, if not only for that purpose."

I open my mouth to say something, but he cuts me off.

"Do not deny it. I felt you in my head."

He closes his eyes and the emotion, the pain, the happiness, lust, and everything in between is gone.

I gasp from the air being taken from my lungs and hold a hand against my heart.

"The pain in your chest is me freezing the ability for you to feel me at all, to hear me, to sense me—" he begins to walk away before pressing a hand to my throat where his mark is "—to want me. Even when I need you, my body needs you, craves you, you will not be able to tell."

I stand to my feet. "I deserve to know."

"My business lies with your father. It has nothing to do with you."

"It has everything to do with me!" I roar, pounding my chest. "I am your firebond. You are mine. We have Rarity. How can we make this work if you hide the most important piece of information?"

"Do you not know me well enough to figure out the truth on your own? I let you mate me, fill me, knot me, mark me, scar me, disrespect me, hate me, burn me, and whatever else you seem fit to punish me with. I let you kill me!" he roars. "It is not my fault you could not go through with it. I never don't follow through." His teeth are tight, his lips barely moving, and his gaze dances between my eyes before turning around and walking away.

"I never wanted this anyway!" I shout at him, hating how bad the lie tastes.

He does not look back. "Good. Business is taken care of. We do not need to be mates now that claiming is out of the way. We can go our own ways. We can figure out Rarity. Have a good life, Dovenyx. I hope

the need for the truth instead of a mate haunts you for the rest of your life."

I have nothing to say to that because there *is* nothing to say. I rub my throat, already missing the man who changed the course of my life so long ago.

Fair is fair, is it not?

Now, I've changed his.

And I've never felt emptier.

Chapter Eight

RARITY

"Rarity?" Uncle Luca asks, bringing me a glass of water as I stare at the flames in the fireplace.

I came home a few hours ago, stronger than I've felt since meeting Cailian, fed, yet instead of happiness, loneliness hits me hard. I've learned I have another beloved, one who didn't seem too happy to see me there, and who wanted Cailian all to himself.

I'm not jealous. I'm not upset.

I'm resigned because once again, I am an outsider.

To my family. To my mates.

I take the glass from Luca, the water instantly freezing from the touch of my hand. Frustration hits me, anger, confusion, and with all my vampiric strength, I throw the glass into the roaring fire. The fire flashes before dimming from the ice, the wood sizzling, and smoke rises, mimicking my emotions.

"I can't fucking touch anything without it freezing!" I shout, tears prickling my eyes from how I can't seem to control the freak of nature I am.

"Rarity," Uncle Luca whispers, taking a step forward, and then reaches out to touch me. "You are not a freak. How can you say that?"

"How?" I sneer, turning around so fast, I grab his hand before he can reach me. "This is how." His skin begins to freeze, the icy path spreading down his forearm. He lets out a breath and it's cold, frozen, a forgetting cloud dissipating just as another takes its place.

I let go before I can cause real damage. "That's how. How do I even know if I'm related to any of you? How do we know I'm Severide's? What if mother stepped out and fucked some other vampire? They weren't beloveds. She could have."

Before I can say another word, my father, Severide, is standing in front of me, eyes crimson with rage. He grabs me by the arms and blurs us outside, past the lake, into the forest, until we are at Shallow Cove, the portal that changed everything for all paranormal creatures.

"I can't believe you'd speak that way about your mother, my mate, my everything. She sacrificed her life for you, for us, to live, to be safe, and this is how you repay her?" He points at the Cove, the water reflecting our distraught images. "She died here. Right here, Rarity. I watched her get ripped apart holding onto you and you dare say she isn't your mother."

"Like you have room to talk? She died for you too. All you do is mope. All you do is stay with Atreyu in the catacombs. Is that how you are going to repay her? Wasting away your life?" I sneer, finally able to throw guilt his way.

"I have struggled," he admits, taking a seat on the ground, staring into the abyss of onyx water that seems to have an endless depth. "The pain of losing a mate is unlike any agony I've ever felt. I've been so lost in my grief that I've forgotten how to be a father to you, to Alexander, to Atreyu. I failed the twins and that's why we will lose Atreyu when the time comes." He swallows, eyes swimming with our rare tears.

"I haven't prepared you for the world." His fingers run through his ragged beard before rubbing over his tired eyes. The blood he was forced to have has barely worked from what I can tell. "How can you be ready for the life ahead of you, your beloved, when I haven't taught you anything."

I take a seat next to him at the edge of the Cove, trailing my fingers over the surface. "I'm sorry," I croak in a whisper. Every spot I touch on the water ices over. "I'm so sorry for being such a bitch." I wipe my cheeks with one hand and swirl the water with my other, a whirlpool of ice forming.

"Don't call yourself that."

"It's true." I turn to him. "I'm letting everything I don't know upset me. I'm even more upset with myself because…" I hiccup, hoping Cailian doesn't hate me. "I forced a partial mating on Cailian. I couldn't control myself. He wanted me to feed because I hadn't. He wanted to take care of me."

"That's good, Rarity. It's good of him to notice you needed sustenance."

"He just…" My mouth waters from the memory, my taste buds dancing in impatience, wanting more of his elixir. "He tasted so good, and I lost control. I shoved my palm into his mouth and made him ingest my blood."

My father smirks. "Truly, I don't think he minds, Rarity. Cailian has always shown his willingness to be a good beloved to you. I'm sure that made his soul very happy."

"Yeah, well, my news doesn't end there," I mumble.

A frog jumps onto a rock at my feet, croaking loudly into the night. His chin expands with every sound. Crickets begin to sing and fireflies glow, flashing their bodies in the dark. This place is so beautiful and for the first time, I don't feel like this is my home.

He wraps his arm around my shoulders, and I sink into my father's side, placing my head on his shoulder. "Take your time, Sweetheart. It's okay."

The words grip my throat. I'm trying to speak them, to admit them, but when I open my mouth, silence follows. I know why too because when I think about the dragon being my beloved, I see him look at me with such rage, such despair, and how much he hates me.

And fuck, it hurts so much.

My father runs his fingers through my hair, giving me all the time I need. "You know," he begins wistfully. "When I met your mother, Esmeralda stole my heart and soul from the moment I saw her. She was the most beautiful woman I had ever seen. Her beauty was more than a thousand sunflower fields. And you know, I don't know if I've told you because talking about Esmeralda hurts me so much, but I think I need to be better at it. Anyway, I was there for her sister, originally."

I turn to him, shocked, and I can't help the laugh that escapes me because he has never told me that before. He is still in love with my mother and thinking of him with anyone else doesn't make sense. "What? Her sister? I didn't even know she had a sister."

"Because she was a raging bitch," he spits.

"Father!"

"She was. My parents wanted me to mate before I became coven master. I was holding out for my beloved, but I wasn't getting any younger, so I agreed to go to a mating ceremony. The Russo's were extravagant. They flaunted their wealth. When I arrived, I wanted to leave, but I couldn't. I had a responsibility. And then I saw your mother. I knew. I couldn't believe she wasn't my beloved when everything inside me felt like she was, but the bond didn't snap into place. I didn't care."

I take his hand when a profound sadness weighs him down, the dark circles of his eyes becoming heavier.

"She was and is my absolute everything. In the moment we danced, I never wanted to let her go, and then her sister saw us. Gods," he rolls his eyes, still annoyed all these years later. "She threw a fit. Luckily, Esmeralda's father was on my side, and I was able to keep her for myself." He stares into the Cove, sighing. "I miss her so much."

"I know," I reply, squeezing his hand. "I'm sorry I've been so insensitive."

He shakes his head, giving me a small, forced smile. "You haven't been. No one has. I've been grieving and I'm not sure if I'll ever be able to stop."

"Not even if you meet your beloved?" I dare to ask.

He whips his head up, his eyes shifting from brown to red. I rear back, wondering if he's about to attack.

"My beloved is dead."

"Father—"

He holds up his hand. "—If fate ever brought me someone who wasn't your mother, I'd rather die. Your mother, no matter what Fate says, was my beloved. I'll take that to my grave."

I drop the subject, not wanting to upset him further.

"What I'm saying is, don't ever let your beloved slip through your fingers, Rarity. I lived before Esmeralda, but I didn't truly see life the way it was meant to be seen until I had her by my side. She made everything better, brighter, and beautiful."

I pluck a piece of grass, wishing I could have known her, and then a thought occurs to me. I press my cheek against my knee, staring at my father who appears so young that I wouldn't doubt people would think he was my brother.

"What happened to mother's family? You never talk about them. Do I have a grandpa?"

"I have no idea. I haven't checked. They haven't checked." His brows pinch together. "I guess that's something I should look into. You all deserve to know your family, just not Esmeralda's sister. She's terrible. She probably got staked."

"Father!" I chuckle, slapping his shoulder. "I can't believe you just said that."

"Eh," he shrugs a shoulder. "I would have done it myself if I had the chance."

"You're terrible."

He grins, flashing a bit of fang. "And it feels so good." He bumps his elbow against me, the tension easing. "So, tell me, what's this other piece of information?" He holds up a finger to stop me. "And before you start, please just start calling me Dad. The Father thing makes me feel old."

"You are old," I mumble.

"Brat."

Slow laughs fade to silence, and I take a minute to gather my thoughts to get this over with.

A big, heavy, end-of-the-world sigh escapes me. "I have another beloved." I tug on another piece, ripping the green blade in half. "A dragon." I cut my eyes to my father's stunned face. "And he hates me," I choke, his face a permanent image in the front of my mind. I could feel how much he wanted to kill me. "He barged in on Cailian feeding from me. I was able to leave before he burnt me to a crisp. He wasn't happy to know he had another mate."

Father remains silent, but then eventually says, "Hmm."

"Hmm? That's it? Hmm?" I ask hysterically.

He leans back on his hands and stares up at the sky. "A mating of three is rare. It makes sense you'd have two beloveds. You're special like that and you deserve all the happiness. What makes you think your dragon hates you? He probably realizes now that you're his mate. I can bet he smelled you on Cailian after you left. Dragons don't have the greatest sense of smell, Rarity. They have to be very close. They are so used to smelling smoke, that it's ruined any ability to scent you. You should go back," he says. "Don't stay away because of fear. Fear is a dangerous prison, Sweetheart. You'll never see the light of day once you lock yourself inside."

"I want to go back. I want to meet him. I just... I don't want him to be disappointed when he sees me."

Father slips his fingers under my chin and gently applies pressure to turn my head, making me look at him. "Why would he be disappointed seeing you?"

I drop my eyes, tears jostling free down my cheeks, and like a good father, he wipes them away.

"Because... look at me," I say quietly. "I'm so different and I don't know why."

"And that is what makes you so beautiful. You are a mate to two princes, correct? That makes you royalty. You are destined for power, Rarity. You'll find your truth in time. I wish I had it for you, but I don't. He will be so happy to know you are his mate because there is no other like you. You are unique. You are rare. Nothing, no one, could ever come close to you for him. You are the gem humans and creatures alike spend eternity searching for, Sweetheart. Your power, is for purpose, your appearance, is for reason, and while you might not have the explanation yet, life will speak to you in time. Tell me, does it truly matter? Why you are the way you are? When you are surrounded

by people who don't care what you look like? You have two beloveds that will protect you until death."

"I know it doesn't matter in the grand scheme of things. There's a void." I pat my chest. "Wondering how I am so different than Lexy, than Atreyu, than all other vampires, and knowing would bring me peace."

"Peace is also rare," he states, melancholy hanging on his smile. "Don't waste your life looking for it when you could have had it all along."

A hum fills the air, and an orange circle appears, sparking like a live wire, and a silver elf tumbles free.

"Holy shit—" he grumbles, rolling right into the Cove.

Water splashes onto me and my father. Of course, my mouth was open to reply to him when the elf rolled into the Cove.

It's surprisingly cold and refreshing, nevertheless, I spit it out, not knowing what's in the water.

The elf pokes his head above the surface, his ears wiggling, his white hair flattened and slicked back on his head, but it's the annoyance in his blue swirling eyes that has me swallowing a chuckle.

"Of course, I'd land in a damn puddle," he gripes, swimming to the edge, and Father helps him out of the water.

"I'll have you know, that is the portal that opened all portals. Be happy to be drenched in such magic," Father quips.

The elf raises his brows, water dripping from the tips of his hair as he bows. "Apologies. I did not know. I have never left the kingdom before."

"You seem familiar," I say, getting to my feet.

"I'm Zyrl. Zy, Cailian calls me. I am his brother."

Makes sense. They do look alike, but Cailian is graceful and has a sleek, feminine structure while his brother has a hard jaw, a wider frame, and thick muscle. He reminds me of a warrior, not royalty.

His eyes widen in fear. "Apologies for soaking you, Princess," he falls to his knees, hanging his head. "Forgive me."

My father chuckles and crosses his arms, staring at me to see what I'll do.

"Um…" I pat Zyrl's shoulder. "You can stand. Please, stand," I rush. "I am not a Princess. Just call me Rarity, please."

He does as I say, straightening to his full height that towers over me. "But you are a Princess, the first ever in Elementalu history." He narrows his eyes. "Surely, Cailian told you that."

"He did not," I grumble under my breath.

"I see. Cailian likes for people to recognize their truth and place before having to confront them." He fans himself. "It's hot here. Where is this?"

I begin to notice the water on his body isn't the water from the Cove but *from* him. That's right. It's too hot for him here, so I act quickly, shoving him into the Cove again.

Another big splash waves onto the shore, soaking my feet.

"What was that for? Oh— this feels so much better," he groans, floating onto his back. "I understand what you've done. Thank you."

"Cailian said it was too hot for him here. It's why he had to go back."

"Which is funny to me, considering he has a dragon mate who spits fire and another mate who lives in…" he trails off and looks around. "Where is this?"

"Salem, Massachusetts. On a planet called Earth."

"Earth," he repeats. "What an odd name." Zy dips his head under the water before swimming to the edge. He crosses his arms on the

ground which helps him to stay in that position instead of sinking. "I am here to bring you back to Elementalu, Princess Rarity."

My cheeks flush from the formality. "Rarity, is fine. Just strike the Princess from your vocabulary."

Zy tilts his head. "I can't do that. Cailian would not allow it."

"Well, he isn't here, is he?" I spew with attitude. "I'm sorry." I pinch the bridge of my nose. "This has all been stressful."

"It has. I've watched my brother nearly waste away for his mates, waiting for them to come to him. Why did you leave?"

"Because I was nearly barbequed by a dragon and Cailian told me to."

He puckers his lips in thought. "Okay, well, the dragon is gone, and I need you to come back. Prince Cailian has not left his bed. I'm afraid he has mated with the dragon, but they have a very complicated history. He is depressed. Please, Princess Rarity, Cailian needs you. The House of Ice and Snow depends on you. These matings have to work or it will be the destruction of not only our kingdoms, but the planet. We will fall."

"I planned on returning. I didn't know when I could. They mated?" A slice of sadness rips through my heart. "Without me?" I don't mean to say it out loud, but I do. "It seems I might not be wanted, Zy, if they mated without me."

"They did not mate out of love, but out of hate, and now they are separated. Please, you are the only one that can fix this. You are the bridge to the kingdoms."

I chew on my bottom lip, spinning to look at my father.

"Go," he urges. "Don't waste another second because it might just be the last second you'll ever have." My father kisses my forehead. "Be better than me, Rarity." And with that, he's gone, nothing but a blur and breeze.

"Zyrl, just tell me what I need to do, and I'll do it."

He grabs my ankle and yanks me into the Cove. "You come home."

I'm drenched to my skin, the water colder than before since I'm in it now, and it begins to swirl, dunking us under.

I can't breathe.

And all I see is darkness.

Chapter Nine

CAILIAN

I am the biggest fool on this planet— no— in all the dimensions. I can't believe I am mated to my eternal enemy, partially mated to another who probably will not come back, and while the melting inside me has slowed, it has not stopped.

Maybe I do not want it to. Maybe turning into water, seeping into the earth, and being reborn as a tree, flower, or anything else magical, is my destiny. I am never the one to give up or quit, but I cannot make someone love or want me, no matter how much I love and want them.

I do not remember life ever being this hard emotionally. Even when my best friend asked me to end his life, I lived day to day knowing I did what he wanted, even with unknowingly making my fated mate hate me, the hours of breathing weren't this harsh.

A tear drips down my cheek and I rub my face against the pillow, turning to my side. There is a slight ache in my backside left from Nyx.

My Dove.

His hate runs deeper than I ever imagined. I know he is ashamed of being mated to me. I am not sure how he will cover my mark, but I have no doubt that he will— just like I will cover his.

I cannot stop thinking about what will happen when we have to tell our Houses that we are now one. If it is up to Dovenyx, he will not want to say anything. He will want to rule as if nothing has changed, as if nothing monumental has happened, as if... I never happened.

The realization has me grabbing the pillow, fisting it as hard as I can before I bury myself in it and scream. Even if I could turn back time and kill my best friend all over again, I would. I would relieve him from his pain and misery.

Even if it means being punished for all eternity by my dragon.

Nothing in this life prepared me for the pain that accompanies a mate who rejects you. The irony of my best friend's son being my mate must be Fate laughing at me or Karma giving me a taste of my own medicine for choosing to kill my mate's father.

Now, Dovenyx has my heart in his hands and his heat is slowly killing me, squeezing and melting the beating drum until it's nothing but a puddle in his palm.

"Get up," I whisper to myself, staring at the wall with swollen eyes. "Just get up and your day will be better."

I try to move, but all I end up doing is pulling the covers to my chin. It is nice and cold under here. I am safe from reality in the confinement of my bedroom. Within these four walls, hurt and pain can no longer get to me more than it already has.

Forget my duties as Prince. Forget the importance of the kingdom. Forget all the responsibilities I have to my House. My brother can rule. He wants to badly, and I believe he is better suited. He is a bit hot-headed, a stubborn horned bull that likes to charge into a crowd rather than speak. I have never been the type who loves controversy. I

am a peaceful soul, one who believes that if the right words are spoken, then all will be right on Elementalu.

Yet it seems allowing myself to speak freely has gotten me nowhere. I do not know what happened to loyalty in fated mates, but I have received nothing from mine.

It is because you hold a heavy lie. Tell the truth. His father would understand.

The voice in the back of my mind is strong, whispering the truth I have been trying to bury deep.

I cannot go back on my word. An elf's word is known on this planet. It's more than a promise, it's a vow. All beings know they can count on the elf's loyalty even in their last breath. If I break the vow and word gets out of the truth, my reputation will be ruined.

My kingdom will fall.

The House of Ice and Snow will be worthless.

This secret isn't only about me, it's about the elves I rule.

They count on me to be what they need me to be. They are more important than my own happiness. A good leader, a wise leader, puts their citizens before themselves, so no matter how much I want to yell the truth to my dragon, to weep the words that have plagued me for eight hundred years, I cannot.

My responsibilities as Prince of the Ice Elven outweigh the need for love.

"If I truly believe that, then why am I not getting out of bed?" I ask myself, my entire body numb. I am sinking further into the mattress, the cold foam forming to every curve I have, and the blanket wraps me in the comfort I long for from my mates.

I hold the ice-woven comforter around me, wrapping myself in its embrace, and imagining the covers are arms holding me tight.

I am pathetic. Truly.

A knock on the door has me groan in dismay.

"Go away. I do not wish to see anyone."

Another knock, only this time it bangs harder, shaking the iron bolts.

In a move unlike me, I reach behind my head and snag my pillow, tossing it against the door. "I order you to leave. I am not available for anything. Come back tomorrow. Go to Zyrl if you must. He is in charge for the day."

The lock on the door breaks, followed by a loud bang that vibrates my aching head.

"Am I? I had no idea," my brother exclaims.

I turn my face into the pillow. "Zy, please leave. I am not in the mood for your antics."

"That's too bad because I brought you a gift."

I like gifts.

I peek my head over my shoulder to see him standing in the middle of the doorway. Seeing him soaking wet has me sitting up for the first time in hours. His hair is dripping, his robes are clinging to his body, and a puddle grows where he stands.

"What happened to you? Did dragons do this?" I toss the covers from my body, swinging my legs over the edge of the frosted mattress then stand. "I will declare war. I no longer care—"

"—No, brother. Stop. Relax. I am wet from traveling through the portal. I have retrieved one of your wayward mates."

I look at him longer than necessary without blinking. "What did you do to Rarity? Did you have to tie her up against her will? Zyrl, I will not allow such things to be done to my mate."

My baby brother wipes his face of water and steps aside, revealing a very wet, very beautiful Rarity. Her skin glistens, and her clothes form to her body, leaving nothing to the imagination. My tongue twists in

an adolescent way of not knowing what to say when confronted with something that has my mind unable to think or process.

Her violet eyes steal around the room, glowing vividly from her pale face. Her lips are the color of a pale rose and when she sees me, the last thing I expect her to do is smile.

My breath is taken from my body as I stare at what cannot be real.

"I'll leave you two alone and I'll do those duties I am apparently in charge of. Rude, brother. Thank you for the forewarning."

"Giving a fortnight would be too much," I manage to push the words from my throat as he shuts the door behind Rarity.

We stand in silence.

Water drips from her clothes, adding to the growing puddle on the floor.

Our breaths collide in clouds we cannot see, meeting eagerly to become one, a secret dance we are not privy to.

She smiles again— well— more of an uncertain smirk that causes her left fang to press against her bottom lip. A faint purple hue appears on her cheeks, a sign that tells me I am the luckiest elf alive if she reacts to me in such a way.

I bend down, take her hand in mine, and kiss her knuckles. "My Snow," I whisper against her soft skin. "Saying I am happy to see you is an understatement. Words cannot describe how I feel. What made you return? I thought since you saw the dragon—"

"—We need to discuss him, Cailian." She laces her fingers through mine, taking me by surprise as she steps forward, initiating closer contact.

My heart grows warm in my chest, a welcome delight from the lonely cold. My veins ease from bright orange to a dull yellow with her here.

"I need you to explain everything to me. I am here, Cailian. I am not going anywhere. We need to figure this out soon because I ache for you, and now I'm aching for a dragon who hates me."

"He hates everyone," I say, cupping her face, and darting my eyes all over her unique face until I land in the haze of lavender. "But not you, Rarity, as you are impossible to hate."

She looks down, her white lashes shadowing the tops of her cheeks, and when she peers up at me, I see the iridescent hue of tears.

"My Snow. What is wrong? Talk to me. I cannot stand the sight of you in such despair." I place my free hand on top of hers and much to my surprise, she scoots closer until our bodies touch, then turns to me. "What is it?" I kiss the tip of her nose watching a ghost of a smile tilt her eyes.

"You and the dragon seem to be very comfortable with one another, as if you are already mated. I feel like I'm the extra mate, the one on the outside. I don't want to be. It's why I'm here. Now that I've been with you, being anywhere else is wrong. How can I compete with you and the dragon when you both have so much history? I don't even know him." She blows out a breath and tucks a wet strand of hair behind her ear. "I guess I don't know what to do. Do we mate and I leave you two alone so you can be happy?"

"Rarity." I pick her up and set her on my lap. She's facing me, her breasts pressing against my chest, and I can't help but react to her nearness.

She gasps, wrapping her arms around my neck as she settles against my cock. I know she can feel me growing harder for her.

"Cailian," the hushed tone of my name falling from lips I dream of tests my control.

"I won't rush this," I struggle to say through my lack of restraint. "Not like I did with the dragon. You need to understand something,

our history is an ugly one, a long one, a never-ending war of him hating me. We mated because we had to, to avoid death." I wrap an arm around her waist and tug her against me. "I do not wish that for us, Rarity. I wish us to want one another, surpassing the need to survive and choosing to truly *live*."

I inch closer to her mouth, wanting to take advantage of her parted lips. Just as we are about to touch, her words are a breeze against my mouth.

"Why does he hate you so much?"

I sigh, leaning back on my hands to put much-needed distance between us before I rip her wet clothes off.

"He has every reason to hate me, Rarity. I killed his father."

I expect disgust, recoil, shock, something that tells me I have lost her forever.

"You don't seem like the killing type, Cailian. What did he do to make you feel so violent?"

I shut my eyes so she cannot see how vulnerable her question makes me feel. I want to spill it all to her. I want to tell her I didn't feel violence, but sorrow. Killing him went against everything I believe in.

"He asked for the unthinkable," I state, forlorn, omitting details.

This is my burden to bear. Not Rarity's. I will not do that to her.

"You must have had a good reason. I don't see you killing for the fun of it, Cailian."

"The reason is mine to take to the grave, My Snow. I hope you know; I would never hurt you. You do not ever need to be afraid of me because of what I did eight hundred years ago."

She presses her forehead against mine, the scent of the rain draping over us. "I know you wouldn't. I can feel that in my heart." Her hand presses against my chest, no doubt experiencing the raging beat of my own. "Just like I know you would never hurt him."

"We cannot dwell on what we cannot change. In time, I hope he sees that I will never hurt him intentionally."

"Time," she whispers, grazing my cheek with her fingers. "Something I have plenty of. Something we have plenty of."

"It is not that unheard of for vampires to live a long time, no?" I ask, ghosting my lips down her neck.

"Yes, but I never thought I would be able to get that time. I never thought I'd be here." Her voice becomes higher when my tongue flicks out along her neck, following the vein that fills her body with life.

Something so sexy yet so overlooked.

I press a kiss against the quickening pulse. "And what are we going to do with all this time, My Snow?" I gather her hair in my hand, draping it over the other shoulder as I move to the exposed side.

"I can think of a few things." The words are spoken to the ceiling in a breathless whimper from her head tilting back, giving me more room to appreciate her beautiful form.

"Is that so?" My own fangs nip at her neck. They are not as sharp as hers, but they can inflict pain if I bite hard enough.

"Yes," she hisses.

My fingers clench her shirt before sliding under, her skin cold from being drenched in water. A shaky breath is shared between us, and I do not know if it is coming from me or her. All I know is with every exhale, I inhale, needing her in my lungs, bringing me to life over and over again.

"I want to consume you," I whisper against her ear before nibbling her earlobe into my mouth. "I want you to scream my name for all the kingdoms to hear, Rarity." My fingers sink into her flesh, grabbing ahold of her body as lust courses through my veins.

She grabs me by the neck, crashing her lips down on mine, and we both moan in relief. The kiss is powerful, planet-shattering, and way

more gentle than Nyx's. He kissed me with hate and regret. Rarity kisses me as if I am her entire world, her reason for breathing, and as she deepens the kiss, wrapping her tongue around mine, she moans into my mouth as if she can't get enough.

The way she's grabbing me, clutching my robes, rocking her pussy against my cock, I finally know what it is like for someone to truly want me out of love and not spite. My hands become disrespectful, changing from a smooth, unsure caress to a demanding need.

I bite her lip, sucking it into my mouth, igniting a moan that travels down mine.

"I—I—" she stutters, pushing me down on the bed in a blur.

I love that vampire speed.

Her sentence is cut short. Rarity decides to take my lips again in a scorching kiss. I become too needy. Her body on top of mine is too much and I crave more. Her hair falls to my chest, tickling the skin just enough to drive me insane.

With both hands, I tug her shirt over her head, stopping her from kissing down my jaw for a split second. When her mouth is free, she's on me again, teasing my bottom lip with her fangs.

"Your blood is a song that makes me high, My Love." She grazes the sharp points against the edge of my jaw causing me to gasp then moan, my cock aching to the point of pure agony.

"Take all you need. Take all of me. I do not care. My blood is yours." I turn my neck, daring her to drink from me, to take, but instead, she only kisses my throat.

"You don't know how much I want you," she whines, palming my cock in her hand.

"You can have me. You can. I really—" I swallow hard, sounding so unlike myself "—I really do not mind, My Snow."

She giggles, kissing down my throat, to my chest, then tugging the fabric of my robes apart to show my body. Her laughter falls short, her delicate fingers covering her lips, trapping a small gasp.

"Oh my gods, Cailian. You are beautiful." A slight tremor shakes her hand as it falls slowly to my chest.

Her fingertips are a feather touch, grazing down in unison until she's tracing my abs.

I squeeze my eyes shut when she teases the waistband of my undergarments. I snag her wrists, breathing so heavily, my lips become dry.

"I have never had sex with a woman, My Snow. Our dragon was my first. I have no idea how to please you, but I promise you, I will learn to make you sing and beg for me."

She unbuttons her jeans. "Good because I have never had sex at all. I am clueless on what to do, but I thought—" her brows pinch together, the air changing from lust to something else.

My fingers slide under her chin. "You thought what? You can tell me."

"I hate I wasn't here for you and Nyx. It bothers me more than it should. I admit, I'm jealous that he got to have you, to see you, and that you got to experience him. I want us all to be together for this. After we are together once, then I don't mind we have each other separately. It matters to me. You matter. And even though I don't know him, he matters."

"You need his blood too, do you not?" I ask with realization. My blood can only go so far but since Rarity has two mates, she can only feed from me for so long before her body begins to break down.

Her answer does not come right away.

I slide my hands up her arms and play with her bra straps, sliding my fingers under them. My thumb rubs back and forth along her

shoulders before I tug the straps down, yet not enough to show her breasts.

"Do not be ashamed of needing him, My Snow. I need him as well. Do not forget that. You can always be honest with me."

"Then, yes," she admits. "I need him too. I crave his blood just like I crave yours. You will get me by, though," she says, a little too hopeful for anyone to believe.

"Until I will not be enough to even get you through the day." My hands begin to roam, becoming free thinkers. I cup her breasts, yanking down the fabric covering them. "If you want him here, then you really need to make the lust travel through the bond I have with him. Can you do that, Rarity? Can you make me so out of my mind, I let him know how good you make me feel?"

Her eyes turn a beautiful shade of crimson, reminding me of what I have forgotten for a split second.

She is a predator.

And I am her prey.

One thing I know for certain is, that I will never make her chase me for what I want to give her so freely.

With her vampiric strength, she rips my undergarments from my body, leaving me bare to her. I am able to track her, and I snag her at the right moment before she is able to take off her bra. I flip her onto her back, hiking her leg over my waist, and clutching my hand around her throat to keep her still.

"Now, now, Little Vampire," I tsk.

She hisses, pushing against my hand to get free.

If she wanted to get away from me, she would. Vampires are much stronger than elves.

"Do not undress when I have been lost in thought of getting you naked beneath me. You are not allowed to move so fast. This is not only about you; do you understand me?"

Her eyes are still the color of a blood moon, but she relaxes under me, settling against the bed. Her fangs poke from her mouth, and I can't help myself, I bend down, licking each point.

She arches beneath me, one hand slipping down my back and grabbing my ass while I pin the other above her head. I transition, slipping my tongue between her lips, dying for her kiss once more.

Her fingers dig into me, squeezing the left cheek so hard, I know there will be bruises. She blurs us across the room, slamming me against the wall.

"What did I say about that?"

"I can't control it. I want you so much." She drops to her knees, wraps a hand around my cock, and purrs innocently. "You'll tell me what to do, right? You'll tell me what you like."

I wrap her long white elven hair around my wrist and pull her to me. "I will tell you but if you have to, suck me first, Little Vampire. Earn your guidance."

"You have such a pretty cock," she compliments. "I bet you're going to feel so good inside me. I can't wait. You're going to fill me up perfectly and give me all your come, aren't you?" She licks down my shaft, moaning before tracing the snowflaked ridge.

"Fuckkk." My head hits the wall with a soft thud.

Her warm, wet tongue pampers me, lavishing long licks of attention down every inch of my cock. She experiments, palming my sack in her hand, and squeezing lightly. I hiss from the slight pressure, then groan.

Rarity tightens her grip, testing how much pressure I can handle, then gives them a slight tug. She hums, lifting her eyes to meet mine.

Something about this view nearly has me on my knees. Her lips spread wide, spit dripping out of the corners of her mouth, her gaze so uncertain yet full of enthusiasm to pleasure me.

My princess kneels before me, worshiping my cock like it's royalty. Her enthusiasm makes up for what she does not know. There is nothing I want to correct. Even the scrape of her fangs against me has me wanting her to bite me.

"Such a good girl taking my cock. I know it's different, but you aren't letting that affect you. You're going to make me come down that whorish little throat if you keep going. Or is that what you want?" I wrap a hand around the front of her neck and squeeze. "You want my frost, Little Vampire? Do you want to know what my ice tastes like?"

She nods, whimpering, picking up her speed. She has no rhythm. Rarity sucks and strokes with awkward head bobs. The wet sounds of her spit slicking my cock is erotic, adding to my heightened desire and pleasure.

"Do not make me come," I grit between tight teeth. "I want inside you first."

Her eyes glaze and narrow with rebellion in effort to disobey me. I tighten the grip I have on her hair, warning her to stop.

"Rarity," I snarl, bending down as far as I can, then applying enough pressure on her head until she can't move, and her throat is stuffed with me. "You need to learn to listen. I think you've been on your own for far too long if you think I will let you do whatever you want, whenever you want." I yank her from me and push her away, my cock slipping free from her mouth.

She flashes her fangs at me, eyes blazing red, and she launches herself at my cock to suck me down again, but I move out of her way, so our bodies do not touch.

I want to use my abilities and if she touches me, I will lose this little war we have going on. Rarity has the upper hand when it comes to power. She simply has more of it, so the time I have to act needs to be quick.

I flick my hand and a thick piece of ice wraps around her neck, then pins her against the wall. Rarity grabs at it, trying to break it, but it is too cold for her to touch for longer than a second. Tilting my chin, I prowl towards her.

I stop when I am directly in front of her, witnessing the gift of watching her squirm.

"It's cold," her teeth clink together as she shivers, her entire body alive with goosebumps.

She manages to crack the ice, and I slide my finger across it, mending the restraints together. I slide my entire hand across it, adding more ice to withstand her strength.

"Good," I say, marveling at the beauty before me. "Maybe then you'll learn."

"Cailian," she whimpers, arching her body to touch mine.

I step away, my cock swaying between my legs. I look down at her, noticing how small she is compared to me, realizing that she'll look even tinier next to our dragon since he is taller than I am. I touch her cheek with the back of my finger and ever-so-slowly, graze it down her jaw, neck, and to her collarbone.

I trace the slender ridge. Back and forth. Back and forth. Memorizing how she feels, how her skin is silk, and how I want her draped over me like luxury, or how her breath hitches when I get closer to her neck.

"Please," she begs, stretching out her arms to touch me.

"Hands at your sides, Rarity. I am not done admiring you yet," I demand, giving her a stern expression.

And to my shock, she listens.

I smile, which is no effort at all when it comes to knowing that not only is my mate here, but she wants me. "Good girl. As a reward—" I step closer and give her my wrist, pressing it against her mouth. "You can have my blood."

Her tongue flicks out, tasting my skin before she peeks at me through her lashes, and slices her fangs into the vein.

I groan from the sweet sensations of pain and pleasure. I stand closer, pressing my wrist harder against her mouth. Red rivulets spill down her chin. With every drag she takes, my cock jerks, precome dripping heavily from the broad tip.

"That's enough," I tell her, trying to pull my hand free.

This time, she doesn't listen.

She takes more.

I pinch her nose so she can't breathe. "I said that is enough," I growl.

She releases me, mouth wide open as I tilt her head back. Her teeth are red, fangs dripping with blood, and the pupils of her eyes are blown wide. I wipe the blood from her lip and suck my finger into my mouth.

"Are you high off me, My Snow?"

Her tongue sucks over her teeth to gather the excess blood, her eyes close as if she's swallowing the best liqueur this planet has to offer.

"I love that I do that to you." I keep her trapped against the wall with the ice collar, not ready to let her go just yet.

I drop the barrier in my bond to the dragon since we have mated, pushing aside my anger and betrayal for Rarity. I refuse to be selfish when she deserves both her mates. We can love her, she can love us, but as far as he and I are concerned, love will never be in the picture.

Lust strums the strings binding me to the dragon, echoing the pleasure I am feeling as I stare at my vampire mate. Every time I blink, I send an image through my mind of what I see.

I trail my fingers down her neck, my touch a ghost over her breast, and a shaky breath causes her stomach to tremble. Her nipple hardens, and more goosebumps arise on her skin, reminding me of a fresh blanket of snow after a blizzard.

Pinching the pink bead, Rarity moans, and she grows louder as I slide my hand further down her torso.

Shock rolls through the bond and I smirk, cupping her virgin pussy.

A roar thunders in my mind.

I have awakened our dragon, but it is me who will have her first.

Chapter Ten

DOVENYX

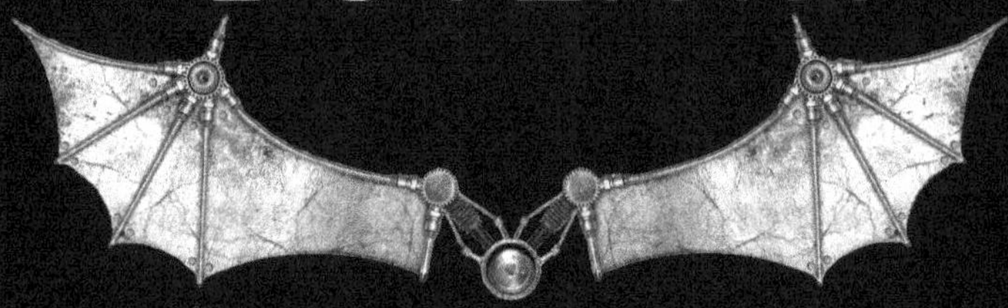

I sit at the head of the table that was cut from the volcano of where our kind originates. The long onyx glows with an array of colors, just like our scales, but lava flows through the middle eternally.

"I want an update on the trolls," I state, staring at Raiden, who is eying me curiously as to why I'm wearing a shirt with a collar that buttons up the front of my throat.

I have to hide Cailian's mark for now.

"They have stopped in Fog's Forest." Raiden taps his claws on the table. "As of an hour ago."

"So they are still a day or so away from us?"

"Yes, Prince Dovenyx," he formally answers since my other dragons in command are sitting with us as well.

I sit back in my chair, tilting my head back as I blow black smoke in perfect circles. "I wonder what they are waiting for."

"If I may, Prince?" Zoren, the commanding officer of the elite dragons sworn to protect the kingdom, raises his hand.

"Please." I hold out my palm in a gesture that tells him he has my attention.

Zoren nods his head in a respectful manner. "What if they aren't coming to attack? There are so many of them. I can't help but wonder if they are moving to a different part of the planet."

"Impossible," Willox, the treasurer of our hoard, snarls with fire brimming his mouth, slamming his hand on the table. "Trolls never have good intentions. History has proven that when they are close, they start a war. They are planning something, and they have grown in numbers. They are not stupid creatures. They are surprisingly sardonic with their strategies. You should know that, Zoren."

Zoren stands, splaying his hands on the table, growling in a low warning. "You don't think I know that? I have fought them a hundred times but this time, this new pattern they are making doesn't fit what I know. They have stopped in the densest part of Fog's Forest. There are no caves, mountains, or rocks where they are. Trolls thrive in those places not some forest with thick trees and questionable creatures."

Sylas, my traveler, the dragon that keeps communication with other beings on the planet speaks. "I've spoken with the Woodland Elves. I told them about the impending danger. The trolls are in a forbidden part of the forest that not even the Woodland Elves step foot in. They are barricading parts of their territory the best they can. Not even they are willing to risk doing nothing."

"Where is Erelix? Perhaps, it is time to barricade the castle to protect the den and the hoard." Down below the castle, nearly to the middle of this planet, near the molten heat of lava, is where we keep our gold.

Willox only comes up for air when we have these meetings, otherwise, he guards what is so precious to us.

"I haven't seen the wizard today," Raiden states, leaning forward. "In fact, I haven't seen him in a while."

I lift my brow. While it isn't unlike my wizard to take a few days to gather herbs, spices, or whatever else he may need, he usually always lets me know if he will be gone.

"Send a search party for him. I want answers to his disappearance. That causes issues when it comes to protection. We are left vulnerable without him." I rub my temples as a headache begins to build, when suddenly something snaps in my chest, pain spreading through my skull.

I gasp for air, placing a hand to my chest as agony thrums through my heart.

"Nyx?" Raiden is at my side just as I slump to the left, nearly falling from my chair.

He catches me, grunting from my body weight.

The table erupts in worry.

"The prince is unwell. This meeting is cancelled."

"Perhaps we need to go to the elves, ask for their witch."

"The ice elves? Are you mad?"

Voices raise until arguments become a meshed sound that I can't understand.

"Enough!" Raiden bellows. "Leave and go about your duties. I will care for the prince. If I have any news, I will let you know. Zoren, I want hourly updates on those trolls."

"Yes, Second. Understood."

I hold my head, a sizzle of white noise exploding in my mind, and it stops my ability to breathe. Sweat breaks out all over my body.

"Talk to me, Nyx. What's happening?" my friend whispers low. "What can I do?"

I'm about to beg him to trespass on the elven property to steal ice and drape it over my body when the ache stops and desire rams inside me instead.

I gasp for breath, thankful I'm not dying, but now I know why.

My firebond has lowered his guard to allow me in his head once more. Images of a beautiful body bombard my mind. Cailian is touching her— Rarity— our firebond and is sending me pictures of what he sees.

Her breasts come to view, her nipples beading under his touch, and in the distance of the bond, I hear her moan for him.

There's no hiding how hard my cock has become. Lust swirls around me in a thick aromatic spice that Raiden will be able to smell any moment. I won't be able to hide the truth from him now.

I roar to him in response when his hand disappears between her legs, making a sweet cry pour from her body that I want to break, bend, and bury beneath me.

Raiden rips the buttons closed around my neck, staring at the glittering light blue snowflake in the middle of my throat.

"You're mated," he whispers, completely dumbfounded. "What the fuck?" he questions with wide eyes that finally meet mine before turning into fiery slits. "What the fuck, Nyx? You mated an elf?" he asks harshly.

I cover his mouth with my hand, glancing around to make sure no other dragons are in earshot. Hanging my head, I get to my knees, a power wave of pleasure almost making me fall again. I'm not sure if I can carry a conversation with him sending me images of him finger-fucking her.

"Shhh," I hiss, not wanting anyone to hear. "I can explain."

"Explain? How do you want to explain the Prince of Dragons has mated to an elf and hasn't told anyone because that means the kingdoms are now joined? How will you explain keeping a secret like this from your best friend?"

"Because my firebond is the elf that killed my father," I snarl at him, covering my throat in shame. "I had to. We had to because we would have died if we didn't."

He sits back on his legs, his wings outstretch, just... staring at me.

The moment becomes uncomfortable. My cock is hard, I'm angry, and every time I blink, I see images of his fingers slipping in and out of her, his silver skin wet with her nectar.

"Say something," I snarl, managing to get to my feet.

"I don't know what to say. Are you okay? How are you doing?"

My wings settle against my back, a bit of the weight of the secret I was carrying is lifted and knowing Raiden cares for my well-being— well— that means more to me than I thought it would.

"I'm not sure," I say honestly, rolling my neck when beads of sweat begin to drip down my throat. "I can't be here much longer. Our other firebond —"

He catches himself on the table. "Another firebond? Another? Jesus. No wonder you've been so damn moody lately."

"She's here," I grumble. "And he is letting me see what they are doing right now so I can't really focus on your questions when my firebonds need me."

"We can talk later."

"Thank you."

I step toward the window, preparing to fly when Raiden grabs my arm. I turn to look at him and his face is contorted in worry.

"I think it is good that the kingdoms will be united. I think it is good that the war between us will be over. It brings hope."

"There is no hope for what he did."

"Elves are loyal creatures, Nyx. Loyal until death. Their word is what they live and breathe by."

"And dragons aren't?"

"You know that's not what I mean. They live by it like a book, like it's their constitution. An elf's promise is one of the greatest gifts to have because you know they will fulfill it. I'm saying, what if there is more to your firebond? Fate wouldn't be so cruel to you to give you the firebond who killed your father without reason."

"Sometimes Fate doesn't make sense. Sometimes there are no reasons. Sometimes, Raiden, the world is against you, and you learn to live with the pain of knowing the universe will never be on your side." I jump onto the ledge and launch into the sky before he can say another word, bursting into my dragon form.

Raiden has always been the most level-headed dragon I've ever known. He is rational, calm, and sees our world in such an optimistic way. More often than not, it angers me because I know I could never have such light. Bitter memories darken the chambers of my heart and the only force that makes this organ beat is venom.

"That's really cynical and pessimistic," he shouts out of the window, and in my dragon form I manage to roll my eyes. "I will be finding a solution to this!"

I huff my flame from my mouth in annoyance. His damn positivity is like a thorn in my side I can't reach. It's always there, fucking poking at me.

Flying around my castle, I reach the boundary, flapping my wings to keep me steady as I stare at the invisible ward. Unless, maybe, if it isn't too much wishful thinking, that Cailian dropped the wards.

Sending me those dirty images of him and Rarity together might be his evil plan to get me to fly into the wards. No doubt I'd have a few bumps and bruises— a little payback for how I treated him during our mating.

My mind fills with another sinful image of Rarity crying out, her mouth parted as she orgasms.

A growl fills my chest, want tugs at my heart, and instinct wins. Mating drives my issues to the back of my mind, the air drifting over my scales as I pass the boundary without injury.

He lowered the wards.

I circle his cold kingdom, trying to find where his scent is the strongest. Elves look up to the darkened sky, covering their eyes to block the bright moonlight. They run inside the iced castle, and they scream for the prince so loud, I can hear the chaos from up here. I land on a large balcony, my claws digging into the iced surface. A slight sizzle of hot meeting cold has me quickly shifting into my human form. This body gives off less heat, but as I step forward to the oversized iced French doors, my eyes instantly landing on Rarity and Cailian.

He has her pressed against the wall, finger fucking her so hard, I can see her dripping from his palm.

"Come on, My Snow, come for me again. I know you can," he commands her in a low, sultry voice that is so seductive, I have to stroke my cock a few times to give myself friction— to try to ease this ache Cailian's teasing has caused.

I step inside his bedroom, the air so thick with their scents, and take a deep inhale to gather as much as I can to memory.

"Yes, come for him, My Darling Jewel. We have to see just how much you can take."

Her purple eyes land on me, glassy with sex and need. "Nyx," she whispers, then lifts her hand to Cailian's chin, forcing him to peel his eyes away from her tits. "Look." Rarity turns his head to look at me. "Our beloved is here."

Cailian doesn't smile at me. "Yes, he is. He's here just for you."

I open my mouth to correct him because those words hurt me much more than I ever thought they would. The lie I told myself on the way over here was that I am only here for her.

I'd be a foolish man not to admit how starved I am to see Cailian orgasm again. The emptiness in my stomach is only the beginning of the abyss Cailian has created inside me. He has no idea that I'm growing to forgive him for killing my father— and that is something I will never say out loud— because now it isn't just about hating him, but myself too.

"Nyx," my name is a whimper on her sweet, swollen lips. "I need you."

Those three simple words are all it takes for me to close the distance between us. I don't ask, don't hesitate. I cup the back of her head and slam my mouth down on hers, giving in to the pull of our bond.

I know nothing about her and the taste of her has me wanting to know everything. My heated split tongue slips around hers, twisting until I have the tip in a tight hold. She moans, her hand reaching below to wrap around my cock.

The fervent rumble in my chest is low and long, a never-ending baritone that my dragon wants to sing for her.

Her fangs nip my bottom lip, my massive hand wrapping around her throat. I lick and suck her bottom lip in return before biting it. "I didn't say you could bite me, My Darling Jewel. You'll do as I say, when I say, and how I say. If I want you to feed from me, you will, if I want you to taste me, you will, if I want that pretty mouth around my cock, you'll fucking suck it. But only if I tell you to." I trail my claws down her throat, one that seems so small in my hand.

Her eyes flash red with discontent, hissing at me.

"She doesn't like to listen, My Dove. You have to force her," he states, pulling his hand from her pussy. "Taste her. She is so good. You'll never want anything else as long as you breathe."

I take his wrist in my hand, staring directly into his swirling blue eyes. "I could think of something else," I state, unlike anything I would

say to him. Having Rarity here is too much. I can't deny the pull to him when we are together as a true trio.

Not breaking eye contact, the side of his palm settles perfectly between the split in my tongue. I flick each end, licking up his palm before sucking the fingers he had inside Rarity into my mouth.

A burst of sugar hits my taste buds, giving me a slight rush, and blood pools to my cock. My sack of three grows larger, filling with enough come that I could easily give my firebonds what they need. When they are in heat, I'll produce as much come as I need during that moment, so they'll never have to wait to have me.

The thought of them going into heat, constantly wanting, moaning, and begging me to knot them has me taking Cailian's fingers to the back of my throat.

He gasps when the tips of his fingers hit the back, his eyes going wide in shock when he realizes I don't have a gag reflex. I smirk, slipping his fingers from my mouth.

"Step away from her and go lie down on the bed. Rarity." I take her hand as if I'm about to ask her to dance.

"But I don't want to," Cailian defies, stepping closer, his thumb stroking her nipple back and forth.

I wrap my hand around his long white hair, then yank him until he is bent backwards. "I don't give a fuck about what you want right now. Do not be a brat. Step away from our firebond so I can lie her on the bed. After that, I will give you instruction on what to do."

"I don't want instruction," he battles me, a tint of light blue glossing over his cheeks as he blushes.

Cailian is tall, but nowhere near as big as I am. I wrap my arms around his waist and lift him, tossing him on the bed. His cock bounces, the thick vein protruding from the shaft as it pumps blood.

Precome gathers at his slit and with his right hand, he wraps it around his cock.

I blow fire at him, not enough to hurt him, but enough to warn him. "What did I say earlier, Little Elf?" I snarl, picking up Rarity by the back of her thighs.

She wraps her legs around my hips, her arms around my neck, and that fucking mouth is on my neck, licking and sucking the place she wants to bite.

And I want to let her.

"Soon, My Darling Jewel," I ease her onto the bed, the tip of my expansive head glides over her wet cunt, daring me to fuck her relentlessly.

But I won't be the first inside her. It will be Cailian for a multitude of reasons. They have a bond that Rarity and I do not have yet. Taking him first will prepare her for me.

"Hands above your head."

She listens beautifully, the motion causing her breast to bounce ever so slightly. I can't help myself. I pinch her nipple between my claws, and she gasps, arching her back from the sweet pain.

"She's never been with another," he whispers, reminding me that neither had he before me.

A possessive force overcomes me, the need for us to be one, and I reach for Cailian, holding the back of his neck while I kiss him.

It's harder, a bit brutal with teeth and hate.

I pull away and bring his pointed ear to my lips. It flutters again and I can't help but to hide my grin. I find it so adorable. "Go fuck her mouth, Little Elf. Give me a show." I suck his earlobe into my mouth, the cool temperature of his skin easing the burn on mine. "Go. Let me see you take what you want before I take the both of you— and you can't do anything except bend for me."

Cailian falls to his hands and knees, crawling up Rarity's restless body. Her legs rub together, her hands grip the pillow under her head, and she already has her mouth open for him.

"Good Boy." I rub my hand over his plump ass, then give it a little slap. "And Good Girl." I knee-walk to the side of the bed they aren't using, and take Cailian's cock in my hand, guiding it to her mouth with a little force.

"Oh, fuck, Nyx," he whimpers, tossing his head back in pleasure from the cruel tug.

"When I am with you, Cailian, I am not Nyx. What am I?"

"My Dove?" he asks, his lips parting as he gasps for breath when his cock presses against her lips.

"That's right."

"Prince Cailian!" is shouted from behind his locked door. "Prince, there is a dragon here! Are you safe?"

A toothy grin stretches across my face as I shove him forward, forcing Rarity to gag on his cock. "No." I hold a hand over his mouth, catching his scream. "You aren't safe with me." My nose feathers down his cheek, then I lick his jawline to his ear. "I'm going to ruin you, Little Elf." His body trembles as my fingers slide down his spine, then graze the crease of his ass. "Tell your people." I nibble his shoulder, wanting to bite him for all to see. "Tell them how you're in danger with your big, bad dragon."

His hips canter, followed by a breathy curse as he fills Rarity's mouth. I look over his shoulder, watching his cock disappear between her lips. Her eyes water from the angle. When he slips out, she eagerly sucks the unique snowflaked crown between her lips.

"I'm fine!" he groans, falling forward to catch himself on the edge of the headboard. "Fuck. I am so fucking fine."

"Liar, liar," I tsk softly, kissing my mating mark.

"Are you sure, Prince? You sound like you're in distress."

I tease his hole with my finger, barely pressing against the tight rim, not enough to enter, but enough to make him push back wanting more.

"I am fine. Leave!" he growls the best an elf can, holding onto the top of the headboard with both hands. He grips it tight, his lean biceps flexing as he uses it as leverage to fuck her mouth.

"Yes, Prince Cailian." The elves behind the door murmur to one another before their feet tap down the hallway, finally leaving us alone.

I chuckle, watching Rarity suck his cock with vigor. Cailian begins to lose control, moving his hips faster. He slams forward, filling her mouth, and tries to sit on my finger.

"Don't be so greedy, Little Elf. I'll give you what you need in time, don't worry." I slip my hand between Rarity's legs, appreciating how they part for me. Her pussy is drenched. Her lips give way to my curiosity, slipping back and forth. She's soft as the finest silk.

I glance over Cailian's shoulder to see her eyes shut and a whine encompasses Cailian's cock. "Do you like that, Rarity? You love having two men adore you, don't you? Such a whore for us." I pinch her clit before circling it in a steady rhythm. I don't want to go too fast, or it won't feel as good. This will give her the build, the warmth, the impending explosion in her body that she craves.

Just as she's about to tip over, I pull my hand away. Her thighs tremble from her body being so stimulated.

"Nyx," she calls out for me.

"It's okay, Rarity." I lie down between her legs, my face full of her pussy, yet if I look up, I have the most perfect view of Cailian's ass.

Oh, what men would give to be me.

I hook my hands around her legs and tug her to me, my mouth kissing her cunt.

"I'm going to give this pussy what she needs." I lick my tongue from her clit to her hole, driving it forward to feel her virgin barrier. My eyes shift, losing control of myself at the thought of her only being ours.

I dig my claws into her ass, eating her like a starved dragon. Sucking her clit into my mouth, I roll it between my forked tongue.

"Oh gods, yes," she cries out.

I stop, growling, displeased. "I didn't say you could stop sucking his cock."

"Nyx, I can't focus. It's too much."

"It's far from too much. It's never enough, My Darling Jewel." I feast once more, sucking on her clit.

Her cries become higher, and her legs try to tighten around my neck, but I keep them forced apart so I can have full access to her sensitive sweet bundle of nerves.

"You look so fucking good sucking my cock, Rarity. So pretty with your mouth stretched open. I cannot wait to fuck you, to claim you as mine. You are divine, as beautiful as the moonlight shining off the ice, but you're as sinister as the heat that lives within our dragon, aren't you?" he quickens his pace and I'm able to hear the garbled efforts of Rarity trying to take his cock.

Rarity's body tightens, her hips arching as an orgasm controls her next moves. I catch her release, her cunt squirting her come directly into my mouth. She tastes so good, it would be completely selfish to keep her to myself. I get onto my knees, tug Cailian's head back by his long hair, and open his mouth by tugging on his bottom lip with my thumb.

He obeys, and I spit half of her come down his throat.

I tighten my hand around his neck, feeling him swallow before kissing him again. I lick his tongue before sucking it into my mouth, wanting to drain his taste buds of her.

"Doesn't she taste good?"

"Yes. So good," he slurs with deep blue cheeks as his body becomes heated.

My hand drops to his chest, pushing him back until he slides off her body to drop between her legs.

His cock leaks with that icy precome, the shaft engorged and dark silver, wanting nothing more than to come. I swipe my finger over his slit, gathering the juice that quenches my thirst.

"Fuck our firebond, Cailian. I want to be able to feel her screams in my bones." I grab his chin, forcing his eyes to lazily slide to mine. "Can you do that?"

"I— I want to. I have never— I do not know—"

I silence his uncertainty with a kiss. "Do not be afraid of what you don't know. Do what comes naturally, and we will guide you the rest of the way. You will be taught to fuck her how she wants, fuck me how I want while telling us how you want to be fucked. Our time together is young, and I doubt it will ever grow old."

"What... what about you?" he asks, trying to catch his breath.

His hand shakes as he lifts her leg around his hip, guiding his cock to her pussy.

I palm her tits, bend down and tease the seam of her lips with my tongue. "I have more than enough to keep me occupied. And believe me, I'm nowhere near done with either of you."

Growling in approval as he begins to inch in, Rarity fists my cock, her thumb and index finger unable to touch.

"Three?" she gasps when she sees my orbs, palming them with her free hand.

"And all three are filled for my firebonds." I turn my head to set my sights on Cailian in time to see the hurt flashing across his face. "And

for you. Every drop," I say to him past the lump in my throat, trying to pull honest words back down my throat.

But it is true, no matter how much I want to deny that my father's killer is my firebond, every part of me needs him now.

Whether I like it or not.

Chapter Eleven

RARITY

I can't help myself. Three large, swollen balls swing between my dragon's legs, and I lean in, sucking half of one into my mouth because I can't get the rest to fit. I know I have no finesse when it comes to this, but I trust my beloveds will tell me if I need to change tactics.

"Squeeze me harder," Nyx says, tightening my fist around his cock. "I love tight places I can barely fit into. Make me work for it."

I do as he says, and he groans, rutting his hips to slide his long, thick shaft in my palm. His heavy balls slap against my hand with every stroke and Cailian is mesmerized, his cock kissing my entrance while he stares at Nyx fucking my hand.

"Enough," Nyx growls, grabbing us by our hair at the same time. I whimper from the sting and Cailian groans, the head of his cock slipping inside me. We both gasp.

"Watch him fuck you, Rarity. Watch that pretty cock take your virginity just like I took his."

I flash my fangs at him, not liking that they fucked without me. "I don't know if I'll ever forgive the two of you for letting me miss that opportunity."

He presses his palm against Cailian's chest, his oversized hand covering the middle of the defined plains, and his fingers drag along the elf's throat while Nyx leans in closer to my face.

"I don't remember asking for your forgiveness, My Darling Jewel. If I had to choose between life and death again, I'd choose life, and gods," he groans into my ear. "Life feels so good inside our Little Elf."

I whimper, closing my eyes and waiting for him to kiss me, but it never comes.

Fingers land on my clit, the electrical current causing me to snap my eyes open a second later. Cailian inches his way inside me, his crown stretching me as a cool, tingling sensation spreads through my pussy.

My fingers dig into Nyx's arm, dragging across his glimmering scales as the pain becomes more intense.

"You're doing so good, Rarity. Look at you taking his pretty cock. What a good girl taking her firebond's dick. You're going to feel so good soon. I promise," he whispers, latching his lips around the meat of my shoulder. "I can't wait to mark you here."

"Cailian!" I cry out his name when he reaches the barrier. If we do this, there's no going back. Nothing will be the same.

And I don't want it to.

His irises swirl with silver around the pupil while the rest shines a bright blue. Frost decorates his forehead where he is sweating. I touch his face, ice sparkling in the wake of where my fingers glide. It doesn't hurt him.

Biting his lip, he drives forward, breaking through my virginity, and slipping to the hilt.

"Rarity," he groans, gasping for breath as he stares down at where we are connected, his hands clutching my hips. Cailian stays pressed against me, shaking with the need to move.

While he enjoys pleasure, I have to endure the momentary pain.

"I know. I know it hurts," Nyx says, palming my right breast before swirling his finger around my nipple. "You're so fucking beautiful beneath him, Rarity. I wish you could see what I see."

"You can show her after you are bonded," Cailian reminds him.

"We'll all be in trouble, then." Nyx's smile is sardonic, as if he has an evil plan to make sure our day-to-day lives are interrupted by his wicked thoughts.

Cool air is blown on my nipples just as hot air follows, giving me the warm and tingly sensation immediately. I relax around Cailian's cock, my painful whimpers turning into erotic gasps.

"So full. Cailian. Oh, fuck, you feel so good. Are you going to fuck me? Are you going to show me who I belong to?" I lift onto my elbows, licking up his chin and onto his mouth before forcing my tongue between his lips. "I hope so." I inhale deeply when the scent of blood fills the air.

Reaching between us, I slip my fingers across his cock, and pull them away. "Look what you did." I show him the light sheen of red. "Does this make me yours?" I suck my fingers into my mouth, locking eyes with him and my dragon as they watch me lick my own fingers clean.

Cailian slides, easy and gentle as if he's still afraid to hurt me.

"More," I groan, stretching my arms up to wrap around his neck when Nyx stops me, pinning my hands above my head.

"And he'll give it." Nyx crashes his mouth against mine, his tongue splicing along mine. He's fast, the two ends swirling in my mouth in a frenzied dance.

Cailian grabs my hips harder, gaining confidence with every stroke. Nyx trails kisses down my jaw, his hands cupping my breasts as he moans.

"So perfect." He continues, his hand trailing down my throat where the shoulder and neck meet. "I'm going to mark you right here. Right here for all to see."

Cailian's hips stutter and a momentary pass of sadness crosses his face before he schools his features. He notices me staring at him before smirking. Cailian picks up my legs to hoist them over his shoulders, wraps one arm around my thighs, and slams into me.

"Your pussy is so tight," he grunts, fucking me harder, driving his cock further as if he's trying to reach my womb. "I never knew it could feel this good."

In a blur, I flip him on his back, but Nyx catches me by my throat before I can straddle Cailian's cock, and throws me down on the bed, fire burning bright in his eyes.

"Lie down, spread your legs, and let Cailian fuck you like the good little firebond you are."

"I want to ride him."

His hand tightens around my throat, choking me like a necklace that's a bit too tight. He forcefully turns my head, dragging his tongue over the shell of my ear. "Didn't I just say that I didn't give a fuck about what you wanted?" Nyx pushes my right knee down, then my left.

Cailian settles between my legs again, slipping his cock into me easily as I'm soaked for him.

"Nothing in my way, nothing stopping me from filling you, nothing daring me to own you." Cailian rams into me, his cock plunging deeper with every stroke. He grabs one of my breasts before twisting my nipples between his fingers.

He owns my body, using it to fulfill his needs when our dragon slips a finger in Cailian's mouth, soaking it before easing it free. Nyx's arm vanishes behind Cailian and his other hand slides around his hip. Cailian trembles, crumbling to insignificant pieces right in front of me when he experiences Nyx's touch.

Cailian stills, arching his body as his mouth parts, his beautiful pink tongue licking his lips.

"Dove," he gasps Nyx's nickname for him.

"I wish you could feel how tight his ass is, Rarity," Nyx groans to me, towering over Cailian's head.

I can't get over how large our dragon is and how small he makes me feel.

"Still virgin tight, isn't that right, Little Elf?"

"For you." Cailian moans, pushing his hips forward to sink further inside me, only to pull out to fuck Nyx's finger.

Nyx's hand slides up Cailian's beautiful swimmer-esque body, slow, soft, and gentle, touching him as if Cailian would break if he applied too much pressure.

I wish I could fix the issues between them because together, they are like looking through a kaleidoscope, a colorful show I can't possibly tear my eyes from. Their sighs are lost within each other, desperately grabbing onto the flesh they can so neither floats away into the past that keeps them apart.

They are a reckoning for my heart, a devastating love that leaves scratches on the bone, clawing its way from the inside to prove itself.

Nyx bends more and Cailian has to move with him. The tips of Cailian's hair graze over my nipples, the phantom sensation kissing each breast. I wrap my arms around him, then slide my hand down to his ass, wanting to feel where he is being touched by Nyx.

Cailian gasps when Nyx adds another finger.

"Does he feel good, My Love?" I lick up his neck, his vein teasing me by pulsing in a loud beat.

"Both of you do. I cannot last like this. You feel so good, Rarity. So wet, so fucking tight, you make me want to lose myself inside you." His hand glides up my body, his hand locking around my throat. Cailian tightens his hold until black swims at the edges of my vision and a small breadth of space allows me to breathe.

He sneers against my lips and the air he exhales slips down my throat like an illegal drug, poisoning me for his own benefit. "I am going to fill you with so much of me, my frost will be leaking out of you for days. When I reach between your legs at any time of day, I will feel how slick and ready you are for us."

I moan in response, feeling myself drench his cock.

"You like that? You want to be used? What if Nyx and I had our way with you, tag-teaming you like the hungry whore you are until you cannot stand on your own two feet without us." His words fall into my chest, veining across my nerve-endings like a live wire.

And it's finding its way to my clit, heat causing me to throb. A constant needy ache builds between my legs, and even with Cailian's cock slipping in and out, it's a teasing rate while Nyx prepares him with his fingers.

A warmth spreads across my stomach from his filth-infused words, an orgasm looming just beyond the storms they reap inside me.

Yet, the storm will not allow me to rain.

Cailian finally releases my throat, enough for me to inhale before strangling me, safely, again.

"Our Little Elf loves making you submit, My Darling Jewel. I have to say, I do love seeing you pliant," Nyx informs between kissing down Cailian's back. "Be there for him, Rarity. He's about to take my cock and it won't be easy, will it, Cailian?" He kisses the tip of Cailian's ear,

and it wiggles in response. "Tell her how you feel like you're about to be split open. Admit how my cock is too much for you to handle." Nyx gathers Cailian's hair, moving it to the other shoulder to expose the elegant curve of his neck. "My marks aren't nearly enough for either of you. I need more. I need to possess your fucking bones and come inside your marrow. Only then will my scent be permanent, not just in your blood, or your mind, but your fucking soul. When we die and our bones turn to ash, I will still be there, claiming your grave as mine."

"What about in the afterlife?" I ask him with a slight attitude, tweaking Cailian's nipples. I want him to say more. I need more details of how serious he is about me and Cailian. I need the reassurance.

My dragon curls over Cailian, reminding me how small we are compared to him, and a rush of danger swims through my veins. My dragon's eyes meet mine, fire dancing behind the pupils as he sneers, his tongue flicking out to touch my cheek.

"In the afterlife, we'll be born again, and I'll be able to find my fire-bonds because I would be in your DNA, embedded in your existence forever."

My heart prepares for death, to experience Nyx for the first time all over again: his intensity, his anger, and his possessiveness.

Nyx's arm reaches out, slips under my head, and pulls me forward, kissing me roughly before pulling away. Cailian's hold on me is still there, his hand never letting go of my throat.

"Now, stop being a brat or I'm not going to fuck you when I'm done with Cailian. Do you want to take Cailian's mind off what's about to happen, Rarity?"

I nod, wanting to ease Cailian's pain, and rolling my lips together so I don't ask any more questions.

"He is going to be a sore, good boy when I am done with him. Aren't you, Cailian?" Nyx hisses the question in a demanding threat,

yanking Cailian's head back by his neck. The move jostles Cailian deeper inside me and I clench around him, needing more.

"Rarity— I am too close." He licks his lips, the icy stencil on the chiseled edges of his cheeks turn to beacons as the sapphire hue deepens.

I clench around him again and he moans, pressing the back of his head against Nyx, and our dragon's claws pet through his hair before gripping it tight. The onyx-dipped nails contrast so beautifully with Cailian's white hair.

Darkness collides with light sliding against one another like two different shades of ink.

Cailian slams inside me causing me to cry out. The trimmed white hairs of his happy trail slightly tickle my upper inner thigh while Cailian is planted inside me.

Desperately seeking someone to hold onto to, he grabs my hand, lacing his fingers through mine as a guttural groan spills from him.

"Slow, slower, you are so much to take," Cailian whimpers, squeezing my hand harder while reaching his arm back to touch Nyx. "You are so warm. Your heat is in my blood."

Nyx hooks a clawed hand over Cailian's shoulder, gripping the skin so hard that it breaks under the points of his nails.

Red paints Cailian's canvas, tempting me over the edge. I sit up in a blur, licking the crimson streaks from his cool, lean chest.

"Mmmm," I moan in appreciation, his unique flavor fueling my body. "The best blood I've ever tasted. I want to make drinks with it, My Love." I lick the claws still clinging to Cailian, wanting the blood. "A blood, gin and tonic," I whisper, clenching around his cock. "A blood margarita on the rocks. A daiquiri on a humid night while I lie out under the moon." I gather another drop that spills from the claws, groaning in delight. I lick my way up his jaw, so defined and sculpted.

"So many ways to feed me. You'll do it, won't you?" I ask against his lips, mewling when he pulls back because Nyx tugs his hips, forcing himself deeper into our elf. Nyx pushes forward which has Cailian sinking into me again.

My mouth parts in ecstasy and my palm cups Cailian's face, my fingers pressing into the divots of his cheeks. "Cailian," I moan, pressing our forehead together as the bond between the three of us strengthens. "Nyx." Glancing over Cailian's shoulder, I see our dragon, his eyes the color of kindling wood, smoke billowing from his nose as sweat drips down the muscular ropes of his neck.

His shines, like black diamonds glimmering from the scales trailing down his shoulders, arms, and chest. Rainbows reflect in his flesh with every motion, reminding me of the darling jewel he calls me, but it is he who is the jewel, the rarest of gems, the treasure people kill for.

I would kill.

I would maim.

I would freeze people to their cores and shatter their souls if it meant protecting my treasure.

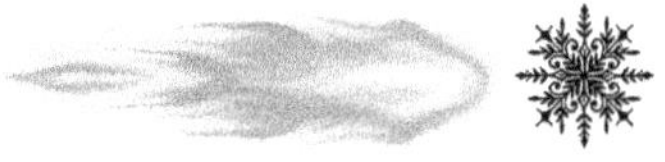

"You're doing so good, Little Elf. I'm almost in. Just a little more."

Cailian shakes his head. "Nyx, there is more? Oh gods, how?"

I clench around him around his cock again just as Nyx inches forward until Cailian's back is against his chest.

"See? Just a little bit more. Now, you're full of me." Nyx kisses Cailian's shoulder. "Such a tight place I can barely fit in to and you know how much I love that." He nips the side of Cailian's neck.

"How does he feel, My Love?" I ask, petting his chest in comfort as his eyes pinch shut. "Tell me everything." I turn my head as Cailian kisses up the middle of my chest and neck. He sucks the flesh into his mouth, moaning before his teeth tease my hopes of him feeding from me. His fangs just aren't sharp enough to pierce the skin.

That's okay. I'll always give him what he needs.

I extend my claw, letting it grow to full length. "Is this what you need?" I press my nail like a knife against my jugular vein, slowly cutting my skin open. "Now that you've had a taste, you can't get enough, can you? It's normal for my beloveds to want my blood since our existence is tied together. Go ahead, My love. Before I heal."

He presses his mouth against my throat, his cool tongue licking the lust-tainted blood, no doubt heating his throat as he swallows.

No sooner is his mouth on my neck, stealing one long drag before Nyx is snarling, clutching the back of Cailian's neck and yanking him back.

Cailian cries out in pleasure, his hips moving lazily as he sinks on Nyx's cock, still keeping me edged.

"I didn't say you could drink from her. I didn't say you could indulge in such fine wine. How dare you try and get drunk from her when I haven't gotten you high yet." Nyx's growl is low and teasing, but the rasp and how he makes eye contact with me over Cailian's shoulder tells me he isn't kidding.

Nyx runs the show and I'm ready to see how it will play out.

Without warning, Nyx splays his hand on Cailian's left hip, applying pressure to silently gesture our Elf back, and then Nyx slams forward. Cailian's cock slams into me with such force, I can't remember how to breathe. My dragon doesn't give me time to think before he's slamming into Cailian again.

"Fuck! Oh, gods. Oh, gods. Oh, gods," Cailian chants, moving his hips to match Nyx's tempo.

"That's it, look at you. What a good fucking boy taking my cock. Every damn day, I'm going to need to be inside you both."

I slap the bed, fisting the sheets to keep my body in place. The force from Nyx fucking Cailian is thrusting him into me by my elf's cock.

Skin slaps fast and hard, Nyx's grunts become louder, and Nyx's eyes roll to the back of his head for a moment before slithering a hand between my legs to play with my clit.

"Cailian! Cailian, more. Give me more."

"You'll take what our dragon gives me. Wait until you… gods—" He rolls his head over his shoulders, biting his bottom lip into his mouth as Nyx continues to fuck him brutally. "Wait until you feel him!" he practically shouts at me as Nyx changes his angle. "He is so big, so fucking thick, Rarity. You will feel like you will die with him inside you."

"Silly little firebonds—" Nyx slaps Cailian's ass before wrapping both hands around Cailian's neck from the back. "—You won't even be safe from me in death." He drives into Cailian's hole, Cailian's cock pummeling me, sending me higher.

Hands are lost between Cailian and I. I'm stroking his chest, digging my nails down the middle to leave thick raised lines on his silver skin. My fangs ache to be inside him, marking him, making our mating official as soon as he comes inside me.

Nyx's wings spread from his back, blocking the moonlight spilling through the frozen windows. They begin to flap, giving him more momentum to fuck into Cailian. The bed moves across the floor, the headboard cracking against the wall.

"Take my knot, Little Elf. Fill our firebond with your come. Mate her. Get her ready for me." Nyx's forked tongue hisses before licking

up Cailian's neck, tasting his sweat. "I want to feel your come drenching the scales on my cock. I want to know that while I'm inside her, you'll still be engulfing me with the orgasm we've made you have."

Cailian's hair becomes damp at the ends from sticking to his sweat-slicked body.

Nyx shoves Cailian down by pressing his hand in the middle of the elf's shoulders and Cailian robs my lips, but we can't kiss, not with the cacophony of the three of us.

"I am going to take his knot," he tells me by whispering it in my ear. "And then I'm going fill you up until you're leaking for him."

Nyx bends my leg, giving Cailian more room and somehow, he manages to sink in deeper.

"Come for me, My Snow. Come for me so I can come for you."

I need more. I'm so close, but there's something missing. Nyx must sense my distress because his hand slides up my thigh as he groans, sinking his knot into Cailian.

Cailian is pressed to the hilt, coming on broken breaths as he fills me just like he promised. A faint cold spreads through my body, his come searching for my womb, and knowing he's there, knowing I am mated sends me over the edge.

"Cailian!" I shout his name, sinking my fangs into his neck in a blur. His blood is sweeter in the highs of his orgasm as it heats his blood. I moan as another orgasm hits him. His mouth is there on my neck again, aching for my blood, and I cut myself with a flick of my wrist.

Feeling his mouth suck me in has another intense orgasm wash over me, my muscles spasming around his cock to pull him in further.

"Look at me breeding you. There will not be a morning and night where I will not rise for you. You will be wet with me, with Nyx, all day, every day. We want everyone to be able to smell us on you, in your body, in your womb."

"We'll have it my way. Both of you will be bred and carrying our children." Nyx glides his hands down Cailian's arm, forgetting the hate he feels to say such dreams. His eyes land on me, simmering with desire. "And I am nowhere near done with either of you."

I never wanted us to be done.

In this room, the three of us can be who we are fated to be. Outside these walls, Nyx is a stubborn dragon who turns hateful and Cailian is a proud elf who refuses to tell secrets. This mating will never go anywhere because of them and our passion, our promises of the future will be locked in this room, and only spoken for the walls to hear.

I'm not sure how long we stay locked like that, Cailian lazily gliding in and out of me while Nyx gives small thrusts with his knot. I can see Cailian's bulging stomach, filling with dragon come. Cailian falls forward, kissing me as if he is high. Our lips meet for minutes, our tongues stroking one another in sweet slides.

Something warm and slick begins to slither up my body, snaking across my skin effortlessly. Breaking the kiss, I glance down to see Nyx's tail, the scales smoother than the ones on his body. The tail reflects as if it's wet. The entire length fades from obsidian scales that hold a hue of different colors to pitch black on the very tip. It's beautiful. He probes my mouth with it, and I suck it between my lips.

The purr that leaves Nyx has Cailian smirking, giving me the idea to stroke the long tail like a thick cock. My tongue rolls over the tip, licking it like I would a bloodsicle.

A sweeping cold chills me from the inside for a moment and that's when I notice the blissed-out expression on Cailian's face before burying his face in my chest, lavishing kisses on my sternum.

I hear a soft *pop* followed by my beloveds groaning in unison.

"Cailian, you took my knot so well. Do you want to see what our firebond looks like all stretched out? Do you want to see me ruin her pretty little pussy?"

"More than anything," Cailian replies, white beginning to drip down his thighs.

Nyx tsks. "We can't have that."

Before I can ask any questions, I'm flipped to my stomach and Nyx is there, teasing his claws along my sensitive flesh.

"She's leaking you too. Oh no, what can we do about this to keep my firebonds full and bred?" he asks rhetorically before smacking my ass. "Cailian, be a good boy and plug yourself. I'll make sure you don't leak another drop from this pretty cunt. Are you sore, My Darling Jewel? Does this pussy ache from Cailian claiming you?"

I bury my face in the bed, embarrassment heating my cheeks.

"How do I plug myself, Dove?"

"Make one from ice. You've nearly killed me with a spear, surely you can conjure a plug."

I turn my head to see Cailian gasp and Nyx lift a brow before wrapping his tail around Cailian's neck.

"Do it."

Cailian holds out his hand, snow swirling with tints of blue. A plug appears, made of ice just like Nyx said.

"Turn around and let us watch you stop my come from spilling free. Go on." Nyx circles his claw in the air, gesturing Cailian to spin.

Cailian winks at me before turning on his knees, and then bending over. The round globes of his ass have a plump arch. Nyx and I share a heated look before staring at the beautiful silver peach again. Copious amounts of dragon come spill down his inner thigh causing Nyx to grumble in disappointment.

The dimples on Cailian's lower back make my lips tingle. I want to kiss them before licking down his crease and sucking his sack from the back.

He is temptation wrapped in a bow and my fangs ache to rip him apart like the gift he is presenting himself as.

Cailian rubs the plug against his inner thigh, gathering the wayward flame-kissed come. He scoops it and guides it between his cheeks, the ice plug vanishing. Come stops spilling a second later and Nyx exhales smoke with flame.

"You have no idea what I'm going to do to you later," Nyx warns. "Now, get me a rag and clean off my cock." The dragon slaps Cailian's ass and the elf chuckles, rushing to the bathroom. The faucet turns on for a few seconds before Cailian rushes back out to us. "Clean my cock. Get me ready for our firebond. I have to make sure I'm nice and clean because when I pull out of her, I want her to witness how filthy she makes me. Then, like the slut you are, you'll lick me clean, won't you?"

Cailian licks his lips, flittering his gaze to mine.

I take the opportunity while Nyx is distracted by Cailian's body, looking him up and down as if he didn't just have his fill. Cailian cleans Nyx's cock thoroughly, stroking the hard length. He pulls back the foreskin, cleaning around the glands.

I crawl across the bed, slow to not distract them, forming a plan in my mind.

Between the three of us, it's obvious that we all like to be dominant at times, but only me and Cailian submit. Nyx is dominant through and through, yet I can't get the thought of me blurring us across the room, slamming him on the floor, and fucking him without him ordering me around.

I'll blur us before he has time to realize what is happening. He won't be able to say a word.

I'm halfway off the bed before a crack in the air sounds and Nyx's tail is wrapped around my neck, sliding me back to where I was.

"I don't know where the fuck you think you're going." His knees push my legs apart as he forces his way between them. "Do you think I forgot about you? Do you think I forgot about sinking my cock into my firebond's pussy for the first time? Do you know…" he bends over me, pressing the blunt tip of his head against my entrance. "After I realized who you were to me, I fucked my fist at the thought of you and Cailian. I have such naughty firebonds occupying my mind like that."

"I wanted to take you by surprise and have my way with you," I admit, pushing onto my hands. Peeking over my shoulders, his nostrils flare.

Nyx drags his claw down my spine. "When I want you to have your way with me, you will," he states as if waiting for that moment isn't difficult.

"But I want you now," I pout, swaying my ass left and right. "Mate me, already."

He slams his cock inside me, pushing me across the bed. My head hangs from the edge, and my vision blurs from the tight hold Nyx's tail has on me.

"How many times do I have to repeat myself?" He slaps my ass, once, twice, three times, and I open my mouth on a raspy inhale of air I struggle to take. "I don't care about what you want. I think you've always gotten your way, haven't you?"

I moan into the sheets, fisting them in my hands. Oh gods, I feel like I'm about to be ripped open. Cailian wasn't lying, Nyx is huge, and I'm not sure if I can take him. My breath catches in my throat, my eyes

water from the pressure, and still, I press myself down, taking more of his cock.

Nyx drapes himself over me, his warm, fire-brewed blood hot under his scales. His body is like stepping into a shower, the water steaming hot and just releases all the stress you've carried in your muscles.

He moves again, in and out, his claws scratching over my hip.

"Cailian, are you watching? Do you like what you see, Little Elf?" Nyx lifts from my body, taking away his warmth, and I whimper, wanting him close again. "Look at your come slicked along my cock. Watch as I push it in and out of her cunt."

I turn my head to see Cailian groan, stroking his semi-hard cock back to life.

"I see it. I hear it too. So wet. She feels so good, doesn't she?" he groans, knee-walking closer to us. "How is it possible we are the only ones that have been inside her? How lucky are we?"

"So fucking lucky. Between the two of you, I'll never want to leave the bedroom."

I hear the sounds of kissing and I'm able to glance over my shoulder, tightening the hold the tail has on my neck which squeezes my windpipe. They kiss and they put on a show for me, their tongues licking one another before plunging into the other's mouth.

A strangled whine escapes me. The tail tight around me as I gasp, clawing at Nyx to let me go.

"You can never stay still, can you? You can't let me kiss my elf and have your pussy warm my cock? What if I wanted to be just like this for hours, Rarity? What if..." he trails off, tugging on his tail like a rein that has my back bending, forcing me onto my hands and knees. "What if I wanted to lie here all night inside a tight place I can barely fit into?" His tongue flicks across my back. "You know I can't resist something so tempting."

"Please," I beg him, sliding myself up and down on his massive cock. "Please, mate me. I am dying for you. I need the connection. I need your blood. Do you not want me? Would you prefer if I left?" Tears spring to my eyes at the thought, the mating taking a swift turn.

I would understand. I'm the outsider here. We don't know each other, not really, and now we have to mate and get to know one another later.

The tail unravels without hesitation, and I suck in a much-needed breath, my face flushing hot from all the blood that was trapped. Nyx flips me over onto my back, Cailian hovering over me too, both of them have concerned expressions on their face.

"Why would you ever think that?" Nyx's large palms engulf my body first, stroking me lightly, in reassurance, while his cock presses against my entrance once again.

"We are nothing without you, Rarity. Without you, we probably would have chosen death," he says. "Nothing is easy about this, but make no mistake, you are ours, and we choose you over dying." He bends down, brushing his lips against mine as Cailian's hands take their turn, skimming down my legs, my breasts, and my inner thigh.

So much sensation, so many hands, I can't tell who is who. Every touch is fading together, but there is always one distinct feeling.

One is hot and the other is cold.

Each one takes turns where the other just touched. My body bends and I gasp, the temperature changes all too much.

"I can't have you feeling like that. Not the Princess of our kingdoms."

"I'm not a princess," I deny, his cock filling me once more, effectively short-circuiting my lungs.

"I have to beg to differ. This body is royalty from where I am." Nyx cages my head in with his arms, his eyes an array of reds and oranges.

"And you will always be treated as such." His onyx lips brush over mine and I moan into his mouth, the space between us becoming slicker.

I wrap my arms around his neck, another purr building in his chest, and it vibrates through mine. I slide my fingers through his hair twisting the shaggy ends, and slide them down the river of his spine. His tail sits at the base, and I wrap my hand around it, stroking it how he likes.

Nyx grunts, his claws tearing into the pillow, sending feathers floating around us.

"Fuck!" Nyx has to turn his head to shout. "Cailian," he growls, more smoke drifting from his nostrils.

Cailian pops his head up, holding Nyx's tail in one hand, smirking. "How could I ignore such a delicious treat?" He sucks the tip of the dragon's tail into his mouth and visible tremors wreck Nyx's body.

"Between that and you're pretty pussy, I don't know how much longer I'll be able to last." He retracts, leaving just the tip of his cock in before driving it inside me. "I guess it doesn't matter. I'll just fuck you through my orgasm, filling you up so much, you beg me to stop."

Our skin slaps together, his heavy triple sack slaps against me with every thrust.

"Just wait until he knots you, My Snow. Just when you think you won't be able to take it, you'll explode with pleasure." Cailian lies down beside us, stroking Nyx's tail while watching us fuck. He teases the tip of the tail down his chest. The dragon slings it around Cailian's length, jerking it in tandem with every drive of his hips.

"Nyx!"

"That's it, Rarity. Cry for all the kingdoms to hear. Let them know the prince has found his firebond."

I want to ask what that is, I do, but I'm too overcome with ecstasy.

"Oh, Nyx. I'm close," I warn him, clawing at his shoulders as my orgasm approaches.

With a sharp, toothy smirk, he flips us until I'm on top. "Go ahead, My Darling Jewel, take what is yours."

I press my hands against his chest, using him as support while I experimentally rock my hips back and forth. I gasp from the fullness. My clit rubs against his pelvis, zipping sparks of electricity down my spine.

"Oh, gods, yes. So good," I moan, fucking him faster, harder, needing more. "Give me more. I want it all. Give it to me."

His eyes roll as he grips my waist and when he opens them again, I know it's the dragon I'm staring at. He rocks me against him faster, the tingling sensations that were far away are now boiling under my skin.

"Cailian, come here. Sit on my face while our firebond uses me," Nyx orders.

"Your face? But... the plug? You will not be able to breathe if I sit on you." Cailian blushes, yet that doesn't stop him from crawling over our dragon, straddling his face. "Like this?"

A rumble resonates in the bed. Thick black claws wrap around Cailian's platinum thighs, slamming him down onto Nyx's face.

"Like this," his deep voice is muffled by Cailian's ass. "I'm going to eat that ice cube right out of this hole, Little Elf. Be a good boy and kiss our vampire."

Cailian's arms shoot out, grabbing my arm as he shouts in shock as Nyx must take his first lick. "Oh my gods," Cailian mumbles. "I never thought— I never—" his words are cut off as he kisses me, the ends of our hair are like magnets.

The white strands twine together, adding more erotic emotions in my mind because his pleasure transfers through my hair, depositing

them right in my mind. His desire has made itself at home inside my skull, swirling around so I can never forget how deep his want for me goes.

I whimper, my orgasm giving me final warning. "Cailian. Nyx! I'm going to— I'm going to—"

"Do it. Let me taste your moans, My Snow." Cailian takes my tits in his palms, his thumbs rubbing over the hardened peaks of my nipples, adding more fuel to the fire.

My fingers trace over the tips of his ears so I can feel them wiggle and for some reason, that's the thing that sends me over the edge.

I clamp around Nyx's cock, crying inside Cailian's mouth like he wanted, a passionate groan replies as he drinks me down.

Nyx growls beneath us, feasting on Cailian, but then his knot begins to swell. The pressure is odd and the more he expands, the more uncomfortable I feel. I try to slide from his cock to save myself, but it's too late.

I can't.

"I can't take anymore, Nyx. I can't. I can't." I shake my head, gripping his legs so hard, I'm not paying attention to his scales frosting over from my touch.

And right as I think I'm going to be ripped in two, pleasure blinds me. I fall against Cailian, orgasming again. My body is sore and tired. I'm not sure I have the energy to continue, yet the scent of Cailian's blood is too much for me to deny. His neck is right here, the vein pulsing as he moans, riding Nyx's tongue.

I strike, taking without asking.

"Rarity!" he calls my name.

Cold splashes of his come hit my stomach. I cup his jaw, pressing him against my mouth so he can't move.

Cailian is lifted from Nyx's face.

"Where's the ice cube?" Cailian gasps.

"I drank it. It melted as soon as it hit my tongue." He places Cailian on the bed, then flips us.

I'm staring up at him, his knot still filling me, and he stares at my face so long, I'm about to ask what's wrong when he roars, biting my neck.

He's mated me.

His neck is covered in scales, but right where his jugular pumps his blood, the skin is beautifully bare. I sink my fangs in, marking him for all to see. He growls, something burning hot around his bite. His blood tastes spicy, hot, like too much cinnamon.

I love it.

It's soothing, pooling in my stomach like lava.

Cailian gasps causing us to break our bites. His forked tongue licks along my throat and I do the same to his, watching my mark become a faded scar. We look at Cailian, and his veins are back to normal, but there's an orange flame on his left arm, working its way up to his shoulder. It stops just at his collarbone, the fire swaying under his skin.

Nyx leans back as much as he can, careful not to hurt me when his brows shoot up as he watches his right arm become covered in snowflakes, glowing a light blue, meeting at the mark in the middle of his neck.

It's my turn to be shocked.

My left and right arms swirl in their marks. One side fire, the other ice, proving who I belong to. The flakes glitter and fall, swirling around my arm constantly as if it's a snowstorm. The fire does the same, flickering comfortably.

"Holy shit, there's no hiding that," Nyx says.

I flinch, turning my chin away. "I didn't know we were going to?"

Guilt flashes across his face, but he doesn't say anything.

This isn't normal. Mating marks aren't so big. They aren't tattoos, but these are more than that. They are alive. They move.

"We need to go to The Veiled Library. They might have a book on what this means. I have never heard of this happening. This seems monumental."

"That is a good idea," Nyx replies to Cailian.

"You know of the library?"

"All dimensions do. It's the only one in existence."

"So they will have answers?" I ask hopefully.

"Maybe. We might need to consult with your witch. My wizard is missing. We don't know where he is."

"I will do that tomorrow, but for now—" Cailian rests beside me, grazing his fingers down my cheek. "—Let us enjoy the rest of the night before reality crashes down on us."

Nyx nods, changing our positions so we are on our sides to get more comfortable. His knot tugs and my entire body trembles, awakening the quieting spasms of my orgasm. I clench around him as a small, yet intense orgasm unravels me one more time, conjuring more come from my virile dragon.

I should feel at ease now that I'm mated, but all of our feelings are bound together now. They crash through me, solidifying the doubt I've been carrying.

Nyx is worried.

Cailian is afraid.

And I'm confused.

Is mating this hard for everyone? I'm wondering if death would have been easier than the journey the three of us are about to go on since this dragon and elf won't speak to one another.

My eyes drift shut but a faint smile threatens me when I feel Nyx's hand on my waist, then Cailian's locking with his.

No matter the pain Nyx feels, the bond wins.

I can only hope that's enough.

Chapter Twelve

CAILIAN

It is the middle of the night when distance grows in my heart. The bed dips from Nyx's weight, the subtle groan of the mattress struggling to support his weight. Mentally I note, that I will have to get a bigger bed for all of us to sleep comfortably. Peeking over the delicate curve of Rarity's shoulder, Nyx's back comes to view. His wings stretch, the damaged one struggling to move at all. The holes in the leather hide seem bigger than they were the other day.

"I feel your eyes on me," he whispers, the depths of his timbre almost not allowing me to hear him. His tongue is hoarse and heavy, breaking like a piece of ice hitting the ground.

I stay quiet, not wanting to give myself away. I can act like I am still asleep, dreaming of our mating instead of facing the impending argument that is no doubt going to happen between me and Nyx. The fated love for us is doomed, a match made to be stricken and lit just to watch two hearts burn.

"I know you are awake, Cailian," he says again, his frustrated voice cutting through the silence. "I feel your emotions coursing throu-

gh me. Although unwelcome—" he turns his head just enough where I can appreciate the sculpted jawline "—Your awareness of me feels good."

"Although unwelcome," I remind him, kissing Rarity's forehead.

I have become a senseless, lovestruck fool for her. I get to fall in love with countless versions of her soul for all eternity and I am curious how many versions of her I will meet. She will never be the same as she is right now, curious and afraid, a little wide-eyed when it comes to the world she does not know. Soon, she will be well-taught and experienced, taking the world for herself. Rarity is strong, but she has not unlocked the true power within herself.

I cannot wait to witness that. I am lucky to know I will be at her side for all her adventures. Nyx on the other hand, counting on him to stay is slim. All we can do is hope he will.

"Unwelcome indeed."

Silence falls again, tension as tight as a rope that is about to snap. Nyx stays seated, his head hanging, his feelings a confusing mess of webs that are tangled and knotted. I try to decipher one thought he is transmitting, yet as his arm pulses with winter across his tattoo, his mind is a blizzard all on its own. I am unable to understand what he is feeling at all.

Kissing Rarity one more time on her forehead, I slowly move from under her arm. The bed barely moves from how quick and light I am on my feet. Soon I am standing without waking her up. Studying my sweet mate, I wonder if anything can wake her up. She takes the opportunity for free space and sprawls out on the bed, taking my side. Rarity snags my pillow and pulls it to her chest. Her cheek is smashed against it causing her lips to squish together and drool begins to spill from her lower lip.

A graceful sleeper she is not.

"I don't want to turn into pizza," she mumbles, clutching the blanket to her chest as she gives us a bit of what she is dreaming about. "Dip me in blood? Blood dip... sounds... good." She trails off into a whisper before a light snore puffs from her.

I am at the foot of the bed, nearly next to Nyx, and place my hand on the footboard. "I wonder what blood dip is made of. Perhaps—" I take a step closer to him, wanting nothing more than to reach out and touch him.

Yet his hesitancy strums the cords of our bond, so I do not dare take another step.

"—Perhaps we can make her this dip she craves with our blood." I keep my voice low, not wanting to disrupt her. She needs her rest. Her entire life has changed. She is mated to two males who will love her, however only one from the pair will get the abundance of love from everyone while the other lives with half.

"Sure. Whatever My Darling Jewel wants, she will get," Nyx replies, never bringing his eyes to mine.

"Just her?" I swallow, rubbing my palm across the edge of the footboard.

The moonlight illuminates the edges of his defined features while shadows play in the crevices allowing me to see how his jaw tenses.

"Do not ask me that." He curls his fists on his thighs, pushing against them as he stands.

His wings tuck behind him, his tail swaying back and forth as he walks to the balcony.

Like the fool I am, I follow him, my secret on the tip of my tongue daring to spill free so I can have his acceptance, his love. The doors open automatically, sensing his royalty, and he steps outside to the cool Elementalu night. He leans against the railing, his long tail swishing back and forth as if it is flicking to the speed of his thoughts.

"I notice you do not sizzle anymore," I blurt out of nowhere, trying to make conversation. "When you walk on the ice."

"Oh," he says dubiously, staring at the ground. "I didn't."

I try not to let those words get to me. He can act careless all he wants. The bond does not lie. I feel him inside me, a constant burn in an array of snow.

"We might be able to use our powers on one another now." I stroll to him, mimicking his stance, and do not pretend to be interested in the beauty of the stars when I have the universe right beside me.

He hums, clasping his hands together while looking up at the sky. "I don't want to use my flame on you, regardless of how I feel, I can't have what I did to you happen again."

I press my hand against his arm and frost takes over the tattooed flame that appeared after we all mated, freezing it mid sway.

"I guess that answers that," I state simply, pulling my hand away reluctantly to give him his space.

"At least I know I can't hurt you."

"I did not realize you cared if you hurt me."

"I shouldn't care." He turns to me, leaning his elbow against the railing, a roar above followed by a flash of light tells us a dragon just flew over. "I am doing my best to accept this situation. I can't just move on from what you did. I don't care if it was so long ago. You took something from me."

"I never knew it would be the piece you would need in order to love me." A sadness twists its way around every word I speak, a poisonous vine killing any hope I have for us ever so slowly. "I did not know Fate would give me you. I did not know that all these years, you were my mate. It makes sense, I suppose."

"How so?" he asks.

"I loved your father. He was my best friend. He was my everything. I looked forward to seeing him every day. Some days, the only good that came from them was if I saw his face."

A growl cutting through the tension has my skin arise in small dots. The hair on the back of my neck stands on its ends, and the familiar slither travels up my spine as his tail wraps around my neck. Nyx's chest is against my back.

The heat from his body nearly makes me melt. His hands slide down my arms, pinning me against the railing as his fingers interlace with mine. The incense of smoke has me inhaling the harsh brimstone. I enjoy it. I want it to fill my lungs, turn them black, and let it be the death of me if he chooses.

"Were you lovers?" he asks, his jealousy potent in the breath he exhales.

"What if we were?" I taunt him, wanting more of his possessive nature, wanting more of his need for me, no matter how fleeting it is.

He yanks my neck to the side with the hold he has on me. "Then if he were alive, I would have to debate if I would need to kill him myself."

A shiver works its way through my body. "No, we were not lovers. We were best friends. I was drawn to him and now I know why."

"Because of me," he explains.

I nod the best I can with the grip he has on me.

He leans in closer, snarling his fangs at me. "Do not entice jealousy from me, Little Elf. It will not end well for you."

"Why would you be jealous? You would have to care. And you do not, remember?"

"I care more than I should. More than I want to. Right now, I'm blaming it on the bond. If I kill you like I've dreamed of doing a thousand times, it will kill me and Rarity. I won't do that to her."

"If it were not for her, would you try to kill me again?"

His nose travels up my neck, a warm sigh ghosting over my cheek. "I have my tail wrapped around your neck. I could snap it. All my pain and suffering are in my grasp. To end it all, one quick twist, and you would be gone." His lips burden the side of my mouth, teasing my lips for a kiss. "But then I feel your pulse beating against my tail, reminding me that the heart inside you was meant to be mine, destined, and no matter how much I hate you, I can't kill what fate made for me. It also means hating you is too exhausting, hating you is killing me, wanting you is hurting me, yet needing you is the only thing that makes sense to me."

My eyes roll to the back of my head as his hands rub down my body, cupping my cock.

"Yet the thought of loving you makes me sick." He shoves me away, unwrapping his tail from around my neck, and I hear the whoosh of his wings spreading.

The bond confirms his feelings. I can feel the waves of unease. Instead of going to him like I want, I spin around and lean against the rail.

He presses his hands against his eyes. "This isn't what I wanted. I never wanted you." When he drops his hand, his watery eyes cut through the dark to meet mine. "Now I've had you. I've had Rarity. Eventually, we will be a family. She will get pregnant, you will get pregnant, and I have to be here for that. I can't... I can't deny myself."

"I won't get pregnant. I can make sure of that. We have elven herbs my witch can brew—"

His snarl cuts me off and his tail whips out, cracking through the air as it wraps around my waist, yanking me across the balcony to where he is standing. The breath leaves my lungs in a whoosh when we collide,

and I am left staring into his fiery eyes. Twin flames dance in his pupils, towers of smoke breeze from his nostrils, and fire licks his lips.

"You. Will. Not. Dare."

"If it is easier for you to be with us for Rarity, then that is what I will do. I know dragons can change the anatomy of their male partners, but—"

He snarls, his wings reaching for the stars. "Your womb is mine, Little Elf. You'll hold every fucking drop of my come. If I ever find out you altered your body taking birth control, I will burn this ice castle to the ground, chain you to my bed, and find a potion that will undo the damage. I will fuck you and Rarity, taking my turns in your slutty holes until I can scent my child inside the both of you. You will not deny me what Fate wants."

"I do not need to deny you when I am giving you all of me."

"Hmm." He tilts his head and backs away. "Not all."

"Kiss him."

We turn our heads to see Rarity standing naked in the doorway, rubbing her eyes of sleep.

"What was that, Darling Jewel?" Nyx asks.

"Kiss him," she repeats herself, stepping out onto the balcony for all to see.

My own growl rumbles in my chest. Nyx leaps into the air, spreads his wings, and lands in front of her, blocking anyone from seeing her body.

"What the hell do you think you're doing, Rarity?" he hisses. "My dragons patrolling the skies could see you."

"They can see the two of you," she points out. "What's the difference?"

"The difference is none of them want to fuck us, but one look at you and they will want to overthrow the kingdom."

Rarity looks me up and down, her eyes landing on my cock, and it begins to stir from having her attention on me.

"I don't know about that. I think you underestimate just how beautiful you two are." She lifts her hands, trailing her fingers down both of our chests. "Your lust for one another woke me up and then I watched you both do your little dance. Denying, accepting, denying—" she grips our cocks at the same time and we both hiss, rocking onto our tiptoes. "So, I want to make this very simple, and every second you wait, I'm going to make your cocks so cold, you're going to beg me for the warmth of my body." She sucks Nyx's dark nipple into her mouth, and he tilts his head back, the tendons protruding from his thick muscle, and my mouth waters to taste the scales shining with sweat.

He cups the back of her head, his claws clicking together as he combs them through her hair. She kisses across his chest to mine, licking her tongue over the gray nipple. Rarity nibbles the hard bead and I moan into the night, alerting all the dragons in the sky and elves on the grounds to what is happening.

A strong inhale has me turning my head to see Nyx bring my hair to his nose.

"You smell like winter," he whispers, the flames in his eyes darkening to the color of soot.

"He smells good, doesn't he?" Rarity says. "He is so beautiful. His skin is silver. Look how it gleams under the light."

"Like treasure," Nyx mumbles, a singular claw scratching down my back.

"Don't dragons love treasure?" Rarity probs, pinching my nipple between her fingers.

"Love treasure. Treasure..." Nyx almost sounds like he's in a trance, staring at me in a whole new light.

"Kiss him, please," Rarity practically begs.

Nyx pulls me to him, crashing his lips against mine. His forked tongue wrapping me in a seductive embrace. Sparks fly into my mouth, the taste of flames warming my throat. I moan, clutching his biceps as he kisses me within an inch of my life.

I hear a yelp from Rarity which has me break the kiss to see what is going on.

"Nyx!" she cries his name, lying on the ground with her legs spread.

His tail slips in and out of her pussy, her legs shaking. "You like to see us kiss, Darling Jewel?"

She nods quickly, her hair falling down her shoulders and covering her breasts.

"Like this?" I whisper, turning his head with my palm against his jaw.

I suck his bottom lip into my mouth, igniting a growl from our dragon. He is so damn big. I do not often see anyone taller than me, but he makes me feel small and fragile. His fingers fully wrap around my cock, stroking me, once again making me feel so small.

"Such a pretty cock, Treasure."

I tilt my head back and close my eyes.

"Look at me touch you. Please our firebond."

Rarity moans as she gets tail fucked. "He's talking to you, Cailian."

I open my eyes in shock, not expecting to have a pet name like Rarity does. I figured "Little Elf" was what he would always call me. I have grown fond of it.

Opening my eyes, breath catches in my throat when I glance down. His claw slips in and out of my slit. He brings the long claw to his mouth and licks my precome from the sharp nail.

"Delicious. Look at Rarity." He tilts my chin down to see her on the floor, grabbing her breasts, and rocking her hips against his tail. "I

think she needs us more. What do you think? I think her greedy pussy can't get enough of us. She's begging for our cocks, Cailian."

Rarity cries out, slapping one hand on the floor as his tail pulls out, then glides up to her clit. Nyx rubs it in a circle causing her thighs to tremble, building yet another orgasm within her.

"So how about you lie on your back and—"

"No!" Rarity cries out, interrupting Nyx. "I want you on your back. I want him on top of you."

Nyx kisses my temple before answering her. "Having you on top of me is no hardship, Treasure. Let's give her what she wants." Nyx wraps his tail around Rarity's waist, tugging her closer to us as he lies down in the middle of the balcony.

I am stunned to stillness when I see him there, nearly taking up the entire space with the enormity of his form. His cock is erect. The thick shaft somehow becomes bigger, the veins in his cock pumping it so full, the knot at the base slightly swells.

He is already close to losing control.

"You want to see him ride my cock, Rarity?" Nyx asks her, stroking himself.

His wings spread out across the ground so he can be more comfortable. The moonlight spills onto his onyx body, reflecting the colors in his scales, and at that moment, I do not know where to look. Every part of him is beautiful, a piece of art that deserves to be appreciated.

"Yes. I want to see him ride you. I love seeing the two of you together."

"You better do as she says or I'll blister your ass, Treasure. Get down here and ride me."

I do as he says, straddling his lap. Rarity sits beside us, legs spread, her fingers teasing her pussy.

I reach behind me, grabbing his cock to hold it steady while I lower myself onto him. My breath catches in my throat, pain blooming as I stretch to accommodate him. This time it is easier. My hole is still wet and stretched from before.

Thunder rolls from his throat, followed by the eerie fog of smoke.

"Still ready for me." His hands run down my body until they settle on my hips. "Yet still so fucking tight for me." He sounds pained, speaking through the tight grip I have on him. "I can still feel my come inside you," he snarls, pressing me down the rest of his length.

"Dove!" I call out into the night, my voice echoing into the distance of the mountains.

"Look at you," he rumbles in approval, his hands touching every part of my chest in appreciation. "What do you think, Rarity?"

"I think I want him."

"That's too bad. You will need to wait your turn. You wanted this so you're going to sit back and watch like a good girl, aren't you?" His tail slithers up her leg, binding her wrists together. "And don't touch yourself. I want you aching and drenched by the time you're sliding onto Cailian's cock."

Rarity whimpers, her fangs biting into her lip until it bleeds. Red tints her skin, staining it in long crimson trails down her neck.

"Move, Little Elf," he orders me again. "Give our firebond a show. Ride my cock."

I rock forward, the broad crown brushing against that spot inside me that makes stars blind me. My cock slides along his abdomen, the scales providing a smooth surface. The unique head of my cock is exposed as the extra skin is pushed back, and Nyx traces the glands with the tip of his claw.

"That feels so good," I tell him, pushing back, then forward, then back.

"You like this?" he continues, stroking a spot under the head that has my knees giving out.

I lie down on top of him, my hair falling as a curtain to lock us in each other's space. Our eyes meet and then his drops to my lips. He leans up, kissing me so hard, so brutally, a fever replaces the cold that lives within my bones.

Something soft touches my lower back and it has me lifting from his chest. Rarity is behind me, watching Nyx's cock slide in and out.

"He really is stretching you so wide, Cailian. It looks like he is going to split you open." Her fingers press against my hole, making me groan from the slight pressure. "He is such a big dragon. He has so much come to give us, My Love. I want to see it drip from you."

"You two are going to be the death of me. I have no doubts I will vanish into a snowstorm if you keep it up."

"You aren't allowed to go anywhere." He clutches my hips and uses his strength to rock me faster. "You are only allowed here."

"On your cock?" I smirk, sinking into Rarity's touch as she places a kiss on the back of my neck.

He punches his hips up, pain followed by pleasure overcoming me. "Your throne, Treasure." His cock spears in and out of me. Faster and faster he moves, his heavy sack filled with the come I crave slaps against my ass. "This ass deserves to sit right here until my dying day." His claws bite into the sensitive flesh of my ass, gripping the thick meat in his palms as he uses me.

My cock slaps against his stomach, clear liquid constantly dripping from me.

"I can't stop watching. Oh gods, please, Nyx. Please, I need to touch myself. I can't take anymore." Rarity tries to pull free of his tail, but his hold on her is too strong.

He tugs her to our sides from where she was watching us from the back. "Let me see," he says, jutting his chin out. "Spread your legs and let me see how wet your pussy is. Prove to me just how needy you are."

Rarity tries to spread her legs and Nyx tsks. "Stand over me. It's the only way I'll really be able to tell. Bring that cunt as close to my face as possible. I want to feel you drip onto my lips before I feast."

Our mate wastes no time climbing over him, running her hands through his inky hair.

"Mmmm," he growls. "You weren't lying. You are so sweet. Give me a taste. Sit on my face, My Darling Jewel. Suffocate me. Ride my tongue."

She lowers herself without hesitation and by the sound of her cries, he has already plunged into her pussy. I have a wonderful view of her backside as she rides his tongue. Her ass shakes with every motion, tempting me to claim it.

I want to.

I want to possess all her holes.

"One of these days, Rarity, your ass will be mine." I slap it, watching the skin heat to a light purple.

"Oh, she likes that, Treasure. Do it again. She gets so wet."

I do as he says, wanting to listen to my dragon without hesitation. The more I show him how I am, who I am, the more he will wonder if I am truly the man who would intentionally hurt him. He will see in time that I am not the villain he has made me out to be.

Loud slaps sound over and over. Rarity's screams carry through the forests, no doubt allowing the Woodland Elves to hear.

A violet handprint arises on the right cheek, showing my claim.

Her breathing speeds up, and she moves against him, grinding harder onto his face, her sounds a symphony. Her volume increases,

threatening climax when Nyx pushes her from his face, and down his body.

"Give yourself to Cailian. Let him fuck you as he fucks me."

"Oh fuck, I will not last, Dove."

"This isn't about lasting. It's about taking. Take her like I am taking you, Treasure."

Rarity lies down on Nyx, arches her back, and scoots down until her entrance is aligned with my cock. I rock my hips forward, sinking into her effortlessly.

"Fuck, your pussy feels so good. How long do you think it will be before she goes into heat, Nyx? I cannot wait until she needs us like that. So desperate."

"She'll be our little whore just like you'll be ours when your heat strikes."

I want to tell him that the chances of me becoming pregnant are low. Even with the power dragon's hold to change anatomy, males becoming pregnant is very rare, and with my age, it is not likely, but Nyx will not listen to me. He will see that Rarity will be the one to carry our children and that is something I am more than okay with.

"I do not want to wait. I want her to burst into flames right now with her need. I want her to be hot to the touch, sweating, coming over and over again on our cocks. I want it now." I yank her head back by her hair, ramming my cock into her as hard as I can before sliding back down on his cock.

"So impatient, Little Elf. You can wait. Fate will give us what we need when we need it most."

"I need it now," I snarl, scratching my nails down her back, ice forming along the lines.

"You will behave, or I'll rip her from your cock and leave you dreaming of filling her up."

I keep my mouth shut, drilling said impatience into Rarity.

"You're going to make me come," Nyx warns, his tail slithering up my body to wrap around my neck. "Take my fucking knot. Take it. Fuck, oh, fuck!" he roars, his knot pushing into me just as he spills heat inside me.

"Cailian, I'm— Yes— Yes— Yes!" Rarity clenches around me, coming so hard, I feel her muscles massage my shaft, beckoning for my come.

My vision darkens as I shout, pushing into her in short strokes as every wave of frost ices her. I can hardly move because of his knot, but the small tugs at my rim, while I fill the deepest parts of Rarity, have my orgasm lasting longer than ever before.

Rarity collapses and I follow, pressing my cheek against her back while trying to find my breath.

"I never want to be anywhere else." I can hear the faint smile as Rarity speaks.

"Me either, My Snow." I kiss the middle of her back, stroking her sides to show her affection. I know she thinks she is on the outside, but she is the only one keeping the three of us together. Without her, I have no doubt Nyx and I would be strangers for most days.

Nyx remains quiet, and I know why. He is struggling to accept that he would rather be with us too— me— specifically. He will always see Rarity, but admitting he likes the company of his father's killer is too much for him.

My eyes become heavy, and I fall asleep, only when I wake, it is to a blood-curling scream.

Chapter Thirteen

DOVENYX

Rarity's scream awakens my dragon, calling the beast forward from a calm slumber when I feel her agony in the bond. The smell of burning flesh fills my nose. Looking down, I see her crying, screaming at the top of her lungs as her skin blackens like charred wood.

"Rarity! It is okay. It will be okay." Cailian runs into the bedroom adjacent to the balcony, snagging the blanket from the bed.

I cover my firebond with my good wing, hunkering down low to give her as much shade as possible from the sun. Swinging my head down, I press my cheek against hers, the wet tears streaming down her face are warm against my skin. Her body trembles, her teeth clinking together from the agony of the burns on her body.

My own tears threaten. Worry and fear build in my chest, wondering what will happen to her. Will she die? Gods, she can't die. I just found her. She gives me so much happiness in the murky waters of my soul.

Cailian is back, gently covering her body with the blanket, and even the pressure from the blanket against her marred flesh makes her scream in agony again.

"I know. I know, My Snow. I know it hurts. We are going to take care of you. Okay? You will be okay. I will make sure of it. I am so sorry. I am so fucking sorry. I cannot believe I forgot about the sun. I am a bad mate. It will not happen again." He rambles his guilt, tucking his arms under her back to lift her.

"Cailian!" she shouts his name, another wave of tears spilling down her cheeks. "I can't. I can't. Please," she sobs, pressing her head against his chest. "Don't move. Please," she weeps, her pain is much, so heavy and sharp, it nearly makes my dragon's knees weak.

"We have to get you inside. Dovenyx cannot stay in his form all day. The sun will shift, My Snow."

And I only have one wing that will help shade her.

"Dovenyx," she whispers, a hint of a smile on her dried, cracked lips. "Such a pretty name. Why don't we call him that, Cailian?" she asks him, her eyes barely open, and half-dead from the pain.

Enough talking. Why isn't she inside yet?

I huff with impatience at Cailian, a bit of sparks tickling my lips.

Cailian understands. He's brilliant catching on to what I am trying to portray. He somehow sees past my grumpy, moody behavior for who I really am.

And that bothers me. He bothers me.

I am falling hard for my firebonds, and I don't think the hate inside me is strong enough to fight it. Not that I could ever fight my love for Rarity. Our bond was born out of realization, not violent history. My love for her is natural, like how the leaves rustle in the breeze. It just happens. An inevitable force that will always make itself known.

He smiles at me, a bit forced, but I can tell he is trying to remain positive and slides his gaze to Rarity.

"You heard our dragon. He does not want you out here anymore, and I cannot blame him."

She whimpers again, shivering from her flesh turning to ash. "Please, don't move. Please. It hurts so much. It hurts. Nyx, please, tell him not to." Rarity manages to turn her head, the skin around her neck cracking from how dry it is. Blood drips from the open wounds. I huff again, a small growl rumbling in my chest because I wish I could give her what she wants.

He has to move.

I shake my head, swinging my head down to press my cheek against hers. The pain strumming the bond has my dragon in a panic.

"I am sorry, My Snow. We have to move you inside. Being out here is too dangerous." Cailian takes one small step, and she buries her face in his chest, screaming so loud, that the birds in the trees caw and fly away.

I want to freeze the sun for hurting my Darling Jewel. Perhaps Cailian can do that. If I fly high enough, if he can take the blazing heat, maybe it can be done.

A ridiculous thought, I know, but I want revenge on the sun for hurting my firebond.

I always want revenge for those that I care for.

Cailian continues to walk, gritting his teeth as her shouts of agony continue. The delicate curve of his jaw tightens as he bites down. He is too beautiful for the ugliness that lives inside me.

He lies her on the bed, bending down to ease her gently onto the soft mattress. I shift into my human form, tucking my wings to enter the bedroom. I close the door and shut the curtains, protecting the vampire that has wiggled her way into my heart.

Cailian takes the blanket from her body, her mouth parting as another torturous shout makes my ears ring.

"I am so sorry," he repeats, the guilt in his tone nearly has me pulling him against my chest to tell him it isn't his fault.

This was an accident. The sun only rises twice a week in Elementalu. We did not do this on purpose. We would never harm her in that way.

He tosses the blanket to the floor— covered in burnt skin and blood. Rarity's flawless skin is unrecognizable. Only her eyes and hair are the same as they were last night as I took her body as mine.

My eyes follow Cailian's movements. His long, lithe body elegant even in panic. We're all still naked and even with the urgency of Rarity's wounds, this fucking bond still wants me to gravitate toward him.

Unlocking my feet from the ground and ignoring the need, I kneel next to the bed by Rarity, not wanting to jostle the mattress with my weight. "What do we do?" I ask her as her body shivers.

Her eyes roll to the back of her head, her breaths broken as she gasps, and then her entire body stills.

I hear nothing.

"Rarity!" I yell, placing my hands on either side of her head. "Rarity? My Darling Jewel, answer me." The desperation leaks into my words. I press my ear against her chest, breathing a sigh of relief when I hear her heartbeat.

"She's breathing," I whisper, not wanting to leave this spot because I have the reassurance of her song against my ear. "She must have passed out from the pain."

"I know. We would feel it in our bond," he explains, coming out of the other room in a simple, blue robe that ties around his waist. "I am getting my witch. If you wish not to be seen, I suggest you leave. I can take care of Rarity."

"The hell I will," I snap, blowing black smoke from my nose in fury. "I am staying right here. Plus, everyone knows I have been here. It is no secret any longer. The entire kingdom heard you come on my cock while I roared your name. Let's not pretend that didn't happen."

"It is not me who is pretending." He narrows his eyes at me before tightening the belt around his robe. "I am going to get Raltena, my witch. She will know what to do and perhaps we can protect the castles with a spell to protect Rarity. This is my fault. I forgot that her capability in the sunlight was taken from her when her brother, the coven master, was bitten by a werewolf, fell into a coma, and was awakened by his beloved. She mentioned it briefly. I cannot believe I forgot such an important thing. We should not have fallen asleep outside. I should have known better."

I realize he knows her much better than I do, and I want that to change. I want to be around her more, even if it means being around him. The more I try to push him away, the closer to him I want to be. As I get to know him, I am questioning whether he truly killed my father in cold blood. My instincts are telling me something more is at play here and he won't tell me the truth.

I hurry to him, grabbing him by the wrist before he leaves to fetch the witch. "I don't understand how her ability to walk in the sun was taken from her. I will need to ask her when she is healed, but this isn't your fault. The sun rises twice a week, and it isn't consistent. We never know when it will rise, time or day. You can't blame yourself for something you couldn't predict, Treasure."

His breath catches when I call him that. He does look like treasure, all silver and shiny, and I love things that shine.

"Still, I should have been more thoughtful. This would not have happened if I had been thinking about something other than—"

"—Fucking?" I growl low in my throat. "Nothing could have stopped that from happening. It is only going to get worse. That need you feel inside, the one wanting you to fall to your knees and suck my cock like the good boy you are, even if our firebond is writhing in pain. It is hard to ignore, isn't it?"

He clears his throat, his eyes casting to Rarity. "I am going to get Raltena. I will be back. Keep her company."

I nod, lifting his hand to my mouth, I kiss his knuckles. I miss the orange in his veins. They are back to being a dark blue, but the orange signified how much he needed our mating. "I will be here by our firebond. Don't worry."

He nods before leaving, the long trail of his robe is extravagant yet classy just like Cailian. He is a pampered prince. He doesn't deny himself luxuries. Perhaps, I need to start treating him as such.

I rip my attention from the door and in five long strides, I eat the distance between Rarity and me. I kneel next to her again, keeping my weight off the bed so I don't harm her. Her hair is untouched and perfect still, unbothered by the sun. The long white strands hold the color of the moon and stars, a brilliant glow that only the Ice Elven holds.

My brows pinch together while I study her naked body. Only hours ago, it was perfect, her body rocking back and forth while she took our cocks. I know vampires heal, so why isn't she?

"Rarity," I whisper her name, tucking her hair behind her ear. "Why aren't you healing? What do you need from me? I will do it. I will give it to you. I don't know what to do," I choke, swallowing the lump in my throat when another wave of her pain shoots through me. "Fuck." I press my hand over my chest as my fire builds. My dragon wants to purge. There's too much building inside me, from her pain, to my conflicting emotions, I have needed to breathe more fire than usual.

"Rarity, please. I am not the kind of man to beg or plead. I am not the kind of man who likes to look desperate. I don't like to look weak, but I am here right beside you, My Darling Jewel, and I am begging you to open your eyes and tell me what I need to do to make your pain go away. I can usually kill those who hurt you, but this time I can't. So tell me." A tear breaks free, and I lift my hand to touch my cheek, the liquid foreign to me, but as another drops, then another, I realize I am also in pain.

I might lose my firebond before I ever get to truly know her.

"Please," I ask her again, pressing my forehead against the mattress.

The rush of conversation coming from the hallway has me lifting my head. My wings spread in defense and I step in front of the bed, blocking Rarity from whoever is coming. Cailian rushes in first which has me tucking my wings in place.

Then an older woman steps from behind him, wide eyes creasing her temples.

I snarl, huffing fire because I don't know her.

"Relax dragon. I am not here to hurt you or your mate. I am here to help. Though from what I sense," her eyes slide from me to Cailian, "It isn't only her I can help."

"She is first. Always." Cailian strolls with his spine straight and head high. As he walks, he looks like he is floating, so quick and graceful.

"Of course." The witch eyes me again, humming as she heads to her patient. She presses her hand on Rarity's head, closing her eyes in deep thought. The necklaces around her neck are large gems, varying in size and shape, but they all begin to glow, clinking together as magic swirls around the room. "There is nothing I can do for her personally," she says in disappointment.

I charge forward. "What the hell do you mean there is nothing you can do? You better fucking figure it out."

"I don't like to be spoken to like that, *dragon*." She turns to Cailian, ignoring me and putting me out of her sight. "I can't do anything because only you and your mate can. She needs your blood. That is how she will heal. After that, she'll be fine, but she will need a lot of blood. If you weren't her mates, I would be worried, but your bodies replenish whatever she takes immediately. For her. I will see if I can find a protective shield for the kingdom to protect our Princess from the harshness of the sun."

"What about the ability to walk in the sun again?" I question with excitement. "Her entire family can be healed. They won't be trapped in the dark anymore." It is the one good thing I can do for her.

"I am afraid, not even I have that kind of power," she says in disappointment. "There is only one spell. It has only been written once. I do not know where it is. The best I can do is form a protective barrier."

"Do that, please. At once. Everything or anyone else can wait."

"Of course, Prince Cailian. I will let you know when the shield is active." She takes a step toward the door and pauses. "I will warn you, she is going to be violent and thirsty when she wakes. She will use you and you will have to take it. Her true nature will control her. Reasoning with Rarity will not be possible, not until her vampire is sated. Do you understand?"

I nod, knowing I can handle anything my little vampire throws at me.

"Thank you, Raltena," Cailian says, shutting the door behind her.

For good measure, he slides the lock into the place, then unties his robe. The velvet blue fabric falls from his body, pooling at his feet, and I feast on the view. He walks by me and against my better judgement, my arm wraps around his waist to stop him.

"Your witch said she would be violent. I should go first. I— I don't want you to get hurt."

His eyes are captivating, a soul-stealing shade of blue, and the silver swirls like molten treasure, shining brighter than any gold I have ever come across.

"Careful, Dovenyx. I will think you care if you speak like that to me."

I release my hold on him, kneeling on the bed. "What did I say about calling me that?"

"Apologies. Nyx," he corrects himself.

I bite into my wrist, shifting my teeth into the sharp points of my dragon's fangs. Blood pools, dripping onto the bed. Holding one hand under my wrist to capture the liquid, I rush before the wound can close. I force her mouth apart, her fangs sharpening when she senses blood, and I press my wrist between her lips.

"I don't like that name either."

"Surely, you don't like it when I call you, Dove? Last I remembered, you didn't like that either."

I grunt. "I don't know what I like when it comes to you."

"I will keep that in mind."

We wait a few seconds, the blood filling her mouth until it spills from the corner. "I don't think it's working, Cailian. Maybe my blood isn't strong enough? She has to be okay, Cailian. She has to be," I whisper. "Please, My Darling Jewel. Drink me. Heal. Let us take away your pain." She doesn't move. Her eyes don't open. Her body remains eerily still, reminding me of the air when danger is near— quiet and fierce. If I hadn't heard her heartbeat, I would think she was dead.

"Look, Dove. Her body. She's healing." Cailian grins, pointing to her legs where the skin is morphing slowly from being a step away from slipping from her bones to stitching itself together. "It is working. It is working!" he shouts in happiness, small pebbles of ice rolling down his cheeks as he cries in relief.

I also get emotional, my eyes burning with the familiar fire of wanting to cry with happiness knowing she will be okay. "So when she is injured, blood. Near death, blood. That seems to always be the answer. That is good to know. I'll need to study up on vampire knowledge so I know everything that can harm her and save her."

"Or you can let her tell you herself when she wakes up. I am sure she will be glad to answer any questions."

He bends down to pick up his robe, the curve of his back awakening my want for him, and I growl in warning. "What the hell do you think you're doing?"

He turns his head to me, brows pinched in confusion, and his hair falls into his face like long icicles. "I am getting dressed. As Rarity is okay now, I am no longer needed."

I puff out a breath of smoke. "I didn't say you could get dressed, Treasure. You're to remain naked for me while I heal our firebond."

"What if I do not wish to be naked in front of you, Nyx?"

I close my eyes in frustration, chuffing at the audacity of the question. "Do not fool yourself, Little Elf. You and I both know being naked for me is one of your favorite—" My sentence is cut off when Rarity bites down on my wrist. Her fangs sink to the bone. "Fuck!" I roar out, my dragon's baritone slipping through. "Rarity. That hurts. Can you please let—" She cuts me off again, holding my wrist to her mouth, snarling with red eyes, and the more I try to pull away, the more pressure she puts on my arm.

And it isn't regular pressure. She's using her vampire strength and if she presses any harder, she might snap my arm.

In a whirlwind blur, she slams me against the wall, yanks my head to the side, climbs up my body to wrap her legs around my waist, and bites my throat. Her fangs are knives at first. Pain ricochets off all my bones before swiftly turning into pleasure. My cock hardens beneath

her, the tip grazing her wet entrance. I want nothing more than to canter my hips and sink inside of her again, but not like this. She is healing. She isn't thinking clearly.

A cold begins to seep into me. I shiver, sliding my eyes down to see what she is doing. My entire body feels frozen. I try to lift my feet, but I can't.

She's made me immobile.

"Rarity. You are freezing him. You have to stop. You might kill him," Cailian protests, but since we are mated, I don't think I'll die.

Rarity jumps off me and tackles Cailian to the ground, biting his upper thigh to drink from his femoral artery while keeping a hand against his chest so he can't move.

Our vampire is much stronger than I thought. She's able to keep both of us still with her force.

"Rarity. Rarity—" he gasps, his chest rising and falling heavily.

She moves up his body, swallowing his cock before pulling back. The once silver shaft is tinted red with blood from her mouth. I'm still frozen in place. I can't help him. I watch from against the wall as she rakes her nails down his chest, cutting open his gorgeous flesh.

He cries out and his agony can be felt in my chest as if it were my own. Blood spills from the new wounds. Too much of it. The red begins to pool under him, creating a sea of death.

"Cailian! Cailian, look at me. Look at me."

He trembles, his eyes losing all life and becoming distant. My elf is strong though and manages to meet my gaze.

"You're going to be okay. I will make sure of it. She doesn't know what she's doing. We can't hold this against her."

"I— I would never," he says while Rarity licks up his torso, drinking the blood leaking from his chest.

The gauges begin to heal, and she picks him up effortlessly, throwing him on the bed. To my shock, she doesn't follow. It's as if she is getting him out of the way. Rarity falls to her hands and knees, pressing her lips against the ocean of Cailian's blood, and drinks it. She flattens her tongue, moaning before rubbing her face through the thick liquid. The tips of her hair becoming a murderous red, a crazed need gripping her tight.

I watch in horror and fascination as she rolls her body in his blood, cupping her breasts before sliding her hand between her legs.

"Rarity—" I growl, my cock still hard and wanting even if she isn't her usual self.

When she hears me call her name, she turns her head, grinning to show me those pretty fangs before launching at me again. She's so fast, I can hardly see her. She's in front of me, her body dripping in crimson, her hair wet with her desire for it, and her eyes blaze the same color as a fresh fire.

They are rubies, staring at me as if she has no idea who I am. She tilts her head, analyzing me, before pushing me off the wall and onto the bed with Cailian. She exudes so much force, that the bed moves a few feet across the room. She saunters over, swaying her hips, her tits slightly bouncing with every step, her thighs shaking. Rarity must sense my desire because she inhales, pinning me with her gaze.

"I am afraid and slightly turned on," Cailian admits in a shameful whisper. "I feel like she is either going to fuck us or kill us."

"Or both," I mumble, sliding my arm around his side to pull him to mine. "Are you okay, Treasure?" I rub my thumb in circles on his hip. "I felt your panic. You were scared."

The bed dips as Rarity crawls toward us, her mouth, chin, and cheeks are smeared with our blood. Like a cat, she crawls over me, forcing me to lie down until I'm on my back. It isn't often I'm intim-

idated, but I'm staring into the eyes of a predator for the first time in my existence.

"Rarity—" Cailian's words are cut off when Rarity wraps a hand around his throat to keep him quiet.

She licks her lips, gathering the blood before biting into my chest. I try to push her away, her strength more than the trolls I've fought, and then I succumb to her demands. Rarity licks and bites down my body, keeping a close eye on Cailian to make sure he doesn't move.

I slither my tail up her back and just as I'm about to wrap it around her waist to yank her off us, her hand snaps out. A brief dark thought swoops in my mind. What if she breaks my tail? I don't know what she wants or is capable of right now. She's too hard to fight and too beautiful to deny. I guess I'll be letting her do whatever she wants to me as long as she remembers we are her firebonds.

In such a blood thirsty state, I'm wondering if she will feel the bond with us. I push what I feel for her through the bond, tugging the colorful ropes intertwining our souls. Rarity's eyes blaze brighter, the rubies glowing a neon red.

She slips her mouth over my tail, sucking me just like she would my cock.

I toss my arm over my eyes, groaning from how fucking good her mouth feels. She lifts off, then spits directly on the tip. I toss my arm onto the bed; a whisper of a chant escapes me. "What are you doing? What the fuck— Oh, gods," I start blubbering like a young dragon finding their fire for the first time.

Blood still stains her body, coating her face like a crazed killer. She licks her lips before spitting onto my tail again, the saliva tinted a shade of her favorite drink. She guides my tail to Cailian, letting go of his throat just to roughly part his legs.

"I think I am blissfully terrified," Cailian whispers as we watch her settle between his thighs.

"She looks so fucking breathtaking like this, but yes, I'm afraid if I move a muscle, she'll cut me open and feast on me," I admit lightly, groaning when Rarity sucks Cailian's cock down her throat.

He shouts, tossing his head back then laughs. "I also have that feeling—" he moans.

Her fangs scrape along his cock before biting down on the hard shaft. The muscle gives under the weapons, cutting into him. Blood flows down his cock and Rarity drinks him eagerly. He comes too, ropes of it arching into the air, landing on his chest.

I lean in, licking his come from his pecs. Rarity shoves me back, flashing those blood-coated teeth at me.

"But I want him," I growl, not liking being denied of what I want. "And I want you. When you snap out of this, your ass is mine, Rarity." I try to launch at Cailian again, wanting to gather more of his frost across my tongue.

It tingles, adding a cooling sensation as if I have breathed in mint. I want more of it.

Rarity scratches my chest with her talons, the pain making me pull back and grab my chest. Smoke angrily breezes from my mouth when I see blood. She strokes my chest before leaning in, sucking my skin to gather the river she's drawn from me. Cailian gasps, his hand slapping down on my thigh, then rakes his nails down to my knee.

I break eye contact with Rarity, staring at the beautiful firebond destiny has given me. The valley between the top lip deepens as he pouts his lips, sweat gathering along the top, and he moans internally. Rarity grabs his aching dick, slicking it with the reminisce of his come and blood. Using him like a toy, she grinds herself over his cock. Back and forth she slides along his length, soaking it with her need.

Rarity takes my tail, lining it up with Cailian's hole, forcing me between his cheeks. Cailian lets out another low groan as I fill him and Rarity rocking her soft, wet pussy over his cock. The unique head showing after the foreskin is pulled back with every glide of her hips. I do as she wants, which is no hardship, and fuck Cailian's ass. My tail hits the spot he loves so much over and over again, his shouts gaining volume.

Rarity snakes her hand around my throat to tug me forward, claiming my mouth for herself. Her tongue dives between my lips, her mouth moving with determination across mine. This isn't a simple kiss. This a claiming kiss, the kind that proves I am hers, and she'll kill anyone who dares to get in her way of me.

I suck her bottom lip into my mouth before letting it go with a soft pop. She whimpers, rocking her hips faster, and I look down to see Cailian's cockhead appearing with every stroke she gives him. His hands are on her hips, helping her move faster. His silver cock is red just how she likes it. He must hit her clit every time she rocks back because with every other stroke, Rarity calls out his name.

Her body tenses, an orgasm shocking her body. She tenses, digging her claws into my shoulder. She continues to rock against him, prolonging the good she feels. Her teeth break the skin on my throat again, messily drinking from me. Warm trails of my blood drip down my body, wasted on my vampire's need.

Her bite has my cock tensing before an orgasm hits me on the next drag she takes.

"Rarity, don't ever stop this," I mumble, my eyes hazed from the bliss.

I would think her heat had her if I could smell it, but since I can't, I know this is the behavior Cailian's witch warned us about. I'm

noticing if we follow Rarity's lead, we don't get shoved across the room or claw marks across our chests.

Rarity hums, gathering my seed pooled on Cailian's stomach. She wraps her come-covered palm around Cailian's cock, then slides her hand across her pussy, getting it slick. Grabbing his length, she slides down on it, taking all of him to the hilt.

"So fucking good. Nothing feels better than this," Cailian gasps.

Rarity tugs me by my tail, gesturing me to get behind her.

Who am I to deny her?

I continue to fuck Cailian's hole with my tail while I stare at her round ass as she bounces on his cock. My hand drifts up her left side, pinning her down against Cailian's chest. She tries to fight me, but I shush her.

"Quiet," I growl, giving her ass a hard smack. "I'm going to give you what you want." My gaze locks onto Cailian's cock filling her pretty pink pussy. Spit, come, and blood make a mess between them. "What do you want that will calm you down, My Darling Jewel?" I press my finger against the rim of her hole. "Do you need me here?" And with a different finger, I press it inside of her, sliding against Cailian's cock. "Or do you want me to stuff this pussy full of my big cock, stretching you until you feel like you're about to break?"

She looks over her shoulder, narrowing her possessed eyes at me, daring me to try.

I slide my hand down, pressing it against her lower back to keep her still. "Don't move, neither of you. This is going to take some time." I align my cock to her entrance, dripping with all the things I love most, sliding against Cailian's cock. They shout in unison. Cailian thighs tremble from the stimulation. His balls tighten and I grab them, squeezing the orbs in my hands until I know it hurts.

"Don't you dare come for a second time. You can wait until I'm about to knot her."

"You're making it tighter. Nyx, Dove," he stutters to correct himself. "This feels so good. You are so fucking big. Gods, Dove. I have no clue how she is handling this."

I slip my hand up her spine as I sink in, making her snarl before biting Cailian's chest. I look over her shoulder to see dozens of bite marks bleeding profusely down his ribs and onto the blanket. It's ruined.

Clutching her hip against me when I'm finally seated, I tremble all over. Sweat beads on my temple. My orgasm wants to burst free, coating her and him together. Rarity tries to move, but I hold her tight.

"Don't. You might hurt yourself. I am going to take care of the both of you." I curl over her, kissing her shoulder before biting it into my mouth, sucking the flesh until a bruise is left. I'm pleased to see my marks on her. I sink deep until my sack is pressing against Cailian's. "Your pussy and his ass are my favorite places to be. You're strangling me with how tight of a fit this is." I look down, her pussy stretching so much I'm afraid she'll rip.

Testing the position, I slide out, my cock right against Cailian's, grinding together in too tight of a hug. The three of us moan when I thrust in, the deplorable wet sounds of us joining, erotic and wicked.

She lifts slightly, trying to use Cailian's chest as leverage, but her hand slips across the blood. I catch her by her hair, bringing her up until I can lick my mating mark on her shoulder. In an awkward attempt, I bite her bottom lip since she isn't turned enough.

I flatten us again, needing to be closer to her and Cailian. My body simmers as flames heat my veins. I curl over them, able to see Cailian and Rarity beneath me. Cailian's eyes are closed, his white

lashes fanning delicate shadows across the tops of his cheeks. He bites his bottom lip, groaning every time my cock thrusts against his. I cup the back of his head, grab Rarity's hip, and drive in faster.

"Fuck, that's it. Both of you are taking my cock so well. Even when you're being bad, Rarity, you still treat me so well. How can I be mad when your pretty pussy is filled to the brink. If you want to prove you're a good girl, you'll come for me, and then I'll let you have all the blood you want."

Our skin slaps together, panting and gasps filling the hot air.

"Cailian, your cock fits just right against mine. Are you close?" I ask him, my strokes becoming longer and harder.

"So close. Please, don't stop."

"I won't, Treasure. You need to tell me why you want to come so badly. Do you want to fill her sinful pussy with your come? Are you hoping she'll become pregnant?"

"I want that. I want— I want to be too—" he admits just as Rarity bites into the right side of his neck. I hear her audibly swallow and Cailian cups the back of her head, turning to give her more space.

She moans, her orgasm rippling up and down our shafts. My knot inflates and Cailian must feel the pressure from my cock swelling because he yells so loud, the veins in his neck protrude as he comes. His release drenches me, tingling my shaft with how it cools. I bend over and capture his lips, gasping for air from how good this feels. He slips out of her, giving me room to knot Rarity, and the moment I have the space, I lock us together. I sit her up, giving Cailian the best view on the planet.

I cup her breasts, placing my chin on her shoulder as I stare directly into my elf's eyes. "Look at her, Cailian. Look how fucking beautiful she is. She's all healed now from taking all that blood from us. I mean, look at these tits, Treasure." I pinch her nipples between my thumb

and index finger, and she arches her back, pressing herself against me harder. "Give me your hands—" I order him, and he lifts them willingly, allowing me to guide them until he is squeezing her soft mounds with me. My thrusts are shallow, my knot tugging at her entrance. It causes her to practically sob with pleasure, so I increase the pace. "Isn't she like fucking silk, Cailian? This gorgeous vampire just came all over your cock and you got to fill her womb cause she is yours. How does that make you feel?"

"Possessive," he snarls, drifting one hand between her legs to give attention to her clit. He leans forward, taking her right nipple into his mouth.

She moans, cupping my cheek with her hand. I know what she needs. I bend forward and she's latching onto my vein, drinking more of me again. It takes our intimacy to another level. Knowing I'm in her body, her blood, giving her what she needs to live has me falling over the edge. The bond explodes with ecstasy from our orgasms, and I come harder than I ever have. I give her every drop I have left, filling her until her stomach bulges. I collapse, catching myself with my hand right next to Cailian's head.

We lock eyes, and I notice the sweat beading along his temple. He's trying to catch his breath, blood stains him practically all over his body, even his lips. Leaning down, I crush my lips against his softly.

Another piece of me vanishes into my firebonds, changing me from this day forward.

Chapter Fourteen

RARITY

I stand in the shower, letting the night wash away from me. Red tinges the water before disappearing forever down the drain. My eyes hood with exhaustion and I can't seem to get warm even under the scolding hot water I'm standing under in Cailian's shower. I blame it on nearly dying and then pumping myself with so much blood, that I think I got a little high.

Luckily, my beloveds can't die if I take too much blood from them. Fate thought of everything when giving vampires beloveds. Their blood replenishes so vampires can take as much as they want without killing their beloveds.

I shiver, turning the handle to make the water hotter but it's already maxed. The door to the shower opens, allowing cool air in and I tremble again.

"Is My Darling Jewel, cold? I feel your bond shaking, Rarity." Nyx steps into the stall leaving plenty of room for Cailian if he wishes to join.

"I don't know what's wrong with me," I say through clattering teeth. "The water is as hot as it can be."

He tucks his wings as tight as they can be, lying them flat against his back before stepping forward and wrapping his arms around me, followed by his wings. They wrap us in a cocoon and his body heat becomes so hot, that the water from the shower evaporates before hitting the floor.

I groan in relief, pressing my head against his chest as I let his warmth envelope my body. "You feel so good," I say on a blissful sigh, holding him tighter.

"Hmm," he grunts, running his claws through my hair. "So do you. Having you in my arms negates all the anger I feel."

I lift my head, placing my chin on his upper stomach. He's so much taller than me. I have to crane my neck back just to look at him.

"Do you feel that way about Cailian?" I whisper, tracing the edge of a scale with my finger.

"He is a difficult topic to discuss. How I feel about him is difficult."

"I bet it isn't. Come on," I urge, sliding my hands to his lower back. "Talk to me. I want to know everything about you. I want to know how you feel. I know how Cailian feels. I know more about him than you. I want to change that."

He tilts my head back, unwrapping his wings from me so the water hits my back.

My eyes widen, pleasantly surprised. "The water is hotter."

"You have dragon blood in you now. You need heat."

"But I have ice elven in my blood. The cold shouldn't bother me."

He lifts his shoulder. "Maybe. Could just be the side effect of all the blood you drank yesterday."

I blush as he untangles my hair with his claws, letting the water rush down the strands.

"I can't remember much of what happened. I mean, I do, but it's all a blur. It's like I was there, but I wasn't."

"Your natural instincts to survive and heal were in full force. That's nothing to be embarrassed about. You can use me like that any time of the day. I promise you won't ever hear me complain." His free hand flattens across my stomach. "How do you feel? Are you sore from taking both of our cocks." The words are thunderous as they leave him as if he is reliving that moment.

I'll never forget it. I was full, so damn full, and I truly thought they were going to rip me apart. Thinking about how I had both of them at the same time, I know I will want that to happen again.

"No. Remember, I heal fast." I trail my finger down his chest, and he circles my wrist with his thick, long fingers. One quick flick of his wrist and he'd break my bone.

"As much as I love that idea—"

And according to his semi-erect cock plumping, he most definitely does.

"—We need to shower and go to The Veiled Library," he says, squeezing shampoo in his hand. He washes my hair, his fingertips lightly massaging my scalp.

I shut my eyes and groan from his touch. I've never had anyone wash my hair before. "Why?" I mumble, half asleep.

"Because there is no way that sun spell has only been written once. I'm determined to find it. I refuse for you to not live life to the fullest. And we need to see if we can find anything regarding how you have Ice Elven abilities, but you are clearly a vampire."

"I don't think they will have the answer there."

"Maybe not—" he tugs my hair in the back, signaling me to tilt back toward the water. "—But it is better to try than to not. We might leave with more than we know now, right?"

"That's true. Maybe while we are out, we can go see my coven? I'd love for you to meet my family."

"I'd love to," he says, brushing his thumb across my lip. "Fate was kind to give me you. I'm not the nicest man. I've done horrible things over the last..." he trails off "...few centuries. Including the war with Cailian."

"Are you ready to let that go? And move forward?" I suds the soap in the loofa, dragging it across his impressive chest.

"I want to be, but I'm not sure I'll be able to give him all of me without the truth of what happened to my father."

I can't say I'm not disappointed. "How can this work if you and him can't meet eye to eye? I can't be torn between the two of you."

"You won't have to be. I won't ever put you in that position. I can only be angry around him so long before I forget about it and want to be with him. I can't promise tomorrow I'll feel the same, but eight hundred years of fury, war, death, and sorrow do not disappear overnight. Many of my dragons died just like Cailian lost the lives of his elves. I'm thankful no one has to die for us. I never wanted others to pay the price. I don't know how it got so out of hand. It just..." he blows out a breath that smells like a bonfire. "It just unraveled and every day my hate for him grew more." Embers begin to flash across his lips as his emotions become stronger. "And now—" his jaw tenses, sharpening that distinctive edge that has my mouth watering for a taste. "Now the more I *feel* for him, the more I want to hate him more, and I just—" he hangs his head as he tries to gather his thoughts. "—I can't. I just can't hate him more and that makes me so damn—"

"—Angry," I finish his sentence for him.

Smoke drifts from his nostrils, swirling high like tall towers before dissipating above us.

"It's infuriating," he growls, his dragon coming forth and tinging his words. "The more time I spend around him, the more I question myself. The more I question if someone like him is capable of killing someone without reason."

I stop him, pressing my finger against his lips. "Did you hear yourself? Without reason." I repeat. "Without reason. Keep that in mind for me."

"It's all I think about," he admits, the water shining from his chest reminding me of a vast inky pool I want to dive into. "You and he consume me, but whatever he hides, it replays in my mind nonstop. And that damn elf would rather die than to speak the truth."

"He will one day. We will figure it out. All we can do is take this one day at a time, right? We're all fated, but we are still getting to know one another. The truth always comes out, Nyx. Maybe not when you want, but what we want never has a sense of time. Be patient."

He takes the loofah from me, squeezing some type of floral-scented body wash onto it before cleaning me. "And what if he killed my father out of hate? What do I do then?"

"I don't know," I whisper honestly, wishing I had a better answer for him. "Either you let it go and hope he isn't the same elf he was eight hundred years ago."

Nyx's hands take their time across my breasts as he washes me, his stare searing into mine. A quick flash of realization ghosts over those embers from my words.

"Perhaps, I need to let the past go," he says, sliding the loofah down my stomach. "You make it easier to do that." He drops to his knees, lifting one of my legs as he cleans, then the other. "You are my peace that takes the place of the pieces I've lost of myself." He turns me around, taking his time to clean my backside. His lips kiss each cheek before following the trail of my spine with his lips. "You make me see

color when I've only ever seen life and death as the goals I need to accomplish. And I don't mean living life, My Darling Jewel, I only mean breathing and waiting for death after I've accomplished the one thing I've wanted to do."

"Which is?" I turn my chin to my shoulder, glancing up at him through wet lashes.

"Killing our firebond." Shame riddles his tone, his black eyebrows pulling together.

The thought of not having Cailian in my life, in the bed next to me, to feel his skin against mine, to experience his kiss, to see him smile or laugh, to feel him experience passion, the torture that twists my soul is unthinkable. The agony knocks the breath out of me.

Nyx must feel it because he squeezes the back of my neck, and then kisses my temple. "Don't fear. I don't have it in my soul to kill him."

I blow out a breath. "That's a relief."

He grins, showing a sharp row of teeth. "It is. Now, I just have to figure out how to live my best life with you and him. I promise you, I will try to put the past behind me." His fingers dig into my hip and yank me forward, pressing against him. "You both are worth the effort."

We take turns rinsing our bodies under the steaming hot water. I can't help but to sneak a little grab of his bubbly butt.

He grunts, quirking one eyebrow at me as he pushes his wet hair back.

I steal another grab. "I didn't know dragons had so much cake." I move my hand to the right cheek, squeezing that globe too. The scales are different on his ass, smooth and faded with a faint rainbow shine like the rest of him.

He snags both my hands and wraps my arms around his waist, sliding my palms down until I'm cupping both cheeks.

Ooooh, that's… that's amazing. These cheeks are a work of art.

"This is the only cake you're allowed to have, My Darling Jewel. Do you understand me? You won't be looking at any other dragon."

"Why would I? I have the Prince's ass in my hands. Squeezing each cheek. So soft…" I mumble, practically lost in the softness as the flesh gives under my fingers. I giggle as I knead. "So when I say you're a royal pain in my ass, that will be so accurate."

His tail wraps around my waist. It slips down my crease, teasing me. "I'll give you a pain in your ass if you aren't careful."

I flush, the thought of something *there* has me flustered.

"Don't worry—" his tail brushes up and down between the crease. "I won't take you there until I know you're ready— until you're prepared. It isn't something that just happens. We will have to prep you." He rubs the worry lines between my brows, his own chuckle escaping him. "Don't look so afraid. I won't let anything happen to you." His tail unravels and I turn around, my palms empty and missing the weight of his cheeks as I shut the water off.

"You wanted me dead, if I remember correctly," I joke, reminding him of how we met.

He closes his eyes in regret and shame. "I am so sorry, Rarity. I tried to kill you and I haven't even apologized for it. I am such an asshole."

"It's okay. Really. I understand—"

"—It isn't okay," he growls, his eyes glowing bright orange as smoke drifts from his nose. "Nothing about how I acted is okay. I shouldn't have lost my temper. I was already irritated with Cailian being my firebond and I saw you drinking from him. I couldn't smell you—"

I kiss the middle of his chest since it's the closest surface on him I can reach. I tilt my head back, getting a view of the bottom of his chin. "Will you look at me?"

He huffs, a small flame blazing forward before he listens to me. Finally, those eyes lock onto mine.

"I know you couldn't smell me. My father explained that your sense of smell is— and I mean this in the best way— crap."

He chuffs, duel flames flickering from his nostrils. "I don't know how that's the best way. I wouldn't say it is crap." He pouts, sticking out his bottom lip slightly. "It's just... not the greatest unless someone or something is close to me."

I pluck his bottom lip, snickering. "I don't blame you, is what I am trying to say. I understand. I'm glad you didn't kill me though or we wouldn't be here."

He opens the shower stall door, and I shiver when the cool air hits my bare skin. Nyx steps out, dipping his head below the top of the doorway. He turns to me and glorifies me with a view of his nude body. Everything about him is impressive. His muscles are defined and thick. The water travels from his onyx chest down to his heavy cock hanging between his legs.

"I wouldn't have killed you. I would have realized." Nyx holds out his hand, the water sizzling on his scales before steaming, evaporating in thin air.

"That's convenient." I step out of the stall, sliding my hand across his rough palm. The bond hums in content, happiness coming off Nyx in waves. "But I need a towel."

He wraps his arms around me, then his wings, and everything becomes hot. I watch as the water dries on my arms.

"You only need it for your hair. I'm afraid if I try to dry that, I'll burn it off."

I yelp, shoving away from him. "You better not. I wouldn't look cute bald." I snag a towel, flip my hair over my head, and twist it.

"You could never not look beautiful. If you ever lost your hair, and if you wanted, I would travel the depths of all dimensions to find the finest, softest silk strands and make you a hairpiece. Do you want them made of gold? The strands of hair of those I've killed for you? You name what you want, and it will be your crown, My Darling Jewel."

The thought of wearing a dead person's hair should scare the hell out of me, but coming from Nyx, I am only reassured of his feelings for me.

"A crown of our enemies hair if I were to ever be bald? You sweet talker."

He lifts his shoulder, a bit bashfully, and scratches the back of his head. "I'm only being honest."

The door to the bathroom swings open, allowing more cold air in. Cailian stands there in fresh robes. They are light blue with hints of white detail on the hems. His hair is combed, cascading down his shoulders. On either side of his head, there are two braids pinned back. His unique eyes roam over both of us as we stand there naked.

Lust plucks the strings of our bond, and he takes a deep breath to calm himself. Nyx growls, taking a step forward to take him, but Cailian holds up his hand to stop our dragon.

"We can't. We mated and it was hectic, but we can't stay here forever. My elves are curious about Rarity, and I know your dragons are too. We have responsibilities. She hasn't even seen the castles. We haven't given her a tour of our lands. We've just been—"

"—Fucking," Nyx finishes for him in a low rough voice that has my thighs clenching together. "We've been fucking, Treasure. Last I checked, she got to explore our bodies which was important, don't you think? For the mating." Nyx is standing in front of Cailian now, his wings twitching as if he is stopping himself from wrapping them

around our elf. He drags his fingers down Cailian's arm. "You're hiding your mating marks. My brand can't be seen."

"Your brand? Last I checked, it was on the back of my neck where it couldn't be," Cailian snaps, narrowing his eyes at Nyx.

The fire and ice swirling down his arms is covered, but I didn't think it was intentional. I frown at Cailian, wondering if he is ashamed to be mated to us, a brief thought that creates splinters in my bones.

"Is it just Nyx or is it me too?" I ask him, wrapping a towel around my body to cover myself. I feel exposed. "Are you ashamed your beloved is a vampire? A bloodsucker that could kill any of your elves? Anyone on this planet? Or are you ashamed you're mated to a dragon?"

Cailian's eyes widen in shock when he hears me, but he straightens to his full height, the crown on his head sparkling against the bathroom light. He looks like royalty in this moment, a man, who when he speaks, everyone listens, and he is always correct. No one dares to challenge a royal.

I'll challenge him every day to remind him he is more than royalty.

"It has nothing to do with that. I do not care that you are a vampire. I love it, Rarity. Don't for one second think I am ashamed of you—" he slides his eyes to Nyx "—Of either of you, but we cannot pretend anything about this is simple. I am not ashamed of what you are, or who you are. I am proud that Fate thought I was worthy enough of not one, but two mates." He takes a step forward and Nyx takes a step back, closer to me.

"The fact, the truth, the reality of this mating is that it contains two royals, one who hates the other, and a new princess."

I open my mouth to argue with him, but he stops me by shaking his head.

"I know you say you are not a Princess. You are humble, kind, and you have a lot to learn about this world, but Rarity, you *are* a Princess. You need to accept it because not only will you be ruling the elves, but the dragons too. You make our kingdoms one."

I swallow, my throat suddenly dry, and for the first time in a long time, I want some water. The pressure weighs on me.

Cailian turns to Nyx. "And that is another thing we need to discuss. How are we going to join the kingdoms? It is an issue we have to face. We cannot live separately."

"I— I don't know if I'm ready for that, Cailian—"

"—Then you better get fucking ready for it, Nyx because that is the truth. You do not have to love me so be a good prince and pretend you do for your dragons so they can trust us to take care of them," Cailian yells so loud, I flinch, icicles begin to form from the ceiling as his anger whirls.

And to my surprise, Nyx doesn't get upset. He doesn't say a word.

"I understand you want me to be your well-kept secret. The elf who killed your father has to sleep next to you every night, but you know what really perplexes me?" Cailian invades Nyx's space, standing toe to toe with him. "Your hate obviously has its limits because you love fucking what you seem to dislike so much."

Smoke spills from Nyx and steam rises from his shoulders.

Cailian turns to me, the anger vanishes when his eyes catch mine, and then holds out his hand. "Come on, I will give you a tour of the kingdom, and then Nyx can take you to his den."

"I will see you both later then—"

Cailian shakes his head. "You have to meet everyone too. This is the first time they will have to be led by a dragon. Some will not react well, including your dragons. It is best if we get it over with."

Nyx nods, bending over to pick up his pants. He slides them on, having to do a little dance to get the material over his ass. His tail slithers through a hole that seems custome made to his form.

"This isn't going to go over well," Nyx mutters, buttoning, what looks like, torn black jeans.

I reach out to touch them, my fingers gliding over material that's so much softer than denim.

"I'll tell you all about how clothes are made for us dragons later. After."

I pull my hand away and nod, not really looking forward to what "After" entails. I was. I mean, I am, kind of. It's hard to explain. I was feeling excited and now there is this underlying sense of dread. I haven't forgotten how far back Nyx and Cailian's history goes but I didn't think about the elves or dragons and how they are going to react to the two being mated.

"Will this be bad?" I grab the brush on the vanity, the clear handle cold to the touch with snowflakes embedded inside. The bristles are surprisingly soft as I brush my hair.

"May I?" Nyx asks, pointing at the hairbrush.

I hand it to him, and the biggest smile stretches across his face. I prepare myself for him to be too rough with hair tugs and tangles with how large his hands are, but he's gentle and soft. I can't remember the last time someone else brushed my hair.

"It could be bad," Nyx begins to say. "Cailian isn't wrong. I think our kingdoms will be surprised. A few might cause issues, but mostly, I think confusion will be an issue. Everyone will ask a lot of questions, questions we might not have answers to."

Silence falls, the only sound is my hair being untangled.

"Which is why it is best to address it now, rather than later. You will have to meet some of Nyx's... female night quests," Cailian states with a bit of jealousy. "I am sure they will not be happy to see us."

Nyx stops brushing when I turn around.

He gives Cailian an annoyed, tired look, and sets the hairbrush on the vanity. "Dragons aren't like other species. We can fuck whoever we want. We can have children with whoever we want if we choose, but we can only knot our firebonds. Yes, I laid a few female dragons over the years to scratch an itch, but I never felt for them what I feel for you."

"I never expected either of you to be saints. What about female elves? Have you ever had any relationships with them, Cailian?" I'm curious, not angry.

"Female elves are rare. We only have three. They are very well protected." He bows his head. "So no, I never had any sort of relationship in my life."

"It's me. I'm the whore in this trio," Nyx grins, showing a flash of fang. "Which my experience seems to come in handy when I make you come, Little Elf. You don't seem to mind it then."

"That is hardly a fair comparison when we both know I cannot help my response to you. It is the bond. Face it, without Fate, we would not dare to be in the same room."

Nyx taps his chin, wraps his tail around Cailian's waist, tugging him until our elf is flush against his chest. His finger traces his jaw, fire spreading in the wake. "I don't know. I happen to like seeing how I make you melt, Treasure."

Cailian tries to shove away from him. It's no use. He isn't stronger than a dragon, although, he could use his power, yet he isn't.

"I won't let you go until you stop this."

"Stop what?" Cailian hisses.

"This jealousy. This anger. This disobedience. The denial. It ends now because there is only you and Rarity now. My cock can't rise for anyone else ever again."

Cailian eyes water and still, he shoves Nyx again, and Nyx unravels his tail from Cailian's waist. Without a word, Cailian leaves, shutting the bedroom door loud enough for us to know we are alone.

"I don't understand," Nyx grumbles. "This isn't easy with him like it is you. I don't know what he wants from me."

"I don't think he is mad or worried you're going to want another. I think he is sad." I feel the heavy weight of emotion plucking on the strings of the bond.

Nyx must too because he rubs his chest. "Why? I thought, after everything, we have made progress?"

"Progress, maybe," I bob my head as I study what Cailian is pushing through the bond. "In here, in the safety of four walls, and with us, there is progress, but out there?" I point to the left where everything outside this room is against us. "There is no progress. You have to pretend to accept him because let's face it, Nyx—" I kiss his chest "—He's accepted you. And now he has to put on a show, a fake smile when his heart hurts. That must be hard."

The door to the bedroom opens again, the light quick steps along with the sense of Cailian coming closer has Nyx visibly blowing out a relieved breath.

"Raltena has managed to place a sun barrier for three hundred miles in either direction. You will be safe now during the day," he informs.

"I'll be able to go outside?" I squeal, running to him. He catches me just as I jump, wrapping my arms and legs around him. "I get to feel the sun's warmth? I get to have freedom?" Tears prickle my eyes and I hide my face against his shoulder. "Thank you. Thank you so much." I lift my head quickly, excitement replacing the heaviness from moments

ago. "Do you think she would teach Maven to create it too? My coven can't walk in the daylight either. She hasn't been able to create a barrier so large like Raltena did."

"Of course she hasn't." He wipes my tears away. "My witch is so much older than Maven. With age comes power. I'll bring her with us when we visit your family. Are you ready to meet the rest of my elves? Are you ready to see the castle? Besides the bedroom," he smirks.

"Yes. I'm nervous. What if they don't like me?"

"What's not to like?" Nyx leans against the wall, crossing his bulky arms. "You're even cute when you talk in your sleep."

Cailian snorts.

I, on the other hand, gasp in horror. "I do not talk in my sleep. Someone would have told me that by now."

"My Darling Jewel," he croons, playfully knocking my chin with his fist before taking my face between his hands, holding me with a barely there strength and caress. "I am telling you now. You love talking about blood dip. What is that? Is it like a cup of blood you dip veggies into? I am so confused."

"It can be any kind of dip with blood added," I mumble, glancing away with a tinge of embarrassment. "I hope it doesn't disrupt you both."

"Disrupt us?" Cailian says. "We love it. We find it adorable. We will make you all the dip you want. You must love it if you talk about it in your sleep."

I shrug. "It's fine."

My head is yanked back, and I inhale a deep breath when I stare up to find an angry Nyx staring down at me. Familiar black smoke leaves him. The heat can be seen leaving his body in waves, pulsing through the air. Even his hands on me gets hot.

"Speak the truth. Hiding how you really feel will only get you in trouble later."

"I think she likes that idea." Cailian's hand tugs on my towel causing it to fall to the floor in a useless heap. His hand drifts between thighs and cups my pussy. His fingers slide along the wet, sensitive lips. "Oh, she does. She is drenched for us." Cailian lifts his fingers to his mouth.

"Watch him," Nyx growls, lifting me enough so I can see. He doesn't release the hold he has on my hair. He likes being able to control me.

Cailian's eye contact never leaves mine. My breathing is faster as if I'm running uphill. I don't think I'm going to make it to the end. I need a break. I need a moment to suck in some much needed air.

But the wicked elf sucks his wet fingers into his mouth, moaning as if I'm the best thing he's ever tasted.

"Still delicious. I can still taste Nyx inside you." The swirling silvers glide to Nyx. "And he tastes delicious." He slips his fingers between my legs again and I whimper, rocking my hips for more. Then he pulls away again. "Try for yourself, Dove."

My gaze follows Cailian's hand stretching over my face to Nyx's lips. The dragon opens his mouth and Cailian's fingers vanish between Nyx's sharp teeth. Our dragon's dark lips close around the elf's lithe fingers.

Nyx hums in appreciation, wrapping his clawed fingers around Cailian's wrist, staring at him as if Nyx wants to eat him too.

His tongue flicks as he pulls away. "She is delicious."

"Please," I groan, wanting one of them to bring relief to the ache they have caused.

"You are pretty when you beg for us," Nyx whispers into my ear, his free hand sliding down my arm until his fingers lace through mine.

Cailian pinches my nipples, rolling them between his fingers. The wicked elf snags my chin in his grasp and tilts his head, his angelic face far from being heavenly in this moment. "You can beg for the rest of the night, but you will not get what you want. I want you to throb. I want you to be in tears with need." He yanks me from Nyx and we collide, my breasts pressing against his chest. "Only then will you get fucked."

"That's so cruel," I whine, rocking my hips against his hard cock. "You want me. I can feel it."

"Wanting you will never be the issue, My Snow." His lips press against mine, pouring want and desire across my tongue until I have no choice but to swallow it and crave more. "Now, go get dressed for the evening. We have a lot to do."

"You're... You're serious?"

"Very. I want to be able to lift your dress and slide inside you so effortlessly because you are so wet and aching from having to think of us having our hands on you."

"Cailian," I whisper his name while Nyx chuckles. "It isn't fun. This isn't funny!"

"It isn't supposed to be." Nyx's voice booms in the bathroom as he follows Cailian. "I happen to like Cailian's idea."

"Your dress is on the bed. If you want, you can go to your closet. It is full of clothes your size."

"I could pout and throw a tantrum," I threaten, even though I know I'd never do that.

"Be a brat and see where it gets you," Nyx growls, eyes flaming, daring me to test him.

"We will wait for you outside," Cailian says, opening the bedroom door.

"Nyx isn't dressed." I point to Nyx's bare chest.

"My Snow, he is a dragon, being shirtless is expected."

They leave me with my mouth open in shock. Nyx gives me a quick wink before closing the door. It's just me alone in the room we have filled with moans and sex. If I breathe in enough, I can still smell our come and their blood. I'm still full from taking so much from them.

Sighing, I lean against the doorway of the bathroom, waiting for them to come back, but after a few minutes, I feel ridiculous standing here naked.

I cross the floor, staring at the beautiful dress on the bed. It's simple. A dark green gown that stops at my knees with a fanned-out top and thin straps. Next to the dress are gorgeous gems. Emeralds if I had to guess, surrounded by diamonds. The necklace holds three giant emerald stones, the diamonds shining against the bedroom light. The bracelet is different. It matches, yet doesn't. In between an emerald there is something dark with a rainbow hue. The color reminds me of Nyx's scales.

These had to be expensive. I knew the princes had money, but I don't think it has set in with how much. My coven is well off. Money has never been an issue for them. I, on the other hand, haven't had a lot of experience with money. I haven't been around because of being trapped in the veil.

I'm experiencing how money is spent now and I'm a little overwhelmed. It doesn't stop me from dancing in excitement and pressing the dress to my body. I run across the floor and stop in front of the full-length mirror that's frozen to the floor.

"Oh my." I hold my breath when I see my reflection in the iced mirror with golden designs painted into the sides, shining dully from the cold temperature. The dress pairs perfectly with my colorless skin yet brightens my eyes and lips. My hair seems brighter, whiter, and as I step closer, I notice a light purple pattern across my cheeks for the first time.

It reminds me of frost.

I smile, feeling more at home than I ever have, and a slither of guilt works its way into my thoughts.

"I wonder what my therapist would say," I mumble, twisting the dress so it flows back and forth.

The more I think about it, the more I know he'd say, "I'm where I belong." I finally feel that way too.

Unzipping the dress, I bring the gorgeous silk material over my head, and it falls perfectly as if it was made just for me.

I can't zip it because the position is too awkward, but I'm able to see myself as someone I've never recognized before. I'm happy and the more I think about it, I haven't used my power since I've been here. I don't feel out of control anymore. I'm grounded.

But then an idea hits me.

What if I freeze Nyx's memory of Cailian killing his father? Maybe then, the two could be happy.

Chapter Fifteen

CAILIAN

"There are trolls in Fog's Forest!" Zyrl shouts through the main living space of the castle as he enters through the main doors. They slam against the wall, a cloud of ice shavings dusting the air. "Trolls!" he shouts again, running out of breath as he stops in front of me.

The icicle pen scratches my signature in a sheet of ice stating that the kingdom is to replenish everyone's food while giving them a monthly allowance to live a better and happier life.

"Riesh, I want to schedule time to see the village. Do people need updates to their homes? Do they need anything from the kingdom? I want to see their homes. It is the kingdoms responsibility to take care of them and I have not done a great job of that as of late."

Riesh, my assistant, bows with his hands behind his back. "Right away, Prince Cailian."

I do not miss how he side eyes Nyx, a question lingering in his gaze. "Riesh, this is Prince Dovenyx." I introduce the two and they stare at one another.

"I know who he is, Prince Cailian."

My brows rise when I hear the disgust. "You will treat my mate with respect, Riesh."

"—Did you not hear me!" Zyrl spins me around and grabs me by my shoulders.

Nyx snarls at my brother from the rough treatment, and for a moment, I think he cares about me. I take his hand in mine and squeeze it.

"It is okay, Dove. This is my brother, Zyrl. He is to take my place when my time comes to an end."

Zyrl, much to my surprise, shoves Nyx in the chest. "Do not take this dragon for his word, brother. He is a liar!"

"In my experience, it is the elves that tend to lie." Nyx spreads his wings, the impressive wingspan nearly taking up the entire room. The very top of his wings almost touch the chandelier, vast and large just as he is.

"The dragons have known about the trolls, Cailian. They have sat on this information for days," he shouts with raw, unhinged fury, the kind that comes from the depths of the soul. "He has known, and he has chosen not to tell you." Zyrl gasps for air, his chest rising and falling in rapid beats. "Go ahead, dragon," he spews. "Tell your mate how you deceived him."

"You mean like how he deceived me!" Nyx roars and the words hit my chest so hard, they steal my breath.

"We don't know what happened all those years ago. That lies between my brother and your father. You are no mate." Zyrl stands toe to toe with Nyx, uncaring that the dragon towers over him by a few feet. Uncaring how small he appears to be, he tilts his head back and conjures a sword from snow and ice, pressing it against Nyx's chin. "I wonder if my brother could live with a mate dead."

Nyx presses his chin to the sharp point of the blade, a bead of blood dripping down it in dark elegance. The dragon doesn't flinch, if anything, he is daring my little brother to drive the blade deeper.

"I wonder if my firebond could live with his brother dead. What do you think?" He tilts his head, narrowing his eyes sardonically. "A life for a life?"

"That's enough!" A soft feminine voice cascades down the swirling steps causing every being in the castle to turn to her.

All of my guards, my brother, my assistant to the crown, the elven royal servants, and Nyx stare at her as she comes down the steps.

"Wow," Nyx whispers, his eyes glued to our gorgeous mate.

There is no hate in his eyes. There is nothing but love and adoration. I wonder if I will ever have the chance to have him look at me the way he looks at Rarity.

The only saving grace is Rarity is not looking at him the same way in return. Fury paints her cheeks and hardens her eyes. Her new heels have spears of ice to make them stiletto and they click against the frosted steps with every step.

"The hate has got to stop, or nothing will get done. It ends now if we care about anything other than ourselves. There are others in this kingdom. Nyx—" she stops in front of him on the steps, still not as tall as he is but with how her shoulders are tossed back and her chin held high, she is every bit as large as he is. "—Why didn't you tell us about the trolls?"

Smoke escapes his mouth in a demonic cloud. "Because there is nothing to tell. The best of my dragons are keeping an eye on them. The trolls haven't moved in days. I had no updates to give."

"It doesn't matter if they have sat on their asses for a year," Zyrl's voice echoes in the chamber.

Rarity lifts her hand to silence him, and I hide my smile. She is a natural in a leadership position. She was born for this.

"Zyrl, please. I will take care of this." Rarity turns her lavender gaze to Nyx, presses her hand against his jaw, and a cold pattern etches across the sharp point. "Would you have said anything if the trolls began to move closer to the kingdoms?"

"Yes."

"Only because he would have to," I inform, not allowing the sadness to leak into my words. "Because trolls love dragon hearts. It is a delicacy for them. His kingdom would be in chaos, and we would wonder why. We would have been unprepared and if the trolls came while we had no idea, we would have lost too many to count." I turn to Nyx and give a soft smile. "And I do not know if you would have cared or if you do at all. I think it might be best if we go our separate ways right now. Rarity will come to you later—"

"—Rarity will do no such thing."

My Snow steps towards the doors, her violet eyes storming with anger. "We will deal with our differences, but right now, I would like the tour of the kingdoms. We will do it together, so everyone sees us together."

"I don't think that's a good idea," Nyx states, glancing around the living room chamber to see all of my elves who stay in the castle staring at him. "Tension is high right now. I doubt I am welcome—"

"—You are always welcome," I cut him off from saying anything else and Zyrl huffs in frustration. "You are my mate. My mates, no matter what, always have permission to be here." I turn around and look each of my elves in the eye. "Do I make myself clear? You are to answer to me, to Rarity, and to Nyx."

"Yes, Prince," they state in unison, bowing their heads.

A young elf, not more than sixty years old and his ears not even fully pointed yet, raises his hand. "Can I ask a question?" he asks, his voice timid and unsure.

"Of course, Laliel," I reply.

"Will the vampire eat us?" he asks, and a wave of murmurs follow by my fellow elves.

Rarity snorts, which is not very royal-like, and begins to laugh. "I'm so sorry. I'm sorry." She clears her throat, still trying not to snicker.

Nyx smiles too, rubbing his hand over his mouth to hide it.

Rarity strolls to Laliel, the green dress giving her skin an ethereal glow. "Do you see my fangs?" She curls her lips back to show off the impressive points, the memory of them sinking into me causing my cock to harden.

"I can smell your want," Nyx rumbles from beside me.

"Do not worry," I reassure him, keeping my focus on Rarity. "It is not aimed toward you."

A sharp sliver of pain radiates through the bond and Rarity turns around, furrowing her brows as she gives us a glance.

Nyx does not say a word because really, what could he say? The fact that he willingly put my kingdom in danger, and not even the bond was enough for him to have the courtesy to tell me the truth about the trolls, speaks volumes.

This will be a mating of convenience for the two of us, nothing more, nothing less, no matter how much my heart loves him.

My elves gasp when they see Rarity's fangs, keeling backward to get away from danger.

"It's okay. It's okay," she rushes with her hands out. "I won't hurt you. Ever. You do not have to worry about me feeding from you or hurting you in any way. I only desire and crave my beloveds. I can

only drink their blood. I physically do not want you. The thought of another's blood makes me ill."

"Who is to say you won't kill us? We do not know of your kind."

"Xalizar," I hiss at him. "Apologize to your Princess at once."

"It's fine, My Love," Rarity tells me, walking toward Xalizar. He's tall with silver skin like me but darker. His veins are a deep blue too and he has earrings, studs, and bars from his earlobe to the point. If I'm not mistaken, he is wearing black eyeliner which makes the blue in his eyes pop. His white hair is the same as my own but curly. It truly is beautiful.

He leans against the wall wearily as Rarity approaches him, tensing but remaining as calm as one can be with a vampire near him.

"What have you heard about my kind, Xalizar?" Rarity asks.

"That you're faster than a blink of an eye and can kill even quicker."

Using her vampire speed to prove him right, she blurs until she is behind him. "That would be correct."

Other elves gasp and Xalizar spins around, the gold beads in his hair clinking together from the force.

"I could kill you just as you could kill me, but the difference is that I won't. Like anyone, I am not violent unless I have to be. You can trust me, unless you attack me—" She saunters her way back over to me— us— I mean, then stops before turning around. "—Then I will rip your throat out with my claws, Xalizar."

Xalizar bends his knee until he is kneeling, bowing his head in respect before crossing his wrists over the other, aiming them down to the floor. All around the elves begin to follow his lead.

"What is happening?" Rarity whispers in a way that tells me she is afraid to move.

"They are showing you respect. The crossing of the wrist is a sign of trust. They are promising they are bound to you, and you will keep them safe."

"I will. I promise, I will."

I cup her slender jaw and kiss her cheek. "I know you will. You belong here. This is what you are meant to do. You have effortlessly brought every elf to their knees in this castle."

She beams, her smile bathing her face in happiness, and it pours light into my heart where Nyx has darkened it.

Rarity looks me up and down. "Not every elf."

I bark out a laugh before nodding in agreement. "What a fool I must be." I kneel, placing one wrist over the other and point my hands to the floor. "I am bound to you, Princess."

She slips her fingers under my chin. "And I will always take care of you."

Much to my surprise, movement to my left causes me to turn my head away from Rarity to see Nyx kneel, who also crosses his wrists.

All the elves whisper to one another, too low for me to hear and understand, but it is obvious they are shocked to see the dragon on his knees, surrendering to Rarity.

"I do not know what this means in extent," he begins, huffing smoke. "Dragons do not do this, but I am *your* dragon and there will not be a day where I will not get on my knees and surrender to you, Princess."

Rarity takes her free hand, cupping his jaw before bending down and kissing each of us on the forehead. "I am a lucky vampire. Now, I believe I am owed a tour."

I stand which has the other elves standing. Nyx is slow to get up, his left wing trying to spread, but the pain is debilitating, and he falls to his hands. A growl fills the chamber, shaking the frozen crystals of

the chandelier. His claws grow longer, scratching deep grooves on the floor. Nyx is fighting his change.

Rarity and I both rush to him, taking each of his hands.

"Let us help you," I whisper.

"I do not need help," he bites between tight teeth. "Leave me be. I can get up on my own."

"But you don't have to be on your own," Rarity says, brushing her fingers through his hair. "You will never have to get up on your own again, My Love."

The steam rising from his back softens until it disappears and his fingers curl over ours, allowing us to help him to his feet.

"I can fix your wing, Dove. All you have to do is allow me."

He shakes his head, denying me. "Dragons are born with their wings and to die with them damaged is an honor. It means I have done my duties."

"You will not be able to fly soon if you do not fix this, Nyx," Rarity urges, reaching to touch the decrepit wing, gently petting the bone that is showing. "I never want you to be unhappy."

He takes her and kisses her inner wrist. "Happiness is only found in who Fate has given me." Nyx takes my hand, squeezing it tight. "I am learning."

I understand what he means, learning how to be happy, to accept how life feels when it feels good. I can understand the guilt too of him wanting those things and then remember it is me that is his mate.

The reason for so much of his unhappiness.

"I am too," I answer.

"So?" Rarity's upbeat voice changes the tension and momentum of the situation. "I want a tour. Tell me everything."

"Wow," she spins in the ballroom that has collected too much elven dust over the years.

I cannot remember the last time we used it to dance, eat, drink, and celebrate. Nyx spins Rarity in the middle of the dance floor under the chandelier.

"Why have you let this room go to waste?" she asks, running away from Nyx and to the window. Quiet squeaks sound when she rubs her arms across the dusty glass. "Woah, what is all this land? What is that little village? Is that a village? Why does that forest look so spooky? Is it always cold? We should clean this room and plan a party."

Nyx chuckles from her tenacity but I am trying to remember the first question.

"One question at a time, My Snow." I smile at her enthusiastically and she skips her way over to me, a jovial grin pointed directly at me. I am one lucky elf.

She wraps her arms around my waist and leans back so she can look at me. "Why haven't you used this room? It is beautiful. The ceiling reminds me of an old cathedral back home. The detail, the artwork. What is the scene from?" She tilts her head back and looks up at the sculpture and painting that my great-great- grandfather had put in place. If I remember correctly, he hired an elf from the village.

Swirls of ice are carved to replicate Elementalu. Our neighbors are included, the dragons soaring the sky, the trees accompanying the Woodland Elves, the wolves howling and creating wind. We are all there, painted on the sculpted ice as if we are all friends.

In those times, we were, I suppose.

I catch Nyx slowly walking in a circle as he stares at the art, his thoughts no doubt matching my own.

"We stopped celebrating a long time ago," I answer sadly, trying to think back to a time when we had something to celebrate. "We have been at war for a long time, Rarity."

"Well, we have something to celebrate now," she says, pointing her gaze at Nyx while she slides her hands up my back. "Isn't that right?"

He gives a lazy half-smirk. "That's right, My Darling Jewel. If you want to dance, we will dance. Whatever you want."

Rarity frowns. "I want you all to want it too."

I study the abandoned room. It looks old from being ignored. Time truly has gotten the best of it. The windows are covered in thick grime, old flowers are dead in tall clear vases, frozen in place. Even old wine glasses are abandoned on the piano made from a glacier itself. The four legs are sharp like an icicle, the body is clear so the wires can be seen that are connected to each of the keys.

The bar on the other side of the wall, once alive with a few bartenders pouring elvish ale and heartsnow-infused mulberry wine, stands empty beside fallen barstools with red velvet cushions.

This room is frozen in time.

"I can have this cleaned up for you in no time, Rarity. Come, I want to show you the rest of the castle." I begin to walk toward the tall entryway with enough room for one of the trolls to walk through, but she does not move causing me to tug her arm.

"I can clean it faster than your elves can, Cailian. That isn't fair to them when I can get it done in half the time with my vampire speed," she explains, crossing her arms in defiance.

Nyx blows out a breath mixed with smoke and flame before chuckling. "My Darling Jewel," he states, flying across the room to get to her in haste. He lands behind her, and his lips pinch together from tucking his injured wing.

Stubborn dragon. If he would just allow me to fix his wing, he would not be in pain.

"You cleaning will not happen," Nyx says the words fluttering through my mind, but I did not want to say them.

I have a feeling Rarity will not be inclined to accept what we are about to say.

Nyx places his hands on her shoulders, massaging them gently, and Rarity shuts her eyes, groaning.

"Not fair," she mumbles, hanging her head. "You're distracting me."

"That's the point." Nyx winks at me and my insides do something funny, something I have never felt before.

I place a hand to my stomach and inhale deeply, yet keep a relaxed demeanor so I do not give myself away.

"You are a princess, Rarity. Princesses do not clean," I inform, wanting to get the image of Nyx's wink further from my mind.

We are not friends, and we are barely lovers. With his announcement earlier, it is clear he will never forgive me, and I will remain the person whom he despises most in this life.

"That's ridiculous. I am capable of cleaning my own home. That's nonsense. We will tell them not to worry about cleaning—"

"—Then those elves will be out of a job and pay. You would be comfortable with that?"

She lifts her head and frowns at me. "Of course not. Maybe I can just help them, then? I don't want anyone thinking I'm here ordering them around. I don't like that they are doing work I don't mind doing. Isn't there a compromise? Can't I help them? It would allow me to get to know them better."

I sigh, unsure of what to say.

"That's not how things are done here, Rarity," Nyx says. "It would change how things are done around here. The rules are here for a reason. You aren't part of a normal family anymore—"

"—I'll have you know I was never part of a normal family. My coven has a Wildes Witch. We are practically royalty to others—"

"—But you lived a normal life." I take her hand in mine. "And there is nothing wrong with that. But you no longer live that life."

Her eyes harden when she glares at me, then slides the maddening gaze at Nyx. "I'm not wanting to give up my life. I will help the others. I will continue to be independent in my own way and you—" she shoves her fingers into my chest "—and you—" Rarity tries to shove Nyx, but he does not move. "Can't stop me."

"You are a stubborn vampire," Nyx grumbles.

"You haven't even seen stubborn yet. This is only the beginning," she huffs, crossing her arms.

"That I have no doubts about." I bring her hand to my mouth and kiss her soft knuckles. "I cannot wait to see every stubborn side of you."

This time when she smiles, Rarity takes my hand and Nyx's, tugging us out the ballroom doors.

"Okay, show me everything about the castle and the land. Then, we will go to Nyx's. Also, how can we join the two? There has to be a way."

Our footsteps echo down the hall and one of my guards nods at me when we walk by, yet Rarity stops in her tracks.

"Hi, I'm Rarity," she introduces, holding out her hand. "I am their mate, so I guess your new princess, but please call me Rarity," she says.

I shake my head behind hers so my guard can see me.

"Princess Rarity," he bows. "I am Taygen, one of Prince Cailian's guards. It is nice to meet you. If you need anything at all, please, let me know."

"Rarity," she corrects him. "Only Rarity."

"As you wish, Princess Rarity," he says with a smile.

"I see how this is going to be. I will wear you down. You just wait and see."

"You can do your best, Princess Rarity. It will not work. I am trained for that."

"Challenge accepted. I have a feeling we are going to be friends."

"I am afraid I cannot be your friend. It is not appropriate," he explains, politely, switching the iced spear into his other hand.

"That is nonsense. We are friends. Have a great day, Taygen." Rarity walks away, flipping her long white hair over her shoulder, and leaving us in the dust.

"Prince Cailian, I can reassure you—"

"—It is okay, Taygen. She is a force, it seems. If my mate says you are friends, you are friends."

Nyx stands beside me, growling. "You will be the best fucking friend she ever had, understood?"

"I do not take orders from you. I am not your guard."

"You do take orders from him, Taygen," I rush to speak before Nyx can lose his temper and burn my guard until he turns to ash. "He is my mate which means we rule our kingdoms together."

Taygen dislikes what I have to say, setting his jaw to the point that it flexes, and casts his eyes away. "Understood, Prince Cailian."

Nyx blows out a slow, deliberate breath of black smoke that drifts into Taygen's face. I slap Nyx's chest before standing in front of Taygen, blocking the brimstone-scented cloud.

"Do not treat my guards and my people the way you want to treat me." Grabbing his arm, I tug him down the frozen corridor, away from Taygen's deadly grip on the spear.

"I was only—"

"—Do not try and make excuses for how you really feel. No matter how you fluff your words, I know your true feelings because I can feel them as if they are my own. You cannot fool me, Nyx. You might be able to fool everyone else, but not me. You hate my kingdom, you hate me, you hate my elves. I understand that." I turn around before we reach Rarity, who is currently leaning against the railing, looking out to the vast view of Elementalu.

Vampire hearing is advanced, and I have no doubt she can hear every word I am saying to Nyx.

I crowd his space, standing toe to toe with the massive specimen that's Dovenyx. "But while I understand that I will not stand for you to treat my elves with so much disrespect. Whether you like it or not, you are here. You are one of the leaders of my kingdom, no matter how much it still surprises me Fate would destine us. You do not like me, fine, but you will take that out on me. Do I make myself clear, Nyx?" I keep my voice as low as a whisper, my heart thumping wildly in my chest, no doubt that he can feel it as if it is his own, betraying my bravado.

"As clear as ice, Treasure." The nickname drapes over me like a warm blanket causing a blip to stammer my heart.

"Do not call me that. We both know you do not mean it. I am far from being someone who you treasure." Before he can say another word, I turn around to give him my back, then take a step to walk toward Rarity.

Our eyes lock and she tucks a piece of wild hair behind her ear before pinching her lips together as if she is stopping herself from laughing.

A hand lands on the back of my neck, gripping me without remorse with how bad it hurts before yanking me backward. Nyx causes me to spin around, his grasp on me so strong, that I feel the threat of it in my bones. One flick of his wrist, and I'll be dead.

He growls as he lowers his head until he is nose to nose with me. "You are my treasure. I apologize for treating you and your kingdom with disrespect, but never say I do not mean something because I never speak false truths. We have a lot to work toward, but you are mine, Little Elf." Nyx turns his head, his warm breath ghosting over my lips. "And what did I say about calling me Nyx?" His lips crash onto mine and the hold on my neck helps him control the kiss, his forked tongue slipping between my lips, teasing me with his want before he pulls free. "Now, let's go see our much more reasonable firebond, *Treasure.*"

He lets me go, leaving me missing the calculating grip on my neck, and my cock aching for him.

Damn him.

Gathering my thoughts and lust, I run my fingers through my hair and take a deep breath before glancing to the right. Snow-covered mountains are in the distance, sitting happily behind the frozen forest. Blankets of snow lie for miles. Ice clings to the leaves. A quiet peace settles in the air, and it is almost hard to believe that on the other side of the castle is Nyx's fiery kingdom where the trolls seem to be camping in Fog's forest.

Rarity's giggle makes me turn towards her to see Nyx making her laugh by brushing his scales against her neck. She must be ticklish.

"Nyx! Nyx, stop," she pleads in laughter, turning her neck and body to try and get away from him, but it is in poor attempt. She loves his attention.

I know that feeling all too well.

Her purple eyes are lighter outside, leaving the faintest hue of the color I have found myself obsessed with. She reaches her hand out, inviting me into their space.

"Cailian, come here. It isn't the same without you."

"What do you mean? You two seem just fine without me," I tease, taking a step closer because denying them would kill a part of my soul.

Nyx takes his turn, pressing his cheek against hers as his embers against his coal-colored scales pierce me.

I cannot help but wonder if our lives would be easier if we loved her separately. I would yearn for him, but I know he would not yearn for me, not in the way mates are supposed to.

To my surprise, his fingers trail down her forearm before sliding across her palm and then pointing at me. One long claw gestures in a come hither motion, the nail changing color as the light reflects off it with every bend of his finger.

"Come here, Little Elf. Our firebond has made my cock hard and while we look out onto this beautiful view, you're going to get on your knees and suck me down your throat."

This dragon has me submit to him in ways I have never submitted to him before.

"And while you suck my cock, I'm going to finger fuck our firebond until she comes and then I expect you to lick her clean. After that, we will finish this fucking tour, and go back to my castle. Do you understand?"

Do I understand? I cannot stand it when he asks me that because no, no I do not understand. What the hell is happening? In a place that is so cold, why do I feel as if I am on fire?

I glance around the corridor, looking left and right to see guards posted at every corner, swallowing the lump in my throat.

"Nyx—" He growls in dismay, and I correct myself. "Dove, someone will most likely see us. The village is not that far. There are people in the winter gardens just there," I point to the courtyard where there are a few elves enjoying their day, stopping to smell the blue roses with frozen stems. "And the guards," I whisper, my eyes sliding to the closest guard, who just happens to be Taygen. "They will hear."

Nyx slides his claw down Rarity's chest and stomach, then dives his hand between her legs and slowly lifts the emerald gown. His hand rubs against her thigh, the skin soft and smooth. I remember it well when I settled between her legs the night before and feasted.

I take another step forward, my eyes locked on where his hand has disappeared under her dress. Her thighs pebble from the cold air and while she's looking at me, her lips part as she moans.

He must be touching her pussy, rubbing his fingers across her clit to ignite such a filthy noise.

"Let them hear. Let them see. I hope they watch. They will know who you two belong to so be a good boy and get on your knees, Treasure. My cock is aching for your mouth."

"But the tour," I say weakly, my voice breaking on the simple three words.

His eyes flame and his wings spread from his back.

Fire escapes him like a lasso and the heat wraps around my waist, then yanks me to them. The flaming limb slams on my shoulder, forcing me to the ground.

"I said to suck my cock while I make our firebond come." His dragon speaks for him, dark and rough as if he has breathed in way too much smoke. "Everything else can wait. Isn't that right, Rarity?" His arm moves further between her legs and by the sound of her gasp, he has slipped his fingers inside her tight pussy.

I turn around to see, wanting a view of Rarity in pleasure, but Nyx wraps his hand around my throat.

"Focus, Little Elf, and then maybe I will let you see her."

A moan slips from me as I fumble with his pants to free his cock. The material leaves nothing to the imagination. His want, his need, how large he is, is very clear. There's a wet spot forming from precome on his pants and the ridge around his crown is easily seen. I scoot closer, my mouth watering, and hide his cock from anyone else who dares to look.

I undo the ties eagerly, having to tug his pants down his hips in order to free him. His cock is down his thigh, and I tilt my head back to look up at him, fishing my hand down his pants. I expect to get the view of the base of his sculpted jaw. Instead, I find him staring at me, his arm moving back and forth while he finger fucks Rarity.

She runs her fingers through my hair, gasping and groaning as he moves his arm faster, fucking her in earnest with his fingers.

I pull his cock free at last, taking my eyes from his handsome face before staring at his cock. It's intimidating and much bigger than I could ever fit in my mouth.

"Go on," he orders.

"I will not take orders from you, Dove. I will do this on my own time."

When he scoffs, flames lick his lips. He grabs the base of his cock and presses it against my mouth, then thrusts his hips forward, silencing me as hits the back of my throat.

"Do as your told, Little Elf, before I fuck your mouth so hard, you won't be able to speak, and when you can't speak, you won't be able to pretend to deny me." He slides out, only to slide back in, groaning in delight. "I do like it when you pretend to act like you do not like orders because you sit so pretty for me, Treasure. Doesn't he, Rarity? Tell him how pretty he is when he obeys."

She holds onto the space where my neck and shoulder meet, making those erotic sounds that echo through the corridor. Everyone can hear and yet, that only makes my cock throb.

"Cailian, you look so good, so—so—" her voice becomes higher as he plunges his fingers deeper. "So sexy, so gorgeous when you are on your knees for him, when you listen, when your mouth is full of his cock," she manages to say.

"Such a good girl," he praises with a grunt. "One of these days, I am going to fuck you both right here, over this courtyard for all to see."

I hum around the mouthful of cock, wrapping a hand around the base to stroke in tandem. Licking and tracing the crown, I suck him as if he is my favorite icicle.

His claws rake across my neck, leaving a slight burn in their wake. My lips stretch wide, my jaw begins to ache, my knees begin to hurt from being on the hard floor, but no amount of pain could stop me from being in this position. My dragon's cock tastes so good, so warm and smooth, and all I want is to swallow his come; to feel the warmth of it spread in my stomach.

I lick the tip, swirling my tongue around the glands before bobbing my head faster.

"Fuck," he growls. "That's it. Suck my cock, Good Boy."

"Nyx, I'm going to— I'm going to come," Rarity warns, lifting one of her legs to drape over my shoulder.

All I want to do is kiss up her leg until I am locking my lips around her clit, but I am not allowed. My order is to be here, sucking our dragon's cock.

"Not yet," he states. "Don't you dare come yet, My Darling Jewel. Once I fill his mouth, Cailian isn't going to swallow, he is going to turn around, and eat that pretty pussy." He grips my chin, stopping me from taking his cock any further. "And you're going to try to spit as much of my come inside her as you can, aren't you?"

My eyes glaze over as I nod.

"Such a good boy." He turns his head to the left, continuing to finger Rarity all while standing there as if this isn't out of the norm. "Do you like what you see, Elf? Are you shocked to see your prince on his knees for a dragon?"

Oh my gods, someone is here. Who is it? Parts of me don't even care. This is one of the hottest, most embarrassing moments of my life.

"He is good at sucking my dick. Are you jealous you have never experienced his mouth?" His hand cups the back of my head. "And you never will—" his hips stutter. "Fuck, I'm about to royally fill his mouth if you want to stick around and watch. It will be more come than you have ever seen."

The hurry of feet retreating tells me whoever it was, ran away as fast as they could.

"Cailian. Cailian, fuck, fuck!" he roars, his voice bouncing off the empty hallway walls, alerting everyone of his orgasm.

Warmth slides across my tongue, never-ending streams of it. His seed leaks from the corner of my mouth and I go to swallow, not wanting a drop to hit the floor, but again, he uses his hand to squeeze my throat.

"Don't fucking swallow. Let it leak. I want to see how messy I can make the Ice Elven Prince."

My eyes roll to the back of my head in ecstasy.

"Please, Nyx. Please!" Rarity begs to come.

"Not yet, My Darling Jewel. You'll get yours. I promise and then you're going to fall to your knees and suck Cailian's cock. I have no doubt it hurts. Isn't that right, Treasure?"

I nod in quick beats causing come to slip from my mouth and down my chin.

"Look at you, making such a mess." His finger slips through his come, brings it to his mouth, and sucks. "Do you want some, Princess?"

"Yes, yes, yes," she chants, rocking her hips against his hand which shakes my body and more of his seed drips from my jaw.

My robes are a mess. They are wet from my spit and all of the come his three balls keep for us.

He swipes his finger across my chin again and her hum of appreciation has me squeezing my cock through my robes.

"Mmmm, such a good boy getting on his knees. I know they must hurt. I'll massage your legs later." He slips his cock free, the massive member taking ages to leave my mouth before slapping against his thigh.

He turns me around, pushing me between Rarity's legs, and lifts her dress for me to dip my head under.

"Feast, Treasure. Experience your firebonds orgasms. Let us be a cocktail that buzzes through your veins." His finger slides free, leaving her empty and wet.

Gripping her thighs to spread her legs, my eyes lock on her trimmed hair and all I want to do is bury my nose in it and inhale.

But I have orders and I want to be a good boy for the dragon who hates me.

I plunge my tongue into her drenched cunt, and she cries out, gripping my head with her hands. A savage, primal, animalistic roar

rings in my ears, and then I hear the smacks of lips together. I want nothing more than to look up and witness my two mates kissing each other until they can't breathe.

Yet I have my own kissing to do.

I do my best to spit his come into her, driving it deep inside with every stroke of my tongue. Licking my way through her lips, I suck her clit into my mouth, and her knees give out. Between Nyx and I, we keep her on her feet, and I suck her bundle of nerves harder, nibbling it between my teeth.

She sobs. "Cailian. Cailian. You have to stop. Oh my gods, I'm so close. Oh, don't stop. Don't." Rarity contradicts herself, pushing me away and pulling me against her in the next second.

Nyx chuckles. "What is it, My Darling Jewel? Is it too much? Can you not take it? That's too fucking bad."

I groan unexpectedly when I feel his tail slip under my robes and tease my crease. I nearly choke on his thick come but as Rarity's thighs tremble, I keep my pace, wanting my mate to come for me, for all to hear, for the kingdom to know my vampire is claimed.

"You're so fucking beautiful when you're about to come, Rarity. Flushed lavender cheeks, pouty pink lips that make me want to fucking eat you, glazed eyes, messy hair, those goddamn noises that fall from your soul. I want to drink them," Nyx says as his tail wraps around my cock until it constricts it, making me mewl in pain.

And then he lets go causing me to groan.

Plunging my tongue inside her again, my sack pulls to my body, my cock burns with a painful throb from Nyx teasing me, and if she does not come soon, I am afraid I am going to die if I do not get relief.

"Cailian!" she screams my name.

My. Name.

And it is music to my pointed ears as my mouth is graced with the taste of her orgasm. I drink her down, allowing her to rub her pussy on my face, using me to get every spasm of pleasure.

I swallow, dipping my head out from under her dress and Rarity's eyes glow a magnificent bright red. Her fangs lengthen and snarling, she slams me against the wall across from the railing we were just at in a blink of an eye. Her strength overpowers my own. Claws rip my robes, freeing my cock for all to see.

In a blur, she lowers herself to her knees, swallowing me whole, and I lose the ability to think or string a thought together.

"Rarity—" I moan loudly, my vision blurring for a moment before I'm able to focus on Nyx.

He's standing across the hallway, leaning against the rail, his muscular arms crossed over his chest, wings spread, as he stares at us as if we are his favorite thing to watch.

I'm starting to think he loves a good show and I do not mind giving it to him at all.

A sharp pain of her fangs slicing into the vein that pumps blood to my cock has me hissing, but then she sucks, relishing in long drags.

She's beautiful as she drinks from the most intimate spot.

Her bite, how she drinks, the pain and pleasure mixed has my orgasm finally ripping from me. She swallows the blood and come concoction, moaning from my taste.

"So, who is ready to finish that tour?" Nyx laughs at his own question.

I mumble something. I'm not sure what it is, but I'm ready for a nap.

Chapter Sixteen

DOVENYX

I couldn't control myself after Cailian got mad at me. I couldn't help myself when I saw Rarity leaning against the railing, enjoying the view of the mountains.

The view of her distracted me. The anger rolling in the bond from Cailian fueled me. I needed them. I felt distant and it is no one's fault but my own. I am trying to accept Fate yet at every turn, I am reminded that the elf I yearn for, the creature I want in my bed and on his knees, is the one who changed my life forever.

The only normalcy I feel in this mating is Rarity. She's solid ground, a place where I can feel peace instead of chaos. She's a welcome breath of fresh air and stability. Because of that, I don't think she will ever know how much her presence, her being, her mind, her soul, and everything else about her, means to me.

She is peace.

He is violence.

I shouldn't be surprised that I can't live without both.

The walk to the village is quiet and a bit comical. Rarity and Cailian are dazed, still riding the high of their orgasms. I feel a bit smug Taygen and a few other guards saw us, saw me claiming my firebonds. I am not a fool. I know Cailian is one of the most beautiful elves I have ever laid eyes on.

And I know Taygen feels the same. I could see it in how he stared at My Treasure. There were hearts in his eyes, and I had to break them.

"Can't we go back and take a nap?" Cailian asks for the third time since we left the main castle to walk down the path leading to the village. "The village will be here tomorrow. We can just go cuddle in bed all day. Does that not sound delightful? And we can listen to Rarity talk in her sleep."

"I don't talk in my sleep that much."

"You're right." I pat the top of her head. "You don't talk in your sleep. You're silent. It's all in our heads."

"Thank you. I am so glad one of you is being reasonable." She laces her fingers through mine, her other with Cailian, and we walk hand in hand.

It's so domestic. I don't think I have ever held hands, but I will hold theirs until death rips me away from them.

It is on the tip of my tongue to tell them I love them, to admit to Cailian that I have somehow fallen more in love with him; that it has surpassed the centuries of hate I've bottled up inside. I want to tell Rarity that she saved me from becoming a darker version of myself, that her love rescued me from swimming in the fires of hate.

I can't tell her I love her without telling Cailian. I don't want to see the pain on his face, thinking I am rejecting him. I'm not ready to tell him how I feel because I'm not ready to accept that I love the man who took my father from me.

And I don't know if I'll ever be ready for that.

"It is so beautiful here," Rarity says, cutting through my depressing thoughts.

She stops in the middle of the walkway, snow up to her ankles, and hiding the heels she is wearing. As if she can read my mind, Rarity bends over, and takes her shoes off, holding them in her left hand.

"The snow feels so good. It's like… It's…" she tries to find the words as she wiggles her toes in the snow.

Even her toes are fucking sexy.

I growl, rolling my neck over my shoulders when my cock takes notice of her damn feet. Their heats must be coming soon because I feel like I'm about to enter a rut. Every move they make right now sends me over the edge. I want to slam Cailian on his stomach and fill his ass, fucking him until he screams for help and his guards rush to his aid, only for me to burn them alive for daring to take him away from me.

I want to fuck Rarity's cunt with my tail, preparing her, stretching her wide for my knot. I want to see her stomach swell, my seed locked into her womb, and I want her to carry my children.

Needing a moment to breathe, I give the two gorgeous, breathtaking, stunning firebonds my back. The air escaping my lungs is a frozen cloud with every exhale. My lungs feel the slight sting of the cold weather, but not as brutal as it used to be.

I squeeze my cock until a sharp pain has me releasing and my erection deflates.

"It's healing, is it not?" Cailian asks her.

Even his voice is causing me to lose control. Now every breath is laced with a growl as I try to control myself. All I want to do is fuck them all day, all night, until they are mindless and tired. I want them to be unable to speak full sentences as they take my cock.

"My Love?" Rarity's sweet, gentle voice wraps around me, not helping my fucking problem at all.

Her hand caresses my arm, her silky fingers stroking my scales and I have to hold my breath while closing my eyes.

"Nyx, are you okay?" she asks, taking my hand in hers.

"Dove, you seem unwell. Your scales are very bright right now."

A sign I am close to being in a rut. I give it a few more days before I have them locked in my room and drowning in my come.

Cailian slides his hand down my spine, and I shiver, his touch innocent yet electric.

"This is going to sound bad and please do not take it that way, but if we are to make it through the day, introducing Rarity to everyone and showing her the kingdoms, I need you two not to touch me for a few hours. Possibly the rest of the day."

I take another deep breath to calm the fire brewing in my chest, wanting to purge itself from sexual frustration.

I see the light go out of their eyes. The happiness that was there just moments ago has retreated into their laugh lines around their lips.

"Of course," Cailian states, looking away to stare at the wintery slush on the sidewalk.

"Sure. Whatever you want. Wouldn't want you disgusted with us or anything," Rarity mumbles under her breath, taking Cailian's hand.

My firebonds begin to walk in front of me, leaving to head toward the village. It begins to snow, a slight irritant to my dragon. Spreading my wings, I leap into the air and fly through the cold, the snowflakes hitting my cheeks. I land in front of the pair and lose my damn temper.

I whip my arms out, taking each of my firebonds by the throat, and with my wings, fly them to the nearest tree. Their backs thud against the thick trunk, the vibrations of the force shake the snow from the heavily weighted branches. All the trees are hidden within cloaks of

snow. That is why it is called the frosted forest. Nothing can be seen except acres of white.

Rarity flashes her fangs at me, her eyes bleeding to red in fury from being taken by surprise.

"You think I don't want your touch? My firebonds get themselves in trouble, I see." My forked tongue flicks out, tasting their confusion, lust, and... what is that?

A tiny dose of fear.

My eyes roll to the back of my head from how fucking good it tastes across my tongue, sending me that much closer to a rut.

"I didn't realize my firebonds were so foolish. Don't you understand?" I snarl, my need clawing at my chest as if a succubus has climbed inside me and is begging to get free. "I fucking want you." I roam my eyes down Rarity's body, then slide them up Cailian's. "I am close to being thrown into a rut and when that happens— not if— there will never be a second where you will be free of me. I will fuck you. I will knot you. I will not stop until I do not have a drop of come left to give. So when I say, 'Please, do not touch me' it is not because I do not want you but that I am saving you from the beast inside me that is nearly too far gone. So be good and do not tempt your dragon." I release the hold I have on them and they slump against the tree.

The lust is so strong, I have to take a step away.

They like the sound of that.

"And if instinct is all I have to go by, your heats are close as well. We need to get this over with. Does it really matter if we meet everyone today? We have the rest of our lives. Can't we go back to my castle? I'll bathe you both in the hot spring I have running through my property. You'll love it."

"I want to see everything. And if you're right, then we don't have much time before we are locked away in the bedroom for days." Rarity wiggles her eyebrows. "I have no complaints about that."

"You'll most likely be pregnant after the fact. The both of you," I state, my blood boiling with desire. I want to see them round with my child. I wonder what our children will be, what they will look like.

I've always heard species can only be one, but what if our child had all three DNA traits? I wouldn't care. I only want them to be healthy.

"I am more than okay with that. I would love to start a family with you both," Rarity says.

"Even if we have so much to learn about one another?" Cailian asks. "Even if we—" he stops speaking, glancing to the left to look out into the frozen forest.

"Even if we what?" Rarity wraps her arms around him, pressing her cheek against his back.

"Nothing," he says, forcing a smile. "Let us go before it becomes too late. With the trolls in the forest, I do not want to risk anything."

I cup the back of his head while placing my hand on Rarity's arm, needing to feel their skin against mine. "I won't let anything happen to you. I promise."

"It is not us I am worried about," Cailian leans in, pressing his forehead against my chest before turning his head and placing his ear against my heart. "It is you," he whispers.

"Me?" I kiss the top of his head, smiling at Rarity who is standing behind him. "There is no need to worry about me. I'm nearly eight feet tall in this form and too many feet to count in my dragon."

"Not if they get to your heart," he exhales a shaky breath. "And I happen to like the sound of the strong, rugged beat. I do not want it taken from us when the song soothes us to sleep."

"I feel the same," Rarity speaks, her voice nearly covered by the slight static of the snow falling. "I don't want to risk you. How many hours do we have before it is considered late? I— I don't know what I would do if anything happened to either of you. I— I— can't think about—" Her eyes begin to well with tears, and they shine like colors reflecting in a kaleidoscope.

I wipe them away, pulling my firebonds to my chest. "Nothing will happen to me. There is no heart for those trolls to take." I lean away cupping their cheeks with my oversized hands that seem to engulf them. "You two have already taken it so how can they take what is not there?"

"Your words are sweet even if they are false," Cailian says.

I urge them forward. "Come on. Let's go to the village. Then we will stay in my castle tonight."

A wave of fear drifts from Cailian as he hurries ahead of us. Is he afraid to go to my castle?

"Cailian," I say his name with an edge, and yet, he keeps walking away from me. I pick up my pace to catch up with him only to slip on a sheet of ice. "Oh, shit—" my breath is knocked out of me when my back slams against the ground.

It doesn't end there.

Rarity bends down to pick me up— and she could with her vampire strength— but I begin to slide down the hill.

"Rarity! Rarity—" I reach for her hand and once I grab it, the speed I'm sliding at begins to increase so I tug Rarity down on accident.

She yelps, slamming her elbow into my gut and I groan. Rarity's claws sink into my chest as we somehow move faster. Snow covers my face and flies on either side of us. I try to stop but the ice is too slick. I can't seem to get any traction.

Cailian turns around when he hears the commotion and his eyes widen, knowing what is about to come because it is too late to move. Rarity and I ram against his legs, and he hits the ground beside us. His hair is no longer perfect, and his crown is tangled in braids. I snag his ankle, pulling him to me so I can make sure he stays with us.

I didn't know our kingdom was so.... steep. I need to get out more.

"Ahhhhh!" Rarity screams when we hit a bump and catch some air.

The sky passes above me, my lashes are coated with snow, my cheeks are frozen, and I can't feel my tail.

What if it isn't attached anymore? What if it got frozen solid and snapped off?

That's ridiculous.

Tails just can't snap off.

"Nyx... Nyx!" Cailian screams before we fly over another bump, only this time, we all get separated.

Cailian flips.

Rarity's limbs are windmilling.

I try to get my wings to work to get some stability, but my left wing won't stretch. We hit the ground one after the other, our grunts following the last, and I somersault until I finally land on my back, coming to a complete stop.

I gasp for breath, arms spread out, thank my lucky stars that— Cailian's elbow slams into my ribs, and Rarity flops between my legs, her fist hammering down on my balls.

Inhaling until I gasp, I roll to the side and cup my dick, gagging a little. My head swims from the pain.

"Oh my gods! Nyx. Nyx, I am so sorry. Are you okay?" Rarity crawls around me, flipping me to my back. "I didn't mean to. I had no control." She covers her mouth with both hands.

"It's— It's fine," I mutter through a held breath. "I need a minute."

She looks so disheveled. Her dress is soaked. The hem is torn. Her hair is a tangled mess. And she has a scratch on her cheek but before I can say anything, the skin stitches itself together and heals.

Why can't my balls do the same?

"Will you be okay?" Cailian asks through a smile he is trying his best to hide but failing.

"I don't know. Maybe you two should check for bruising." I tuck my hands behind my head, smirking as the pain fades. "Maybe give it *three* kisses. I might feel better then." I wink at both of them.

"Ugh," Rarity nudges me playfully. "Men. You're all the same in some capacity."

Cailian snorts as he laughs, shaking his head. "You're a menace."

"You love it," I say, catching his eyes.

We lock gazes and he stands, holding out his hand.

"You love it," I repeat, brows furrowing as I stare at his palm. I need him to tell me.

"You know I do," he mumbles so quietly I can hardly hear him. "You're still a menace."

Slapping my hand in his, I allow him to help me up.

"I'm your menace." I slip two fingers under his chin and force his head up. "Yours."

That faint blue hue dusts his cheeks as he nibbles on his bottom lip. As I look at him, I realize the hate I've been carrying around all these years is no longer there. There isn't a voice in the back of my head whispering he has another agenda.

I believe anyone is capable of being a killer. Cailian? He is not a murderer. My heart is telling me that. I'm getting to know him and while I'm afraid I could be wrong; I don't think I am.

"You always have a way of making me feel so... fragile," he says.

"Now you know how I feel when it comes to the both of you." Rarity twists her hair before wrapping it in a messy bun on top of her head.

I shake the snow from my wet hair and heat my body, warming my veins and eventually drying me from head to toe.

"You should be able to do the same," I inform, finally spreading my wings. I choke in the agony in the middle of my back, knowing that my flying days are numbered. "Focus on my dragon fire inside you. Imagine it is me making you warm."

"I cannot," Cailian scoffs. "We are too close to the village and imagining you making me warm is a recipe for disaster."

"Is that so?" I growl, the urge swelling back inside me to hide them away in my room. "If you want to be dry, focus, Treasure. Imagine I am swimming through your body, igniting a fire in every crevice, in every bone, in your marrow. Pretend, I am melting the ice that lives inside you." My own words turn against me. The thought of being so close to them, inside them, exploring every aspect of their cells has the threat of the rut creep forward.

Their scents hit me at the same time, mixed with steam, surprise, and desire. I have no doubt Rarity is wet and Cailian is hard.

"It worked," Cailian says, patting his dry chest.

"That's an impressive trick," Rarity agrees, touching every part of her dress, including sliding her hands down her breasts.

I know she doesn't mean for it to be sexual, but I'm hanging by a fucking thread. I want to burn that dress from her body, sit her on my lap, and watch as she rides my cock.

The rut is way too close. I can't imagine how it will feel when it hits if my want for them is already like this.

"Prince Cailian?" An older, broken voice sounds from behind us and we turn around in unison.

I stand in front of my firebonds, covering them with my wings just in case this creature is a threat. Cailian gently lowers my right wing, taking a step forward.

"Anleer," Cailian greets. "It has been too long, my friend."

Anleer bows the best he can, holding the hand-carved cane in his hand. He leans most of his weight on it, but Cailian stops him by grabbing his wrist.

"Please, do not bow to me when it is me who should be bowing to you."

"I might be old, Prince Cailian, but I still have a few bows left in me," the old elf argues in a huff. "But my back hurts today, so you win, for now." He arches a bushy silver eyebrow as he looks at me, then Rarity.

If Cailian is over eight hundred years old, how old is Anleer? His hair is no longer white, but streaked with silver and black. His skin lacks the shine Cailian's does, and he has hundreds of wrinkles on his face, neck, and arms. Even the tips of his ears droop from age.

"You're staring, dragon. You're wondering how old I am." He hits me in the knee with his walking stick.

"Ow, fuck." I hold my knee and hop for a second, snarling at the crazy elf. "You have lost your fucking mind."

"My age is none of your business."

"You could have just said that." I glare at him, debating if I want to set his body on fire. It would be quick. "Hitting me in the knee wasn't necessary."

"Ah, yes," he shakes his finger. "But I wanted to. I'm too old not to do what I want."

The ache in my knee pulses for a few seconds before going away. "That's fair," I grumble just as Rarity snickers. "You get hit by a wooden cane and see how it feels." I begin to tickle her ribs, and a loud

squeal echoes before turning into fits of laughter that is music to my ears. The joyful notes remind me of the stories my father told me when I was just a little dragon still trying to find my wings.

Every night before going to bed, he'd tell the stories of the mag-mayas, similar to sirens in the sense that they have human-like upper bodies and a fishtail. Where one swims in water, magmayas swim in magma, living inside the volcano itself.

He would say, *"They have fire for hair and long black tails similar to our scales. They are beautiful— the deadly kind of beautiful. They would lure men with their laughter, a unique song that only a man with a broken heart can hear. The men would wander through the forests for miles until they finally got to the magmayas, who would be lounging on the volcanic rocks, waiting for them. The dragons and magmayas lived peacefully together since we come from the same place, so the dragons never interfered. See, all magmayas are female, and in order to have young, they have to seduce human men with their songs. After the men were used, magmayas would throw them into the volcano so their bodies would become one with the magma and rock. It is the magmaya's belief that killing the men seals the mating. They are dangerous and breath-taking but be careful when you hear laughter. You never know where you'll go."*

Rarity's laughter reminds me of all of my father's warnings because I would follow her to the doomed depths. I would burn if it meant being with her, even once. Rarity might not physically be magmaya but she has me under her spell regardless.

"Why are you looking at me like that?" she whispers, side-eyeing the elder elf.

"Like what, My Darling Jewel?"

"Like—" she can't find the words.

"—Like I can't get enough of you?" I grip her chin with my fingers before staring into her eyes and leaning in for a kiss. Just as our lips are about to touch, I whisper, "Because I can't." And I press my lips against hers, forgetting where we are and who we are with. I need to feel her.

I need...

Fuck, I don't know what I need.

I deepen the kiss, raking my hands down her body, my claws tugging on the material of her dress. Settling at her hips, I grab them, twisting the fabric in my palms.

A throat clears.

"We keep getting distracted," Cailian says as an explanation.

"If I were a few thousand years younger, I would get distracted too."

I snort in laughter and Rarity hides her face in my chest, embarrassed.

"Anyway, what are you doing in the village, Prince Cailian? Without your guards. That is dangerous for you. You know that."

"He has me," I explain, tucking Rarity to my side. "He doesn't need his guard."

Anleer rolls his damn eyes at me before tapping his walking stick on the ground. "Typical dragon. Always so confident to protect, but you are no ordinary dragon. You are royalty too. Two of our royals, here, unprotected with a vampire who has purple eyes. Yes, yes, I can see where you would think you wouldn't need protection."

"Your sarcasm wasn't asked for." Fire begins to warm my chest and Rarity rubs the middle of my sternum, trying to get me to calm down.

"Oh good. I freely gave it if you did not— or could not— catch on. I hear dragons are a little—" he hits his head with his cane.

I step forward, snarling at the elf I could turn into a fucking kabob by shoving that walking stick right up his—

"—Okay, I think that is enough taunting our dragon, Anleer. We are here for a quick tour to introduce Rarity and Nyx to everyone."

"Right, right. Apologies. It's been a while since I had some fun. Apologies, Prince Dovenyx. You know, you look a lot like your father. Not as kind or even-tempered, but I can see where you are his son. This must not be an easy mating, considering..." Anleer implies.

"We are working through it," I bite, hating to be reminded. Every time I think I am getting ahead of the damn past, it catches up with me.

Anleer nods, whistling as he turns around and walks away. His walking stick thuds against the ground, leaving small circular indentations in the snow.

"He was lucky to have survived that conversation, Cailian. Next time, he might not be so lucky."

Cailian pats my shoulder. "He is an old elf. His manners are long gone. He's been around long enough to see me and all of my ancestors on the throne."

"Oooh, what are these beautiful creatures?" Rarity asks, skipping down the slick road where Icebergsa's are tied to poles. "Looks kind of like a horse."

She raises her hand to pet its neck and Cailian snags her wrist before she can touch the Icebergsa. "You cannot touch an Icebergsa without its approval. They are very loyal to their masters because the master gives a slither of their magic to them, binding them for life."

"I have always found Icebergsa's temperamental. I have yet to find one that is accepting of anyone that isn't their master. It is best not to risk it, Rarity," I state, agreeing with Cailian for once.

She stands in front of the Icebergsa, its long white mane nearly touches the ground, and the muscular legs hold up its thick frame. The edges of their hooves are jagged and uneven, frozen like a chunk

of ice. Their tail is unique as well, the long strands morph from hair to icicles halfway down. The eyes mimic a blizzard. There is no pupil or iris. The entirety is just a snowstorm blazing in each eye.

"It is said if you can hold its stare for more than a minute without losing your mind and getting lost in the storms they hold, it will accept you."

"That doesn't seem too hard."

"I see that look." Cailian snaps his fingers. "I know that look. Do not dare," he warns in a way that has the hair on the back of my neck stand up. "I have seen too many elves and men alike fall to the attempt."

Rarity grins, lifting her chin as she meets the eyes of an Icebergsa. "I am neither, Cailian. Do not compare their weaknesses to me."

I rub a hand over my mouth, wondering just how dumb he must feel right now. It's too late to say anything. Her gaze is in the Icebergsa's grasp.

Captivated, I step closer, seeing the flecks of snow reflecting from the creature's eyes against Rarity's. The area around us is quiet, nothing but the heavy huffs from the Icebergsa and the snow gently falling to the ground. In the distance, music and laughter echo, tempting me to take my firebonds there to see the fun that can be had.

Fun.

I can't remember the last time I had a genuinely good time. Being a royal comes with too many responsibilities. My duties do not get done just to make time for fun and I know Cailian must experience the same.

"Rarity," he whispers painfully, waiting for the last few moments to tick by.

He shuffles his weight from his left to the right, placing his hands on his hips before pacing back and forth.

"Treasure." I snag the back of his neck— something I notice I very much like to do— and tug him against me.

His back fits perfectly in the divots and nooks of my body, his ass curving like a puzzle piece against my pelvis. I gather his hair and tug his head back, a sweet gasp escaping that panicked mouth.

"Do I need to fuck you out here in front of everyone to get you to calm down?" I slide my claws down his cheek, the other down his back, tracing the scars I left there. "Will that get you to see that our firebond is stronger than you give her credit for?" I tug his head to the side and ghost my lips down his throat, the smell of an iced forest lingering on his skin. Being alone in the cold, the frozen air stinging our lungs, and with every pant, the puffs of air clouds our vision. The sun shines against the blankets of snow covering the ground. Each small flake glitters like diamonds, a variety of colors bouncing off one another.

The sun promises spring with fresh wildflowers that are waiting to bloom under the cold, waiting to be warm.

That is the closest I can get to describing how he smells— the promise of a field of wildflowers after an ice age, that peaceful promise that can only be found when alone, lost, and exploring the end of winter.

It's a cold scent I want to bottle so I can smell the morning sun mixed with winter.

"That wasn't so hard," Rarity says out of nowhere.

Hearing her voice brings me back to reality, but not enough to stop my lips from pressing just below his ear.

"I live to see another day." She strokes the Icebregsa's neck.

It neighs before bumping its nose against her cheek.

Cailian clears his throat, straightening out his robes as if they are a mess from us fucking. Oh, how I would love to lift the material and bunch it around his thighs while I drive into him over and over again.

"No one can know of this," he hurries. "No one can know you are accepted by the Icebergsa. It means you can take any from their master. The more you have, the more powerful you are. Icebergsas, once trained, can be a deadly force to any army."

I'm trying to listen to him but his voice keeps getting further away as I stare at him.

He looks perfect. Not a wrinkle crinkling those expensive, elven-made robes. Even his hair is lying down on his shoulders like the mist from a waterfall. The braids he has neatly weaved through the crown before falling to his jawline, the golden jewels clipped into the strands clinking together.

Cailian can fool everyone right now with how put-together he is.

I know better.

His eyes are glazed and hooded with desire, a distant expression captivating his features.

Physically, he is in control, but mentally? Emotionally?

That's in *my* control. I *own* his desire.

"We won't tell a soul." I finally manage to rip my tongue from the roof of my mouth in order to speak.

"We should get going," Rarity says, kissing the Icebergsa on the snout. "I want to see everything. Cailian, Nyx, I want an Icebergsa." She takes our hands and turns us to walk down the cobble-iced road. "The village is beautiful." Rarity is looking in every direction, taking it all in and finding every last thing she sees fascinating. "That looks like an old, gothic cathedral." She points to a tall building with a pointed frame.

"Let's go back to you wanting an Icebergsa. They aren't inexpensive and once you have it, others will want it, or simply kill it because it belongs to royalty."

"We can protect it, can't we? If Icebergsas represent power, why don't we have any?"

"Well, dragons don't ride them due to the temperature changes."

"But you can now that we are all mated. Imagine the three of us riding them to any battle or meeting. We would be making a statement to all who challenges us."

"You are taking this role on quickly."

"Well, last I checked, I was destined for this role." She playfully flips her hair before snickering.

"She isn't wrong," Cailian says, stopping in front of the cathedral.

"You'll come to learn that I am never wrong," she sasses.

I smack her ass, giving her a taste of what will happen for when she is wrong. "I wonder if you'll feel the same when I have you bent over my knee, punishing you for that attitude."

"I'd like to see you attempt to put me over your knee."

My brows rise at her challenge and a dark chuckle escapes me as I take a step closer to her. I lean down, twirling her hair around my finger but tightening my grip and yanking her head back.

I breathe in her shocked gasp.

"I have no doubt that if I told you to lie over my lap and count each time my hand hit your cheeks, you'd submit to me, My Darling Jewel."

"Guess we will have to see about that," she whispers through a rasp, licking her lips.

I step away, my cock swelling beneath my pants, and it only gets worse when I notice how flustered she is.

"The... the cathedral." Rarity stumbles over her thoughts as she collects herself, remembering where the conversation left off. "It seems—"

"Gothic?" Cailian smirks, rubbing her plump bottom lip as he looks us up and down knowingly before giving us his back. He stares at the large building for a few moments before saying another word, allowing the sounds of the music and laughter to drift to us again.

The silence allows me to really appreciate the old ice building. Icicles hang from the roof, nearly touching the ground. The stained glass is an array of different colors and as the light hits it, the orange and reds reflect on the snow-covered canvas of the ground.

"It is one of the first buildings of the village," Cailian explains. "It's where our female elves live. The building is protected well. Nothing can hurt them there."

"They stay in there? All the time? That sounds terrible." Rarity frowns, stopping just at the bottom of the steps that lead to the wrap-around porch of the cathedral. "Why can't they leave? I understand there are only a few females—"

"—You do not understand how rare female elves are. They are better protected here. They are not able to walk this planet alone. Every creature, every being knows that female elves possess abilities that no other elf can. They can heal, take away pain, freeze memories, and so many other things, including fertility. If in the wrong hands, a female elf can give birth every three months. She could be a breeding machine. I will not allow my sisters to be sold on the black market. They have a good life here. A bit isolated, but I do what I can for them."

"Your sisters?" I ask, a bit confused because I do not remember him mentioning that he had sisters.

He stares at the building, watching it as if it is going to come to life and take him too. "I do not speak of them. It is also safer that way. The less people who know about them, the better, so you cannot tell a soul. Their lives will be at risk. Female elves are the equivalent of your gold, Dove. Their blood is silver and too many of our females in the past have been drained so hunters can sell it and make a fortune. It is also a hallucinogen so it gives the person who is taking it a fantastical high. Everything about them is worth money and cannot be found anywhere else in this dimension. Do you understand? I need you to understand," he practically yells, his eyes narrowed and raged. "Nothing can happen to them."

Rarity grabs his hand, but I want more.

I wrap my arms around them both and pull them to my chest, pressing my cheek against the top of Cailian's head so I can look at the building imprisoning his sisters.

"Let's go meet them," I say. "They are allowed to have visitors, right?" I lean back to see him but his gaze is cast downward. Slipping my fingers under his chin, I apply the slightest amount of pressure, and force his head up. "Right?"

"Approved visitors, yes."

"We are approved, are we not?" Rarity questions, taking the first step of the stairway to the porch. "I want to meet them."

"The last time I saw them, we had a big fight, so it has been a while."

"How long is a while?" I tuck my hands in my pockets to keep myself from reaching out again. I want to hoard my firebonds. I want to keep them close to me, skin on skin, it is the only way I know they are protected.

"A few— a few hundred years— give or take three hundred?" he shrugs, lifting an arm to scratch the base of his neck.

"My gods, Cailian. What happened?" I step in front of him to cut him off. "We aren't going further until you tell me."

He steps around me. "They did not want to speak to me after what happened with your father."

"Why did they care about my father?" I try to keep my temper, my panic, and my desperate curiosity in check.

He begins walking again. "Because his death might have meant you'd want retribution. They thought I would have to sacrifice one of them to you, as an apology."

"There's too much to unpack in that statement. I didn't even know about the female elves, so I couldn't have asked, not that I would have. I'm not too intent on having someone with me against their will."

He gives a tight smile. "Like you are with me, Dove?"

"That's... that's not what I mean. Can we not talk about that? How could I have gotten one of your sisters if I didn't know about them, Cailian?"

"Because I was supposed to offer one of them to you. I was supposed to come to you with my offering."

"But you didn't," Rarity says, wondering why we are still deciphering this. "So?"

"So he broke tradition, I'm guessing."

"I wasn't going to sacrifice one of my sisters to you when you were on a war path. If anyone was going to sacrifice themselves to you, it was going to be me. I won't allow them to become pets."

"Is that what you are to me, Treasure? A pet? Do you want me to treat you that way? How about you can sacrifice yourself to me later and I'll show you what a good boy you are for protecting your family."

"Nyx—"

"—Dove," I correct him. "I won't answer to anything else."

"You are not mad that I didn't bring them to you?"

"Why would it have mattered? You are my firebonds. They wouldn't have meant anything to me at the time."

"But to have one is—"

"—I don't care about that. Why would I want to possess someone who doesn't want my possession?"

"You don't have to worry about that with me," Rarity flirts, placing her hand on my bicep, kindling a growl in my chest. "I will always want your possession." She has an uncanny ability to obliterate any tension so Cailian and I don't get stuck arguing.

When we get to the top step, I'm about to throw Rarity against the wall when the guards in front of the wooden doors take a stance. Their spears clash together, forming an X so we can't enter.

"It is fine," Cailian appears at my side. "They are my mates. You can lower your weapons."

Without argument, they stand down, without a hint of emotion on their faces.

"You are aware of the Prince of Dragons and our mate, Rarity, the new Princess."

They bow, their gold and silver amor clicking together as they show their respect.

"They don't talk?" I ask as one of them opens the doors for us.

Cailian shakes his head. "The guards have had their tongue's cut out."

"For what?"

"You should ask your dragons that."

Chapter Seventeen

RARITY

I sigh when I hear Cailian's response, the never-ending digs they poke and prod at one another a few times a day. No one will ever move on if we can't put history behind us.

I step between them before another random fight occurs. "Now isn't the time or place for this. We know the issues here and there is no need to reenact them. Fighting can wait." I know I sound exhausted, but I suppose I am. I'm not sure how much more of this back and forth I can take with them.

They give me whiplash. One minute they are at each other's throats and the other they can't keep their hands off of one another.

"My dragons? Why would they do that?"

"I assumed they were taking orders from you," Cailian sneers, making my chest hurt with anxiety.

I truly can't stand this. How have they managed this for eight hundred years?

Interrupting their bickering, I push myself in front of them. "—We can make this quick and go to Nyx's firelands." I whip open a

velvet curtain with enough force that the rods and clasps grind together, matching my annoyance.

My beloveds fall silent, and I thought it was because of what I said, but when I finally see what the simple curtain was hiding, I gasp.

You can tell the living area used to have pews because of how the stained-glass windows are placed. They must have removed all the seating because now it's all rich colors. The floors are black and white marble, the colors swirling together. The ceiling are high, reminding me of the ballroom at Cailian's castle.

Only it is the décor and what is happening that has my lips parting.

A circular couch is in the middle of the room with blankets and pillows in the middle. More sofas line the wall, a few orange, some purple, and more chandeliers hang low with dull lighting. A long bar is frosted over, and a shirtless ice elf is behind it, wiping down the bar top. A naked elf hangs upside down from silk sheets, using them to pull himself into acrobatic positions. His large cock hangs between his legs and then I see the piercing on the crown when it glitters against the light.

Nyx covers my eyes. "I don't like this place. My firebond only sees our cocks."

I peek my head around, watching the elf flip again, giving me a view of his strong backside.

"Firebond," Nyx growls low in warning. "You have one second to put those lavender eyes on me before I bend you over."

Moaning comes from the couch with the bed in the middle and a gorgeous female elf is naked, fucking another elf. She's on top of him, moving faster, her groans louder as her hips rock back and forth.

"—I just don't know where to look," I reply honestly, getting distracted by all the open sexual encounters.

He slips his finger under my chin and blocks my view of anyone else. "Me. You look at me. Or Cailian."

"But…" I peek around his body when I hear another thud.

A female elf is slammed against the wall, her legs wrapped around the male elf's waist, his well-defined ass flexing with every thrust.

I expect Cailian to freak, to scream, but all he does is grab us by the arms and rush us away from the curtain.

"What the hell is going on?" Nyx whispers. "It is a brothel in there."

"I didn't realize they were trying to conceive. I've lost track of time."

"Conceive? I'm confused. What about their mates?" I ask.

Nyx hangs his head and scratches his neck. "The chances of them meeting their mates are low, Rarity. This is their home. If they want a family, they have to mate with elves here or anyone they pick."

"They could save the species but as of right now, a mating has not been successful. Two of three of my sisters wants a mate, the other isn't sure what she wants."

Another moan rings out, the kind that's loud and full of relief.

One of his sister's just had an orgasm.

My cheeks burn and Nyx buries his nose in my neck, inhaling. "You like what you hear, My Darling Jewel?"

"Nope. No, do not answer that." Cailian wrinkles his nose in disgust.

"She doesn't have to. My filthy little vampire loves hearing them fuck, don't you?"

"Nyx," I whisper in shame.

"It is okay." The velvet curtain is peeled back to reveal a woman, as she tightens the belt of her robe.

Her nipples are hard and pressing against the silk material.

"You get used to the smell and sound of lust." She flips her hair over her shoulder and smiles, her face somehow more beautiful the longer I stare at it. "Long time, no see brother." She doesn't smile at Cailian before her eyes land on Nyx and she lifts her chin. "Seems you have come to collect. Is that right, dragon?"

Nyx shakes his head, pulling Cailian to his side, then me. "No. Cailian is my firebond. I am Dovenyx, Prince of—"

"I know who you are. There is not a need to introduce yourself." Her bright blue eyes find me, and she takes a step forward. "I'm Leasyn. Call me Lea. I'm glad to know my brother has settled down and is not going to auction us off to your dragon mate."

"I would not have done that. What else can I do and say for you to believe me?"

"I believe you now because now the dragon is mated to you, taking my worry away from me," Lea replies just as another loud moan interrupts this... friendly encounter. "Azorwyn will be here in a few moments."

"Lea, I promise, I would have never given you to anyone. You have been here all these years, and you think I am going to be so evil as to do that? What have I done to you—"

"—We are prisoners!" she yells, her face morphing into something more sinister. Her cheeks become gaunt, her eyes sunken in, and her teeth are sharp before she turns into herself again.

Her long white hair emanates the glow of the constellations in darkness. Lea's body is curvy with wide hips and thighs. Her lips are plump, her eyes a shade of blue that reminds me of the sky back home.

I can see why the female elves are wanted. Sex appeal oozes from her without her trying.

"Cai! Is that you?" An elf with short hair cut above her shoulder stands by Lea, only this sister seems friendly. She has a big smile on her

face while tucking the hair behind her ears. "I have missed you. Where have you been?" She hugs him tight, and he does the same in return, squeezing his eyes shut in their embrace.

"Staying away like Lea wished."

Azorwyn scoffs, slapping her sister on the arm. "Don't mind her cranky ass. She knows our position and wants someone to blame. That's all—" Azorwyn turns, genuine happiness spreading across her face. "Oh my. You must be Rarity, my brother's mate. Word has traveled fast, and you are a knockout!" She grabs my hand and then gives me a spin. "Oh, I bet my brother cannot keep his hands off you."

"Neither of us can." Nyx snags my hand and yanks me away from Cailian's other sister, clearly jealous.

"Two mates? Really?" Azorwyn leans against the wall, looking me and Nyx up and down. "That makes sense. Fate would give you your best friend's son. Uniting the kingdoms. This will be good. I'm so happy for you, Cailian. Really. It's so good to see you." She kisses Cailian on the cheek. "Perhaps do not wait so long to come say hi because of our bitch sister."

"Hey, fuck you. I am doing what I can to protect us, and I am getting blamed? Unbelievable. Cailian will forget all about us now that he has his mates. You think we went a long time without seeing him before now? We will mean nothing to him soon." Lea storms away, leaving a trail of ice in her wake.

Azorwyn sighs, giving a half smile. "I am so sorry. I like our situation. I love it here. Cailian takes care of us. He gives us everything we need and more. You are a good brother, Cailian. Lea will come around."

"Where is Faerora?"

"I am here." Someone comes running down the steps so fast, I'm not able to see her as she wraps her arms around Cailian's neck. "I have missed you."

"I have missed you too. Faerora. I want you to meet my mates, Rarity and Dovenyx."

She turns around and I don't know why I'm so taken aback. Maybe because I don't expect elves to wear glasses, but Faerora does. The black frames are almost too big for her face and her hair is tossed into a messy bun. She reminds me a lot of Maven for some reason.

"It is nice to meet you. I cannot tell you how happy I am that Cailian has his mates. He deserved happiness out of all those years mourning his best friend."

"Fae," Cailian hisses her name with a stern tone.

"What?" she shoves her glasses up her nose with her finger. "You didn't want to kill him. You have been so miserable since that day."

"Fae—"

"—What is she talking about?" Nyx asks, cocking his head.

"Nothing. She is speaking of things she has no idea about."

Fae rears back, offended. "I'll have you know, I know many things and that is one of them."

"Is that so?" Nyx is curious, getting closer to the truth, and the discomfort on Cailian's face is enough for me to drag him out of this building.

Nyx grabs Cailian's shirt sleeve and tugs him to the front doors. "It was so nice meeting you all but we have to go to my kingdom. It has been such a busy day. We will come back soon."

"Bye— I love you, Cai. Come back soon, please!" Azorwyn yells just before the doors open.

The uneasiness infiltrating the bond tastes like sour fruit.

Once we are outside, Cailian runs down the steps, but Nyx is right on his heels. The guards on either side of the door try to stop him by blocking Cailian.

"Nyx, wait. Stop. Just take a second," I try to reason with the dragon, but it's too late. Smoke is coming from his nose and mouth, and his body becomes bigger as he fights the shift.

He roars, flames lighting the air and the guards dive to the right, barely missing being burnt to death.

"What the hell was that, Cailian? What did she mean by that?"

"Nothing. Fae is the youngest sister. She has no idea what she is talking about."

Nyx grabs him by the neckline of his robes. "What won't you tell me?"

The way his voice breaks reminds me of ice cracking and melting, drifting off into the water before vanishing until the next cold season.

The bond becomes itchy as if static is wrapping itself around me before numbing the cords that tie us together.

Cailian breaks free, straightening his robes. "Nothing. I am telling you nothing. I won't ever tell you the truth. No matter how much time has passed, no matter what you hear, what you want me to say will never leave my lips. You need to come to terms with that. No matter how many times you ask. No matter how much pain there is on your face—" Cailian chokes on his own emotions, the want of the truth trying to break free strangling his heart.

Nyx takes a step back, spreads his wings, and shifts, his dragon growing so large, that I have to duck to miss the swinging tail. He snatches me in his oversized hand, the ground suddenly too far away from my feet. I scream when I am lightly tossed through the air, the ground moving fast beneath my eyes.

Landing on the moody dragon's back I grab a hold of his wings where they protrude from the middle of his shoulders. I pinch my eyes shut because the thought of falling from massive heights might cause heart palpitations.

I've never ridden a dragon before.

I mean, I've *ridden* a dragon. This dragon to be exact, but that's a whole other, much more pleasurable scenario.

Without a word, he flaps his wings, and we lift into the air.

"Cailian! Cailian!" I scream for him, my heart aching for my Ice Elven Prince. Snow begins to fall in a blinding amount, the clouds darken, visibly filling with snow— or Cailian's emotions—because in the bond I feel the heartache. "Don't you dare fly away without him you stubborn dragon," I shout through the loud *whoosh* his wings create.

He spews fire, completely ignoring me, and flies higher, leaving Cailian staring up at us which breaks me.

"He never would have left you." I press my face against his back and cry. "Why can't you take him for his word?" The ride to the firelands is filled with silence, the only comfort is the cold air we are slicing through, giving me the faint presence of Cailian.

I'm starting to realize Cailian's word will never be enough.

Forgiveness is nonexistent when it is buried beneath so much pain and suffering.

The two men I love will never *love* each other. I'll have two separate lives and perhaps it isn't them who needs to face reality, but me.

They will always be broken and forcing them together will not make us fit.

Chapter Eighteen

CAILIAN

That dragon is insufferable. I cannot stand him or his damn moods. He is mad that I mourned his father? He is mad that he found out I never wanted to kill my best friend? Unbelievable. He is mad thinking I never cared at all. He is mad thinking I cared too much.

An elf cannot win.

I storm through the village again, being left alone without protection. Next time, because I am sure there will be a next time, I will bring Taygen, one of my best guards.

"Maddening fire-breathing asshole," I grumble, walking swiftly down the sidewalk, away from my sisters and toward where we saw the Icebergsa's.

If Rarity wants one, I will get her one. I will get her a hundred if that is what it takes to make her happy and if this is how things will be, then keeping her happy might be a challenge. That will not be anyone's fault but Nyx's.

And mine. To a point.

But mostly that damned dragons.

An elf stumbles out from a door to my right, laughter filling the empty cobble-iced street, reeking of ale.

He is not too far gone not to realize who I am. His eyes are almost comical with how wide they are.

"Cai... Prin... ze..." he slurs, giving me a drunken, yet somewhat well executed bow for someone in his state.

I am not in the mood for formalities. I give him a slight tilt of my head to acknowledge him.

"Wha—What?" He hiccups. "You doing... doing... doing—" he repeats himself, trying to find the right pitch in his voice. "Here."

"I am only checking in on the village," I say with a smile, not wanting anyone to know about the fight I had with my mate. I am sure word will spread fast enough. Right now, I want to ignore my problems.

Another elf stumbles out of the cave door, slamming into, whom I can only assume is his friend, the one who has been speaking with me.

"Ravarie, you missed it. You missed the greatest score in Freletch. Traxidor slammed the froster on the other team."

Ravarie clears his throat, grabs his friend's head, and turns it until glassy elven eyes are staring at me.

"Oh, fuck," he curses, straightening the best he can in his inebriated state. "I mean— I apologize, Prince Cailian. Seeing you—"

I hold up my hand to stop him. "It is fine. There is no one else around. I am glad you two are having a good time. Freletch is on? It has been since I was in my early hundreds that I watched it. Is the team doing well?" I ask, eying the cave to the right that has a wooden sign nailed above it.

Ockard's Tavern.

"Yea—Yeah," he stammers, swallowing nervously. "Graveleers and Snowtops are playing. Did you hear? Now that the portals are opening again, they might take Freletch dimension-wide?"

"Really? That's interesting news. Thank you, Ravarie... and?" I step forward, wanting the young elf's name and he steps back, oddly afraid of me.

"Tasar," he replies.

"Tasar," I repeat, nodding my head to his friend who nearly bumped into me. "I think I will go in and watch the match. Thank you."

"What— Huh— no— I mean— you—" Tasar grabs my shoulder and I cut my eyes to him, lifting a brow.

"Touching royalty without permission could mean your head."

A bead of sweat plays on his temple. "Apologies, Prince. It is that you are alone. You are vulnerable. This bar is for the villagers. It gets..."

"Unkept?" Ravarie answers. "Wild." He hiccups again. "Definitely wild."

"Perfect. I need to get my mind off things. I think I will get a pint of ale or wine. I have not decided." I smile, clapping my hands together in excitement. I have not been on my own in too long. It is freeing to do what I want without someone breathing down my neck.

The two young elves follow me inside the dark tavern. It is a cave of ice painted black on the inside and out. The lights inside are dim followed by a few candles lit on the tables. The moment I step inside, the crowd inside roars, cheering in happiness while downing their drink of choice.

The happiness is short-lived because all eyes fall on me.

One man burps, covering his mouth in horror. No one moves. I am not sure if anyone breathes. The live footage of the game still plays on

the large wall to my left. In order to get the game, the elf who owns this must pay a witch to siphon the live footage to the bar with her magic.

I remember watching games like this when I was younger, but only now do I know how illegal it is. Matches should only be seen live. If someone is caught, they could be thrown in the dungeon if found guilty.

The giant man behind the bar tugs on a rope and a sheet of canvas falls down, covering the wall— as if I have not seen the game.

"Please, turn it back on. Your secret is safe with me." I begin to walk through the crowded tavern, inching my way by people who continue to stare at me. "Excuse me. Apologies— oh my—" I chuckle, smiling at their confused faces.

Finally, I make my way to the bar.

The counter is a long tree trunk. It is not sanded down, but there are worn places in the bark where drinks have been made and poured.

I tuck my robe and take a seat on a wobbly stool. A giggle slips free. It wobbles.

I sigh in content and tap my fingers on the bar. "Can I have a glass of your best wine? And please, turn the game back on. I am not here to get anyone in trouble. I am just passing through."

"You will not arrest me for siphoning magic?" he asks, his hand on the rope again.

"I have more important things to worry about than you siphoning a little magic," I mumble. "Please, I need that drink."

"Of course, Prince Cailian." He rushes, tugging on the rope to lift the canvas to show the match. The large elf has a scar running down the side of his face and a lip ring that he is nibbling on while he pours my wine. "On the house. It isn't every day I get royalty in here. We appreciate the living wage increase. You really do help your people. It is good to see."

"Nonsense. I will pay just like any other customer." I dig into my robes and grab a few elements for the bartender. "How much?"

"For our finest wine, that is fifteen eles," he states, shortening the term for what we call our money.

"Not a problem." I hand him a hundred. "Is that sufficient for a few more glasses and a tip?"

He gathers the elements and stuffs them in his pocket. "You can't flash around that kind of money, Prince. Not here. You're safe, but this isn't the castle. Everything is up for grabs here."

I nod, feeling more out of place the longer I sit here, but I refuse to leave. "Understood. Thank you....?"

"Ockard," he replies, holding out an overly large hand. His fingers are covered in tattoos and silver rings. His wrists are bound in leather and other metals that must have been expensive. The sides of his head are shaved, and the rest of his long hair is tossed in a high bun that oddly works for him.

"*The* Ockard who owns this establishment?" I meet his hand with my own, giving it a friendly shake.

Another typical gesture I do not get to do.

He tosses his head back, his laughter an echoing bellow through the tavern. His hand lands on his belly.

I readjust on the hard, uncomfortable stool, flushing with embarrassment. I sip my wine, telling myself to be quiet. I do not want to be the laughingstock in the tavern. That is the last thing I need.

"I don't think anyone has thought of me as 'the' anything. It feels nice." He places his elbows on the bar, leaning in. "But yes, I own this tavern. I am proud of it. I look forward to coming here every day, but today, I didn't think I would see the Ice Elven Prince or speak to him for that matter."

His forearms are riddled with scars as if he has seen and been in battle.

I am curious and want to ask him about his life, but I refrain. He is not my business.

The patrons roar again, and I almost spill my wine as I look toward the wall. The two elves whom I spoke with outside are seated at a table, eyes on the match, and I am envious of their freedom. They are able to do as they please and one would think I would be able to as well because I am royalty.

Yet freedom does not apply to me. I have to always be on my best behavior, and watch what I do and say, or it will be used against me.

The teams playing might as well be new to me because I have not kept up with the sport in centuries. Eight players are on either team. The Froster is the muscle and there are typically two on either team. They play on rocky terrain, covered in snow and ice with obstacles like freezing water and dangerous creatures. The field is always different, never the same one twice.

On either side, at the end of the field, are Shivers, members of the team that protect the goals. The goals are made up of four elements. Earth. Wind. Fire. Water.

One goal is made of a tree, a small slit in the middle for the crystal disc that the team is so possessive of. If the disc is thrown successfully in the opening, the team gets a point. Shivers are able to protect their posts with shivs, a deadly sharp object made of ice.

Killing is illegal in the game, but you can maim if someone gets close enough.

The other goal is a wind tunnel, it is hard to see, fast, and constantly moving. Next is fire, a small opening left in the middle of the ring and with every shot missed, the fire will grow. Lastly, there is water. Magic

keeps the water flowing like a waterfall but every few moments, there is a small break for the disc.

The rules are simple. Get the crystal discs in each element and the team wins, other than that, the only rule to follow is there can be no killing or a wound that can end up being deadly.

"You drank that fast."

I stare into my empty glass, handing it to Ockard. "It is delicious wine."

He pours me another. The red liquid spills over the rim and onto the bar, soaking into the wood.

"You should be proud of this place. It is a pleasant change of pace compared to my every day. Thank you for allowing me here."

"Thank you for coming." He wipes down the bar top, his eyes lock onto my hands, noticing the flames on one and snowflakes on the other. "Where are your mates? Surely, they wouldn't leave you alone. I hear dragons are protective." He tosses the dirty rag over his shoulder.

A short chuff escapes me right before I take another drink of the sweet, smooth wine with flavors of marigold flower and velvelore berries, a rare berry that grows under the snow on top of the mountains of Elementalu.

"That is a story for another day, my friend," I tell him, downing the glass of wine a little too fast at the thought of Dovenyx.

The constant burn on my soul.

"Understood." He pours me another glass. "I'll have to stop you here, Prince. This wine is strong. You might have had too much already."

I lift a shoulder and shrug. "Not like anyone would care anyway." My lips are loose and slightly numb. I cannot believe I just said that. "Do not mind me. It has been a long day."

"I don't know much about being mated," he begins to explain, grabbing the bottle of wine and walking around the bar to take a seat next to me. The stool groans under his weight. "I imagine it is not easy, even if it is given to us by Fate."

"It is not," I agree.

"But good things take time for them to be what they are meant to be. Do not give up yet. You can't expect love in a few days when he has hated you for centuries."

I play with the stem of the wine glass. "I know that, but my heart does not."

The tavern roars when the Graveleers score again. I lift my glass in the air and cheer with them, not knowing exactly what I am cheering for, but the hell with it. I am having a good time.

The door to the tavern bangs open and standing there are four of my guards. Taygen is in front, his sword clipped to his belt, and his spear in the other hand. Before I am able to say a word, Taygen throws his spear so fast and with such force, it is nothing but a blur.

Ockard bends backwards, the spear missing his face by less than an inch. The sharp arrowhead slams into the icy wall, but not before shattering a bottle of the wine I am drinking.

I stick out my bottom lip. "Damn it, Taygen," I slur, pointing at the mess. "I really liked that wine."

Everyone in the tavern stands abruptly, chairs screeching across the floor. Taygen and his men unsheathe their swords, and my lead guard crosses to the bar, pressing the tip under Ockard's chin.

"You dare get the prince drunk. I should cut your head off where you sit," he seethes.

"You…" I poke Taygen's chest. "Will do… no…" I shake my finger in his face. "Such thing." I flick the sword next, hiccupping. "Ockard is my friend. He has been kind."

"He is using you." Taygen lifts his elbow, pressing the blade closer to Ockard's throat.

"For what? I am here drinking his wine, watching his illegal…" I cover my mouth with my hand and chuckle, slipping out of the chair. Taygen catches me in his arms. "I mean, not illegal. There I nothing illegal here. Also, I love this wine."

"I make it myself, Prince," Ockard states. "I will gladly send some to the castle."

"No!" I stand on wobbly legs. "I will come here."

"Prince Cailian, I suggest—"

"—You suggest nothing. Who is watching the castle?"

"Zyrl," he answers.

"That's a good choice."

"It is the only choice, Prince Cailian, as you are not there, and you have no other brothers. He sent a party out to search for you when he saw that damn dragon in the sky."

"That damn dragon is right." I finish the rest of my glass of wine. "Hey, Ockard?"

"Yes, Prince?"

"I am going to pass out." The glass falls from my hand and my body is weightless, falling against Ockard's chest.

Ockard lifts me into his arms and a blurry vision of Taygen appears in front of me, angry and worried by how he is staring at me. His sword is still against Ockard's throat, debating if he wants to kill him.

"He is royalty, but he is still an elf. He is a being like the rest of us. He deserves to blow off steam."

"I have him. Give me the Prince."

"I will once you take that damn sword out of my face."

Taygen sighs and I know that sound. It is him relenting. The sharp scrape of him sheathing his sword has my ears ringing.

"There. Is that better?"

I am handed over like a child into Taygen's arms. "I like it here. Ockard is nice."

Taygen grunts. "I will get you back to your mates, Prince Cailian."

"Why?" I whisper, my eyes closing from too much wine. I have so much to say about going to Nyx. My tongue is twisted from the wine, the velvelore berries still sweet in my mouth.

"Why does not matter," Taygen answers, his boots thudding against the wooden floor.

"Bye, Ockard," I say to him in a whisper, wanting to thank him for giving me a normal experience.

The wine wins my body causing my eyes to fall shut. My mind darkens yet my heart still feels just as much as it did when I entered the tavern— even though I wish it didn't.

Chapter Nineteen

DOVENYX

I dodge the snowball Rarity throws at me in the den, my fellow dragons watching in humor while my firebond attacks me with anger. I have never seen her use her powers and while snowballs aren't exactly deadly, they are cold, and if I'm lucky, she won't figure out how to turn them into solid ice. I duck again, the next round of snowballs aimed right at my face, but they miss me.

Raiden grunts as three hit him in the face one after the other, after the other.

The entire den roars in laughter, a few of them laughing so hard they are on their sides, gasping for air. They know that if this were anyone else attacking me, I'd be killing them.

But it is my firebond, My Darling Jewel, the rare piece of my soul that paranormals are lucky to find. I have to let her take her anger out on me, and if I am honest, I want her to. I deserve it.

"You stubborn, angry, conceited, rude, thoughtless, selfish dragon!" she yells, lifting both hands to conjure snow.

She is so similar to Cailian.

I am a doomed dragon.

She throws her hands through the air and the snowballs launch, smacking me right in the chest, neck, and face.

My dragons continue to laugh as I allow her to make a fool of me. I will never punish my firebond for being upset with me. I will always allow her to put me in my place. My dragons deserve to see her angry. They need to see her put me in my place.

"I know, My Darling Jewel—"

She tosses another snowball, hitting me square on my ass.

"—Don't you 'My Darling Jewel' me, you pompous, arrogant, asshole!" She throws six snowballs at me one after another, one hitting me directly on my cock.

I groan, completely folding to the floor with my hands cupping my aching balls. This is the second time I've been hit today and if the hits keep coming, children might forever be out of the picture.

My dragons groan in sympathy pain, cupping their own cocks in phantom agony. I bet they are glad they aren't me right now.

I wish I wasn't me right now. Rarity is brutal when she is upset.

She ices the floor, gets a running start, and slides her way directly in front of me. This time, it is her hand wrapping around my throat. Her palm barely covers the middle, but she manages to squeeze my windpipe enough to leave me gasping for breath.

"You will go get Cailian and you will bring him here."

"Rarity—"

She squeezes, ruining my ability to speak. "You will go to him. You will apologize. You both will stop this nonsense. And we will all be happy together. Do you understand me?" Ice begins to form on my neck, slowly traveling up my jaw. "Or so help me, Nyx, whether you like it or not, I will freeze the memory of how your father died, and the only thing you will feel when you look at Cailian is love."

My fire brews in a wicked fury, heating my skin to melt her ice. "You wouldn't dare invade me in such a way. You and I both know I need to come to terms with Cailian on my own."

She leans down, the tip of her nose touching mine. "Then you better figure it out soon. I have frozen memories before and I have no issues doing it again." With a rough shove, she lets me go, and gives me her back.

The dragons watch her in awe as she saunters to my throne, her spine straight, her head held high, and she sits proudly on the obsidian chair forged from lava.

"I will go get him." I go to stand, but two spears of ice emerge from the ground, nearly piercing me under my chin. "My Darling Jewel, what is this?" I have to tilt my head back to keep the sharpened points away from my neck.

My dragon is beginning to feel testy from this treatment.

"Crawl to me and tell me that," she states before leaning forward, her violet eyes electric with her own flames. "Crawl to me and convince me you will go to him. I want you to beg for my forgiveness for taking my heart and breaking it when you left him behind and alone. Mates do not do that, no matter the pain."

I blow smoke from my nostrils, not because I would never crawl to her, but because the thought of submitting in such a way has the beast inside me anxious. I have never been seen in such a position in front of my dragons, my elites, my chain of command below me.

"Crawl. To. Me," she repeats, her fingers digging into the chair until her knuckles are white.

All the dragons surrounding the den turn their heads to me, waiting to see what I will do.

I crack my neck, knowing when I do this, everyone will know that it is Rarity who is in charge. It is the Princess that will be in control.

I fall to my hands, my palms cooling against the iced path Rarity left. I keep my eyes forward and locked on her. I can feel the small shockwaves of surprise when I begin to move, lifting my knees as I place one hand in front of the other.

She never expected me to crawl, but what she doesn't know is I would crawl across troll territory if I meant bowing at her feet, worshiping her.

The same for Cailian, no matter how conflicting my emotions are.

So I crawl, my nails dragging across the ice, chipping it away with every motion I make. The dragons I rule whisper to one another, their conversations too low for me to understand. Inch by inch, I make my way toward the Princess. The ice is cold against my palms, and whereas before I couldn't stand the low temperature, it doesn't bother me anymore.

I welcome it.

Rarity's smirk is cunning and admirable as I get closer, her finger beaconing me to keep coming.

Nothing can get me to stop. I actually find it arousing. My blood begins fill my cock as I get closer to her. Her bare legs are right there, soft skin waiting to be marred with my marks. I imagine lifting one leg over my shoulder, kissing her inner thigh, and feasting on her pussy. She can stay right where she is, sitting on the throne while I stay on my knees, sucking her clit into my mouth until she cries out in orgasm.

I want her to soak the chair royalty only sits on. I want to be able to smell her every time I take a seat to rule.

When I finally reach her, I growl when she uncrosses her legs, the view I have of her lace panties has me dragging my eyes to hers. She's playing a very dangerous game.

"You'll go get our beloved and bring him safely to us," she states, wanting reassurance.

My fingers drag up her left leg, enjoying how her skin reacts to my touch as it pebbles beneath my scales. Wrapping my hand around her calf, I bring it to my mouth and kiss her shin, then her knee. My claws dig into her flesh as I get higher, stopping just before I would have to lift her dress and show all the dragons here her pretty pussy.

I'm not in the mood for anyone else to see what belongs to me.

"I vow on the magma that pumps my heart, My Darling Jewel. I will get him and bring him to you."

"To us," she corrects me, lifting a cold, white eyebrow at me.

I bow my head. "To us. He is ours."

She eyes me for a moment, debating if I mean what I say. "I want to say this out loud for all to hear." Her gaze roams every dragon in the den. "If you know elves, then you know their loyalty, their honor, and their word is how they define who they are. They are elegant, honest, and faithful. I believe Cailian isn't speaking the truth about what happened because of this. I do not need to know his truth because I know him, his heart, his soul, and his mind. I trust him." Her eyes land on me before staring into the crowd again. "And everyone here should too."

A loud bang sounds from the front door, three solid knocks that reverberate through the entire castle. The iron hinges shake from the force.

Someone clearly isn't happy.

A violent growl trembles my entire body as I stand. "Stay here. Do not move from this spot, Rarity." I bend down and kiss her cheek, whispering. "And don't worry, My Darling Jewel, you'll pay for making me crawl to you, but it's okay, because later, I am going to make you crawl to me." My voice is on edge, meshed with my dragon.

She gasps when my lips graze the bottom of her ear.

The loud bangs at the door sound again causing me to straighten, ruining the moment with my firebond. "Raiden. You're with me. Be at the ready when I open the door."

"Obviously," he rolls his eyes, his dragon shining through his eyes while he walks toward me.

Rarity tries to get up to follow me and my hands hit her shoulders, forcing her to sit down. An icy blizzard reveals the anger in her eyes, the muscle in her cheek flexing.

I lower my voice to a rough edge. "Sit. Down. And don't you dare move or so help me, I will have one of my dragon's take you underground where we keep our hoard. It is so dark, so grim, your eyes wouldn't be able to adjust to daylight for days."

"You wouldn't dare," she seethes.

I lean in until I can see the different shades of purple in her irises. "I would for your safety."

The knocks come again, louder this time, and I lose my fucking temper. I spread my wings, roaring to the sky and the castle shakes. I fly across the community den, down the corridor, and land in front of the door.

Raiden is right beside me.

Baring my teeth, I swing the door open, ready to attack with I see Taygen standing there with Cailian in his arms. I'm not sure if I have ever felt so much rage and jealousy in my entire life. The firelands burning behind Taygen don't even compare to the blaze swirling in my chest. I want to burn him where he stands and watch his body turn to ash, but I can't. I won't dare harm Cailian.

I inhale, smelling wine on my beloved's lips. My wings spread and my dragon threatens to emerge. I lunge for Cailian, to take him away from the arms of the man, whom I know, loves him.

"What did you do to my firebond!" I shout, fire lacing through the air as I speak.

The skies darken with smoke and lightning as a volt storm rolls in, clouds carrying drops of lava and lightning to feed my lands.

Taygen backs away, the heat clearly getting to him as sweat builds at his temple. "I did nothing," he spits at me, pulling Cailian away from my reach. "It is what *you* did!" he shouts just as a bolt of lightning strikes behind him, giving life to the tree that blooms embers. The trunk comes to life with glowing crevices, feeding the branches until the veins in the leaves kindle like a freshly made fire.

"Me?" I snarl. "I didn't leave him drunk. And you arrive on my doorstep, carrying my firebond? Having his cheek against your chest instead of mine?" I reach for Cailian again, yet Taygen tests the thin control I have over wanting to kill him when he pulls my firebond away again.

"Maybe if you didn't leave the Ice Elven Prince alone and vulnerable, this would not have happened because he was drinking to rid the feeling of abandonment you gave him. He is drunk and in my arms because his brother sent a search party for him when he noticed you in the sky without Cailian. I found him at the tavern. Luckily, there was good company there. This time. That might not be the case next time. And you know what?" He places Cailian in my arms, tugging a piece of hair from my firebond's face.

I growl at him for touching what is mine.

"He deserves more than you. He deserves someone like me, someone who would never leave him alone and in danger. There are threats everywhere, even in our kingdom. I would never let my pride control me like how it controls you. Cailian deserves better but unfortunately, he is stuck with you. I will never and would never interfere in a mate bond. I believe Fate has her reasons, but know this, dragon." He steps

closer, uncaring he is threatening royalty. "If it ever came down to me choosing between you and Cailian, it will be Cailian every time. And if the world finds a way to break a mate bond, there are a thousand Ice Elves who would gladly take your place. Cailian is an amazing leader, a kind soul, a strong elf so many admire. He is smart and lethal, yet gentle with peace. He is everything you are not. Continue to treat him how you treat him, and he can stay mated to you so he can live, but I will be there to pick up the pieces and loving him for who he is."

"You are lucky to still be breathing speaking to me in that manner," I state, pulling Cailian against my chest.

He releases a soft breath smelling of velvelore berries and it tickles my chest. He buries his face against me, a small smile appearing on his unconscious face.

"Nyx," he whispers, snuggling further.

"And yet I speak to you that way and you do nothing because you know I am right," Taygen states before turning away. "Take better care of your mate before I do it for you." He steals one last glance at Cailian, his brows pinching together in heartache. He grinds his teeth together before he hurries down the steps, trudging through the firegrass before crossing the heartsnow.

I knew Taygen felt deeply for Cailian, but I didn't know how deeply. I look down at the beautiful elf, his lips stained a dark burgundy from the velvelore berries.

Oh, how I want a taste.

I cup the back of my firebond's head, pressing him against my chest, and close my eyes, hating myself for how I treated him.

How I continue to treat him.

"I'm so sorry, Cailian, My Treasure. Please, forgive me," I whisper into his ear, but all he does is snuggle deeper, his wine-colored lips parting on a soft exhale as he sleeps.

Raiden closes the door behind me, sliding the lock into place. I usually don't mind the grinding echo of the metal but this time I can't stand it. It's too quiet and all eyes are on me.

"He will forgive you," Raiden says, patting my shoulder. "You two have more to overcome than most. I can't imagine it is easy."

"Easy or not, I shouldn't have left my firebond alone. Anything could have happened to him." My heart clenches, struggling to beat at the thought of him battered and bleeding. "What would I have done?" I force out with a catch in my throat.

"You don't have to worry about it, Nyx. He is okay. He is safe. Drunk, but safe."

"He shouldn't have gotten drunk alone."

"Is that Cailian?" Rarity sprints across the den, her hair flowing behind her as she runs. "Is he okay?" She skids to a stop in front of us, placing her hand in the middle of his chest.

"He is fine. Drunk, but fine."

Her shoulders sag with relief before pressing a kiss against his forehead. "I know he is. I needed to feel his heart against my palm. I needed to feel for myself." She takes a step back, giving me a sad, forced smile.

"Nyx?"

I turn to Raiden and he has a grim expression pinching the corner of his brows. "There are a few things I need to discuss with you."

"Raiden, I just got my firebond here. I have a lot of apologizing to do. My head is killing me. My wing is on fire. Just let me be."

"It has to do with the trolls."

I freeze mid-step, careful not to jostle Cailian.

"Nyx." Rarity grabs my forearm. "Can I not stay for this?" she asks, a weave of hurt in her question.

"Anything you say to me can be said in front of my firebonds, Raiden. What is it?" The rush of wings whoosh, sending a breeze through the air. "Where are they going?" I yell over the strong gusts.

"I ordered them to do a final patrol tonight," he replies. "I want us—" his voice becomes louder when silence falls meaning the last of the dragons have left. He clears his throat, lowering his voice so as not to wake Cailian. "I want us to always have dragons in the air. Constantly rotating. No breaks. We need to keep up with the trolls."

"You just said you had information on the trolls." I side-step, repositioning Cailian.

He moans from being disturbed and proceeds to climb up my body, wrap his arms around my neck, his legs around my waist, and buries his head in my neck.

"Nyx." The way he says my name is a tickle against my neck. "My Dove."

When I hear the name he calls me, my soul breaks with relief. I wrap my arms tighter around him, sliding one arm under his ass and the other around his waist.

"I'm right here, Treasure. I'm here. You can rest. I'm not going anywhere." I squeeze my eyes shut, doing my best not to tighten my hold on him more. My arms shake from resisting. I want to crush him but in a way that has all my love for him exploding from me just so I can be closer.

"The trolls still haven't moved and there's no sign of your wizard."

"That's all you wanted to update me on? You stopped me with a false threat and now I'm minutes behind on lying with my firebonds in my bed for the first time. What is your reason?"

Raiden coughs into his fist and his cheeks flush with embarrassment of being caught. His tail wraps around his waist and his hair falls

perfectly over his eyes to block eye contact. This is unlike Raiden. He does not get shy.

"Raiden. Out with it," I demand, wanting to strip both my firebonds down, feel their skin against my own, and sleep soundly with my arms wrapped around them.

"Be nice," Rarity murmurs at me, leaning her head against my shoulder.

"This is me being nice," I snarl as kindly as possible. "If my arms weren't carrying my firebond, I might be wrapping my hands around your neck, Raiden. Tell me," I say louder. "And if My Treasure wakes up while you're standing there—"

"—So remember when you told me about you and Cailian? How it was going to be difficult, and you were pretty angry."

"I wasn't angry," I correct him. "I was confused."

"Ehh," he tilts his head back, nodding his head as if he is thinking about it. "Sure, but mostly angry."

I suck my tongue across my teeth, breathing in and out while Raiden works through his way to tell me what is so important.

"And?"

"And well, I just, want you to know I listened and..."

"—And?" I clip. "I am becoming more irritated with every word that leaves your mouth, Raiden. I'm going to sleep. Come, My Darling Jewel. Let me take you to bed." My tail slithers across her lower back, draping over her hips.

I spin on my heel and begin to stroll toward the staircase.

"I sent invitations out to the other kingdoms!" he spills in a shout.

I freeze, staring at the brimstone staircase, the edges chipped with age. "Invitations to what, Raiden? I don't remember planning anything with you."

"It was supposed to be a surprise. I know this isn't a good time. It really... really isn't. Cailian is drunk, you three have your stuff to work out. It can wait. Some. It can wait another... day."

Rarity snickers when I close my eyes and take a long, deep, calming, relaxing, much-needed breath.

"I can't kill him. I can't kill him. I can't kill him," I chant to myself. No one else could ever take Raiden's place as a friend and second in command. My chin hits my shoulder, my eyes peering over at him, "Invitations for what?"

"A ball."

Rarity rolls her lips together to swallow her laughter. She can't hide anything from me. I see her laughter in her eyes.

"A ball?" I ask in disbelief. "A ball for what? Where? When? Raiden, now is not the time for a celebration."

"Now is the perfect time. The trolls haven't moved. We can't stop living while they are sitting. You and your firebonds deserve celebration. You are uniting two kingdoms out of the four on this side of the planet. That is something to be celebrated. I think everyone here needs to have fun. It's in two days where the wind wolves used to live. There's enough room for all of us. Rarity's family has already been invited. The Woodland Elves were sent an invitation too, but they only decided to come because I said the true woodland prince would be there after speaking to Alexander, so let's hope he shows, or I'll feel horrible for lying to them. I'm sure word has spread through the forest to our allies, so it will be busy and if not, we can call it an early night. I'm getting wine, ale, and the best food."

The old me before having my firebonds would tell Raiden to shut it down yet as I look at Rarity's face, the excitement, the happiness—I know I can't.

I'll do anything to make her smile like that, even if it means going to our clothsmith and getting fitted for a suit.

"Fine, but I want my firebonds to have the best material for the clothsmith and want the clothsmith brought here to the castle. My firebonds will not leave the comfort and safety of these walls with the trolls in the forest."

Raiden beams, swiping his finger over his brow before flicking his hand away from him. "Whew, you had me worried there. Yes, I will have the clothsmith come here first thing tomorrow."

"Great." I climb up the steps, needing away from the drama and responsibilities. I only want to be with my firebonds . I need the world to shut off. The noise is all too much and the doubt within myself is too hard to listen to on my own.

Only my firebonds can bring me peace.

"Goodnight, Nyx. You won't regret it!" Raiden shouts up from the bottom of the staircase.

I keep climbing, not wanting to give him anymore time.

"I've never been to a ball! I don't know how to dance. I never have before." Rarity flings my bedroom door open and squeals. "I can't wait. Oh, it's going to be so much fun." She runs to the tub, her fingers trailing over the faucet. "How should I do my hair?"

"Rarity?" I set Cailian on the bed, then pull the covers over him so he stays warm.

"What?" She stops in my closet, fingering through the few clothes I have.

"Be quiet. Get undressed. And join your firebonds in bed."

She peeks her head out of the closet and grins, her fangs showing adorably. "Can I have a snack?"

I stretch my head back, showing my throat. "Please do."

She blurs across the room, straddling me before digging her hands in my hair then yanks my head to the side. Her fangs tease my throat, her tongue wetting the area where she's about to feed.

Grabbing her upper thighs with my hands, I pull her across my aching cock, wanting her to feel what she does to me.

Just as she sinks her fangs in my vein and moans, I lace my fingers with Cailian's, needing to feel him.

With every drag she takes, I promise myself I'll be better for them.

Chapter Twenty

RARITY

I pick up a small piece of fruit from my plate, my nerves getting the best of me at the table. I didn't know they always had a giant buffet of food for breakfast for any dragon to come down and eat with Nyx. What I also didn't know is how Cailian and I would be all they stared at as they chewed into thick, bleeding meats.

It's nearly unsettling.

"Why do you have purple eyes?" one of them asks.

"I— I don't know."

"—Why do you look like the elf?" someone else asks from the end of the table.

I tuck a piece of hair behind my ear and push my food around my plate. "I don't know."

"Stop asking my firebond that. She doesn't know why she is different. We are looking into that later. We've been meaning to go to the Veiled Library to see if we can find any answers there," Nyx says, washing his breakfast down with something called velvelore juice.

A drink Cailian hasn't touched. He is staring at the cup, debating on drinking it. The sweet prince is a bit grey in the face and he has messy tangled hair. He must not feel well after having all that wine last night. He hasn't said much either. Nyx has dazzled him with affection, yet Cailian has remained quiet. Whether it is because of Nyx or drinking too much wine, I miss him. I bet if he saw himself in a mirror, he would be terrified.

He doesn't strike me as the kind of elf that likes to seem messy or unkept.

"Fine." A different gruff dragon wipes his mouth on his arm before pointing a long claw that has pieces of meat stuck to it at Cailian. "Is it true you killed Nyx's father? He was a good prince."

"Do not bring up my father to Cailian. That topic is off limits!" Nyx slams his fist down on the table so hard, the volcanic sheet of rock cracks in half. "Do not ever bring that up again or I will rip your wings from your back."

Claws stop scraping plates. Conversation halts. Breathing is no longer a choice. Everyone is frozen to their seats, staring at Nyx and waiting to see what he will do.

Cailian stretches his arm across the table and takes Nyx's hand. "It is fine, My Dove. They deserve to hear the truth from me since I am now one of their Princes."

"You don't have to answer them. You don't have to answer to anyone." Nyx brings Cailian's hands to his lips, giving it a kiss.

His free hand finds a home on my knee, and I have to hide my happiness because he is always finding a way to touch the both of us.

"I do not mind." Cailian turns to the dragon staring daggers at him, picking up the glass of water and taking a sip before speaking. "I did kill his father. It does not get easier to say. No matter how much time has passed. No matter how many times I answer this question. No matter

how many times I see the sadness in my mate's eyes every time he looks at me. The guilt of killing my best friend is with me every day. I dream about it all the time, wishing how it could be different, wishing how he were still here with us." Cailian wipes his cheek before anyone can notice he is crying.

"That's enough," Nyx says, grabbing our chairs at the same time and tugging us to him. "He doesn't deserve to get interrogated for something he did eight hundred years ago."

"Why did you do it?" A female dragon asks, and she doesn't sound rude, just curious.

I'm not sure of her name. I need to make note of it so I can learn all the female dragons. Apparently, they patrol most of the time which is why we don't see them often. Nyx said last night while we were falling asleep that the women while smaller, are quicker, and are far more brutal than any male dragon of his.

I laughed because that aspect of being a female seems to be the same across all species, not just one.

She stares at Cailian, sipping her velvelore juice while waiting for him to answer. She is fucking beautiful. Her scales are just as dark, but there is a faint blue hue to them that Nyx doesn't have. Her eyes are a bright hot blue, the same color as the hottest part of a flame. Her wings are smaller and more compact, tucked down her back. Her long dark hair is up in a ponytail, and she drags her claws through the strands.

Cailian shuts his eyes for a moment, a massive wave of emotions filled with sorrow and guilt have me gripping the edge of the table. The pain takes my breath. I glance over to Nyx to see him rubbing his chest, his amber eyes glowing with tears.

"I want to tell you, I do." He nods, giving her a sad smile. "I am not trying to be difficult, but I can't tell you why. Loyalty is a component in my blood. Please, know I mourn my friend every day. I think about

him constantly. We would always have breakfast or lunch in the middle of the heartsnow. He would stay on his side, I would stay on mine, and we would talk. He was my best friend and I have to live with what I did every day until death takes me."

Nyx growls, dragging his claws across the table. "You won't be dying on my watch, Treasure."

Cailian takes a sip of water and blows a kiss at Nyx. "Always be ready for the unexpected. Death is by far the biggest surprise one ever receives." Cailian looks down at his food, the faint color on his cheeks retreating. "I apologize. I am not feeling well. If you will excuse me." His chair grinds across the floor before he dashes to the staircase, leaving the table in silence.

Nyx stands, watching Cailian retreat, his wings spreading so fast, the breeze from them cause pieces of hair to dance in front of my face. I blow them out of the way, tucking the loose strands behind my ear.

Nyx's breathing speeds up, his shoulders rising and falling with every inhale and exhale. Black smoke swims in clouds as it leaves his nose and fire begins to dance across his scales.

"Nyx," I whisper, placing my hand on his arm to bring him back to me. His fury is building, and it is hot. Literally. I can feel it and I'm beginning to sweat. "Nyx, it is okay."

"Duck," he orders, and I don't dare to disobey him.

His body trembles as his muscles grow. His tail becomes longer, and his growls become deeper. With a savage roar, he purges the flames inside him while picking up the table and tossing it through the air, sending a few dragons along with it.

I duck just in time, falling to the floor to crawl behind him. I rest my back against his massive legs. His tail wraps around me, a gesture that has me relaxing, knowing I am safe from his wrath.

"How dare you!" he shouts at his fleet. "How dare you upset my firebond after I said not to ask him questions. I should send you to the dungeons myself, so you never see the light of day. No, better yet, I should chain you with an iron bracelet laced in troll blood, and watch as you wish you could shift, but can't. I want to see you struggle for how you just made my firebond struggle. You clearly defied me. I do not care if you don't like my firebond, but disrespecting him, disrespects me. This is your warning. Do it again and I will kill you."

"No you won't."

I gasp when I hear another say that out loud.

"I won't? Do you forget I am a Prince? That I have royal blood inside me? Apparently I don't use the power often enough. I'm connected to you all as you have pledged yourself to me."

My back becomes warm, my skin begins to sweat, and I scoot across the floor to get away from him. I exhale with relief. Damn, he gets hot.

"Burn," he states.

"What? N-No-Prince Dovenyx, please, I—"

"I said burn!" he roars.

I peek around Nyx's body, past the meats and vegetables strung across the floor, to another dragon to the left.

Smoke begins to lift from him, his scales drying, rolling tightly as they lose their moisture.

"Pl— ease," he begs, and I cover my mouth to hide a whimper, tears falling down my face as the dragon screams in agony.

Flames cover his body until no more screams are heard. Silence rings in my ears.

And all that is left is a pile of ash.

"Does anyone else wish to defy me?"

"No," the deep voices say in unison.

"No, Prince Dovenyx."

Nyx rolls his neck, cracking it before tucking his wings. "Take his ashes and spread them across the firegrass," he orders, turning around, then squatting to become eye level with me. "Are you okay, My Darling Jewel? Did the heat get to you?"

I shake my head, remaining silent, shocked, a bit scared, and a little turned on. I shouldn't be turned on by him killing another, but it was the possessiveness, the protection he exuded for Cailian, for us that acted as an aphrodisiac.

"Did I hurt you? Did the flames get to you?" He grabs my arms, turning them to assess the damage, but there is none.

"No, no. I'm fine. I'm just shocked. You can do that? You can burn them where they stand?"

His lips form a grim line. "I don't like to. I haven't done that in many centuries, but I will when it comes to my firebonds." He holds out his hand to offer me help up and I take it, sliding my fingers across his massive palm.

Electricity crackles between us as he helps me to my feet.

He cups my face, tilting his chin down to look at me. "I would never hurt you. I would rather burst into flames myself and turn to ash than ever do anything to harm you."

I lean into his touch, taking a deep breath to calm my heart. "So I guess that breakfast didn't go over too well?"

Nyx tiredly chuckles before sighing. "It went as well as I thought it would."

"Nyx?"

We both turn to Raiden and next to him is an older female dragon. She's short, her scales wrinkled, and her hair grey. Her wings have gone from onyx to an aging silver to match her age, rolling in a large trunk behind her.

"The clothsmith is here," he announces, giving a strained smile.

"I apologize for the mess. My dragons and I had a small... disagreement," Nyx states. "Thank you for coming on such short notice."

"Anything for the crown, Prince Dovenyx," she bows the best she can. "I have brought all my finest materials. Where shall we begin?"

Nyx's hand lands on my lower back. "If you will give me five minutes. I need to check on my other firebond. Raiden will bring you to my chambers and we will do measurements there. Raiden, offer our clothsmith a drink. Make her feel at home, please."

"Yes, Prince," he bows, guiding the clothsmith to the kitchen.

"Let's go check on Cailian. On top of being bombarded, I don't think he feels very well. Come on." He laces his fingers in between mine, tugging me through the den to get to the steps.

Like always, I'm in awe of this old castle. I never know where to look. The den is my favorite spot. It's a huge circle with couches, pillows, and blankets where the dragons come to either sleep or hang out. Everything is stone except for the low obsidian wall in the circle. I glance up to the opening where the dragons fly out to see a few soaring in the sky, blocking the moon.

There are so many different wings in the castle that lead to hundreds of rooms where the dragons stay. Unlike the elves who have a village, this castle is everything to the dragons. Other dragons do not live outside of it unless they run a specific business, like the clothsmith.

I take one last look at the den, a dragon coming down the chute lands in the middle of the circle. He shifts into his humanoid form, giving me a brief wave before sitting on the pillows with his hand tucked behind his head.

The windows surrounding the den give the perfect view of the firelands. The flaming grass, the smoky air, the darkened sky, the embers blowing in the wind. You would think it would look like hell, some-

thing sinister and unforgiving, but it is oddly beautiful and brings me the same peace the tundra does.

My attention is ripped away from the beauty of the old castle when Nyx tugs me up the stairs to the bedroom. The lamps attached to the wall glow, the wick igniting, allowing us to travel down the corridor. Every few feet there are low-hanging lights, but they aren't chandeliers like the elves have. These look like black tree roots swinging down from the ceiling and on each end is a flame.

Nyx pushes the doors open to his room and Cailian is just now getting out of the tub, wrapping a towel around his waist.

A snarl has Cailian looking over at us, his wet hair sticking to his arms.

"What's wrong, Nyx?" Cailian asks. "What is it?" He straightens, waiting for us to deliver bad news. "Rarity?" His gaze falls to me.

The doors slam shut behind me and I jump from the loud bang. Nyx stomps forward, charging Cailian in determined strides. Our elf stumbles backward, his back hitting the window that overlooks his kingdom. Nyx stops directly in front of Cailian, muscles tensed, jaw clenched, smoke fuming from his lips. His hand binding Cailian's neck so he is pinned against the wall.

"We don't have the time for you to look like this."

"Like what?" Cailian gasps.

"Like you're readying yourself for a feast." Nyx tugs the towel off, letting it fall to the floor at Cailian's feet.

My mouth waters when I see his cock freed, lying semi-hard against his thigh. His stomach trembling with every inhale of air.

"You're naked and wet from my bath, you've draped yourself in my towels, and your hair is dripping water down your skin, and you expect me to stand here in front of you unbothered? I just killed one of my dragons for disrespecting you and now all I want to do—" Nyx reaches

between Cailian's legs, grabbing his cock "—Is disrespect you." Nyx turns his head, leaning in, ghosting his lips over Cailian's. "Wouldn't you like that, My Darling Jewel?" He cuts his coal-burning eyes to me. "How much do you want to see me fuck our firebond? Will you get wet watching us? Will you fuck your fingers while I fuck him? How badly do you want to hear him scream my name?"

I whimper, my clit throbbing and my hole aching to be filled as I become wet imagining them in the bed.

"I want that very much," I manage to say as Nyx's arm moves up and down while stroking Cailian.

"Now Rarity and I don't have time to enjoy you, Treasure. I hope you realize how much trouble you're in because of this." Nyx grabs Cailian by his plump ass, lifting him fast and pressing him against the wall.

Cailian's tongue flicks out to wet his lips before they part. He wraps his legs around Nyx's waist, his eyes wild with confusion and want.

Our dragon slides his hand around Cailian's back, the elf's nipple hardening from the quick caress Nyx's thumb steals. He hooks his hand around Cailian's shoulder pressing his body down until Cailian gasps.

"Do you feel what would happen if I wasn't dressed? I could just slide into you, filling you until you tighten around me, begging me to stop, begging me for more, just begging me to do whatever I fucking wanted to you."

Cailian rocks his hips, sliding his hard cock across Nyx's stomach. "Nyx, please. Look what you've done. I need it," he groans.

"Me too. We can be fast." I slide my finger down Nyx's crease before clutching his tail and stroking it.

Nyx looks from me to Cailian, debating if we have enough time before making up his mind. His hand locks around my throat and

slings me against the wall next to Cailian. His hand slides up my thigh while his mouth latches onto Cailian's.

They kiss with desperation, their tongues colliding, and Nyx's forked tongue teases the bottom and top of Cailian's. Nyx's fingers slide under my panties, pushing through my wet lips, and he growls into the kiss at the same time.

"Gods, my firebonds are going to be the death of me." Nyx peppers kisses down Cailian's neck, sucking on the space just below his ears. "Too tempting for me. How will I survive a day without being inside you both?"

"Best not to risk it," Cailian mumbles. "I feel like I'm burning up. Nyx, fuck me, please— please—"

Nyx inhales Cailian's scent before his finger slides free from me, slips up to my clit, and rubs the bundle in small circles.

"Your heat is closer. I smell it in your blood," Nyx says, burying his nose against my throat next. "Fuck, you too. We have to be careful. We can't force the heat forward. We have to control ourselves."

"I don't want to."

"Me either," Cailian agrees, grabbing Nyx's erection through his tented pants. "Please."

"My firebonds will never have to beg for me." Our dragon fumbles with the ties of his pants and just as he frees his cock, there's a loud knock on the door. "No," he yells, pressing his forehead against Cailian's. "Go away. I am with my firebonds."

"The clothsmith, Prince Dovenyx."

"Fuck!" he curses, taking a step away from us.

His ink-colored hair slightly tangled and messy from Cailian's rough attention. His lips are swollen, the familiar coals of his eyes are lit with arousal and he's aiming them right at us.

"Later, when we have no obligations, I expect both of you to lie down and present yourself to me."

Cailian swallows, taking my hand for support, and I eagerly take it.

"Are we clear?"

"Crystal," Cailian replies.

"Grab a robe, Treasure. No one is allowed to see your beautiful body but me and Rarity."

"I would be decent if you had not taken off my towel."

Nyx tugs Cailian to him by the wrist. "And if you put that damn thing back on, I will rip it off, burn it, and fuck you in front of my second in command. Do not tempt me, Cailian. Get. Dressed. I only have so much self-control."

"Whatever you want, I will gladly do, My Dove. Do you want to fuck me in front of everyone? I will gladly bend over for you and make sure they hear me scream. What about you, Rarity?"

"I will ride both of you in front of them, proving your come will take hold and your bloodline will be safe."

We are playing with fire because Nyx seems like he is about to break. Steam rises from his shoulders, and he drags his claws down the wall, leaving white grooves in the rock. Dust and pebbles fall to the floor.

"You two have no idea what you have just agreed to." With every step he takes to the closet, he growls.

Cailian and I share a knowing look. We enjoy tempting the dragon too much, but we love the trouble it gets us in.

Nyx snags a robe from the closet and strolls to us again, holding it open for Cailian.

Cailian spins around, sliding his arm through one sleeve, then the other. Nyx lifts the material over his shoulders, wrapping the belt around his waist, and ties it.

"You better keep this on before you regret everything you just said." He nips his ear, snarling in delight as if he is ready for a hunt. He stops in front of me, forcing me to look at him by cupping the back of my neck. "And you better stay on your best behavior or so help me, I won't let you feed from me or Cailian for days."

"That's cruel. You wouldn't. I need you both." I can't believe what I'm hearing. He would cut off my food supply? The thought of going a day without tasting them has my stomach clenching and my mouth watering. I already feel my mind becoming numb at the aspect of not being able to sink my fangs into their necks, cocks, thighs, or anywhere else I choose.

"Then you better be a good girl." He kisses me, the quick kind, a peck where I barely have time to move my lips before he is gone.

I'm left flustered and discombobulated.

What just happened?

Nyx opens the doors to his room and Raiden is standing there with the clothsmith.

"Excellent. I need everyone to get naked," she announces.

Cailian clutches his robe together and my jaw drops in shock at what she just said.

"Excuse me?"

"Prince Dovenyx, I had... I had no idea she would say that. I'll escort her—"

"—Oh, please." The old female dragon pushes her way into Nyx's room. "Calm your tails. I don't want anything to do with your fire-bonds, but I need accurate measurements in order to create the clothing you wish. Anything in the way will be problematic. I already have your measurements, Prince Dovenyx. You don't need to be naked."

"My firebonds will not get naked in front of you. I don't care how old you are. Their bodies are mine unless a discussion has happened, and an agreement has been made."

"I don't mind," I say, stepping in front of Cailian, and then gathering my long hair to get it out of the way. "Cailian, can you unzip me?"

"I will just... I will go, Prince." Raiden turns, only to slam into the wall next to him. He rubs his head, chuckling. "I'm fine. I'm going. This way." He spins, nearly running down the hall to get away from us.

Nyx grumbles before slamming the door. "If you touch them—"

She wrinkles her nose in disgust. "I have no need to want to touch them inappropriately. I am a happily mated dragon, Prince Dovenyx. I am only doing my job."

"Fine." Nyx takes a seat on the couch situated in the middle of his room. The area is so big we are free to do whatever we want with when it comes to decor. There's a mirror framed in black rock leaning against the wall and that is where she is standing, preparing for the measurements.

"Cailian, can you unzip me?"

"With pleasure, My Snow." Cailian kisses the back of my head as the metal teeth of the zipper release, grinding down until the tight-fitted dress is loose. "You are fucking gorgeous," he admires, kissing my neck which has me stretching it in the other direction to give him more access. "Everything about you." His hand slides up my back. "So soft." He drifts his fingers back down my spine and my skin arises in goosebumps. "Do you think they will notice if I just..." His cock nudges my entrance. "Real quick." He nibbles the back of my neck, groaning as he tries to control himself. "Just so I can feel how wet you are for us."

"Cailian," Nyx yells across the room, no doubt feeling the sexual tension in the bond.

Even the way Nyx sits has my heart thrumming like a humming-bird's wings. His legs are spread, arms draped over the back, and he's watching us intently, an air of danger surrounding him that pulls us closer.

Cailian and I both head to him as if he is a magnet and we have no choice but to follow the force. His gaze is dark, trailing over Cailian and I slowly as if he is undressing us with his mind. The bond is electric, firing back and forth with so much desire I can barely breathe. The lust is drowning my lungs, suffocating me softly.

But what a way to go.

My dress falls from me and Nyx's nostrils flare when he sees me.

"You better make this quick, clothsmith," he says. "The longer I see them naked, the more I want them."

"Oh, stop acting like an adolescent dragon. Get yourself together." She waves him away dismissively. She unlocks her trunk and on top of the silks, she snags her tape measure. "Lift your arms, please."

I do as she says, never taking my eyes from Nyx. He bites his bottom lip, cocks his head, and gives it a slight shake as if he can't believe what he is seeing.

Cailian takes a seat next to him, rubbing his hand down Nyx's leg only to stroke Nyx's hard cock.

"This is the worst kind of foreplay," Nyx mumbles, readjusting his cock in his pants.

"Arms down," she demands and to my shock, they fall to my sides as if forced.

"What—"

"—It is clothsmith magic. Not many have it," Nyx explains. "She is one of the few, minus her granddaughter, Gwelyn. She's too young to take over for her grandmother, but she will one day."

"Clothsmith magic is only hereditary. No one knows who will get it, but my line has been successful." She wraps the tape measure around my chest, down my arms, my stomach, legs, and even my neck.

The measurements don't take long at all.

"Excellent. I believe a shade of purple would look wonderful on you." She digs through her trunk of treasures, pulling out a beautiful lavender sheet. "Yes, yes, this one."

The clothsmith moves quickly as if she has vampire speed.

"It is part of their magic," Nyx explains. "It is why they can produce clothes so fast. They get the measurements and—" he snaps his fingers. "Bam, just like that you have a dress."

A few minutes later, the whirlwind stops.

Her silver hair is kindling with flames before it regrows.

"They sew the material with their hair. Their hair is the thread, once it is sewn, the thread disappears." Nyx stands, drifting his finger across the hem. "Watch."

The stitches blend themselves into the gown. I touch it, astounded, and look at myself in the reflection.

"How do I get out of it then?"

"The zipper in the back. What am I, stupid?" The clothsmith busies herself with making sure the belt across my hips is just right. She takes her claw and cuts the neckline a bit lower before she is happy. "There. Now look." She guides me to the mirror, and I'm stunned.

"Oh my gosh. This is... this is beautiful." I run my hands down my waist. The dress makes my eyes and hair seem brighter. The dress stops at my ankles and there is a high slit that goes to my thigh, showing off my long legs.

"Made for a Princess," she says, right before shoving me to the couch. "Okay, yes. You're lovely." She snaps her fingers at Cailian. "Prince Cailian. Please, will you stand... just here." She points to the middle of the floor. "And undress please."

Nyx tucks me to his side. "Don't mind her. They like to get their jobs done."

"I don't mind," I say, snuggling against his side. "Do you like the dress?"

"I'll like it more when I get to rip it from your body and use it to bind your wrists together, but yes, I love it. You look beautiful."

"Nyx," I giggle, hiding my face in his chest.

Cailian stands in front of the old lady and unties his robe. I sit forward, staring at him as if he is prey. I hiss under my breath with want, my fangs lengthening to prepare to bite.

"Easy, My Darling Jewel." Nyx pulls me back, wrapping an arm around my shoulders. "He will be ours soon."

But he still has a constant rumble in his chest, especially when the claw marks show on Cailian's back.

"I can't tell if you are a dress man or a suit man. For the first time, I am perplexed as a clothsmith."

"Dress." Nyx crosses his legs, but the movement doesn't hide his erection. "I want him in a white dress that shimmers like the snow. You remember, don't you, Treasure?" he asks Cailian.

"I remember. I am not sure if that is a good idea." Cailian's cheeks are a deep blue.

It is so funny to me how shy and submissive he becomes with Nyx. I love it. I think he loves having someone else in control after being in control of himself for far too long. He likes someone else to make the decisions after being a leader all day, but with me, Cailian is different.

He takes charge just like Nyx does.

Our dynamic is a recipe for a sex marathon.

"Arms up!"

Cailian's arms reach to the ceiling as her voice changes to a demonic, powerful tone. He has no choice but to listen.

She takes his measurements, even measuring his cock, but doesn't touch it.

Nyx snarls in warning.

"I need to know how much material to use everywhere. As this will be skintight. I am very uninterested. No offense, Prince Cailian."

"None taken," Cailian grumbles, tilting his head back to stare at the ceiling.

In another rush, materials are tossed in the air, and she moves at a speed I have only seen a vampire move. Her hair is a rush of sparks as she works and when she is done, Cailian has on a very tight white dress that glitters just like snow when the lights hit it.

"Oh my," I'm left speechless as I stare at him. He is beautiful. The thin straps hug his shoulders, the neckline's cut down to past his sternum, the back cut down to just above his ass, and the rest of the gown stretches over everything, his cock is settled to the right against his thigh.

"Maybe, showing so much is a bad idea."

"No fucking way," Nyx stands. "I want everyone to see you. I want everyone to be envious. You both are rare forms of obsidian, hardly seen but deserving of being noticed for your beauty."

"My work here is done. Don't ruin my gowns, Prince Dovenyx. My fee is not cheap." She slings the door open and hobbles down the hall, back hunched as she drags her trunk.

"You have two minutes to get undressed before I rip them off you," Nyx warns, low and deadly.

Cailian rushes to unzip my dress and then I do the same to his while Nyx is untying his pants.

A knock sounds at the door, interrupting us again.

Nyx roars, fire spewing from his mouth before he swings the door open. "What?" he barks at Raiden.

"The dragkins have come back with the RSVPs."

"Does it look like I give a fuck about the dragkins?" Nyx roars. "Do you see me with my firebonds? I'm fucking naked, Raiden. Twice. Twice you have interrupted me. Can you understand my rage?"

"What are dragkins?" I ask.

"Miniature dragons that didn't mature because the eggs didn't fall into the magma, so they couldn't grow. They can't shift. They are only dragons," Raiden explains. "But you'll want to know the trolls aren't there anymore. The dragons can't find them as they patrol."

Nyx sighs, resigning to his duties. He bends down and snatches his pants from the floor. "I'll be right back. Don't move. Don't even think of leaving."

As if.

Where would I go that would be better than being sandwiched between two men?

Exactly.

Chapter Twenty-One

CAILIAN

I stare at myself in the mirror, nervous and excited to see how the night will play out. For the first time in centuries, elves and dragons will be in the same space peacefully. We will not be fighting. We will not be killing one another.

We will have fun.

I hope.

Oh gods, I do really hope nothing murderous happens. That is a setback we do not need.

Everything will be fine. It will be a wonderful night. We will laugh, heal, and love. Everyone will get along and it will be the event we all needed to bring the two kingdoms together.

"Everything will be fine," I say to my reflection, brushing my hair down my shoulders.

The strands are straight and soft. My crown is settled on top of my head, the blue gem shining bright against my hair. The dress hugs my body, the neckline low to show the definition of my pecs. The glitter shimmers as the candlelight glows, flickering and swaying.

I grin when the bond hums with Rarity's excitement. She is not nervous at all. We decided to get ready in different rooms to surprise one another and I am slightly afraid Rarity will not like this gown on me. What if she does not find me as manly? I still want nothing more than to bend her over and fill her cunt while Nyx lifts my own dress, wraps his hands around my hips, and slides into me.

A knock on the door sounds, pulling me away from my fears. They are ridiculous. I should not have doubts about Rarity.

"Prince Cailian?"

I grin when I hear Raiden's voice. I set the brush down, take a deep breath, and walk to the door. I swing the door open, my hair fanning from the slight gust of air. Raiden's eyes widen and he looks me up and down.

"Nyx is going to lose his mind when he sees you. You look lovely, Prince Cailian." He gives a slight bow.

I return it. "You do as well, Raiden. The color gold looks good on you."

He's wearing a sheer golden shirt, the material is made up of small links, like chains. His pants and blazer are black, his wings shining brightly behind his back as if he has had them polished.

His cheeks darken. "Thank you. I will take you to Nyx. He is pacing a hole in the floor waiting for you and Rarity. I have never seen him so nervous."

I close the door behind me. "Really?" I blow out a breath before laughing, relieved I am not the only one. "Me as well. It has been a long time since I danced. I am afraid I will not remember how."

"Nonsense." He holds out his arm for me to take when we reach the staircase. "You will find your footing. I have no doubt."

I slip my arm through his and lift the bottom of the gown while we cascade the steps. "Why are you so kind to me?"

"Why wouldn't I be?"

"You know why."

"Because it is exhausting to hold onto pain. I refuse to do it. I also know how much his father meant to you. I was here. I saw how you two interacted. Nyx might have his doubts because the pain is so personal, but I think there is more to the story, and because of that, I will not punish you when it seems you punish yourself enough."

I glance away, blinking away the tears.

"Don't cry. Nyx might burn me alive, and I rather like living."

I bark a very unattractive laugh, wiping the corner of my eyes. "We can't have that."

"No. His wrath is unlike anything I have ever seen."

"I would have to agree." I remember the battles over the years and while I never saw him directly, I saw what his fleet could do. I knew their leader had to be vicious.

We finally take the turn on the staircase, the den coming to view. I hear the fast thuds of Nyx's steps come to a halt.

"Presenting Prince Cailian of the Ice Elven to you, Prince Dovenyx," Raiden announces, slipping his arm free.

My hand slides down the rail while I take the last few steps alone. Nyx is at the bottom, hand held out, his eyes darting from the tips of my toes to the top of my head. He does not know where to look. It is almost comical.

Almost.

If the awe and lust were not so overpowering in his embracing gaze, I might be able to laugh.

I slide my hand across his palm, the bond buzzing with happiness. Nyx lets out a slow shaky breath as we touch before bending down and kissing my knuckles.

"You have stolen my breath, Treasure. You are by far prettier than any snowfall, for you are my own pattern of ice, specially made for all my likings." He kisses my knuckles again before pulling me against him.

The wind is knocked out of me as I land against his body, my palms gliding across his chest. His claws slide down my back, a slight tickle causing me to shiver.

"This is very low cut," he growls, tapping his claws right above my ass. "How do you expect me to focus when you look like this?"

I bring my lips to his ear, flicking my tongue across his earlobe. "Silly dragon, I do not expect you to focus at all."

His hands travel, curving to my ass before gripping each cheek. "I am going to ruin you tonight. This ass is mine, Treasure."

"We will see." I pull from his arms and try to walk away when his arm slings out, tugging me back with a firm grip on my hair.

I am dipped over his leg, forced to look up into his handsome, chiseled face and luminescent irises.

"There will be no seeing, Little Elf." He cups my cock through the gown, and I moan, heat pulsing through my body. "Your body is mine. Don't think for one second you own yourself when you and I both know—" he ghosts his lips over mine "—I own it."

He lifts me to my feet, placing an arm around my waist, and awaits Rarity's presence as if he did not just change my life with three words. My heart is racing. Blood is rushing through my ears. The tips of them wiggle and I pinch them to get them to stop.

They always give away all my damn secrets.

Nyx spins until he is standing in front of me. He takes my hands and drops them to my sides, smirking as the tips of my ears wiggle. I have no doubt my cheeks are blazing blue. My entire body is on fire. Going to the ball seems ridiculous right now when I feel like this.

"I love to see them wiggle." He brushes the shell of my ear, and the touch only adds to the fire in my veins.

I moan loudly, sweat beading across my forehead.

He sniffs the air, brows furrowing, and just as his nose reaches my neck, the heat fades. "Your heat is closer, Treasure. Taking you to the ball might be a risk. There will be too many dragons who will want you."

"There is only one dragon I want to want me, so I do not see the problem."

"I won't be able to control myself in front of everyone," he warns, playing with the thin straps on my shoulders.

"Then don't."

Another growl leaves his chest, bringing smoke and flames across his lips.

Heels echoing from the staircase has Nyx turning around. We both gasp at the same time when we see Rarity.

"May I present Princess Rarity Monreaux from the Monreaux Coven," Raiden announces.

Rarity smiles, showing the sharp tips of her fangs before covering her mouth. "I'm sorry. I haven't been able to sheath them all day. I don't know what is going on."

Nyx wraps his long fingers around her wrist and tugs her hand away from her mouth. "Don't hide them from us. I love seeing your fangs." He helps her down the steps, shaking his head with a grumble. "How am I going to make it through the night when my firebonds are the most beautiful creatures in all the dimensions." He spins her, the bottom of her dress twirling with her. "You look..." he undresses her with his eyes. "Devouring."

"You look handsome too." She rubs his shoulders, appreciating the tight fit of the tuxedo he is wearing. "And Cailian?" My Snow bats

her beautiful lashes at me. "You look ethereal in that gown. I didn't know someone could look so masculine and so beautiful at the same time." Rarity squeezes my bicep, her fangs playing with her bottom lip. "You are very dangerous to be around." Her tongue slides across her left cuspid, her eyes drifting from red to purple. "You look divine. I just want to—" She turns my hand over and licks her tongue across my wrist. "—but I won't because staining your dress before the night even starts would be a punishable offense."

My cock swells, tenting the gown, and I am unable to hide the evidence. "You two better not keep me in this state all night."

"Oh, you don't need to worry, Treasure. I do not plan to let you suffer." He swipes his finger over his lips as he looks me up and down again. "If anyone is suffering it is me."

"And me," Rarity chimes in, looping her arm through Nyx's.

I loop my arm through hers. "And me."

"Is everyone already there?" she asks, glancing around. "The castle is oddly empty."

"Everyone has left and is awaiting royalty," Raiden announces, flying through the air before landing in front of us. He grips the door handle and swings it open. "Your carriage awaits."

"Carriage? What are you—" I need a moment to process what I am seeing. "Icebergsa's," I whisper, completely beside myself when I see six of the creatures stomping on the firegrass.

"You got them?" Rarity asks Nyx, running up to the horse-like creatures.

"I did. They are ours and will listen to us. I made sure of that. You said you wanted them. I got them. And what better way to arrive at a ball?" Nyx tugs on the sleeves of his suit. He grunts, tugging the collar next. "This thing is terrible."

"Do you have enough room for your wings, My Dove?" I lean back to check, but they seem fine.

He flexes them. "They are fine. It's everything else. The fabric around my thighs is too tight. The sleeves are itchy. The collar is strangling me."

"Now you know how we feel when you collar us with your hands," Rarity mumbles, causing Raiden to trip over his own feet.

"I really need to get used to this or I'm going to end up accidentally walking off a cliff if I manage to listen to the lot of you."

I press my lips together to keep from laughing and he murmurs a few things I cannot understand as he steps up onto the seat, sitting next to the driver who is trained in controlling Icebergsa's. He is not a dragon nor is he an elf. The shells of his ears are jaded, and he has dark blue skin with black and red stripes. I want to ask what he is. The question is on the tip of my tongue, yet I refrain.

That would be a very rude question.

Nyx opens the carriage door. "Every time I wrap my hands around your throats, you don't seem to mind, My Darling Jewel."

Rarity takes the offered hand and lifts herself onto the small step to climb in the circular carriage. It is black on the outside with the same color hues as Nyx's scales.

"It is made from the lands where I was born," he explains, being a gentleman to help me into the carriage.

"It is lovely."

"No, it's fine, you two are lovely." He follows behind me, slamming the door, then knocks on the wall to let them know we are ready to go.

The inside is very different than the outside of the carriage. Lining the floors, cushions, and walls is a beautiful shade of purple. Small lamps hang on either side of the doors, giving us just enough light to

see each other. Nyx looks so handsome in the slight glow reflecting off his cheeks.

He yanks the bowtie from his neck and flicks the top button while keeping his legs spread so he can be comfortable. Something about how he sits has me wanting to crawl on top of him. Spreading his legs like that is an open invitation.

He lifts a dark, groomed brow. "See something you like, Treasure?" Nyx unclasps another button, showing more of his shimmering onyx chest.

Rarity's hand wraps around my upper thigh, nearly touching the tip of my cock.

This night is going to kill me.

I stare down at Rarity's hand, her thumb rubbing back and forth. I groan, licking my dry lips. "I see many things I like, and both are in the carriage, driving me insane."

"I like you on the edge of insanity. It has you…" he waves his hand in the air before raking it through his hair. "Razzled. Usually, you are so put together. I enjoy seeing you like this."

An explosion to the left brightens the carriage. I look out the window to see a swirling tornado of fire, lightning crackling the sky, orange veining through the clouds.

"It doesn't move?" Rarity questions, leaning across my lap and my eyes fall to her cleavage spilling from the low-cut dress.

Heat tempts my blood again, taunting me to lie her across the bench and bury my cock inside her cunt.

"No, they stay just like that. They do no harm," Nyx explains, his eyes following Rarity as she pulls away.

Rarity gasps when snow slams against her side of the carriage. My castle can barely be seen through the blizzard. We pass the iced bridge, following an untraditional path.

To the left, The Flaming Forest burns. The trees are charred, the branches are dead, the grass swirls with every individual flame. A few creatures stand in the middle of the field, chewing on the grass. Their bodies are translucent with one long singular horn in the middle of their forehead.

I can see the flames in their stomach as they swallow. Their hearts beat the same color as Nyx's eyes. "What are those? They are... terrifying. I have seen them on my walks, but I have never approached one."

"We don't know their official name, but we call them phantom feeders."

"Makes sense." Rarity crinkles her nose. "They are kind of terrifying."

"No need to be. They are harmless. They can walk right through you without harming you. Holy— What the hell is that Cailian?" Nyx points to the snowing side of the landscape we are passing through.

A large beast with long hair, long teeth, and one eye walks alongside of the carriage.

"Aw, that is a unifuring. A gentle creature. They love to be pet right behind the ears."

"He is kind of cute." Rarity presses her face against the glass. "Like a puppy."

"A puppy? What is that?" Nyx stretches to peer from the other side of the carriage to get a better look at the beast.

"I'll have to show you when we visit my coven. You'll meet Whiskey."

"I look forward to it," Nyx says, looking at her as if she is his entire world before gliding his eyes to me.

His expression changes slightly. The slightest wrinkles form around his mouth, his eyes becoming bigger for just a fraction of a second before forcing a smile.

The rough road of the lands meeting becomes smooth, the ride no longer bumpy. The large landscape has always taken my breath away.

"Welcome to the land of the wind wolves. The House of Howls and Wind."

Rarity peeks at Nyx before scooting closer to the window. "Wow. This is beautiful. They lived here?"

"They did. I miss our neighbors. I miss hearing the howls and the promise of the wind. I hope they aren't dead and are just lost looking for a way home," Nyx says solemnly.

We travel further into the crater, cutting through a light dusting of snow. The mountainous walls tower over us, nearly cutting the sky. There are no trees, no creatures, no life. It is empty, barren, and waiting for someone to make this place a home.

The carriage rolls to a stop and Nyx climbs out first, he turns and holds his hands out to help Rarity and me down.

"I remember when the howls would echo from the mountains and then make their way to us."

"Me too." Nyx places his hand on my lower back. "Come on. Everyone is waiting for us inside."

"A cave? The wolves lived in a cave?"

"It is actually very nice. Looks a lot like a castle on the inside only it is in a mountain," I explain.

Raiden stays behind us, protecting us to make sure there are no threats. Candles light the pathway inside the cave. Music plays in the distance. Laughter has me grinning from ear to ear.

"Do you want me to announce you, Nyx?" Raiden asks.

"No. Everyone knows who we are. There's no need to remind them."

The cave opens to a giant space. We are on the second floor where a few dragons and elves are gathered, actually speaking to one another.

Rarity peers over the railing, completely enamored with what she sees. Below is a dance floor where no one is dancing which is a shame because the floor is made from the last of the trees that grew on this mountain. The floor is a beautiful light yellow color and in the middle, there is the House of Howls and Winds seal. A wolf howling with three lines to represent the wind.

"Rarity?"

My Snow gasps when she hears her name. She spins around, Nyx and I following her excitement.

"Lexy!" she screams, running to her brother. She jumps, wrapping her arms around him to give him a hug.

The vampire picks her up and swings her from side to side, cupping the back of her head. "Oh, I've missed you, Rarity. We all have missed you so much," he says.

Nyx growls, stomping forward before I have time to stop him.

"No, Nyx! Nyx, stop!" I shout, loud enough for Rarity to hear me.

She spins around, baring her fangs as she takes a protective stance in front of her brother.

Alexander looks nothing but amused.

"He's my brother. This is Alexander Monreaux. The master of my coven. Calm down, Nyx. Please," she begs.

Alexander gently tugs her back, patting her shoulder. "It is okay. He doesn't know me. He reacted as I would. I'm Alexander, Rarity's older brother." Alexander holds out his hand and Nyx huffs a breath of black smoke before shaking his hand.

"Dovenyx, everyone calls me Nyx."

"I do not," I singsong.

"Don't be a brat, Treasure. You know where that will get you," he warns.

"Cailian," Alexander begins to walk towards me. "It's so good to see you. You look wonderful."

Nyx stops Alexander by placing his hand in the middle of his chest. "Respectfully, do not go near my firebond. I don't know you well enough."

Alexander nods. "I understand. No problem."

"It is good to see you too, Alexander. And thank you."

"Anwyll! Ru!" Rarity squeals, hugging the werewolf that needed my help before.

I push by Nyx and Alexander, bowing my head in greeting. "Anwyll. You look well. How are you?"

"I'm good. Thank you for inviting us. I wanted to see this place again. You remember, Ru," he says, wrapping an arm around his mate.

"How could I forget? The leprechaun who sacrificed her luck for love." I bow to her as well. "And your brother?"

Anwyll frowns. "He is alive. His soul is stuck in purgatory, and he has to find his way back."

"He will. I should not say that, but your pack— or coven— is strong. I have a feeling everything will be fine."

"Nyx. Nyx!" Rarity shouts for our dragon, tugging two men behind her.

I remember them.

"That is Greyson and Luca. Luca is Alexander's Uncle. Greyson is just a very close friend of the family," I mutter to him.

"I haven't seen her so happy," Nyx remarks. "We need to make sure she always looks like this."

She stops in front of us, completely out of breath. "This is my Uncle Luca. And this is Greyson. Where is Maven?"

Alexander frowns. "I'm sorry, Rarity. She felt out of the two of us, it was best if I came. She had to be at home with the twins."

"I'll have to come visit. The triplets? Where are they?" she asks Anwyll and Ru.

"Also with Maven, but she has help. Alaric is there with Alistair and Tala," Ru replies, sipping her wine.

"I'm just glad I got to see you at all. I promise to come home soon and visit."

Alexander kisses Rarity's forehead. "We will be there. Your place is here now. With your beloveds."

"And Reuel?"

"He—"

"—I am here." Reuel steps out of a sunset magnolia circle, traveling through the way of powder. Roots swirl along the floor, creeping up the walls until flowers bloom.

"I am sorry. I pop tree roots when I am nervous."

"The Prince of the Woodland Elves," Nyx gasps. "I dare to see him with my own eyes."

I chuckle which sends everyone else into a fit of laughter.

Reuel is not dressed for the occasion. He has on a flimsy, breathable shirt, and his pants are torn at the knee. His locks are pulled back making his piercing white eyes stand out even more.

"Let's celebrate!" Nyx roars, his order echoing through the entire cave. "To fate, to family, and for bringing the Woodland Elf Prince home!"

Everyone cheers and the Woodland Elves form a line to meet Reuel. They are a beautiful species of elf. Their skin ranges from pink, blue, purple, green, yellow, brown, and black. Now that Reuel is here and if he stays, they will be the most powerful kingdom in Elementalu.

The only ones missing now are the wind wolves.

They will come home. The call cannot be ignored at this point.

Reuel greets the first elf and her ears wiggle while tears pour down her face. He hugs her and a bright blue glow pulses between them. That only happens when royalty accepts the responsibility of caring for his kind.

"It feels like a fresh start for Elementalu," I say, smiling as I watch others become overjoyed, especially Rarity.

She hasn't left her brother's side.

"Would you like to dance?" Raiden asks me, holding out his hand.

"Um. I— Um—" I look to Nyx for approval, and he bows his head.

"Have fun, Treasure. And Raiden? Touch my firebond inappropriately and I'll rip your wings from your back."

"Never in a million years, Prince." Raiden salutes, then tugs me down the staircase.

I bump into a few elves and dragons drinking, apologizing because Raiden is not taking his time.

The song changes and Raiden spins me twice before tugging me to his chest.

"Did you not hear him? He will kill you, Raiden. What are you trying to do?"

He twirls me again as the elves pluck the strings on their instruments. My hair flies around me, everyone is a blur, and when he takes hold of me again, his hands find my waist.

"I'm trying to make him jealous so you can see how much he cares about you and how far the past is from his mind."

I want to believe him, I do, nevertheless, actions speak louder than words, and while Nyx is possessive, he keeps me at arm's length.

While stupid, I decide to follow along with Raiden's plan. I just hope he gets to keep his wings after.

Chapter Twenty-Two
DOVENYX

I watch Rarity drift from family member to family member, smiling and laughing. It brings me so much happiness to see her like this and I'm determined to keep my firebonds this happy forever. She deserves more time with her coven. I didn't know how important coven bonds were until seeing them together. She's different. She seems energetic and her cheeks must hurt from her constant grins.

Rarity floats around, greeting everyone, dragons and elves alike.

And that's when she reaches Taygen.

I watch from the other side of the room, my nails tapping on the railing as I wrap my fingers around the iron. He bows, holding out his hand, and I focus on what he is saying. All the other conversations in the room fade away while I lock in on his voice.

"Would you like to dance Princess?" he asks her.

I snarl but remain still. It is common for others to dance with others mates at a ball. I won't ruin the evening because I am possessive. It is no secret Taygen and I do not like one another. I have no doubt if Cailian was available to dance, Taygen would ask him.

"You're going to allow that?" Alexander asks, standing next to me. He brings the drink to his lips and takes a sip. "I could never allow Maven to dance with another."

"It is custom here. Events are meant for royals and everyone else to get to know one another. We are equals here. Friends."

"The way you are looking at that elf is anything but friendly."

"That is because he is in love with Cailian."

"And now he is dancing with Rarity? Do you think it is to piss you off?"

"Most definitely, but I won't let it get to me."

"The flames on your shoulders tell a different story."

I slide my eyes to the right, then left, seeing that he is right. "Fuck," I curse, patting them to extinguish the fire.

"Don't worry, he didn't notice."

I cut my eyes to my new brother-in-law only to see him hiding his face behind his drink as he sips it.

"I don't know why he bothers me so much." I lean against the rail, my eyes trailing the two while they go down the steps to the dance floor.

They look good together, but they will never look as good as she and I intertwined.

"Maybe because he is a better male than you," Alexander states.

I growl at him, debating on ripping his throat out where he stands.

He lifts a hand. "I don't want to start a fight. You and I both know that he probably is the better choice. Fate didn't think so. You should remember that."

I grunt in response, liking how much he is making sense. I relax, letting the tension out of my wings. Still, while everyone is celebrating and having a good time, I remain in this spot as time ticks by. My eyes

never leave my firebonds as they dance. One song turns to two, then three, and they are still dancing with the same partners.

Raiden dips Cailian, grinning at my firebond in a more flirtatious manner than I like. Taygen's hands are too low around Rarity's waist. Every motion, every spin across the dance floor, I follow them. Jealousy rages in my chest at every smile he pulls from her. My unhinged anger begins to pulse. My blood becomes unbearably hot.

His fingers drift down her arm in a yearnful caress. Their palms slide together, and I swear, there is a fucking sparkle in his eyes that I can see shimmer from here.

I push by Alexander, never taking my eyes off Rarity.

No one dares to say anything to me as I shove them out of my way if they are in my path. A few drinks spill on me. The sweet aroma of velvelore berries hits my nose as a wine glass shatters on the ground at my feet.

I don't care.

The glass crunches under my shoes, my sights sliding to Cailian. A male has no business being so goddamn beautiful yet handsome all at once. He is every creature's fantasy. I know Raiden would never cross any boundaries but not noticing Cailian's beauty is impossible. He has to be affected by the ethereal power Cailian holds in his eyes.

Which firebond do I take away first? I want them both equally, but I don't want to disrupt the party.

I'll take Rarity, then Cailian, no one needs to worry about cleaning. I want both of my firebonds to smell of me when they are dancing with others. It will be the only way I will be able to function at this damn event. I haven't decided if I want to punish Raiden for planning this yet or not. My mood is too unstable.

My hand grips the rail of the wide staircase that leads to the dance floor. My claws scrape against the iron, sparking embers and leaving

silver scratches behind. Others step out of my way, staring at me while I descend, not paying attention to anyone as my eyes watch my firebonds drift around the dancefloor with males who aren't me.

I'm not built for this. I don't care what the custom is. I don't care how much of a tradition it is, their touch, their smiles, the graceful steps of their feet, are mine.

Everything about them. Everything that makes them who they are. Every word spoken. Every breath taken.

Belongs. To. Me.

When I get to the bottom of the steps, I snag a glass of wine from a caterer, tossing the entire glass back before crushing it in my hands as a wave of fucking need embodies me. I drop the larger pieces on the platter, yet I stay in the shadows close to the wall, plucking the glass from my skin and tossing it on the floor.

A light trance takes over as I stare at them, smiling and carefree. They have no idea what is about to happen to them.

My scales begin to tighten and itch. My wings have the urge to spread and fly them out of here. My cock hardens, my thoughts focused only on sex and driving into my firebonds. The thought of my come dripping down their thighs while they dance has me rolling my shoulders, a snarl licking my teeth.

Seeing them with other males has had my rut hit full force. My body trembles, the ache in my cock becomes worse, their scent is stronger than all the other bodies in here. Their heats linger under their skin. All I have to do is coax it out and they will beg for me to ease the scorching lust crippling their bodies.

"Fuck," I groan, pressing my back against the wall, rubbing my hand across my cock, squeezing the tip.

Rarity and Taygen loop around again, their feet quick, heads high, elbows out, and just as she is within arm's length, I wrap my arms around her.

"May I cut in?" I rumble, my lips finding the shell of her ear.

Taygen grins, stepping away. "Of course. Thank you for the dance. Find me later, Princess." He bows, immediately grabbing another elf, completely interrupting their conversation.

Rarity spins, wraps her arms around me, and tilts her head back. Sweat beads on her forehead from dancing. Happiness is high in her eyes.

And then when my scent hits her, her eyes morph to red, and the aroma of her heat intensifies. Her lips part, showing the sharp weapons she's teasing her tongue with.

"Are we going to dance?" she whispers in a low, needy groan.

I glance around the room, noticing everyone is occupied either in conversation or dance. I cup the back of her head and lean down, whispering in her ear. "If that is what you want to call it, then yes, we are going to fucking dance."

Wrapping my arms around her, I pull her away from the main floor, taking the first connecting hallway to the left. I practically run, tugging her behind me, traveling further into the darkened cave. The music and conversations are nothing but a distant hum. There is a faint hue from the candlelight from the ballroom that kisses her skin, but it is her that is the light.

The flames embedded in her arms, the proof of me claimed in her soul are bright, swaying, dancing, and swirling as if her skin is ablaze. Her other arm has the peace of a snowstorm, every flake proving they are much more elegant than the rage of fire.

A feral disgruntled howl forms in my chest as I slam her against the wall. Taking her wrists between my hands, I pin them above her

head, and my eyes roll to the back of my head when her heat becomes stronger.

It smells like spiced velvelore berries, nearly too sweet alone. My mouth waters for her. I can nearly taste her aroma, the sugar, the cinnamon, and a deep fucking craving starts that only she can satisfy.

"Dancing with Cailian's guard?" I sneer, leering down at her as I curl my lip. "You've caused my rut." A bead of sweat trickles down the side of her neck and my forked tongue flicks, tasting it before I even lick her dampened skin.

She moans, arching her back, her tits straining against the material of her purple dress. Her legs part, grinding against my knee. "Nyx, My Love, I need you." Her words are full of distress. "I'm burning up for you. It's so hot in here. Nyx, what—"

"Keep them there," I order, dropping my hands from her wrists and she keeps them above her head. "Good girl." I claw at my pants to free my cock, flames licking my lips the closer I get to being inside her.

Grabbing her hips, I wrap her legs around my waist, and her dress inches up her thighs to give me the space I need.

"You are mine, Little Vampire." I nip at her bottom lip, the tip of my cock pressed against her entrance.

A gush of liquid drips down my cock and I groan from its warmth. There's a slight cooling sensation that follows it and I can't help but wonder if it's what Cailian would call frost. Either way, she feels amazing and I'm not even inside her yet.

"You look divine and seeing you dance with another man broke me in all the ways that are dangerous for you." I drive inside her with the force of my need, knowing I'm stretching her wide, pressing into her with every fucking inch.

We groan in unison. Her head tilts back, hitting the wall, giving me the side of her neck that holds Cailian's mark, a beautiful glowing

snowflake. I kiss the mark, lashing it with my tongue, hoping he can feel it through the bond.

I hope he becomes inundated with lust as he dances with Raiden. Oh, I just might punish my second-in-command for taking him away from me.

"Fuck, you feel so fucking good." I slide out, keeping the tip in, and look down. Her cunt is spread wide, her want dripping down my shaft, and a wave of her heat washes over me like a cloak. "Keep your legs around me, Rarity. I'm going to fuck you until you hurt." I wrap her wrists in one hand again, grip her hip with the other, and slam into her.

Her cries echo through the hallway and a small part of me wonders if the party can hear us. I hope so. Let them hear. I want the entire kingdom to know just how a princess sounds when she's being claimed.

"Nyx. Oh, fuck. Nyx, you feel so good. I need more. I need so much more. Give it to me. Give me more." She pushes against my hand to get her wrists free, but I keep her pinned, adding more of my body weight against hers to keep her still. Rarity could easily pin me down and take control. She's stronger than me yet she loves being dominated.

"When we get home, you and Cailian are staying in my bed. I'm locking the door. I'm ordering everyone to stay away and by the time I'm done fucking you both through your heats, you're going to sleep for a week." I lick a bead of sweat from her neck, my dragon purring as her taste bursts across my tongue. "I'll take care of you, though. I'll make sure you're fed." I drive into her, and her body moves up the wall. My hand slides up her torso, her dress covering her body in every delicious way.

I want to rip it from her body but not yet, not now, not when so many people are near and can see her.

My hand hooks around her shoulder, my claws digging into her bare flesh as I use her body as leverage to fuck her harder. My wings spread behind my back on instinct, wanting her to appreciate the wingspan.

She sucks my bottom lip into her mouth, her fang nipping my bottom lip. Rarity sucks the small amount of blood from it.

"Feed me now," her words are long, drawn out, and flirtatious.

"I'll feed you when I'm fucking ready to." I trail my lips down her neck, appreciating where the scent is the strongest.

My own fangs scrape across her skin, her body a tempting snack for my dragon.

I blow fire along the ridge of her collarbone, her flesh reddening from the blaze. Rarity screams, her orgasm unexpectedly gripping my cock. I blow the flame out as if it were a candle and her skin heals in the next instance.

She soaks me, the sound of me easing in and out wetter and feeling it has me move faster.

"You liked that? Mmmm," I hum in appreciation, moving to her next shoulder. "How much can you take, My Darling Jewel? How much heat is too much?"

"As much as you want to give me. Do it. Do it!"

I purge the fire from my chest, the fire twisting along her collarbone.

"You're going to make me fucking come. Seeing my fire on you is more than I can take." My knot begins to form at the base, filling with come, and preparing to lock inside her.

The skin begins to blister, and I wrap my mouth around it, swallowing the heat before it can do more damage.

And she comes. Again.

"Nyx!" she screams, my name reverberating off the empty rock walls.

I have no doubt everyone can hear.

"Rarity. Oh, fuck." I thrust once, twice, and plant myself as deep as possible.

My knot locks me in place, filling her until her womb has no choice but to let me in. After tonight, she and Cailian both will be pregnant.

We'll be a family.

I drop Rarity's hands, flattening my palm against the wall to hold us up while my knot does its job, filling her with jet after jet of my come.

With a hiss, she yanks my head to the side, and strikes, feeding from me while I'm mid-orgasm.

My vision blurs on the edges. I'm unable to form her name as I roar my pleasure. Fire spews from me, darkening the wall of the cave from how fucking good it feels to have her fangs in me, her lips on my neck as she drinks.

Cupping the back of her head, I turn us until my back hits the wall, and slide down it. She's straddling me, moaning and snarling in my throat.

"It's okay, Little Vampire. Take as much as you want. You'll be needing it." Not only for the next few days so we can ride out the heat and rut, but for the child she will carry.

I grin when I feel the arousal through the bond on Cailian's side.

"You taste so good when you're orgasming," Rarity manages to say as she takes a breath. "Oh gods," she moans loudly, leaning back with her eyes shut. Her mouth and chin are red, wet with my blood.

"Let's go get our firebond, My Darling Jewel. I need to knot him and imagine how fucking good he will taste as he comes."

She begins to bounce on my cock, whimpering, loving the sound of that. Rarity strikes the other side of my throat, leaving the pinpricks unhealed so they can be seen.

Let my blood run in rivers for all I care, for every drop belongs to her, and if she wants to drain me to create a sea so she can swim in it—then so be it.

I will die a dragon who fed his firebond and there is no better way to go to death.

Chapter Twenty-Three

RARITY

I ache in all the ways that have me craving more. My blood hums with fire. The heat causes beads of sweat to form on my temple. Nyx's blood coursing through my veins is like adding gasoline to the blaze. I'm an inferno, burning from the inside out, and only the scorching desire from my beloveds will ease this emptiness only they can fill.

"I need Cailian too," I rasp, the material of my dress scraping along the sensitive hardened peaks of my nipples.

All my nerves are raw and exposed. One kiss, one tease, even the threat of Nyx's breath against my neck is nearly too much for me to handle.

"I'm going to go get him. I know he has to be feeling the heat too. Stay right here. Don't move, okay?"

"I don't think I could move anyway."

Nyx's knot deflates and he slowly slips out. We moan together, but immediately I want him back inside me.

"I know, My Darling Jewel. I know. Let me go get him." Black smoke rises from his nostrils. "He's dancing with Raiden," he growls,

jealousy overcoming his bright amber eyes. "I'll be right back." He bends down, crashing his lips onto mine to give me a searing kiss that resonates in my bones.

I moan into his mouth, grabbing at his pants to get them off. I need him.

Nyx breaks the kiss, pressing his forehead against mine, and tries to catch his breath. He lowers my arms to my sides, my fingers slipping away from the fabric of his pants.

"I want you too much for you to kiss me like that," he thunders, his dragon threatening to burst free. "I will grab our firebond and we will disappear far into the cave until we are lost."

I nod frantically, taking a deep breath to gather some sort of control. I let the air out slowly, another wave of heat trying to possess me again.

"Go," I say. "Hurry."

"I love you, Rarity."

Tears prickle my eyes as I cup his cheek. "I love you too, Dovenyx. I love you."

His claws drag across the stone, etching five grooves across the wall setting dust loose. His entire body trembles, flames encompass his body from the lack of control.

"Fuck. Fuck!" he snarls, spinning around and stomping away.

I would laugh if my body wasn't in so much distress.

"Please, hurry," I whisper as more of a prayer than to Nyx because he can't hear me. I slump against the wall, wiping the back of my neck as I sweat. My bones feel like they did when I was young and Dad called them growing pains. It's an ache that can't be relieved. My head begins to swim, a throb forming in my temples.

I slide to the floor, lying on my back, and stare up at the ceiling. My chest rises and falls with quick beats of breath. I groan, sliding my hand down my chest. The simple caress is a brushstroke against every

nerve-ending. Electricity shoots across my skin, bolts of desperate, unhinged desire lighting fire after fire in my body.

My hand slips between my thighs, my fingers becoming soaked with Nyx's come as I drag them up my thighs.

Boom.

Boom.

Boom.

The ground vibrates, shaking the loose pebbles beside me. My entire body freezes. The crazed heat that almost had me out of my mind dissipates. The hair on the back of my neck stands up, my fangs drop, my claws lengthen, and my vision flips red.

Boom.

Boom.

Boom.

My eyes flutter when dust falls from the ceiling, and I hold a hand over my face to block it. I roll to my hands and knees, the earth still shaking under me. Alarm bells ring in my head, my instincts yelling at me to go to Nyx and Cailian.

On wobbly legs, I manage to stand, the heat subsiding to a dull pulse. It's manageable, but why? Aren't I supposed to be overwhelmed with need right now?

Boom.

Boom.

Boom.

The cave shakes and the floor cracks beneath me, traveling all the way down the hall. The thuds become louder, closer, and I lose my balance from the force. A deep roar has me covering my ears, and another violent rumble has me losing my footing. I slam against the wall and wait for the tremor to end.

Is this an earthquake? What the hell is going on?

Screams resound through the cave. Screams of many.

"Cailian! Nyx!" I shout for them, but I'm not sure if they can hear me.

Another crash occurs, breaking a chunk of rock from above me. It hits just on the other side of my feet, and I lose my balance when the floor begins to move, separating into small pieces. Using my vampire speed, I blur across the unstable floor.

"Rarity!" Nyx shouts from a distance but I can't see him.

The clouds of dust are too much to see through, the other shouts of fear drown out his call for me.

"Nyx!" I want to cry. I want to be thankful I can hear him at all. "Nyx, what is happening?" I blur to a thick pillar, one that is stable and not cracked. I hold onto it for dear life, hoping whatever is happening passes swiftly.

"Where are you? Rarity! I need you to follow my voice."

I nod, forgetting he can't see me. "Is Cailian with you?"

"He's safe for now." His voice is closer now and I peer through the thick cloud of dust to see a flaming figure cutting through it. "Where are you, My Darling Jewel? I need to get you out of here."

Sobbing, I blur to him, wrapping myself around his body. His flames wrap around me just as his arms do, embracing me in safety.

"Oh, thank the gods. Thank you," he chants, holding me tight. "You're okay. You're not hurt?" He sets me down, patting my arms, legs, and stomach before spinning me around.

"I'm fine. I'm fine." But he still assesses me. "Nyx! Gods, damn it, I'm fine! What is happening? Talk to me."

"The trolls," he grinds his teeth together. "They are here. They are smashing the mountain to pieces. I'm not sure how long this cave will hold. We have to move. I need you to find your family and go home. Go back to Salem and I will find you, okay? I'll find you with Cailian."

"What?" I duck when I hear another loud roar followed by a shattering thud. "No, no. I'm not leaving you. I can help. I'm quicker. I'm stronger." I don't mean for it to sound as if he isn't strong. He is, but vampires have uncanny strength that is far superior to most supernatural creatures.

"I need to be in my dragon form. It is up to me and Cailian to stop the trolls. They will destroy everything, and they won't leave anything or anyone alive. I can't protect you and fight them. I need to know you're safe."

I blur us, diving us to the floor to miss another falling chunk of rock. "I'm not going anywhere and there isn't a damn thing you can do to stop me."

"Rarity."

"Dovenyx."

He snarls when he senses I'm not backing down. "Fine, but you find your family. Make sure they are okay."

"They are fine. I hear them through the coven bond. They have gone back home through sunset magnolia powder. Alexander can't risk his life when he has Maven and the twins. Wait—" I gasp, sensing Anwyll nearby.

Anwyll has come back."

Nyx rolls us, bringing us to our feet just to push us against the wall, another piece of rock dodged that could have crushed us.

"Find him. Get him out of here."

"What about Cailian? Find him, Nyx. You have to find him!" This time I scream in desperation with everyone else. "Please," I sob, thankful I can still feel Cailian in the bond.

He cups my face. "Look at me, Rarity. Look at me."

I do as he says, bringing my eyes to his.

"I will find him. I will bring you both home. Nothing will happen, okay? Nothing." He gives me a deep kiss, the kind of kiss that might feel like the last one I might ever get.

I pull away, shoving his chest. "Don't you dare kiss me as if this is goodbye, Dovenyx. Don't you fucking dare."

A troll roars, sending rancid breath through the caves.

"Listen to me, rogue trolls are violent. They are slow but still, the power they yield in their hammers could crush every bone in your body. Whatever you do, stay away from them. I don't want you to fight them. I don't want you to take one down. You have nothing to prove to anyone."

"Nyx—"

"Damn it, Rarity. Fucking listen to me." He grabs me by the arms, giving me a good shake. "I don't give a fuck what you have to do to stay alive, you do it. Do you understand me? Prove nothing to no one." His eyes drop to my stomach, and he presses his hand against my belly, a faint smile ghosting his lips. "It isn't just you anymore. Nothing and no one else matters, okay? Promise me."

"Dovenyx!" His name is roared monstrously from a troll.

"I promise." A tear drips down my cheek as I press my hand over his. "I swear." I want to ask how he knows. I know paranormal creatures can sense pregnancy instantly, but why didn't I? What if he is wrong and just hopeful? I need to ask these questions, but now isn't the time.

"I love you, My Darling Jewel." Those are his last words as he backs away into the cloud of cave dust, leaving me alone to find Cailian.

I'm going to listen to him. I wish I had sunset magnolia powder. That would come in handy right now.

Another tremor shakes my legs from the floor moving and I run at vampiric speed, following the connection Anwyll and I share. The

coven bond is useful, but I hate to use it at a time like this. I'm also fighting every damn urge not to look for Cailian.

Every molecule that makes me is pushing me to go to our beloved, but I have to trust Nyx to find him.

I dive behind a large rock and glance up, gasping when I see the large hole in the ceiling that was once a mountain. "Oh my gods," I whisper as dragons fly back and forth, attacking the large arms of the troll who continues to swing his hammer, but to me, it reminds me of a bat. It is huge, but I can't tell what it is made of.

More screams have me flinching and another tear breaks free, rolling down my cheek.

"Stay alive, Cailian. Stay Alive, Nyx. Come home to me," I whisper, pouring my love into the bond in hopes they can hear me. I shut my eyes, needing a moment to calm my racing heart. I've only been scared like this one other time in my life and that's when I was a baby, watching my mother get torn to pieces by werewolves.

"Rarity!"

The sound of Anwyll's voice has me snapping my eyes back open, staring into his bright green eyes. "Anwyll!" I throw my arms around his neck, inhaling him and smelling the scent of home. "Are you okay? Oh my gods, you're bleeding." I touch his cheek.

"It isn't mine. I killed a troll."

I stare at him in disbelief. "But how? They are huge and strong. You couldn't have."

"I couldn't leave you here unprepared for this." A boom in the distance has him crouching more to stay hidden. "I took Ru home to be safe. I can't risk her, not when we have triplets at home."

"I know. I know. I understand. I don't want any of you to stay. You need to go. Go home, Anwyll."

"I did and I grabbed something I think will help you." He reaches behind him and pulls from his waistband a unicorn horn.

I've only heard about this from his adventures while trying to get the treatment for Aziel, his brother, to cure his madness. This horn was used against stone giants, the only thing capable enough to pierce the strong stone hide of the creatures they fought.

"The stone giants and the trolls look a lot alike. I gambled in hopes it would work the same. The magic, the purity, the innocence, I don't know, whatever is in this horn is strong enough to kill them, but one stab won't do it." He takes my hand and places the horn in my palm, wrapping my fingers around it. "Give it to Nyx. He'll be able to do what needs to be done."

I stare at the beautiful horn sprinkled with blood. It has to be twelve inches long and it swirls together in opal shades. When the light hits it, pinks, purples, and blues. How can it be capable of being so deadly?

"Come back with me to Salem."

"What?" I hiss, clutching the horn to my chest. "No. Are you out of your mind?"

"Maybe, but you'll be safe. Rarity, if anything happens to you—" he hangs his head, taking my hand in his, clutching it so hard it almost hurts. "—We don't know what we'll do. I don't know what I'll do. You've saved my life so many times. You're the reason I have the life I have. You're always saving others even when you don't think you are. Let me save you. Let me return the favor."

I hug him, wrapping my arms around him tightly, and memorize what his friendship feels like because if I don't make it out alive, I want to relish in this moment.

Sniffling, I pull away, snagging the sunset magnolia powder hanging on his belt loop. "You have saved me. You risked your life to come back here to give me this. So now I have to return the favor." I toss

the powder bomb behind him, an orange sparking circle forming, and in the distance, I can see the Monreaux Estate. "I'll see you soon, Anwyll."

Using half of my vampire strength so I don't hurt him, I shove him backward, and he flies through the air, falling into the portal.

His eyes are full of fear and anger. His arms flail to reach to me, his hands snagging air. "Rarity!" My name is echoed through dimensions as the portal closes.

"I'm sorry, Anwyll. I hope you can forgive me." I peek over the chunk of rock I'm hiding behind, eyes widening in fear when I see so many elves lying still.

I climb the fallen rubble before jumping down, and running to the first elf I see. His eyes flutter when he sees me, a small, bloody smile stretching his face.

"Princess," he chokes.

"Shh. Shh. Don't. Speak."

"You shouldn't… you shouldn't be here." He swallows before coughing, more blood blooming across his lips.

"My beloveds are here. You are here. You all make up my new home. I'm not leaving. I'm here to take care of you." I run my palm over the top of his head, hoping it brings him comfort. My vision becomes hindered with tears, and I refuse to let them go to waste. "What is your name?"

"Ock… Ockard," he stammers, his eyes beginning to glaze over with the promise of death.

"Ockard. I know you." I force a smile. "You took care of my beloved."

He nods slowly.

"Let me take care of you now, Ockard. Trust me?"

"With my life, Princess."

I hold his face in my hands, look into his eyes, give him the best reassuring 'everything will be okay' smile, and tilt my head, placing my cheek right over his mouth. Tears drip freely, rolling off my jaw to his lips.

He gasps for air as my tears begin to heal him. The wounds on his body stitch together one by one.

"You... You..." he is left without words, sitting up without pain. His hands pat every inch of his body to double-check for wounds. "Holy shit, you healed me."

"Yes, but let's try to keep that between us and the other elves. So many creatures want vampire tears, and they don't care what they will have to do to get them."

He stands, kneeling and crossing his wrists to me, a promise that he is bound. "I promise to protect you and your secret."

"Great. Help me find the injured, okay? The dead..." My breath is strangled and choppy from the thought. "I... I don't know what to do about them. I'm not sure my tears will work for them."

The weight of the horn in my hand reminds me that I need to find Nyx. "Will you be okay without me for a little while?" I dig through the rubble, trying to find a glass that isn't broken or completely shattered.

"What? I need you here. I need... you know," he whispers out from the corner of his mouth.

I lift a wine glass in the air. The stem is broken but the round part that holds the liquid is okay. "I'm going to give them to you. Listen to me, it doesn't take much. One drop, maybe two, that's all you need, okay? Dip your finger in, rub it on their lips. That's it. Okay?"

"Okay."

I hold the glass to my cheek and let the tears roll freely. "Repeat it to me. "

"One to two drops, dip my finger in, rub it on their lips."

"Good. Good." The roars of the dragons, the crash of rocks, the shouts of elves, and the pounding of the trolls have the tears falling faster. Cailian and Nyx are still alive yet all I can think about is seeing them dead, preparing myself, and the thought of them lifeless punches me in the gut.

I'm able to fill the glass enough with about three inches of liquid. I hold it out to him, the light piercing through the hole in the ceiling shines on the specks of glitter. They reflect off each individual piece. Ockard carefully takes the glass from my hand and holds it to his chest.

I grip the material of my dress at the thigh and lift it, so it is easier to walk. "Remember, it doesn't take much, Ockard."

"Your tears will be honored, Princess. I will be very careful."

My gaze bounces around the room, the reality setting in when I really take in the damage. I can't believe barely an hour ago, this place was alive with laughter. Elves and dragons were dancing. Everyone was getting along. Wine was being poured. Ale was being drunk. Reuel was surrounded by Woodland Elves who were bonding with him, getting to know him, and I swear, his silver veins pumped brighter with every greeting.

Happiness filled this room.

And now, half the mountain is in a crumble. Mounds of rock are piled in every corner. I can see out to the landscape now, a chunk of the side of the mountain gone. Two huge feet thud against the ground before a giant roar escapes, the hammer swings in the air followed by a blaze of fire.

I can also smell the blood. I can hear it dripping from the tips of the rock, pooling onto the floor. The scent of death is heavy in the air. Even though my tears will save some, it is too late for so many.

So many that were here to celebrate me, Cailian, and Nyx.

Guilt weighs against my lungs and it's hard to breathe. I roll my rage into a tight fist, gripping the unicorn horn. I want revenge.

I blur through the open side of the mountain, the cold air hitting my face. The circular landscape that used to be undisturbed snow is now a battlefield.

And a black dragon dips between two trolls, legs stretched out and his claws extended.

Nyx.

He roars, snagging me by the shoulders. I yelp being thrown through the air, missing the side of the mountain by a fraction of an inch. We dip below a troll's wrath as he reaches for us, growling when he misses, but his attention is snatched by another dragon who blows fire in his face.

Raiden.

Nyx lands and we skid a few feet across the snow and ice. Cold blasts me in the face, snow plunging into my mouth. I roll until I come to a stop, get onto my hands and knees, and spit the slush in my mouth out. I'm barely able to catch my damn breath before I hear a menacing rumble coming from my right.

I stand, wiping my hands on my dress. Straightening my spine, I prepare for Nyx's onslaught.

"What the fuck are you doing?" he yells at me. "I told you to stay away from the fight. I told you to be safe. I told you to find Anwyll. Why won't you listen to me? What would I do? What would I do if I lost you?" He charges at me, taking my neck in his hand, and yanks me closer to his face. "You and Cailian are all I have. So listen to me," he begs, a plea frowning his eyes. "Because if you don't, if I lose either of you in this—" He stops speaking, rolling his lips together. His eyelashes become wet before cutting those golden irises to mine. "Just take my flaming heart and watch it smoke. Watch it die. Watch

me turn to ash without you, without him. So please, just... just fucking listen to me," he shouts until his voice breaks with emotion.

He clings to me, one hand on the back of my neck while the other cups my cheek. "Please, just listen to me. I can't... I can't breathe at the thought."

"I understand. I feel the exact same way, but I won't apologize for finding you. Anwyll came back to give me this." I press the horn against his chest, and he looks down, brows pinched in confusion.

"It's a stick. What the hell am I going to do with a damn stick?"

"Nyx!" Raiden calls from the sky and we both look up just in time to see him dodge an oversized, light green arm that is followed by a troll's roar.

They are hideous creatures with different shades of muted green skin. They have eyes too big for their head and every time they roar, their breath smells like decomposition. They have straggly pieces of hair, a unibrow, and three fingers on each hand.

The next second Raiden is being held upside down by his legs and the troll swings his weapon, but he lifts his body to miss it.

"I need help!"

"Use this. This is a unicorn horn. It can kill them. Go! Just trust me. I'm going to go find Cailian."

He gives me a look of disbelief before sprinting away, his wings spreading then he takes flight. He swirls around each swing, then dives between the troll's legs, spewing fire at his thighs. The trolls screams, releasing Raiden.

Nyx lands on the troll's shoulder and then stabs him in the temple. Blood oozes down the troll's body and he begins to sway to keep his stance. It isn't enough.

He falls.

And when he hits the ground, the entire ground shakes from the force.

The dragons cheer from the kill, only leaving a few trolls left to take care of when someone presses something sharp against my neck. I hold my breath, trying to calculate who this can be.

"You'll make me a lot of money in The Menagerie Trade on the forbidden market. All the rarities. All the pretties." He spins me around, and I expect this man to be someone I know, but I don't recognize him at all.

I push my fear through the bond to my beloveds. I keep my features schooled as they respond, the strings of our souls thrumming.

"I'm Nyx's wizard, Erelix."

To say I'm shocked is an understatement. I know Nyx has been looking high and low for him. He's been worried, hoping his wizard is safe.

"You've been plotting against him. Why?"

"Why not? I've been trying to kill this bloodline for centuries. Luckily the trolls took care of his father's firebond and then the elf killed his father. It was a win. I am the one with the true power. Me. This kingdom would be nothing without me. I deserve to sit on the throne not some fucking dragon," he spits, the vein in his forehead protruding as his face turns red.

He has sandy blonde hair and an aged face with wrinkles around his mouth and eyes. He has a villain's face, gaunt cheeks, and sunken darkened eyes.

"His father's firebond? What are you talking about?"

Erelix cackles. "That stupid elf is still keeping that ridiculous promise."

"Rarity!" Nyx calls for me just as the ground shakes again with another fallen troll.

"We are here!" Cailian's voice pierces the sky, the ground quaking once more. "It is okay. You will be okay."

"Ah, ah, ah, don't make promises you can't keep, Elf. We all know how you're bound by fucking loyalty."

"Get your fucking hands off her before I burn you alive," Nyx threatens taking another step.

"One more step and this blade stakes her heart and I'd hate that because—" he takes a strand of my hair and inhales. "—She is going to make me rich."

Another troll falls and the tremors shake my legs, the sharp needle of the blade digging a bit deeper into my back.

"You aren't going to make it from Elementalu alive." Nyx's fire begins to dance over his scales.

Cailian swirls his hands to the ground, and large spikes of ice pierce the surface, towering until they reach the sky. His power is immense. Snow begins to fall in blinding amounts. Another ice pillar shoots between me and Erelix, freeing me.

"Rarity? Rarity!" Cailian calls for me, searching for me through the maze of pillars.

I run to him.

At least, I think I am. His voice begins to echo, bouncing off each sharp pillar.

"Cailian! Nyx!" I spin around, closing my hands over my ears and my voice becomes louder.

The pillars begin to descend and something painful rips through my heart and soul. Something that sends me to my knees. I can't breathe. I can't think. All I feel is pain. I hold my hand to my stomach, gasping, struggling to get air. Tears pour from me. An ache spreads like poison.

"No! No!" A guttural cry comes from Nyx, and I turn my head just in time to see Erelix with the blade deep in Cailian's heart.

Everything slows.

Cailian grabs the blade and stares into Erelix's eyes, only to shove himself down onto the knife.

"I love killing mates," Erelix whispers.

Cailian presses his hand against Erelix's chest. "And I will kill you with my dying breath."

"Cailian!" I scream at the top of my lungs until a metallic taste forms in the back of my throat. I stumble as I try to get up, slipping on the ice and snow. The shock of what I'm seeing has me off-balanced. "Cailian. No. No. Please," I wail, slipping again.

Erelix's smile fades as his entire body becomes frozen solid, and then Nyx is there punching his hand into his wizard's chest. He yanks out his heart and it shatters in his hand. But he's too late, Cailian is left impaled, his blood dripping into the snow as if it's rain.

"Treasure? Treasure. I have you. I have you. You're going to be okay. Rarity will heal you with her tears. Everything will be fine. You'll see. You'll see." Nyx pulls Cailian free from the blade and catches him in his arms. "Treasure? Please." Nyx shakes him, patting his face. "Look at me, Cailian. Look at me. I love you. I love you. You can't... please! Fucking look at me," he shouts again, the soul-wrenching agony breaking his words. Spit drips from his mouth as he cries. "Cailian."

"My Dove," Cailian whispers, placing his hand on his cheek.

I slide to a stop right beside him and just as a tear drips from my face, he releases a long exhale, setting free the air he had in his lungs. His eyes get this far-away look in them and one singular frozen tear rolls down his face.

"No. No. No. No. Cailian. Cailian? You can't. You can't go. Please, Treasure. Please. Come back to me. Come back. I'll do anything. I'm

sorry. I'm so sorry for everything. I don't care about what happened, just come back to me!" Nyx pleads, sliding his arms under Cailian's body, and holding him against his chest.

I scream my pain, clutching my heart as it tears itself in two.

"You'll be okay, Treasure. We'll be okay." Nyx runs his hand through Cailian's hair. "I'll fix this. It will be okay. You'll be okay. Everything will be okay."

Denial is an enemy wielding a sword that plunges into me. I pray it brings me closer to death.

I climb on top of Cailian, pressing my cheek against his bloody chest. "I can't hear his heartbeat. I can't hear his song." I bury my face into his sternum and sob, clutching onto his tattered dress.

"Nyx. Let me take him. Let me—"

Nyx spews fire at Raiden for daring to attempt to take his body. "You will not take him. He will be fine. Won't you, Treasure? You'll be okay." He kisses Cailain's temple.

"Nyx—"

"—You will leave us to die with our firebond. You will not touch him. You will not do anything! You will not take him from me. I will kill you. I will kill you and replace his dead heart with yours to bring him back to me."

"That will not work."

I look up to see an older witch, wearing a black robe. She lowers the hood and kneels, reaching to touch Cailian's face.

Nyx pulls us away, so she is left with her hand mid-air.

"Raltena," I whisper with hope, slipping from Cailian. "This is Cailian's witch. She can help, Nyx."

"I don't trust her. Look what mine did. He promised to protect us, to help us, and he took from us instead." He grazes his knuckles down

Cailian's cheek another sob breaking free. "I didn't love him like he deserved. I will die with that regret."

A shadow forms next to Raltena, a figure dressed in black with a skeletal face.

"A void," she sneers at him.

"Lorcan, but I will answer to void as well." He pulls out a cigarette and lights it. "Ya know, there are aspects about my job I don't like. For instance, taking a soul when he is mated and loved. That doesn't bring me joy."

"You aren't taking his soul," Nyx snarls, clutching Cailian to his chest.

"I have to. Do you want him to be trapped in the Phantom Forest." Lorcan points into a shadowed forest covered in fog. "That's where he will be if I don't or if he chooses not to go."

"Why won't my tears help? They aren't working." I rub them on Cailian's lips waiting for him to wake up.

"Because he is dead. Nothing can bring back the dead," Lorcan says.

"That's not true," Raltena states. "I can bring him back."

Lorcan glares, blowing smoke in her face. "You would do that to them? Do you know what they will have to give?"

"I'll give anything. Everything. Whatever it is," I rush, begging and on my knees.

"Me too. I'll do anything. Everything. I'll do anything to have him come back to me. This pain is something I can't live with. Parts of me are dying and if he can't come back, I'd rather choose death, so maybe in the next life, we can find each other." Nyx squeezes his eyes shut, blackened tears streaming down his face. "Remember, Treasure? Remember, that's what you said. We will find each other in the next life, and I swear, I won't care what happened between you and my

father. I just need you. Rarity will be coming too. We can all be happy. We can have the life we deserve."

I take his hand and squeeze. "To the afterlife, then."

"You two won't be dying," Lorcan states. "Not when a part of him lives in you." His eyes fall to my stomach. Trio matings are odd like that."

"It's his?" My hand trembles as I place it over my stomach.

"All of you. Your dna combined."

"So... we have to live our lives without him?"

"No," Raltena says again. "His spirit can be found."

"But you said his soul was here," I say, confused.

"His soul is different than his spirit. His spirit is another form of him. His soul is the purest parts of him, creating energy that stays within his body. That's what I take," Lorcan explains. "Something like that. It's more complicated but none of us have time for that."

"I hate reapers," Raltena rolls her eyes.

"Enough!" Nyx's voice booms across the mountain ranges.

The dragons and elves who are alive kneel as if they are forced.

"Tell me what we have to do," Nyx orders.

"Tell us. We will do it."

"We need you both to sacrifice something dear to you."

"That's it?" I ask. "Like a pendant? What?"

"No, something bound to you. Something you live with every day. Something that is a part of you." Her eyes drag to Nyx. "Would you sacrifice your wings? Would you choose to be flightless if it meant having your mate?"

"Yes," he says without hesitation. "Take them. If I can't fly to him, then I don't want to fly at all."

She nods, moving her attention to me. "I will be taking your Ice Elven magic as it was never meant to be yours anyway."

I rear back. "What are you talking about?"

"You don't know? You only have this magic for this moment. The witch who bound her magic must have foreseen this, so she bound her magic with Ice Elven. The magic must have transferred to you. This moment was always meant to happen. Certain milestones are always set in the future."

"Okay. Take it then. I don't want it. What else do you need?"

"He will need to sacrifice something as well," she says sadly.

"He is dead. Isn't that enough?" Nyx spews his hate.

"No, because that isn't a sacrifice. He won't be able to have children once I bring him back. A future life for his."

My head swims, and my stomach turns from the thought of not seeing what Cailian will look like pregnant. He would have been beautiful.

Nyx rubs a hand down his face, nodding his acceptance. "That's fine."

"The hell it is," an unknown voice sounds next to Lorcan.

"How the hell did you get here?" Lorcan shouts. "You aren't allowed. The only way a spirit can—" he frowns, taking another hit off his cigarette. "His soul called to you," he murmurs, staring at Nyx.

Snow swirls in a small swarm, sticking to a figure I can hardly see.

"Dovenyx." The man crouches, placing his hand on Nyx's shoulder.

"Dad?" His eyes are wide, pupils blown with shock. "What? How? You can't be real. I'm losing it. I'm mentally breaking because Cailian is dead."

"He is here. I see him, Nyx," I reassure, pressing my cheek against his shoulder. "You aren't mad."

"Cailian died keeping my promise and now it is my turn to return the favor. Nyx, look at me, son. I can't be here too long. It takes too much energy."

"How..."

"He chose to stay in the Phantom Forest until you needed him," Lorcan explains, tsking. "I bet that's been a rough stay."

Nyx's father rolls his eyes before he smiles at me. "Rarity. Thank you for bringing my son and my best friend together. They are lucky to have you."

"He's gone. I blamed him. I didn't give him all of me and now he is gone."

"Trust me. Trust Raltena. She has never swayed. She has always been loyal, unlike Erelix. He killed my firebond by spelling the trolls. When she died, I was dying, burning from the inside out. I begged Cailian to kill me because I didn't want to burn to death. It was so painful living without her. He wouldn't do it, so I provoked him. He killed me just like I asked him to. I made him promise he wouldn't tell the truth about what happened, but I had no idea wars would be started because of your hate. Let it go. I've been waiting until you needed me, and now I can be free. I can finally go to my firebond."

"What are you talking about?"

"Take my energy," he tells Raltena. "Use mine and Lorcan, you can finally take me. My energy will be enough, won't it? He'll be able to have kids?"

"Well... yes. A spirit that has been bound for so long will work just fine. Your energy will be enough, but you won't ever be able to make this form again. You'll be gone."

"And I'll finally be with my firebond. That's fine."

"Dad..." Nyx croaks, teary-eyed.

His dad hugs him. "I love you. Be happy. Live a good life. I'll see you again."

Raltena doesn't allow Nyx to say another word before she drives her hand into the spirit of Nyx's dad. Her eyes glow as she soaks in his energy.

"Unfucking real. You Monreaux's make my job difficult, ya know?" Lorcan flicks the cigarette to the ground, stepping on it.

"Dad?"

"It's okay. I feel good. I'm... free." He smiles, slowly fading.

"Thank you," Nyx says.

"Anything for my son."

And then he's gone with Lorcan.

Raltena digs into her bag, grabs a vile, places it to her lips, and a blueish tint fills the small container as it leaves her mouth.

She moves quickly after that, snagging the sword that killed Cailian, and slices it through the air, chopping Nyx's wings off.

"Nyx!" I yell just as he roars, sending fire into the air.

I dab my tears on his lips before he has a chance to feel too much pain. His skin heals over where his wings used to be, but the bones where they belong are still there, flexing from habit.

"Thank you, My Darling Jewel." He is sweating, his onyx scales ashen.

"Nyx."

"It's okay," he says, taking my hand, then Cailian's. "We will all be okay."

"He's... so cold. Colder than usual." I cover my mouth while bile climbs up my throat.

"I need a dragon to burn these wings. I need their ashes. It can't be from the dragon I took them from," she announces to the fleet.

Raiden steps forward and inhales, letting his fire free. I don't miss the guilt, the pain stretching across his face as he burns the wings of his prince.

Nyx buries his face into Cailian's chest. "Anything to get him back for us, right?"

I nod, unable to speak because if I do, I'll sob again, letting go of any hope.

The witch gathers the ashes, places them into the vile, and then whips her head up from the ground, staring at me.

She stands, strolling over to me casually as if she doesn't hold the rest of our lives in her hands. She digs her nails into my chest until I hiss, my fangs dropping on instinct. "This is going to hurt but only for a moment. You don't have much of the magic to begin with, but it is enough to restart his cells."

I can feel her taking the magic, dragging it from my bones, and I scream.

"Stay still or this process will kill you."

At least in death, I know I'll see Cailian again, but one look at Nyx keeps me strong.

We all live together.

Or we all die together.

There are no other options.

Chapter Twenty-Four

CAILIAN

I have no idea where I am. I remember pain and the devastation in Rarity's eyes.

My hand flies to my chest and I glance down, not seeing anything, but I swear, something was there. Something happened.

Something horrible.

"Why am I here?" I whisper, rubbing my chest.

I feel empty. There are pieces of me missing.

I gasp when images bombard me. One by one, the moments come back to me. Erelix stabbed me. He killed me.

I am dead.

Bending over, I dry heave, the excruciating pain and doom of knowing I will never be with them again makes me ill. What am I going to do? How can I get back to them? Can I?

The ground beneath my feet is soft and dark, riddled with black pine needles. The trees are full, the branches thick with life, and fog stays low to the floor.

"Hello?" I shout, cupping my hands on either side of my mouth.

Hello. Hello. Hello.

My voice is echoed back to me.

"Is anyone there?"

There. There. There.

I spin around, looking for something, anything, but I am alone.

The air is stale and cold. Nothing seems to move. Silence is not comforting here. Instead of peace, it brings doubt. Rustling from the right has me turning my head, examining the depth of the woods.

Nothing is there but fog and the skeletal finger of the trees reaching out for me.

"Where am I?" I whisper to myself.

Staying in this spot will not get me anywhere, so I walk, putting one foot in front of the other with home as the only destination. I refuse to accept anywhere else. My time with my mates cannot be up. We have only just started. We were making progress. We were happy. Nyx and I were healing old wounds slowly. Rarity is the healing additive, the glue, the stitching that allows Nyx and I to be together. Without her, I know my journey with Nyx would be more difficult.

I miss them more than I ever thought possible. I miss the way I felt Nyx's jealousy through the bond as I danced with Raiden. I love knowing he cared enough. I miss how Rarity's eyes took on a red hue as she looked at me as if she wanted to devour me.

I miss her bite. The way she fed. The way she needed me. How will she survive?

My feet stop moving when I wonder if they will die because of the pain of losing me. I start running, pumping my arms and legs. Snarling sounds behind me and I look back, wondering what the hell that could be.

Three massive dogs, each with two heads and red eyes chase me. They are triple my size. Their large paws thrash dirt against the trees

as they pound against the dirt. I duck to the right, coming to an open field with a giant building.

Warm breath on the back of my neck has me moving faster.

A huge creature steps out of the building and sees me coming, his wings wider than I've ever seen. His face is stitched and his horns swirl above his head. One moment he is standing there, the next he is gone.

Until he grabs me and slings me behind him. He roars so loud, that the trees shake from the long, deep guttural sound. Fear roots itself in my veins.

The large beasts stop, snapping their teeth at the stranger before turning around and vanishing into the forest, no doubt searching for their next meal.

"Th-thank you," I stutter, trying to catch my breath.

I'm not sure if that is possible.

"Don't mind them. They are hellhounds. They wouldn't have touched you. They only wanted to scare you."

"I have a feeling they would have eaten me."

"No, no offense. They don't like Ice Elven. They like their meat warm."

My brows raise. "I am not sure how to respond to that."

"No need to, Cailian."

I stumble away from him. "How do you know my name?"

"Apologies. I don't mean to frighten you. This is a scary place, but this is a neutral area. The good creatures tend to stay inside Purgatory Pins." He juts his chin to the building, and I turn to get a better look.

It is a huge log-style like cabin, but it's black with a red roof, and a bit run down.

"Purgatory Pins?" I question.

There is a line of bikes parked out front and if I am seeing correctly, each bike is made of bones.

Noted.

Do not get on this creature's bad side.

He holds out his hand, his arm stitched the same as his face is. "I'm Death."

I blink at him. "I am sorry?"

"Death," he repeats. "I am why you are here." He pulls out a cigarette and holds the box out to me. "Want one?"

"No, thank you." I am becoming more confused as this interaction goes on. "You are Death?"

He snaps his fingers and a flame flickers on his index finger to light the cigarette. "You know, Four Horsemen, blah blah blah." He exhales smoke, giving me a sad smile. "I do not enjoy so many parts of my job. Some days it weighs on me. I can feel the love you keep for your mates—" he clears his throat, glancing away.

"Are you... are you crying, Death?"

He wipes his eyes. "Don't be fucking ridiculous, Cailian. I am a Horsemen. I am Death, The Reaper of All Souls. I do not cry about love."

He sniffles.

"Right," I say slowly, narrowing my eyes. "Listen, I do not know why you brought me here, but I need to go back. It is not my time."

He sighs, nodding. "It isn't. You're right. You are actually one of the few that I cannot kill. Any friends or mates of The Monreaux Coven are off limits. They must always live. Bosses rules."

"And your boss is? I would like to speak to him because I am a mate of a Monreaux and yet I am here being chased by hellhounds."

"Lucifer is my boss. He is booked out for the next three months. Sorry, he can't squeeze you in. You are here because I need to speak to you while introducing you to somebody." He wraps his arms around my shoulders. "Let's go play a game."

"Okay— wait— no!" I shrug out of his hold and point my finger at him. "I do not want to play a game. I want to go home. To my mates. They must be terrified."

"They aren't fucking well Cailian," he shouts at me. "Their mate just died. They can barely breathe." He flicks my forehead, and I rub the sore spot.

"Ow. No need for that."

"You are here because you are friends with Anwyll, no? He is part of the Monreaux Coven."

"Yes. Is he here too? I thought you said we were off-limits?"

"You all are but there are loopholes for everything." He wraps an arm around my shoulders, and we start walking to the front door.

The steps creak from our weight and the man kicks the door open to reveal the inside. It is rundown with dull lighting. The floor is translucent. Fire brews and souls scream, pressing their faces against the barrier, moaning to get free.

"Don't mind them. That's Hell and these are the worst of the worst of souls. You know, the rapists and child murders, blah, blah, blah." He tosses his cigarette on the floor, steps on it, then stomps his boot. "Hey, shut the fuck up. Stop groaning. You aren't going anywhere." He gives me a large, toothy smile. "Sorry about that."

I gulp, knowing I am in way over my head. Nyx would do well here, not that I would ever want him here.

To the left is a room full of arcade games and to the right is a huge bar lined with different paranormal creatures.

In front of us are the bowling lanes. It looks so... normal.

Minus the bowling balls. Every ball is a skull and people use the eye sockets to put their fingers into.

"Want to play?"

"I would rather get down to business," I say, uncomfortable at the thought of rolling some dead guy's head down the lane.

"Right. Anwyll's brother is here. You know what happened to him, right?" Death leans against the bar.

A shifter is behind the bar, making drinks with his arms, but his six other tentacles are pouring beers. Without a word, he slides two glasses down the bar top and Death hands me one.

I take it because I need it.

I down half of it.

"It is a shame he is here, but if Monreaux's are off limits, why not send him back?"

"Because of the treatment he had for his madness. I did not bring him here, the treatment did. He has to find his way back."

"Okay? What can I do to help?"

He lowers his voice. "You can't do anything, but you can get a message to Anwyll. I can't do it because I have to be careful sending this kind of information. I am doing my best to guide Aziel to a section of purgatory that has a way out. He is searching for something here, someone, and he won't leave. Not yet. Just tell Anwyll he is okay and to give it time. His brother will come back."

"I do not understand why you cannot tell him yourself."

"Because I am not supposed to be helping him at all. Purgatory isn't easy. You have to kill to stay alive here. Kill or be killed. All that jazz, you know? The longer he stays here, the more anchored he becomes. If he doesn't start listening, he could be stuck here forever. If Lucifer finds out I am helping him, I could lose my damn wings and I'll be under this floor."

"I see. Can I see Aziel myself? Is he here?"

"No. He isn't here. He is out there, fighting. Something he is way too good at. He'd be a hell of a Horseman."

"You better not—"

"—I wouldn't. Just pass the message on, okay?" He pauses, grinning, and setting his drink down. "Our time is up, Prince. See you another time." He snaps his fingers, and everything morphs to black.

I gasp, bolting into a seated position, my hand to my chest as I awaken from a terrible dream.

"Cailian?" Rarity whispers, rubbing her eyes half asleep. "Cailian?" she shouts, straddling me. "Oh my gods. Nyx! Nyx!" she continues to yell, cupping my face. "You're alive. You're here. You're actually here." She crashes her mouth to mine, moaning into it before the passionate relief turns into her crying.

"My Snow. I am here. I am here." I wrap my arms around her, her pain screaming that the dream I had was real.

I had died.

I lean away, sensing something different about her. "Something has changed."

Before she can answer, Nyx's presence fills the room, and I turn my head.

"Treasure."

"Dove."

He dashes to me, jumping onto the bed, and gathers Rarity and I into his arms. Our dragon sobs, clutching us tighter. I wrap my arms around him in return only to pull away and scramble off the bed.

"Your wings! Where are they? How long has it been?"

"It has only been a few days, but I sacrificed my wings, Rarity sacrificed her Ice Elven magic, and my father gave his energy to bring you back to us."

"Wha—what? But—"

"He's been in the Phantom Forest. He is free now, but he won't be able to come back. Raltena preformed the spell."

"Your wings?" My bottom lip trembles. "I know how much you loved them. You can't be without them."

"I can be," he growls. "I can't be without you. I can't be without Rarity. I love you more than I loved my wings. I love Rarity more. If I had to, I would do it all over again. He tugs me onto the bed and Rarity cuddles against my side. "My heart died the day you did. Only Rarity and the baby kept me going. Living has been hard, for the both of us, but we had to." Nyx presses his hand against her stomach.

"You're pregnant?"

Rarity nods, smiling at me. "And he or she is the DNA combination of all of us."

I slip my hand to her flat stomach, tears breaking free in pure happiness.

"But you aren't," Nyx growls.

"I am not what?" I say gently, never taking my eyes from Rarity's stomach.

"Pregnant. How are you feeling since coming back to life?"

"Fine... Why?"

Nyx pins me to the bed, eyes blazing, and he strikes before I can ask any more questions. He marks me, biting my neck with a mating mark for all to see.

"You aren't leaving this bed. Neither of you are. Not for days. I need to reclaim you both."

The words send fire through my body and Nyx inhales as I squirm, wetness leaking from my ass.

"Looks like we get to pick up where we left off, Treasure."

Chapter Twenty-Five

DOVENYX

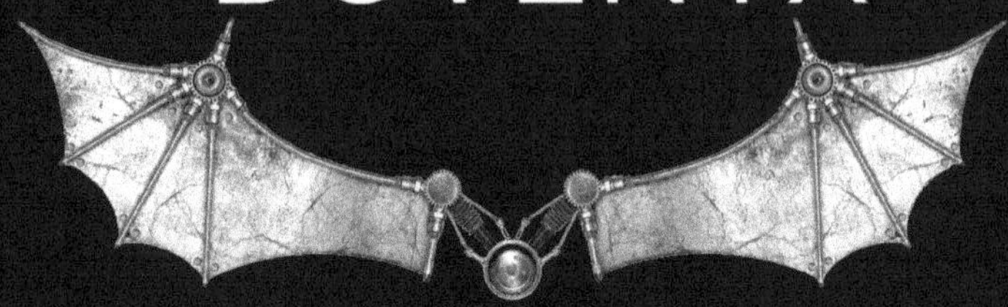

"But— but there is so much to discuss. Where I have been, what happened when I was dead, how many of our people died, what Death said to me."

"I don't give a fuck about anything else. I need you. Everything else can wait. I've spent the last two days thinking you were gone forever and now you are back. I can touch you, kiss you, hear your voice, and now I need to hear your pleasure. Unless you don't feel well?" I ask him, wanting to make sure he is healthy. He died and came back to life. I can't relate, but I'm sure that is exhausting. "Your heat is getting stronger by the second, Cailian. I don't think we can wait." I press our lips together in a bruising kiss and to me, it feels like the first.

There's no hate inside me, no anger, no need for revenge. There's just love. So much fucking love and I try to pour that feeling into the kiss, my lips sliding effortlessly across his. I grip the nook where his neck meets his shoulder, keeping his head still so I can control the kiss. I want him to feel that with every slide, every fucking motion of my lips against his, he can feel my love for him.

I want to erase the hate I've stained on his soul. It doesn't deserve to be there.

"Thank you," I whisper into his mouth, running one hand down his body until I'm gripping his ass. "Gods." A desperate growl of need escapes me. "You smell so good."

"For?" he mewls, arching his back, and the robe Rarity and I changed him into after giving him a bath to get the blood off him, parts.

"My father." I kiss my way down his throat to his chest.

His defined chest comes to view and the scar where the blade pierced his heart, sending him to another dimension is still there. It looks old, as if it has been there all his life instead of just two days. I bend down, kissing the scar, pinching my eyes shut when the image of the blade slicing through him blares in my mind.

He was so close to being taken from me.

Rarity's hand lands on my back, right where my wings used to be, and while I haven't shifted into my dragon form because I don't want to see what I look like, I know sacrificing my wings was worth it.

Fingers lift my chin and gently turn my head. Rarity is there sensing my emotion and her own shines through her eyes.

"He is here. He isn't going anywhere." She bends down and kisses my forehead, before taking a seat in the chair nestled in the corner.

"My Snow, why are you over there?" Cailian asks.

"I want to see him fuck you, My Love. I love seeing you two together. I didn't think I would ever get to see it again, so I want to sit here for a bit, until I'm wet to the point where I can't wait any longer for you to fill me, Cailian. So let me enjoy my view." She spreads her legs and the lavender velvet nightgown inches up her thighs.

She isn't wearing any panties. Her pussy is already a glistening pink, promising warmth and tightness.

"Come sit on my face, My Snow. Let me taste what I missed."

"In time," she replies with a smirk, torturing herself for pleasure.

She glides her fingers along her inner thigh, biting her bottom lip, and her fangs drop. Her tongue rolls over her left one, then right, and her eyes take on the gorgeous crimson hue that gives away how much she wants us.

A grumble purrs in my ribcage, vibrating my bones. "Look at her, Treasure. Look how beautiful our firebond is."

He pants, his hard cock slipping and sliding against my stomach as he seeks friction. "I want to taste her. I want her to ride my tongue. My Snow, please," he begs. "Will you grant an elf his wish after experiencing death?"

I grab his face and force him to turn his head to me. "You will not ever use that against her or me because, in our eyes, you were never dead. We were ready to do anything to get you back, even if it meant killing ourselves to be with you. Don't ever..." My voice wavers. "Don't ever say you died because I'm still healing from seeing you dying. I don't think it is something I will ever forget. Promise me."

He pets my cheek lovingly, his eyes darting over my face as a slow, sad smile just barely makes an appearance on his lips. "I promise, My Dove. I promise."

"You can't ever break that promise," I remind him, lowering myself to my elbows so I'm hovering just over his face.

"To my grave, My Dove. To my grave."

I dip down to rob his lips, parting my own robe to feel his cock against mine. I shuck it off, grabbing every part of his body I can get my hands on. The kiss turns from sweet to needy. My palms roam down the feminine edges of his body, appreciating the small dip in his waist. I groan, rocking us together faster, our cocks sliding together easily from the precome dripping from my cock.

His body becomes hotter and the little noises escaping him have me teetering into insanity. I'm fucking crazy for him and Rarity. There's no other way to describe it. I'm an unhinged dragon and my fire belongs to them.

Rarity whimpers next and her pleasure plucks at the bond, creating a beautiful song only we can feel.

I reach between us, stretch his foreskin, and press my cock into it until I'm covered, then rock.

"Nyx! Holy fuck, oh my gods. What— yes—" he rakes his nails down my chest.

"Do you know what this is called, Treasure?" I bite his bottom lip, snarling before letting it go with a soft pop.

He shakes his head, beads of sweat pooling at his temple.

"Docking. Do you like it?"

"Feels so good."

"Yes, you do," I moan in agreement. "That fucking snowflake for a crown makes me want to come but this tight space won't be able to hold all of it, will it?"

He shakes his head again, unable to speak. His heat hits him full force, probably worse since it has never gotten satisfied the first time before...

Before.

"My Dove, I need you. I need you now. Please, no teasing, please," he practically sobs, grabbing my ass. His fingers dig into each cheek, pulling me against him harder and faster.

"I thought princes didn't beg?" I remind him of his words, sucking his nipple into my mouth.

"I am not a prince right now. I am your mate. I am yours and I need you."

I remove myself from his foreskin, then slip a hand between his legs. My finger runs down his crease. He's wet. His heat in full force.

In frustration, he wraps his legs around my waist and flips me to my back, guides my cock to his entrance, and slams himself down on me.

"Cailian!" I groan low, digging my fingers into his hips so hard, I know there will be bruises. "You could hurt yourself."

"I do not care. I need more. I need so much more." He rocks himself hard and fast against me, his cock slapping against my stomach. He lifts his arms, gathering his hair from his slick shoulders. The ends of the strands are already damp. Beads of sweat roll down his body as he uses my cock to search for the release he needs.

I sit up, wrapping an arm around his waist. My forked tongue stretches from my mouth, licking him from his navel to the middle of his chest.

"You know how to take my cock, Treasure. Look at you." I lean back on my hands, watching him fuck me. "That's it. Use me. You were made for this cock. You were made to take my knot."

He whines so loudly, finally opening his eyes to look at me. Tiny sweat droplets form under his eyes and a panicked need glosses over his silver orbs.

"You want my knot, don't you? That's why you're fucking me so hard." I hold in a moan, but my claws get the best of me as my hands shift into my dragon. I rip the mattress as I watch one of the most beautiful creatures in the world take every scolding inch of me. "Earn my knot then," I sneer at him. "Make me lock inside you and fill you up with so much come, it still won't be enough to sate your heat, and you'll be begging for me again." I wrap my hand around his throat, gripping it tight.

Rarity tosses her nightgown on the bed. Cailian and I both whip our heads to the side, watching as she kneads one breast while finger

fucking herself. She's watching us with hooded eyes, gasping for air every time Cailian moves against me.

"My Snow, please. I need you too. I can't overcome this heat without you."

"I want him to make you come first and then I'll fuck you, My Love. I'm enjoying my view too much. I'm not ready to leave it just yet."

I flip Cailian to his back and drive into him, giving him the hard thrust he is searching for. His cries echo throughout the entire castle. Every fucking time I slam into him, I manage to get him to shout a little louder. The headboard smacks against the wall, cracking in half, and it only gives me the fuel to find the strength to move faster.

He reaches for his cock, and I slap his hand away. "I make you come, Treasure. Me. My cock. My knot. Nothing else. Either me or Rarity's pretty pussy. That's it."

"I'm so close. Please!" he begs again.

I happen to love hearing that from him. Maybe one day I can get him on his knees, begging me to let him suck my cock.

"Look at Rarity. Look at her." I lightly slap his cheek to turn his head. "She's fucking herself at the view of us. Do you hear how wet she is? Look at her body. Look." I slap his cheek again, then press my hand against his head so he can't move. He has no choice but to look at her. "She's pregnant with our child, Treasure. Ours. Imagine what she will look like with a round stomach, our child growing. Imagine how even more beautiful she will look. We won't be able to get enough of her. Will we?"

Cailian groans, his cock flexing as ropes of come paint his chest.

"Rarity?"

"Yes, My Love?"

"Clean up his mess," I order, bringing Cailian's right leg up to kiss his inner leg.

Rarity lifts herself from the chair, my eyes drop to her breasts. Her nipples are hard and abused by the rough attention she has given them.

She knee-walks onto the bed, running her fingers through Cailian's hair. He stares at her, completely enamored.

Cailian lifts, snagging her neck, and kissing her as if his life depended on it. I move slowly, sliding in and out at an unhurried pace.

"Clean me, My Snow." He pushes her down to his chest and she eagerly begins to lick him, flattening her tongue and gathering the seed wasted on his body.

She moans in delight as if his come is the best thing she's ever tasted. She works her way from his chest to his stomach, delving her tongue between each defined abdominal muscle.

"Good girl," I praise her, rubbing my hand down her back. "Now, get on top of him, My Darling Jewel. Fuck him wildly."

"There's nothing more I'd rather do." She straddles his waist, reaches behind, grabs his cock, and guides it to her entrance. She lowers herself onto his aching cock and I'm entranced watching her take more and more of him until she's seated to the hilt.

I reach between his legs and fondle his sack, igniting a groan from him. She lowers herself onto his chest and he wraps his arms around her, gliding his hand up and down her back. Ice leaves his fingertips, freezing certain spots in the middle of her back.

Adding to it, I blow my fire delicately, so I don't hurt her. She moans, wiping her hair as she tosses her head back. The two elements collide, extinguishing themselves on her skin. Her vampire healing soothes the reddened flesh before healing them.

As if fire and ice never met.

I bend down, licking up her spine and gathering her sweat. I'm not sure what it is about their sweat that sets me off, but my firebonds taste

so fucking good. Their scent is the strongest in their sweat. I can taste their aroma and how much desire they feel.

"Mmm," I hum, licking up her neck before pulling away.

My eyes roll to the back of my head when his heat peaks. I ram into Cailian, his cock driving into Rarity from the force.

"Goddamn, I wish you two could see my view right now." I stare down where I'm pummeling into Cailian while also having the view of Cailian disappearing into Rarity. "So fucking beautiful. Look at my firebonds taking cock so well. Do you like his cock, Rarity? Does he feel good?"

"Yes," she shouts. "So good. He's perfect. I want his come."

"So greedy for more when you're already pregnant. Haven't you gotten enough?"

"Never," she hisses at me, turning her head to bare her fangs. "I'll never get enough."

"Such a good girl." I ram into Cailian, his cock doing the same to Rarity.

Watching them is too much. My knot begins to form at the base, and I groan, my hips stuttering because I don't have much longer.

Cailian shouts when Rarity sinks her fangs into his neck, dragging his Ice Elven blood out of him. Come drips down his shaft, leaking from Rarity's cunt, and that's all it takes for me because I never thought I'd be able to see such a beautiful fucking sight again.

I thrust my knot into Cailian, tossing my head back and roar. Flames lick the ceiling, turning it black. The bones of my wings flex out of habit. I fill him with days' worth of come. All three of my testicles give every drop to him, wanting to get him pregnant. I need him bound to me in every single way.

He is mine.

They are mine.

I will kill for them, and I have. I'll do it every day if I have to.

I'll have to show him Erelix's head on a stake outside on the heart-snow. A warning to trespassers not to come near this kingdom.

It is protected.

And this land, the elves, the dragons, and these two beautiful fire-bonds in my bed are mine.

I'll burn the world to the ground if it means I get to experience another breath from them.

We collapse on one another. I kiss Rarity's upper back before turning my cheek, pressing it against her back while I catch my breath. She groans, sliding off to cuddle Cailian, placing her head on his shoulder. She kisses his silver skin, her mouth tainted with his blood.

I fall onto his chest, Cailian wraps his arms around me, stroking where my wings used to be, and I flinch.

"I can fix that."

I swallow, unable to look at him. "How can you fix what isn't there?"

"I can give you wings better than the ones you were born with. All you have to do is say yes."

Rarity smiles at me, nodding, urging me to do it.

"If it means I can fly to either one of you at any time, then yes do it." I take a deep breath and smirk, running my claws through my hair when I scent the change in Cailian. It's ridiculous to feel so proud for satisfying his heat so quickly, but I am.

Loving them is all I live for, but I know if Death came for us, I would find them in the next life, and love them the way they deserve to be loved from the start.

-The end if you don't read epilogues. Kind of like me? Please join my reader group on Facebook: January's Raynestormers

Epilogue

RARITY

Three months later

I rub my swollen stomach, a bit grumpy from not being able to see my damn feet. I'm hungry. I'm tired. I want to fuck my beloveds, espe-cially since Cailian is tweaking Nyx's new wings. Something about the way Cailian works, his movements graceful and smooth as he tightens the last of the screws into Nyx's bone.

Nyx grumbles low with discomfort. Dragons and elves are gathered all around for this momentous day to watch their Prince take flight for the first time in three months. It hasn't been an easy time either. Cailian and his elves worked hard to dig a hole to the core on his kingdom's side, reaching the frozen core.

Apparently, that was where the element for his wings were. It is called icenite, a metal made from ice, frozen at such low temperatures, that only Ice Elven can harvest it.

The wings themselves are lightweight but unbreakable and sharp. He can use them in battle if he chooses like a knife to slice the enemies' throats.

I like the sound of that.

My stomach turns at the thought of blood.

Nope. No, I do not like the sound of that. I've changed my mind.

Relaxed his wings appear metal, with one sharp piece protruding at the top where three other pieces connect. In the middle of his shoulder blades is what looks like a silver ball, but it's that ball that is connected to his spine and nerves to give him control.

Cailian places his hand over the bolts, freezing them for good measure.

"How do you feel?"

Nyx rolls his shoulders. "Good. No pain."

The dragons and elves cheer. Nyx holds up his hand to silence them.

"Can you move them? It's okay if you can't at first. It could take time."

Nyx takes a deep breath and shuts his eyes. His new wings tucked behind his back.

Seconds pass with no movement.

Then minutes.

My heart loses hope.

And then Cailian jumps away when they spread out, bigger than his other pair of wings. The smile on Nyx's face is priceless. Everyone claps, shouting in celebration, and Nyx sprints down the middle of the heartsnow, launches himself into the air and takes flight.

He shifts into his dragon form, barely clearing the castle.

The castles connect now. Dragons and elves can come and go as they please, but dragons are able to withstand the cold more than the

elves can heat. Dragons tend to come to the cold kingdom, so the elves don't have to hurt themselves.

The baby kicks, and I rub my hand over the spot as I look up to the sky, watching Nyx fly in dragon form.

"He'll probably be gone all day. He has a lot of time to make up for," Cailian explains, wrapping his arms around me. "How is my mate?" He kisses my cheek, rubbing my stomach only to feel our child kick.

"I'm tired but I'm hungry."

He takes my hand and gives me a knowing smirk. "How about I feed you, and then fuck you to sleep, My Snow?"

"That sounds perfect."

"I would pick you up if we weren't in the same predicament."

I place my palm on his stomach. He seems much further along than me. "I am lucky to just hold your hand as we walk home." I stretch out my arm and he happily takes it.

The shadow of Nyx above us has me looking up again, a sense of belonging reminding me how this was always meant to be my home.

I can't freeze memories. I can't manipulate the cold. I'm no longer rare. I gave that aspect of myself to him to bring him back to me.

And I'd do it all over again because my life, my happiness, my Beloveds, my child?

That is what is rare.

When we get inside, we stop at the staircase and groan in unison, not wanting to even attempt to go up the stairs. Nyx always carries us when he is with us. Instead, we head to the couch and lie down. Taygen is there so we are protected and instead of feeding and fucking, we fall asleep in each other's arms.

Cailian's heartbeat lulls me to sleep while Nyx's happiness fills my heart.

My peace has the missing pieces it has been searching for and those pieces are priceless.

They are rarities.

The End.

Kind of like me? Please join my group on Facebook: January's Raynestormers

ACKNOWLEDGEMENTS

I want to thank my entire team for working so hard to get this book finished in time for release. Life hit me hard this year and writing Eternally Rare was difficult. To my editor, cover designer, and everything partner who is so creative and talented, Tiff – I couldn't do this without you. This world, these characters, even my day-to-day, you make it better. I appreciate you so much. Thank you for all your hard work and for being an amazing friend. Carolina, you're such a talented PA and you teach me something new every day. This journey wouldn't have started if you hadn't messaged me and asked if I was writing. You made me a schedule. You made me do this seriously. Thank you for everything and always being there. I'm lucky to call you my friend as well.

My husband deserves his own paragraph for dealing with me. He listened to me panic, cry, and become so frustrated while writing. He listened to my fears and worries. He comforted me. Adam, thank you for your faith in me. You believe in me when I never believe in myself. Your love for me, and your support motivate me to write even when I convince myself I can't. Shallow Cove wouldn't be where it is at if it weren't for you. I love you so much. With all my insides.

And thank you to my hype team and alpha readers. You all worked your butts off to get this done in time. You make up such an important part of Shallow Cove. I appreciate you and love you all so much.

ARC readers, thank you for reading last minute. I know it wasn't easy. I am thankful that you made time for me in your life.

I am seriously the luckiest author in the world.

-January

ABOUT THE AUTHOR

January Rayne is a paranormal fantasy romance author who lives in Buffalo, NY with her husband, son, two dogs, and two leopard geckos. Buffalo is freezing, but January loves when it snows as it gives her the perfect atmosphere to write a book for you to get lost in.

Scan here for easy access to follow me on social media:

ETERNALLY RARE

January Rayne

WELCOME TO THE WORLD OF

Shallow Cove™
DIMENSIONS